THE RENEGADES

When an SIS operative is killed in a London restaurant shoot-out, police initially assume it to be no more than a robbery with drug and gangster overtones. But when one of the corpses is found to have more than one name, they suspect a cover-up from within the depths of Britain's secret services.

As British Council offices in Pakistan and then Russia are attacked by suicide bombers, it soon becomes clear that there is a link between an apparently ordinary working lunch and world terrorism.

Talal Asir, a banker who has financially backed almost every known terrorist organisation, and Ali Mohammed Khalef, the bagman who has distributed the monies on his behalf, are two of the most dangerous men in the Middle East. How can Peter Ashton and his colleagues track down and eliminate them?

THE RENEGADES

Clive Egleton

WINDSOR
PARAGON

First published 2005
by
Severn House
This Large Print edition published 2005
by
BBC Audiobooks Ltd by arrangement with
Severn House Publishers Ltd

ISBN 1 4056 1072 7   (Windsor Hardcover)
ISBN 1 4056 2060 9   (Paragon Softcover)

British Library Cataloguing in Publication Data available

Printed and bound in Great Britain by
Antony Rowe Ltd., Chippenham, Wiltshire

This book is for my granddaughter, Harriet

One

Giordano's Italian restaurant was roughly three hundred yards below Harrods and diagonally across the road from the information centre adjoining Hans Crescent. The external appearance of the restaurant with its dark one way glass frontage backed by a shoulder-high green net curtain reminded Quayle of a pokey little billiard hall in some quiet back street. The interior décor was, however, far more welcoming with red cedar panelling on the walls and a floor composed of matching wooden blocks. The tables and chairs were made of yew and had cost a small fortune, but nobody came to Giordano's to admire the furniture. They came because the food was excellent as were the full-bodied Italian reds in the wine cellar.

The good food and wine was only part of the attraction for Toby Quayle. Whenever it was necessary to entertain one of the Firm's overseas associates, he would invariably take the visitor to Giordano's because the restaurant was off the beaten track and had yet to be discovered by Grub Street. Furthermore, thanks to a private arrangement between the Firm's managing director and the proprietor, Quayle could always be sure of reserving a table at short notice. However, things had not gone quite so smoothly this particular lunchtime: he had booked the usual table for two only for his guest, Anwar Farid, to arrive with a lady in tow.

'This is Danièle,' Anwar had said without

1

elaborating how they were acquainted.

Hackneyed though the adjective was, petite was the only way to describe Danièle. Quayle reckoned she was no more than five two in her stockinged feet, and she was slender with it, but not skinny like some emaciated waif from a Third World country. Everything about Danièle was undersized but exactly in proportion. She had a good figure and knew how to make the most of it without appearing the least bit tarty. He thought the charcoal-coloured jacket and skirt she was wearing must have cost a packet but then Anwar could afford it.

Anwar Farid liked to describe himself as an importer of fine goods from the Orient, which was a far grander way of saying he was a carpet salesman. In this capacity he travelled extensively throughout the Middle East, India and Pakistan.

Quayle had invited him to lunch to hear what he had learned on his latest trip to the Middle East. To be more specific he wanted to find out if there was any substance to Farid's claim that he had run into Talal Asir, the man the Firm called 'the Banker'. Distantly related to the Saudi ruling family, Talal Asir had first come to notice in 1989 when he had been the vice president in charge of overseas investments at the National Bank of Saudi Arabia in Riyadh. In those days he had done most of his business in Europe, investing heavily in telecommunications and information technology. He was also known to have acquired property in Switzerland and the south of France on behalf of his relatives. In May 1993 Talal Asir had turned up in London having lost his job with the National Bank of Saudi Arabia. Some said it was because he had been embezzling the bank by inflating the cost

2

of the properties he had purchased, while others had maintained the family had grown tired of his sexual antics with foreign women. Whatever the reason, he had become a currency speculator, buying Deutschmarks and Swiss francs to force up their exchange rate value, then selling the currencies before they peaked and fell back. After three years in London Asir had moved to Paris, where he had continued in the same line of business. He had also organized fundraising activities on behalf of the Palestinian refugee children of Ramallah.

In April of last year Talal Asir had left Paris in a hurry, supposedly for Saudi Arabia. More recently Asir had been seen in Beirut, Amman, Cairo and Islamabad. Now Anwar Farid was claiming to have met him in Damascus a mere five days ago.

On previous occasions when Anwar had something for him their business was concluded long before the restaurant closed at three o'clock. This time round the Egyptian was taking for ever. Everybody else had left, the other diners, the waiters and the hat check girl; only Enrico Giordano, the proprietor's eldest son, remained. Ever patient, ever smiling, he had refilled their coffee cups time and again . . .

Danièle was a major distraction because Anwar was simply unable to keep his hands off her. Quayle couldn't help noticing that whenever the Egyptian began to tell him what he knew about Talal Asir's movements she would make some skittish comment and Anwar would clam up, his right hand then coming to rest on Danièle's thigh. The more Quayle thought about it, the more he was convinced their curious behaviour masked a coded message. Every time Danièle opened her mouth she was warning her lover to guard his tongue while Anwar's hand on her thigh signalled that he knew what he was doing. Although Quayle was not easily riled, his patience was not inexhaustible.

'This charade has gone on long enough,' Quayle growled. 'I know what you two are after but I've heard nothing yet that's even worth the loose change in my pocket.'

'I tell you that Talal Asir was entertained by Walid al-Kasam while he was in Damascus and you say that is nothing!' Farid threw up his hands as if temporarily lost for words. 'You do know who Walid al-Kasam is, don't you?'

'I've heard of him,' Quayle said dismissively. 'What interests me is how you learned Talal Asir was being fêted by Major General Walid al-Kasam, Deputy Prime Minister and Minister for the Armed Forces.'

'If you gentlemen will excuse me,' Danièle said and stood up, 'I have to go somewhere.'

Anwar watched her walk off in the direction of the ladies' room near the back of the restaurant, then turned to face Quayle again. 'Danièle thinks you haven't done enough for me,' he said in a low voice.

'Really? Well, that makes us even because you have done next to nothing for me.'

'How can you say that, Mr Quayle? I have done many favours for you and my stuff has always been good. You have told me so many times.'

'Nothing you have picked up on your travels before has been this big. That's why I want—' Quayle heard a muffled thump as if somebody had

4

fallen down and immediately glanced over his shoulder. 'Are you OK, Enrico?' he enquired.

'Yes indeed. Why do you ask, Mr Quayle?'

'That noise just now . . .'

'It's the wind. One of the window frames out back does not fit properly.'

Quayle nodded, his curiosity satisfied. It was, after all, a typical day in March with frequent rain squalls driven by a gusting wind that could turn umbrellas inside out, as had happened to his on the way to the station. He had caught another heavy shower when he'd alighted at Knightsbridge and had had to run like hell to Giordano's because the damned anorak he was wearing only just reached the hips and he hadn't wanted to arrive looking like a drowned rat. Unfortunately the three-hundred-yard dash had been in vain. All it had done was remind him that he was forty-four years old, overweight and out of condition.

'You were about to say what you wanted from me,' Anwar snapped.

'So I was.' Quayle pressed his hands together, the fingers making a steeple which he brought to his lips as if in prayer. 'See, it's like this, Anwar,' he said and pointed the steepled fingers at the Egyptian. 'There is nothing I would like more than to present you with the kind of big, fat reward you deserve because your information is sensational. But I need to validate it otherwise my board of directors won't sanction the payment.'

'I've applied for British citizenship,' Anwar reminded him sourly.

'I know and believe me we will be happy to lobby the Home Office on your behalf. And on the strength of the information you have provided linking Talal Asir with Major General Walid al-Kasam your naturalization papers will go through on the nod.' Quayle paused, then said, 'Provided we can nail it down. You understand what I mean?'

Farid didn't say anything. Instead he reached inside the breast pocket of his jacket and produced a slip of paper folded in two, which he passed across the table. Quayle unfolded the note and glanced at the name and address inside.

'Miss Lana Damir Rifa, Villa Caprice, 111 Boulevard Hafez el-Assad, Damascus,' Quayle intoned and pocketed the note. 'Who's the lady, Anwar?'

'Walid al-Kasam's mistress.'

'And the Villa Caprice belongs to whom?'

The window frame thumped again. Caught by a sudden gust of wind the noise sounded louder this time.

'Well?' Quayle said, demanding an answer.

The Egyptian remained silent. His head was turned half right in the direction of the ladies' room and to Quayle he seemed to be in a trance. Unable to get any reaction from Anwar when he spoke to him, Quayle leaned forward and jabbed the Egyptian in the chest with a finger. In that same instant, Anwar Farid reared back and a segment of bone roughly the size of a tennis ball parted company with his skull. A millisecond later a second bullet hit him in the neck as he slumped over the table. He was, in fact, already dead when he stretched out his left arm and swept a coffee cup and saucer on to the floor.

Quayle turned his back on the lone gunman and took a shot between the shoulder blades before he could dive for cover under the table. The impact

6

virtually lifted Quayle off the chair and dumped him face down on the floor. He heard the killer walking slowly towards him and tried to crawl away on hands and knees but the effort was too much for him and he froze on all fours, head down and coughing blood while he waited for the coup de grâce. Then the burglar alarm went off with a nerve-jangling warble that was painful on the ears. It was the last thing Quayle heard before the gunman shot him the second time.

*　　　*　　　*

Guardian Services Limited was a private security agency that specialized in protecting business premises in the central London area round the clock. It was the company's proud boast that within ten minutes of a burglar alarm registering in the London control centre two of their security officers would be on the scene. The vast majority of break-ins occurred late at night when the property was unoccupied. Of the alarms triggered in daylight hours, approximately ninety per cent were false. Among the many clients protected by Guardian Services was Giordano's Italian restaurant in Knightsbridge.

The burglar alarm at Giordano's had been tripped at twenty-eight minutes past four. Because it was known that the restaurant closed at three o'clock and reopened at six thirty, the senior watchkeeper at the control centre assumed the alarm had been set off accidentally by somebody on the evening shift who had just arrived. Accordingly he had decided to wait five minutes

7

before taking action in order to give the culprit a chance to reset the alarm. The number of ear-splitting decibels generated by the radio alarm was such that five minutes was the maximum time most people with normal hearing could tolerate the noise. When the alarm was still active after five minutes had elapsed the senior watchkeeper despatched Brown and Gilroy to investigate.

The company's proud boast went by the board. It was that time of the day when the extended rush hour was just beginning and there was absolutely no chance the security officers could be on the scene within ten minutes of being alerted. In fact, given the heavy traffic, Brown and Gilroy had done well to arrive outside the restaurant by ten past five.

Giordano's was part of a small shopping precinct and was situated between a picture gallery and a boutique. Although the security light above the front entrance was flashing and the alarm itself could be heard above the noise of the traffic by pedestrians on the same side of the street as Giordano's, it was evident that no passer-by had thought to inform the police.

'Whatever happened to the public-spirited citizen you used to hear about?' Gilroy complained acerbically.

'They were a dying breed a long time ago,' Brown said.

The front door was locked and there was no sign of a forced entry. When nobody answered the door the two security men walked down the narrow passageway between Giordano's and the boutique to check out the back yard. If there was an intruder inside the restaurant, somebody had made it easy

8

for the burglar, because the back door was unlocked.

Leaving Brown to switch off the alarm at the control panel fixed to the wall just inside the entrance, Gilroy checked out the kitchen before moving into the restaurant. He found the first body in the men's room, though what a woman was doing there he couldn't say. She was sitting on the floor in one of the cubicles, her back resting against the lavatory pan, her head bowed as if contemplating the bloodstained silk blouse and the scorch mark around the entry wound in the chest. There were three male victims of the shooter in the restaurant, one of whom was still alive but only just. While Gilroy did the best he could for him, Brown made a 999 call on his mobile to the police and paramedics, then contacted the control centre to report what they had found.

The police arrived in six minutes, marginally ahead of the paramedics. The media weren't that slow off the mark either and the incident was reported in the six o'clock newscast on Radio 2.

Two

Until nine months ago Ralph Meacher had been resigned to the fact that he would always be a Grade I Intelligence Officer. Back in June 1998 Meacher had already been acting Head of the Mid East Department for almost a year, which had been a tad galling considering subordinates like Toby Quayle were the same grade as him. Although Meacher had been in receipt of extra-responsibility pay, it had been no secret among his peer group that he would never be confirmed in the appointment. Whether or not Meacher was capable of holding down the job had been irrelevant. The Middle East was regarded as the major flashpoint in the world and the Foreign and Commonwealth Office had been determined to exercise tighter control over the activities of the Secret Intelligence Service in that region.

To that end the Permanent Under Secretary of State had paved the way for a career diplomat to be appointed Assistant Director in charge of the Mid East Department. He had then ensured that his man had a clear run to the top. It had also been his intention to fill the vacancy thus created in the department with another career diplomat.

However, as the Permanent Under Secretary knew full well, slotting a round peg into a round hole was never straightforward. The Diplomatic was not so awash with suitably qualified officers that the right man could be produced at the drop of a hat. To make the chosen one available it was often necessary to move three or four other individuals to free the desired round peg. For twelve months commencing the 30th June 1997 Meacher had been keeping a chair warm for the FCO's man. Then a major terrorist incident had changed everything and with great reluctance the FCO had been forced to recall Sir Victor Hazelwood, who had been their pet bogeyman from time immemorial.

As if to cock a snook at the Permanent Under Secretary of State, his first act on being reinstated as Director General had been to promote Meacher and confirm him in the appointment. Eight months on, Meacher still found it hard to believe that he had finally made it to Assistant Director.

It was said of Meacher that in his case a pending tray was superfluous because he never left the office until he had cleared his in-tray. Even though he had dealt with the last file at a quarter past five, he had remained behind waiting to hear from Quayle long after his colleagues had departed. Today was not the first time Quayle had entertained Anwar Farid for lunch but on every other occasion he had returned to the office shortly after three. By four thirty his continued absence had worried Meacher enough for him to call the restaurant. An itchy feeling that something was wrong had taken off when the phone had gone unanswered. As soon as the night watchkeepers reported in at a quarter to six Meacher had sought out the senior duty officer and asked him to arrange for one of his clerks to monitor the newscasts on the BBC and local stations.

Six o'clock came and went. Shortly before five past Meacher heard the measured tread of footsteps in the corridor and assumed a security guard was carrying out a routine check to make sure all classified material had been locked away.

'It's OK, I'm still working,' Meacher said loudly to let the guard know there was no point in him checking the office just yet. 'I'll let you know when I'm about to leave,' he added.

'Actually, it's me, sir, Nancy Wilkins,' the girl said before appearing in the open doorway.

'Sorry. Are you one of the duty clerks this evening?'

'For my sins. I understand you wanted to know if there had been a serious incident in the

11

Knightsbridge area?'

'That's right. What have you got for me?'

'It's not good news. One or more gunmen walked into Giordano's Italian restaurant at approximately four thirty this afternoon and shot four people, three men and a woman. There is one survivor whose condition is said to be critical.'

Nancy looked up from the slip of paper she was holding in her right hand. 'Nobody has been identified as yet.'

An ID was unnecessary. The unfortunate Toby Quayle had been in the wrong place at the wrong time. So far as Meacher was concerned, it was as simple as that. 'Any suggestion of a possible motive for the shooting?' he asked.

Nancy shook her head. 'There may be something in a later bulletin.'

'Could be. Anyway, if you'd like to keep listening I'll look in at Central Registry before I leave the building.'

Just when that might be was entirely dependent on the DG. If there was one man in the SIS who was never in a hurry to go home it was Victor Hazelwood. From the day Meacher had been appointed as the acting Head of the Mid East Department he had learned that, in order to leave the office at a reasonable hour, any business with the DG should be conducted before 5 p.m. If that wasn't possible you could look forward to chewing the cud with Victor for a good hour or even longer.

The five o'clock deadline didn't work for Peter Ashton. Any time Hazelwood felt like talking things over with the Head of the East European and Balkan Department, he would get Dilys Crowther, his PA, to ring Ashton on some pretext shortly before five o'clock. Consequently nobody spent more time in Victor's company than Ashton. The special relationship that existed between the two men dated from the time when Hazelwood had been in charge of the Russian desk and Ashton had been his deputy. The younger man had been Hazelwood's Rottweiler, in the sense that he had conducted more hazardous operations in the former Soviet Union and Warsaw Pact countries than any other SIS officer. Consequently Meacher was not surprised to find Ashton closeted with the DG when he sought out Victor Hazelwood.

'This won't take a minute,' Meacher assured him.

'Take as long as you like, Ralph,' Hazelwood said. 'I'm in no hurry.'

But Meacher was. He had a house in Ruislip to go home to and a marriage that was going through a bad patch. In a few brief sentences he told Hazelwood about the shooting at Giordano's and why he believed Toby Quayle was either dead or critically wounded.

'Who was he wining and dining?' Hazelwood demanded when Quayle had finished briefing him.

'Anwar Farid. He's an Egyptian domiciled in this country. He was born in Alexandria in June 1965.' Meacher pursed his lips. 'By and large he is a pretty good source of information.'

'How highly do you rate him, Ralph?'

'C3,' Meacher said unhesitatingly.

A source was graded from A to F. At the top end of the scale 'A' indicated that the source was very reliable while 'F' meant the informant was inclined to manufacture information when there was a dearth of it. The quality of the information provided by a source was assessed on a scale of 1 to

6. The figure 1 labelled the report as probably true whereas a 6 signified that it was uncorroborated and likely to be false. C3 meant the Egyptian had a reasonable track record and was therefore regarded as a worthwhile asset.

'Do we know when Farid returned to this country?' Hazelwood asked.

'Not really. He rang Toby Quayle at home yesterday evening and said he'd run into the Banker five days ago.'

'And on the strength of that Toby invited Farid to lunch.'

Although it sounded like an assumption Meacher chose to treat it as a question.

'Yes, he did. With my approval I might add.'

Hazelwood opened the ornately carved cigar box on his desk, one of a pair he had purchased on a field trip to India a lifetime ago. The civil service had banned smoking in the workplace but it would be a bold man who reminded Victor of this edict. The upward path of his career could be traced by the number of extractor fans Roy Kelso, the Head of the Administrative Wing, had been obliged to install. As Meacher watched, Hazelwood took out a Burma cheroot and smelled it lovingly. Before too long the cheroot would join the other stubs in the cut-down brass shell case Hazelwood used as an ashtray.

'Is it possible the Banker got to Farid?' Hazelwood asked, drawing on his cigar. 'Perhaps he gave your source a wad of money, Ralph, and promised him there would be more to come if he set up Toby Quayle?'

'And maybe it could just as easily have been an armed robbery that went horribly wrong.'

14

'Are you telling me Giordano's is equivalent to a high street bank?'

'No. I have in mind some drug addict with a gun who was looking for a till full of cash to feed his habit.'

Hazelwood grunted and looked to Ashton. 'What do you think, Peter?'

'I think we should involve the Security Service ASAP.'

'Ralph?'

'I agree,' Meacher said and turned to Ashton. 'Will you start the ball rolling, Peter?'

He wasn't asking Ashton to do him a favour. As Head of the East European and Balkan Department, Ashton was responsible for providing the SIS member of the Combined Anti-Terrorist Organization, commonly known as CATO. The Firm was represented by Will Landon, a Grade II Intelligence Officer.

'No problem. I'll call Richard Neagle now on the Mozart secure-speech facility, then I'll stand up Will Landon. You'll need to brief him about Anwar Farid before morning prayers tomorrow.'

'That's understood.'

'It's gone six thirty,' Hazelwood observed. 'Are you sure Richard Neagle will still be in his office, Peter?'

'Of course I am,' Ashton told him. 'He's like you, Victor, always reluctant to go home.'

*   *   *

Richard Neagle had cut his teeth in the Irish Section of MI5, which he had joined in 1979 after spending four years in K1, popularly known within

15

the Security Service as the Kremlin watchers. From the Irish section he had graduated to a wider field of counter-intelligence operations with special responsibility for homing in on terrorist groups suspected of using the UK as a secure base. In November 1997 he had been appointed to head up the Anti-Terrorist Branch when the then incumbent had been promoted to Deputy Director General of the service.

Neagle was forty-seven but most people would never think it to look at him. Something in his genes had given him the round, puckish face of a mischievous child which time was unlikely to ravage. The same could not be said for his wispy fair hair, which he carefully brushed across the scalp to disguise the number of bald patches that were steadily increasing year on year. His lips always seemed to be hovering on the brink of a smile, but that was a trick Neagle had learned eleven years ago after his wife, Gillian, had suddenly died. She had been full of life and in a bubbly mood when he had left their house in Godalming at the usual time that morning. On his return in the evening he had found Gillian lying on the kitchen floor, her body already cold to the touch. Neagle had learned later that a blood clot had travelled up the artery and exploded like a bomb in her heart. The pathologist who had conducted the post-mortem had expressed it more scientifically, attributing the cause of death to coronary artery occlusion complicated by severe coronary artery atheroma.

In the weeks immediately after Gillian's death friends had urged Neagle to sell the house and move on but that had been something he couldn't bring himself to do, and still couldn't. For the first three or four years he had deliberately manufactured work that would keep him in the office all hours. Even when the pain of not having Gillian by his side had dulled to the point where she did not enter his thoughts for days at a time, he was still the last senior officer to leave the Gower Street headquarters of MI5. He had in fact become a workaholic.

That evening Neagle had stayed behind to work on the file relating to Ali Mohammed Khalef. Born on the 19th March 1953 at Mosul in Northern Iraq, Khalef had allegedly been on Saddam Hussein's death list and had fled to the UK in 1982. After being granted political asylum, he had settled in Finsbury Park. For every newsletter Khalef had written attacking the Iraqi President, he had produced a dozen soliciting funds supposedly to buy food and medicine for the marsh people in the south. Over the years there had been persistent rumours that much of the money raised by Khalef had actually been used to send young British Muslims to Libya for military training. Despite keeping Khalef under observation, MI5 and Special Branch had been unable to provide evidence hard enough to persuade the Home Office that he should be deported.

Convinced in his own mind that Khalef was active in Islamic Jihad, Neagle had continued to keep the Iraqi cleric under surveillance, albeit with reduced cover. On the 1st June 1998 Khalef had given Special Branch the slip and disappeared. Twenty days later he had been spotted in Bahrain and reported to the security officer at the British Embassy in Manama. Since the British had no

17

extra-territorial rights in Bahrain, the MI5 security officer had been obliged to arrange for the local police to watch Ali Mohammed Khalef. Money had obviously changed hands somewhere down the line because one week later the Iraqi had paid his hotel bill at the Tybos, taken a cab to Muharroq and boarded a Middle Eastern Airlines flight to Kuwait. In the eight months since then Khalef had been reportedly seen in places as far apart as Rawalpindi and Beirut. All the sightings had come from low-grade sources and were of little account.

Having studied the file in depth Neagle came to the conclusion that it offered no pointers to where Khalef might be hiding himself. He was about to consign the file to the combination safe and call it a day when the Mozart rang. Answering the phone, Neagle found he had Ashton on the line.

'Where are you calling from?' Neagle asked.

'The office.'

'You must have a problem.'

'We have,' Ashton told him. 'Have you heard about the shooting in Knightsbridge this afternoon?'

'What shooting?'

'It happened at Giordano's Italian restaurant. Four people were hit, one of whom was a woman. There is one survivor who is reported to be in a bad way.'

'Male or female?'

'We don't know,' Ashton told him. 'The fact is we've every reason to believe one of our intelligence officers was hit.'

The victim was Toby Quayle, a name that didn't ring a bell with Neagle. Neither did Anwar Farid, the source who might now be lying next to Quayle in a morgue somewhere.

'We're not sure when Farid returned to this country,' Ashton continued. 'However, he rang Toby yesterday evening claiming he had met Talal Asir five days ago in Damascus.'

Talal Asir: now there was a name Neagle was unlikely to forget in a hurry. Nine months ago MI5 had finally persuaded their French counterparts, the Direction de la Surveillance du Territoire, to enter Talal Asir's apartment on the Rue de Ponthieu in the 8th arrondissement. In a concealed wall safe the French authorities had found statements from the Hispaniola Bank, Port au Prince, Haiti, First National Trust and Investment, Grand Bahamas, the Consolidated Bank, Bridgetown, Barbados and two numbered accounts with the Grande Banque, Estavayer Le Lac in Switzerland. Without exception the accounts had been extremely active and the transactions had involved large sums of money. The statements had been mailed to various post office box numbers in France, Germany and Italy.

Talal Asir had long been suspected of funding such terrorist groups as Hamas, Hezbollah and Islamic Jihad. The evidence found in his Paris apartment had provided sufficient proof of this contention for MI5 to go after him. It had cost the taxpayer a mint of money to hire the best firm of chartered accountants in London and put together a legal team second to none. But Neagle thought it had been worth the expense; between the beginning of June 1998 and the 31st January 1999 every known bank account operated by Talal Asir had been frozen and the monies impounded.

'I expect you can guess what we would like from

you,' Ashton said.

Neagle wondered what, if anything, he had missed while his thoughts had been elsewhere, then said, 'You want to know who's dead, who is still alive and which hospital is caring for the seriously wounded victim. You'd also like to know the prognosis for his or her continued survival. As for physical protection, I think you'll find the police already have the patient under armed guard. It would be standard procedure in a case like this.'

'And as a matter of standard procedure they will undoubtedly question the staff at Giordano's. Right?'

'It would be pretty odd if they didn't,' Neagle said.

'OK. When they get round to it, I'd like the investigating officers to find out if the woman was dining with Quayle.'

'No problem.'

'Good. I'll send Will Landon round to Gower Street tomorrow morning at nine. He'll give you everything we have on Anwar Farid.'

'Including his last known address in London or wherever?'

'Hang on a minute.'

Neagle heard a low mumble of voices in the background and guessed Ashton had referred the question to one of his colleagues. Presently he came back on the line with the information that Farid had a mortgage on the semi-detached at 62 Monk Road, Wood Green.

'How much discretion have I got?' Neagle asked.

'In what respect?'

'With regard to Toby Quayle and Anwar Farid. How much can I tell the investigating officer?'

'Everything.' Ashton paused, then said, 'Just make sure he understands his head will be on the chopping block if a single detail is leaked to the press.'

*   *   *

Landon let himself into the flat at 25 Stanhope Gardens, picked up the airmail letter he had left on the hall table when he'd returned home earlier in the evening and went on through to the sitting room. The answer phone on the combined drop-leaf desk and bookcase that he'd recently acquired indicated somebody had left a message for him while he had been working out at Wilford's Fitness Club on Gloucester Road. When he depressed the play button on the BT Response 300, Ashton said, 'I'm on my way home. Please call me at eight thirty p.m.'

Home for Peter Ashton was Roseland Cottage, Church Lane, Bosham, roughly three miles from the outskirts of Chichester and a mere two hundred yards from the seashore. Landon had spent a night there last June and had come away with the impression that the cottage was exactly right for a man with a wife and young family, a status that had eluded him to date. Landon could understand why this should be so whenever he looked at himself in the mirror. He was six feet three and built like a heavyweight minus the scar tissue around the eyes normally associated with a prizefighter. He had light brown hair with an auburn tinge to it and plain features which could be best described as homely. He was thirty-two years

21

old.

Landon lowered the drop leaf and slotted the unopened airmail letter from America into one of the pigeonholes, then walked into the master bedroom and stripped off. Stepping into the shower, he drew the plastic curtain and ran the water, blending the hot and cold until the temperature suited him. He stood under the rose, flexing the left shoulder while rotating the arm and experienced, as always, a slight twinge.

It was a physical reminder of what had happened last year on Friday 3rd July in Dolphin Square. On that day Landon had arrived on the scene seconds too late to prevent two Chechen gunmen carrying out a political assassination. He had however exacted immediate retribution. Shifting down into second gear, Landon had floored the accelerator and used the Volkswagen as a weapon to run down and kill both men. Unable to stop the car in time, Landon had slammed head on into a parked Jaguar. At forty miles an hour, the seat belt had given way under the impact and he had collapsed over the steering wheel. The next thing Landon had remembered was waking up in hospital with a broken collarbone, three busted ribs and the American girl sitting by his bedside.

The American girl was Ensley Holsinger, whose curriculum vitae read as if it had been prepared with an entry in *People of Today* in mind. Born in New Milton, Connecticut, in 1973, Ensley had majored in English at Boston U where she had been a cheerleader. With massive self-belief she had gone to New York and made the rounds of all the major publishing houses until she had eventually found a niche with Barnes and Wallace, an imprint of the HarperCollins empire. In September 1996, when she was still only twenty-three, she had been invited to join the Julian H. Shubert literary agency.

Twenty-one months later Ensley Holsinger had thrown it all away when she had tried to go into business on her own account. The script she had hawked around London had been borrowed from the Julian H. Shubert agency. If that hadn't been disreputable enough, she had known the script contained highly classified information that would prove a major source of embarrassment for Her Majesty's government if it appeared in print. After everything had gone pear shaped, Ensley had been astute enough to leave the UK before she found herself in serious trouble.

Landon turned off the shower, towelled himself dry and changed into a black sweatshirt, dark grey slacks and a pair of moccasins. Returning to the sitting room, he picked up the phone and rang Ashton. 'It's me, Will,' he said.

'I rather thought it was,' Ashton told him drily, then said, 'Tomorrow is going to be your busy day. First thing you do is look in on Ralph Meacher, then make your way over to Richard's place. OK?'

Landon said it was and put the phone down. Since he was not issued with a Mozart secure-speech facility, Ashton had had to call him on an open BT line. Mindful that his private phone number in Bosham might have been targeted, Ashton had told him no more than was absolutely necessary. The fact that he was required to see Meacher before reporting to Neagle was significant. It told Landon that there had been some sort of terrorist incident involving the Mid

East department.

Landon havered, uncertain what to do about the letter from America. It might be out of sight but it wasn't out of mind. Curiosity about the letter finally got the better of him and, lowering the drop leaf, he removed it from the pigeonhole and examined the envelope more closely. The postmark showed that Ensley had mailed it in Chicago, which probably meant she was staying with Daddy, the hotshot attorney with scads of dosh. For all her professed independence, Ensley always turned to her father when she was in trouble.

Landon could see her now in his mind's eye. Glossy dark brown hair, five feet eight in low heels and blessed with a figure most women would die for. To call Ensley attractive failed to do her justice; arresting was a more apposite description. She could make you feel you were the most important man in her life. Ensley was also hugely ambitious, was ruthless in her determination to succeed no matter what the cost, and dangerous to know. Slowly and deliberately Landon tore the sealed envelope in four and dropped the pieces into the wastepaper basket by the desk.

Three

Landon was no stranger to the Gower Street headquarters of MI5. Members of the Combined Anti-Terrorist Organization chaired by Richard Neagle routinely met there every Tuesday morning at 1000 hours. Other members of the committee included representatives from the Defence

Intelligence Staff, Government Communications Headquarters at Cheltenham and the Commander, Operations, Special Branch or, in his absence, the detective chief superintendent. Since this morning only involved a head to head with Richard Neagle they met in his office rather than the small conference room used by the full committee.

'You'll join me in a cup of coffee, Will,' Neagle said, waving him to a chair. 'You take it black. No sugar. Am I right?'

Landon nodded but he needn't have bothered. Neagle was already on the office intercom talking to someone called Rena who was asked to produce a black Colombian and the usual for himself.

'A bad business about Toby,' Neagle said. 'His chances of pulling through are pretty slim.'

'I didn't know he had survived the shooting,' Landon said.

'No reason why you should. The police have only just released the news. They won't name him of course until the next of kin has been informed.'

'Toby is a bachelor with no surviving relatives in this country. He has a sister living in New Zealand but they haven't seen one another in years. I daresay Roy Kelso, our admin king, will inform her later today.'

Neagle shook his head. 'I doubt if she will get here in time.'

'It's as bad as that, is it?'

'Quayle was shot twice. He took the first round between the shoulder blades, which put him face down on the floor. According to the police, the gunman must have been standing over Quayle when he fired the second round.'

The bullet had shattered the left cheekbone,

25

travelled diagonally through the mouth, slicing off part of the tongue before destroying the lower jawbone on the right side as it exited. The bullet then struck the floor and ricocheted, hitting the right arm sideways on above the elbow.

'He would have bled to death if Enrico Giordano hadn't triggered the burglar alarm ...' Neagle broke off to smile warmly at a plain, youngish looking woman who had entered the office carrying two cups of coffee on a tray.

'Thank you, Rena,' he said and waited until she left before resuming. 'As it was, Toby had lost a lot of blood by the time the paramedics arrived. In fact they thought they were going to lose him on the way to the Brompton Road Hospital.'

'Poor old Toby.'

'Yes, it's all bad news. When the police finally got their hands on Quayle's bloodstained clothing they found a note inside the breast pocket of his jacket.' Neagle passed a slip of paper to Landon. 'This is a copy. The original note had been folded in two and was badly contaminated.'

The way Neagle evidently saw it, contaminated was infinitely preferable to saying the paper was gummed up with congealed blood. All the police had managed to decipher were a few random letters with an indeterminate number of spaces in between. The note began with four question marks followed by a capital 'L' and a lower case 'a'. A further sixteen question marks then preceded a capital 'C' and the numerals 111. After that there was a horizontal line roughly two inches in length and an exclamation mark.

'What does this mean?' Landon asked, holding up the note for Neagle to see while pointing to

26

the line.

'It means that section was so bloodstained the police couldn't tell how many letters had been obliterated before the final group of four. Know any likely words that end in "scus", Will?'

'Damascus,' Landon said promptly. 'And before you ask that's just a wild guess. It could be the blank spaces contained a name and address. But that's even more of a wild guess.'

'Has Anwar Farid been in Syria recently?'

'When I asked him this morning, Ralph Meacher had no idea where the Egyptian had been on his travels. Neither, it seems, had Toby when he left the office to meet Farid at Giordano's.' Landon looked at the note again. 'Is there any chance forensics can enhance the original?' he asked.

'They seemed very doubtful when I spoke to them.'

'Well, if I could have a photocopy of the original we may be able to tell who actually wrote the note.'

'I suggest you ask Detective Chief Inspector John Verco about that. He's our Special Branch link man with the investigating officers of "B" District, and will be waiting for us at the Brompton.' Neagle snapped his fingers. 'Incidentally, the police have established that the dead woman who was found in the gentlemen's had dined with Quayle and Farid.'

'Interesting.'

'Yes, isn't it.'

Knowing Neagle as well as he did, Landon sensed there was more to come. The MI5 man liked to surprise people and would wait patiently for the right moment to drop his bombshell. It was one of his little foibles.

'How many transsexuals do you know, Will?'

27

Neagle asked as they left his office.

'I don't think I've ever met one.'

'Well, you're about to see a dead one. The lady who was shot in the gents has a small penis between her legs.'

*   *   *

Detective Chief Inspector John Verco was waiting for them outside the front entrance to the Brompton. He was a relatively small man, barely five feet seven, and, according to Neagle, he would not have been accepted by the Met had he not earned a Queen's Commendation when serving in the Royal Military Police. If his grey hair was anything to go by, Landon thought he had to be nudging the mid to late fifties. On the other hand, apart from a few wrinkles on the forehead, his face was unlined and there were no telltale marks under the eyes. Shaking hands with some of the men Landon had met was like grappling with a wet piece of fish. Verco however had a grip of steel. He was also blunt and very direct.

'Your man's in a bad way, Mr Landon,' Verco said.

'So Richard told me. Just how bad is he?'

'Mr Quayle is in a critical condition and a long way from being stable. What we would like from you is a positive ID for the record.'

The intensive care unit was on the second floor. As a precaution against a further attempt on his life, Quayle had been moved to the floor above and lodged in a single room. Two armed police officers had been assigned to protect him, one outside in the corridor, the other inside the room. The room itself was just beyond the ward sister's office.

'This is Mr Landon,' Verco said introducing him to the sister in charge. 'He's here to formally identify the victim. It'll only take a minute.'

Verco was wrong about that. Landon had met Toby at Amberley Lodge, the SIS training school on the outskirts of Petersfield, when he had lectured the induction course on the Intelligence setup in the Persian Gulf. Apart from the time Landon had been seconded to the British Embassy in Lima, he had seen Quayle practically every working day for years on end. The shrivelled figure in the bed bore only a passing resemblance to the man Landon knew. The side of his face that hadn't been totally destroyed was the colour of greaseproof paper, the skin stretched tight as a drum under the right eye. Yesterday Quayle had been forty-four years old and overweight; today he looked well over seventy and appeared to have shed at least twenty pounds.

'Well?' Verco said impatiently. 'Do you recognize this man, Mr Landon?'

'Yes, he's Toby Quayle.'

'You're sure?'

'I wasn't at first but now I'm positive.'

'Good. If you gentlemen would follow me we'll take a look at the other two.'

The mortuary was located in a separate block as far removed from the hospital as was possible within the limits imposed by the grounds. There was an overpowering smell of Lysol disinfectant in the air and the room temperature felt almost glacial. But the attendant didn't appear to notice either the noxious smell or the cold. Bodies

29

awaiting a post-mortem were stored in metal containers much like a filing cabinet. On a signal from the Special Branch officer the attendant moved to the nearest bank of three and pulled out the centre drawer, then stepped aside to give Landon a better view of the corpse.

'Do you know this man?' Verco asked.

'Not personally but this morning I was shown a number of photos of him and that's definitely Anwar Farid.'

'Really? Well, for your information, Mr Landon, HM Customs and Excise know him as Mahmoud Hassan Soliman. They pinched him twenty-seven months ago for smuggling Class A drugs.'

'Presumably for his own use?' Neagle suggested.

'You've got to be joking. The amount of H found in his suitcase had a street value of three hundred and fifty thousand.' Verco broke off and gazed pointedly at the mortuary attendant. 'You look as though you're dying for a cigarette. Why don't you go outside and have one?'

'I don't smoke.'

'So go and get yourself a breath of fresh air instead.'

'I can take a hint,' the attendant told him in a surly voice.

Verco waited until the man had left the building, then said, 'Mahmoud or whatever you want to call him was charged with possession with intent to supply. He was wheeled up before the magistrate and remanded in police custody. The evidence the DPP had made it an open and shut case, but it never came to court. Mahmoud had friends in high places and they leaned on the Director of Public Prosecutions. The bastard was back on the streets barely forty-eight hours later.'

Landon was left in no doubt that, in Verco's opinion, the friends in high places were to be found within the SIS. 'Are you certain Mahmoud Hassan Soliman and Anwar Farid are one and the same man?' he asked.

'Mahmoud was fingerprinted as soon as he was arrested,' Verco told him. 'The detective chief superintendent of "B" District had the same thing done to this man when he fetched up here. Within an hour the National Identification Bureau had a perfect match.'

In the last two years the Head of the Mid East Department had changed three times. For much of that time span Ralph Meacher had been keeping the chair warm for a Foreign Office nominee, and no way would Ralph have gone out on a limb for Anwar Farid. At least Landon couldn't see him doing so and he believed Meacher's predecessor would never have countenanced the idea either. That left the notorious Jill Sheridan, whose reputation for being a bit of a chancer had eventually brought about her downfall. If saving Anwar's hide would have furthered her career, Landon could see Jill Sheridan persuading somebody to lean on the DPP. But that was a mighty big 'if'.

'I assume you've seen enough of this corpse,' Verco said and closed the drawer. Sidestepping to the next bank of three, he pulled out the top container. 'This is the mysterious transvestite Richard will have told you about. He calls himself Danièle.'

'When did you learn that, John?' Neagle asked sharply.

31

'A few minutes before you arrived,' Verco told him. 'The murder team has been talking to the staff of Giordano's. They say Quayle booked a table for two and looked pretty boot faced when Anwar Farid showed up with this fruitcake in tow. Anyway, according to the waiter who looked after the table, Danièle was full of herself and kept interrupting the two men. Thanks to her they were still sitting over lunch long after three o'clock when the restaurant should have closed.'

'So in the end there were just four of them in Giordano's,' Landon said and rattled off their names.

'What's your point?'

'Danièle was found in the men's room, where were the others?'

'Enrico Giordano was behind the bar, Farid was still in his chair but sprawled across the table. Quayle appeared to be crawling towards the entrance.'

'Whereabouts is the men's room? Near the entrance or further back?'

It was, Verco told him, on the alley side of the restaurant towards the kitchen but forward of the bar. It was just beyond the ladies' on the other side of the short corridor. Both facilities were illuminated by strip lights in the ceiling and there was no exit into the alley.

'Quayle was trying to escape,' Landon said voicing his thoughts. 'But what the hell was Danièle playing at?'

'He'd gone to the lavatory and decided to stay there when the shooter opened fire.'

'So how did the gunmen effect an entrance?'

'Gunman,' Verco said tersely. 'From the ejected

empty cases it was obvious that there was only one shooter.'

Landon knew it wouldn't have taken ballistics long to reach that conclusion. No two firing pins left the same indentation when striking the primer. Each one had a distinctive signature.

'And he didn't have to break in,' Verco continued. 'The back door was unlocked. Enrico Giordano lived in the flat above; he was always the last person to leave the restaurant and he routinely locked the back door behind him. Mystery solved. Right?'

'Only in part.' Aside from the fact that the shooter must have known the back door would be unlocked, there was also the little matter of the almost perfect timing. Someone must have told the gunman the restaurant was still open and there were just four people inside. 'What did the scenes of crime officers find in Danièle's handbag?' Landon said.

'The usual womanly things.'

'How about a mobile phone?'

'I've no idea. You'll have to ask the investigating officer when we finally catch up with him.' Verco closed the drawer containing Danièle's body.

'It's time we moved on,' he said.

Before they set off to Wood Green and the semi-detached at 62 Monk Road, Landon just had time to call up the communications centre at Vauxhall Cross on the Haydn, the miniature, battery operated, crypto-protected radio he'd drawn from the Positive Vetting and Technical Services Division. The message he left for Ashton concerned the true identity of Anwar Farid.

Even before the Berlin Wall came down the Middle East was regarded as the number one flashpoint in the world. The so-called peace dividend occasioned by the disintegration of the Warsaw Pact had had little effect on Ralph Meacher's empire. Other establishments had been pared to the bone in a cost-cutting exercise but the Mid East Department had emerged from the reorganization virtually unscathed. It had more linguists, clerical support staff, Analysts Special Intelligence, and grade I officers than the combined strength of Ashton's fiefdom and the Pacific Basin and Rest of the World Department. It was therefore not entirely inappropriate that, next to the DG and his deputy, Meacher should have the largest office on the top floor, often referred to as the eyrie.

When Ashton dropped in on him Meacher was busy searching MIDAS, the Multi-Intelligence Data Access System. In order to protect the highly classified information on file, the visual display unit was mounted on a small table positioned against the wall in the far corner of the room well away from the window. Consequently Meacher had his back to Ashton and wasn't aware of his presence until he tapped on the open door.

'Can you spare me a minute, Ralph?' he asked.

'Be my guest.' Meacher waved him to a chair, then blanked out the VDU and returned to his desk. 'Toby hasn't snuffed it, has he, Peter?' he asked. 'I mean it's only a few minutes ago that Roy Kelso assured me he was still hanging on.'

'He still is as far as I know. This concerns the late Anwar Farid. How well did you know him?'

'I never met him. All I can tell you is that the information he gave us was usually pretty solid. That's why I graded him a C3 source.'

'Who recruited him? Toby Quayle?'

'Yes.'

'How long ago?'

'What is this?' Meacher snapped, his eyes narrowing.

'Humour me, Ralph.'

'OK. Farid was recruited by Toby Quayle in February 1995.'

'Does the name Mahmoud Hassan Soliman ring a bell with you?'

'I think you had better tell me what this is all about because I'm not answering another damned question until you do.'

'After Farid was pronounced DOA at the Brompton, taking his fingerprints was the first thing the police did. They matched him with those taken from Mahmoud Hassan Soliman in January 1997.'

Meacher looked stunned, as if he had forgotten to duck when passing under a low arch. He looked even more poleaxed on learning that Soliman had been caught with three hundred and fifty thousand pounds worth of a Class A drug in his possession.

'He never appeared in court,' Ashton continued. 'Somebody with a lot of influence told the Crown Prosecution Service to drop the case. According to Landon's informant the police were hopping mad.'

Meacher didn't say anything. Instead he got up, went over to the VDU and switched on the computer, then accessed the Mid East programme. Under the file dealing with Egypt, he went into the sub-section headed 'Paid Informants'. Arranged in alphabetical order, Anwar Farid's name was the fourth one down from the top. Mahmoud Hassan Soliman however was not on the list. Tapping in the appropriate entry code, Meacher put Farid's entire case history on the screen. Despite the acronym, MIDAS was not all embracing. Agents in place were excluded from the database as was information that could only be released on a need-to-know basis. The latter category was indicated by a star against the name of the informant. Farid carried two stars, details of which were recorded in BM/05/ME/Cairo.

'Let's have a look at that branch memorandum,' Ashton said, reaching past Meacher to tap the screen.

A faint smile appeared on Meacher's lips. 'That's real *News of the World* stuff,' he said.

'Somebody's sexual peccadillo?'

'More like wishful thinking on the part of Louise Appleton.'

'Who's she?'

'She was the cultural attaché at the British Embassy in Cairo from September 1994 to July 1995.'

Twice within a period of nine days Ms Appleton had accused Anwar Farid of indecently assaulting her. The first assault had allegedly occurred at a house-warming party given by a British nursing sister, who had just been appointed to the Children's Hospital in Garden City, a suburb of Cairo. The second incident had occurred at a dinner and dance hosted by a Greek couple to celebrate their twenty-fifth wedding anniversary and had been held at a restaurant in Heliopolis. The celebration had been attended by the Head of

Chancery.

'Louise Appleton submitted a report complaining that Anwar Farid had fondled her buttocks while they were dancing.' The ghost of a smile that had been hovering on Meacher's lips became a definite beam. 'Head of Chancery reckoned it had been six of one and half a dozen of the other the way she had been rubbing herself against Farid. Louise Appleton is nothing to look at but she certainly put it about. That's why the lady only lasted ten months in Cairo.'

'I'd still like to see the file, Ralph.'

'That figures.'

Meacher switched off the computer, then rang the chief archivist of the Mid East Department and asked for branch memorandum BM/05/ME/Cairo. The file that arrived a few minutes later was decidedly slim. It contained copies of the two complaints made by Louise Appleton, an internal memo commenting on the allegations from the Head of Chancery to the ambassador, who had subsequently forwarded it to the Foreign and Commonwealth Office. There it had lain fallow until the 5th March 1996 when the senior Deputy Under Secretary of State had seen fit to provide the SIS with a complete dossier. Two photographs had been included with the papers. One showed a casually dressed Anwar Farid on the sundeck of a houseboat while the other subject was a rangy woman with a long face that reminded Ashton of a horse. Louise Appleton, he learned, had been photographed at a reception to mark the official birthday of the Queen.

'You see what I mean about wishful thinking,' Meacher said. 'What would make a good-looking bloke like Anwar Farid lust after a skinny thirty-six-year-old who appears to have an eating disorder?'

Ashton thought he had a point but what interested him more was the covering letter from the Deputy Under Secretary. It bore all the hallmarks of a Foreign Office mandarin, in that the D.U.S. had drawn attention to the potential security risk involved in employing Anwar Farid, and had then virtually discounted the threat in the next paragraph.

'The D.U.S. appears to think Farid deliberately set out to cultivate Louise Appleton,' Ashton observed.

'Yeah, he obviously believes in covering himself. I mean the lady was a cultural attaché, what could she tell him for chrissake?'

'The answer's a great deal about her colleagues as you know full well, Ralph.'

'Farid gave us some good stuff in his time,' Meacher said defensively.

'I'm sure the DG is aware of that.'

'This business about Mahmoud Hassan Soliman? Is it possible the National Identification Bureau made an error?'

'The answer is no. You're just clutching at straws, Ralph.'

Ashton thought he would probably do the same in Meacher's position.

'Nobody in my department knew of Mahmoud Hassan Soliman's existence,' Meacher said forcefully.

'I believe you.'

'Yeah? Who else will?'

'Victor Hazelwood for one. I reckon Farid had two paymasters, ourselves and MI5.'

'That's ridiculous.'

'Think about it,' Ashton told him. 'Which agency has the most influence with the Home Office? It's no contest; MI5 and the Home Office couldn't be closer if they were housed under the same roof.'

Four

Number 62 Monk Road was a ten-minute walk from both Alexandra Park and Wood Green station on the Piccadilly Line. The three bedroom semi-detached had been built in 1925 at the height of the ribbon development that had begun shortly after the Great War, as it had been called in those days. Similar houses were to be found in towns as far apart as Middlesbrough, Darlington, York, Leicester, Brighton, Swindon and Kidderminster, as well as the outer suburbs of London. In an era when few people owned a motor car, only one semi-detached in eight had been provided with a garage. Seventy years on ninety-five per cent of the families living in the street owned more than one car. Consequently nearly every front garden had been concreted over to give the owner-occupier a hard standing for at least one car. A five-year-old Saab 9000 was parked on the hard standing outside 62 Monk Road.

There was nowhere to park near the house Farid had owned. Alighting from the car with the other two, Neagle told the driver to try his luck further up the road, then stepped over the blue and white plastic tape the police had strung out to fence off the property. By the time he joined the Special Branch officer, Verco had already introduced Landon to the investigating officer.

'I'm Richard Neagle,' he said, advancing towards a tall powerfully built man who dwarfed Verco. 'And you are?'

'Detective Chief Superintendent Roberts from B District. Which of you two gentlemen had dealings with Mahmoud Hassan Soliman?'

'My lot did,' Landon told him, 'though we knew the deceased as Anwar Farid. He had lived at this address ever since we recruited him in 1995.'

'Living here rent free, was he?' Roberts said in a voice that dripped acid.

'Not exactly. We lent him the deposit and he took out a mortgage for the rest.'

'Pull the other one, it's got bells on it. You don't seriously expect me to believe Soliman needed a loan when he had such a sweet racket going for him on the side. He must have been the only drug baron in town who enjoyed the protection of Her Majesty's Secret Service.'

If Roberts had deliberately set out to needle him Landon reckoned the chief superintendent could not have done a better job. In an effort to contain his anger Landon counted slowly up to ten, but for once this didn't work.

'Now you've got that off your chest, perhaps you'd tell me what you've learned from the next-door neighbours. Did they have anything to say about Danièle? And what about Anwar Farid? Did they have any idea where he had been in the last few—'

'Hey, I'm in charge of a murder investigation team,' Roberts said, cutting him short. 'I answer to the commissioner of police not the chief spook. So don't come to me expecting answers to a shopping list of questions. I'll tell you what we learned so far.' A wry smile appeared on his mouth. 'And that's not very much,' he added.

None of the neighbours had recalled seeing a woman answering Danièle's description. However, Anwar Farid had not led a celibate life. According to the people next door and across the street from number 62, the Egyptian had had a long-term partner called Jeanne Wagnall. It seemed Farid had been about to marry her when she had suddenly dumped him.

'This was roughly three days before Farid took off for Birmingham.'

'Birmingham!' Landon repeated incredulously. 'When did he return from there?'

'The day before yesterday, Tuesday the sixteenth of March.' The wry smile made a second appearance. 'That's the one date all the neighbours agree. Apparently some driver hadn't left him enough room at the kerbside for Farid to reverse his car on to the hard standing fronting his semi-detached, and he had scraped the offside of the Saab 9000. Anyway, Farid called on all the neighbours wanting to know if any of them had seen this interloper who'd left his Ford Fiesta in the way. Of course they hadn't: people round here mind their own business.'

Farid had been as mad as hell and in revenge he had inflicted twice as much damage on the Ford Fiesta with a screwdriver. The owner hadn't done anything about it, he'd simply collected his car sometime during the early hours of Wednesday morning. Nobody had seen or heard him

41

drive away.

'The residents are equally vague about Farid's movements. However, the general consensus is that he had spent a fortnight in Birmingham. Farid allegedly has friends and family living in that part of the world.' Roberts gazed at him speculatively. 'Would you happen to know if there is any truth in that, Mr Landon?'

'Not off the top of my head. But the Admin Wing will have screened Farid before he was taken on. I'll see what they have on him and pass the information on to DI Verco.'

'Is there anything else I can do for you?'

'Actually there is. I'd like a photocopy of the original bloodstained note that was found in Quayle's jacket. We might be able to tell if it was in fact written by Anwar Farid.'

'OK. Do I send it direct to you?'

'I think it should go through DI Verco,' Neagle said, jumping in quickly. 'He is, after all, our official liaison officer.'

Roberts grunted. 'First I've heard of it,' he said.

'Do you mind if I look the place over?' Landon asked.

'What are you hoping to find? Or can't you tell me?'

'I don't see why you shouldn't know. The people who were running Anwar Farid reckoned he was a valuable source of human intelligence. Among his numerous acquaintances in the Middle East there were leading politicians, civil servants and businessmen together with a coterie of senior army and air force officers. He had an encyclopedic knowledge of their vices and character defects. Farid didn't pick up that sort of information nosing

42

around Birmingham.'

'I'll let you know what we find, Mr Landon.'

'Am I missing something?'

'In a manner of speaking,' Roberts said. 'We've already taken away his personal effects—cheque book, bank statements, account books, life insurance policy, driving licence and vehicle documents. We didn't find a passport.'

'I'd still like to run my eye over the place.'

'Be my guest,' Roberts said and opened the front door.

A narrow hall led to the kitchen, scullery and pantry that extended beyond the sitting room at the back of the house. The dining room at the front could not have been further away from the kitchen. Upstairs there were three bedrooms, the smallest of which over the porch was little more than a boxroom. Like so many other semi-detached houses in Monk Road part of the loft space had been converted to provide an extra room.

The desk positioned in the dormer window suggested Farid had used the extra room as a study. The drawers were, however, empty and, although two lines had been installed, there was no telephone, fax machine or computer. Under the amused gaze of Neagle, Landon removed and inspected the underside of each drawer.

'What exactly are you looking for, Will?' he asked.

'I'm damned if I know,' Landon told him.

The bedrooms off the landing below were equally anonymous. Landon thought it likely that the boxroom over the porch was rarely if ever used. With a divan single bed, hanging cupboard and chest of drawers in place there was scarcely room to turn round. It was evident Anwar Farid and Jeanne Wagnall had occupied the front bedroom. Her lipsticks, eye liner, moisturizing cream, lily of the valley scent and nail varnish were still on the dressing table, but all her underwear had gone from the chest of drawers. Although Farid had just two suits, a sports jacket and three pairs of slacks, the wardrobe revealed that there were enough spare hangers to open a ladies' dress shop. There was also the best part of another full rack in the other main bedroom, suggesting Jeanne Wagnall could have stocked that as well.

'There's nothing here,' Landon said. 'Let's go downstairs.'

'What about that picture on the wall? Don't you want to look behind it?'

Neagle was enjoying himself immensely at his expense. Telling him he didn't know what he was looking for had been a mistake.

'I can't see the mouse,' Neagle murmured.

'What?'

'Terence Cuneo always puts a mouse in somewhere, it's like a signature.'

The signed print was called *Out of the Night* and showed a steam train hurtling through the darkness with the distant lights of a town in the background.

'There's the mouse,' Landon said, pointing to a parallel track. 'It's jumping the rail nearest the locomotive.'

Acting on impulse, Landon took down the picture and examined the back, half expecting Neagle to observe that changing one's mind was usually a woman's prerogative. There was, he noticed, a small sticker in one corner of the mount that indicated the print had been purchased from

44

Parker's Fine Art Gallery, Richmond, Surrey.

'What do you reckon?' Landon asked. 'Do you think the previous owner left it behind when he moved out?'

'Maybe.'

'But this print is a limited edition and it must be worth a bob or two.'

'Well, in your shoes I wouldn't waste my time trying to ascertain how the print came to be in Farid's possession.'

'I don't intend to,' Landon said.

'Does that go for the rest of the house?' Neagle asked.

Landon ignored him and went downstairs to check out the dining and living rooms. In common with the rest of the house both rooms were totally antiseptic. All the houses Landon had ever seen reflected the personalities of their owners. Farid was the exception; he had not put his stamp on the property. There were no ornaments, no photographs, no books, no bric-a-brac, and no pictures save for the Cuneo print upstairs. The Egyptian had been the embodiment of the classic definition of a spy. In life he had been the sort of man who would not have been noticed by the waiters in an otherwise empty restaurant.

'What now?' Neagle asked.

'There's nothing here for us,' Landon told him.

Roberts asked him virtually the same question as he walked out of the house.

'Just a couple of points,' Landon said. 'There are two BT lines in the dormer room. Do I have to say any more?'

Roberts shook his head. 'Farid had an answer phone and a computer. We removed them early

45

this morning together with a three-drawer filing cabinet.'

'What about his mobile?'

'It wasn't on his person and we certainly didn't find one at this address. For that matter, your Mr Quayle didn't have a mobile on him either.'

Landon frowned, it was inconceivable that neither man was carrying a mobile. That could be bad news, if his presumption was correct.

'Let's hope they didn't programme their most used phone numbers,' Roberts said, as if reading his thoughts.

'What now, Will?' Neagle asked, a touch impatiently.

'I want to go to Heathrow.'

'Fine. We'll drop you at Wood Green station and you can go by Underground.'

'OK. But DCI Verco comes with me.'

'Now just a minute—'

'No, you listen to me,' Landon said, interrupting him. 'I'm telling you Anwar Farid hasn't been near Birmingham during the last fortnight; he was sunning himself in warmer climes until he returned home two or three days ago.'

'How on earth are you going to prove that when you don't have his passport?'

'Anwar Farid becomes the cover name of a terrorist who is believed to have entered the UK. We then persuade every airline to check their manifests for the past week. That's why I need DCI Verco.'

Landon didn't have to point out to Neagle that he would get a lot more cooperation from the police at Heathrow airport if he was accompanied by a senior officer from Special Branch.

'Naturally Chief Superintendent Roberts can't release Farid's name to the press. For the foreseeable future he has to remain an unidentified victim.'

'What if there are next of kin?'

'We deal with that problem when it arises,' Landon said.

From their expressions, it was evident the two police officers didn't like the sound of it one bit. Furthermore, Neagle didn't appear all that keen either and without his support Landon knew he would get nowhere. Somehow he had to get the MI5 officer on his side.

'Look, Richard, whatever profitable sideline he might have had, Farid was a good source of information. He told Toby Quayle he had run into Talal Asir and I don't believe he would lie about that. We don't know where or when this happened and I doubt the bloodstained note will tell us. Our only hope is to discover where Farid has been and we can't afford to ignore even the slenderest of possible leads.'

It wasn't the most convincing argument he had ever made and there was an intolerably long pause before Neagle finally agreed to go along with his suggestion.

*   *   *

As the Admin King of Vauxhall Cross, Roy Kelso's empire consisted of the Financial Branch, the Motor Transport and General Stores Section plus the Security Vetting and Technical Services Division. Among his many duties he was responsible for the provision of clerical support, control of expenditure, claims and expenses, works services, internal audits, collation of estimates under vote sub-heads, disbursement of funds and boards of inquiry. Of these, the disbursement of funds was the job which gave him the most satisfaction together with a real sense of power. In preparing their own estimates, heads of departments always tried to allow for the cuts the Treasury was bound to impose by inflating their budget for the financial year. The Treasury was however wise to this gambit and still made draconian cuts no matter how convincing the department's justification might be on paper. With the next financial year just over a fortnight away, the Treasury had finally announced just how much money the SIS would be allowed to spend in 1999/2000. It was a long way short of what the various assistant directors had asked for, but there was nothing unusual about that, it happened year on year. And year on year Kelso had to adjudicate between the bids submitted by heads of departments. He had already warned his colleagues that money was going to be even tighter in the coming year and was now busy preparing the proposed allotment of funds.

There was not the slightest chance the proposed disbursements would go through on the nod. As in previous years the allotment would be revised several times before agreement was reached under his chairmanship of the estimates committee. It was this role of power broker that gave Kelso such immense satisfaction. Kelso was in the process of correcting the first draft when he was interrupted by an incoming call on the British Telecom unprotected line. The ensuing conversation was brief and largely one sided. When it was over,

Kelso left his office, locked the door behind him and walked to the other end of the corridor to see Hazelwood. If you wanted an audience with the Director General during normal office hours you had to go through Dilys Crowther, the PA, a fact of life that really irked Kelso. He could not forget that when he had been promoted to Assistant Director Victor Hazelwood had merely been the Grade I Intelligence Officer in charge of the Russian desk. To assert his independence it was Kelso's practice to breeze through the PA's office, open the communicating door and walk in on Hazelwood before Dilys Crowther had a chance to announce him over the intercom.

'I've just heard from the Brompton and I'm afraid it's not good news, Victor.' Kelso cleared his throat. 'Toby Quayle died this afternoon at 1513 hours without regaining consciousness.'

'I'm sorry to hear that. Has Ralph Meacher been informed?'

'Not yet. I thought the next of kin should be the first to hear the news.'

'Quite. I imagine it won't come as a total shock. I mean you have already been in touch with the next of kin, haven't you, Roy?'

'I sent a cable to the last known address of Toby's sister.' He wanted Hazelwood to know that in contravention of standing instructions, Toby Quayle hadn't bothered to keep his personal circumstances up to date, despite the usual routine reminder at the beginning of January each year. Kelso had tried to phone the sister but all he'd got was an unobtainable signal, which suggested she might have moved house.

'You should have rung our High Commission in

49

Wellington,' Hazelwood told him. 'They've got a Second Secretary who is responsible for Administration and Consular Affairs.'

'With respect, Victor, New Zealand is twelve hours ahead of us. It was almost eleven o'clock at night their time when we learned officially that Toby Quayle had been shot and was in a critical condition. I shall call the High Commission from my home late tonight when I can be sure the Second Secretary, Administration will be in his office. Meantime I will fire off another cable to Quayle's sister.'

'Have the police been given Toby's address?'

Kelso bridled, quick to take offence at what he thought was a critical tone of voice. 'Of course they have,' he snapped. 'I contacted the assistant commissioner in charge of the Serious Crime Squads at Scotland Yard the moment I heard Landon had formally identified the body.'

'You should have consulted me first, Roy, then we could have spring cleaned his flat before they arrived.'

'Spring cleaned,' Kelso repeated with emphasis. 'Do we have the odd skeleton in the cupboard?'

'One must hope not.' Hazelwood paused as if torn with indecision, then said, 'However, the fact is that two years after Anwar Farid started working for us, he was caught smuggling Class A drugs into this country. He was arrested and charged under the name of Mahmoud Hassan Soliman. Forty-eight hours later the Director of Public Prosecutions was persuaded to drop the case and he walked. We knew nothing of this and weren't involved. In other words, the SIS wasn't the only Intelligence organization Farid was reporting to.

50

That said, we need to satisfy ourselves that Toby had clean hands.'

'What would you like me to do?' Kelso asked.

What Hazelwood wanted from him was simple enough. On the first of each month Quayle's salary was automatically transmitted to his bank account by the pay branch, without disclosing the reason why he wanted the information to his subordinates; Kelso was to ascertain which bank had looked after Quayle, his National Insurance number and the tax office the Admin Wing dealt with.

'And that's all there is to it, Victor?'

'Absolutely,' Hazelwood assured him.

But it was just the beginning. Moments after Kelso had left his office Hazelwood was on the phone to Colin Wales, the newly appointed Deputy DG of MI5.

*   *   *

Although Ali Mohammed Khalef was no stranger to the North-West Frontier Province of Pakistan, this was the first time he had been to Peshawar and he was anxious not to lose sight of his twelve-year-old guide. The boy, who was under five feet, was approximately twenty yards in front of him and from time to time was swallowed up in the jostling crowd. The café he was making for was on Jinnah Street and was said to be above a fruit and vegetable shop, but that could apply to practically every other stall in the bazaar. Should he lose the guide, Khalef doubted if he would find the café.

He was dressed like a Pathan in sandals, baggy trousers, loose-fitting knee-length tunic and an untidy looking turban with long loops coming down round his neck. Beneath the tunic Khalef was carrying two thousand rupees and gold coins to the value of fifteen hundred pounds. Ten days ago he had met with Talal Asir in Damascus, in June of last year he had been living in London's Finsbury Park.

Khalef suddenly lost sight of the boy and broke into a shambling run, elbowing his way through the crowd. Before he caught up with him in an alleyway between a fruit and vegetable stall and an open-fronted shop selling bolts of cloth, he had cannoned into two men and knocked down an old woman in the space of less than twenty yards.

Beckoning Khalef to follow, the boy led him further down the alley to an iron gate in an adobe wall. The gate opened into a small courtyard littered with sacks of rotting mangoes and bananas that had attracted a myriad of flies. An evil looking pi-dog scavenging for food among the sacks snarled at Khalef as he moved towards the external wooden staircase.

'He will not hurt you,' the boy told him.

The animal looked to be frothing at the mouth, which was enough to make Khalef suspect it had rabies. With a fine regard for his own safety he made sure the boy was between him and the animal before he scuttled up the staircase to the veranda above. From the top he could look down into Jinnah Street on his left while in the opposite direction he enjoyed an uninterrupted view of a vehicle repair shop on the parallel road. There were two doors to his front; easing past Khalef the boy opened the right-hand one and waved him to step inside the room. Only the leader of the four men waiting for him was known to Khalef.

'Greetings, Tara Rahim Khan,' he said. 'I salute you.'

Khan nodded. 'You have come from Talal Asir?'

'Yes. With money and gold.' Khalef sat down cross-legged on the carpet.

Raising his tunic, he unclipped the money belt around the waist and passed it to Rahim Khan. From the inside pocket of his tunic he then produced a photograph. 'And this is the infidel who has been sentenced to die in ignominy.'

The infidel was fifty-six years old and married with two children, both of whom were at school in England. He was the British Council representative in Islamabad and was to be taken from his house in the middle of the night and conveyed to a place of imprisonment, there to await execution in the presence of his wife, the American whore.

'The infidel is to be castrated before he is beheaded.' Khalef looked Rahim Khan in the eye. 'I want it clearly understood that he must face the camera the whole time.'

'And what of the woman?'

'Oh, you may hang her whenever it pleases you,' Khalef informed him.

Five

Obtaining what Landon had wanted from the airlines using Heathrow had proved to be a daunting task. If the trawl was to be of any real value the search could not be limited only to in-bound flights from the Middle East. Anwar Farid was a free agent and there was nothing to prevent him returning to the UK via Cape Town if he had a mind to. Furthermore, although Farid had been seen in Monk Road on Tuesday, who was to say he hadn't arrived two or three days prior to that and had spent the intervening time elsewhere? From a practical standpoint what counted was the number of days an airline retained an in-bound flight manifest and that, as Landon rapidly discovered, varied between long-haul carriers.

It was also possible that Anwar Farid had flown into Gatwick, Stansted or Luton. Inevitably they'd had to strike a balance and, at Neagle's suggestion, they'd put Gatwick on hold, dropped Stansted and Luton from the equation and concentrated on Heathrow from the first in-bound flight on Sunday 14th March. As a sop to Landon, Neagle had agreed to check the car parks in the vicinity of the airport where Farid might have left the Saab 900 while he was out of the country. It had taken DI Verco less than ten minutes to discover the long-stay car parks at Heathrow were unable to assist them.

After yesterday's burst of activity, all any of them could do now was sit back and wait to hear from the airlines. For Landon today was yet another opportunity to get to grips with his principal job. Before being transferred to Ashton's department, he had run the South American desk for Roger Benton's Pacific Basin and Rest of the World organization. He had read Spanish and Italian at Nottingham University and had subsequently spent three years in Peru, masquerading as the Third Secretary, Administration at the British Embassy in Lima. What he had known about the Balkans three years ago could have been written on the back of a postcard. A year ago Ashton would not have trusted him to find the linguistic support for the eight SAS deep penetration patrols that were deployed in Kosovo.

The requirement was to provide four Serbo-Croat speakers and four Albanian, which would have been easy enough but for one major snag. The indigenous population had to believe the interpreters were completely neutral. To this end English-speaking Serb and Albanian nationals could not be recruited. Finding the Serbo-Croat interpreters was not difficult, the armed forces had a fair number of linguists on their active and reserve lists and there was also a pool of salesmen who'd done business with Tito and were willing to do their bit. Albanian speakers were, however, few and far between. Until the politicians had seen fit to intervene in Kosovo the armed services had had no need of Albanian linguists, and precious few businessmen had had any dealings with the country.

So far they had got by with a little help from Government Communications Headquarters and the reluctant agreement of both the FCO and the Cabinet Office that the fifty-fifty ratio between Serbo-Croat and Albanian speakers was not sacrosanct. Like the SAS patrols they were attached to, linguists spent six months in the field. The commitment had started in June 1998 and the first relief party had been on the ground for almost twelve weeks. Although he still had three months in hand, Landon was already looking for the next four Albanian linguists. To date he had one definite and one possible, leaving him with two

55

holes he had no hope of filling. The way Landon saw it, the Cabinet Office had three options. They could accept a three to one imbalance, allow Albanian nationals to be recruited or scale down the number of deep penetration patrols in order to achieve a not too disproportionate ratio. All he had to do was draft a letter for the DG's signature, getting started was the difficult part. Lacking inspiration, it came as something of a relief when Ashton rang and asked him to come on up.

Landon had assumed Peter wanted to know if they'd had any joy from Heathrow yet and was caught on the hop when he disclosed that Hazelwood wanted to be sure Toby Quayle hadn't left a nasty mess behind him.

'This has to do with Farid's double identity,' Ashton told him. 'We have to know whether or not Toby was clean.'

'I can guess what's coming.'

'I'm sure you can, Will. As a Grade I Intelligence officer with six years seniority, Quayle was on £54K a year plus three thousand five hundred inner London weighting allowance. He had a two-bedroom house at 3 Mews Terrace, Lancaster Gate, which he was buying with an endowment mortgage. Run your eye over the place and find out what it's worth at today's market price.'

'Seems straight enough to me,' Landon murmured.

'Well, now comes the tricky bit. We would like you to look inside the house and see what Toby had in the way of silver, paintings and other valuables.'

'Have we got a key to the front door?' Landon asked.

'Terry Hicks will be coming with you. He has a whole bunch of keys.'

To all intents and purposes Terry Hicks was the Technical Services Division. Every year he descended on the twelve most vulnerable embassies around the world and swept them for electronic bugs. If there was such a thing as a master class in breaking and entering, Hicks would be an automatic choice for chief instructor. And when it came to wiring a room for sound or effecting an illegal phone tap there was nobody to touch him.

'If I need Hicks it obviously isn't a kosher job,' Landon observed quietly.

'Damn right it isn't,' Ashton told him bluntly. 'Roy Kelso saw fit to give Toby's address to the Assistant Commissioner, Serious Crime Squads.'

'When was this?'

'Yesterday.'

'And when did we decide to look the place over?' Landon asked.

'A half-hour ago. And, yes, we should have grasped the nettle yesterday but there were too many faint hearts on Thursday.'

'Do I have any discretion?'

'Not really,' Ashton said laconically. 'But I'm telling you to walk away from the mews should the men and women from Grub Street be camping on the doorstep. Same applies to any sign of Plod. OK?'

'It is now.'

'Good. Call Hicks when you're ready to go.'

Landon said he would do that and returned to his office on the fourth floor with its unrivalled view of the rail tracks from Vauxhall to Queenstown Road,

Battersea. He cleared the filing trays from his desk and stacked them inside the safe, then closed it up and spun the combination lock. He was about to call Hicks on the internal line when the Mozart rang. Lifting the receiver, Landon reeled off the number of his extension and found he had Neagle on the line.

'Congratulations,' Neagle said. 'You were right, we were wrong.'

'About what?'

'Airways Cranford Parking.'

'Now I'm with you.'

After DI Verco had established that none of the long-stay car parks at Heathrow were able to help them, he and Neagle had been reluctant to widen the search. Landon had argued vehemently that Airways Cranford Parking should be included because it was on the doorstep and, having used it himself, he knew their system of ticketing.

'They found the docket Farid had completed when he left the country on February the twenty-sixth,' Neagle continued. 'And guess what, he returned on Monday the fifteenth of March, twenty-four hours before he was seen in Monk Road.'

Neagle was dragging it out again, seeking to maximize the impact of what he was about to disclose. Ordinarily Landon didn't allow this little foible to annoy him. But this time it was different; he knew what Neagle was holding back and he was in a hurry.

'So what flight number did Farid put on the docket?' Landon demanded tersely.

'United Airlines flight 956. You want to know where it departed from?'

'New York JFK?' Landon said in a hollow voice.

'I thought that would shake you. What price Talal Asir now?'

'Have you verified the flight details with United?'

'Now you're clutching at straws and that's not like you, Will.'

'You're right, it isn't, and I'm not clutching at straws.'

'OK,' Neagle said exasperated. 'I checked with United. As I could give them the flight number and the date and time of arrival they were able to call up the appropriate manifest, which fortunately was still on their database. And yes, Anwar Farid was on flight 956 departing JFK, Sunday the fourteenth of March.'

'Was there a woman with the first or last name of Danièle on the flight?'

'No, but there was a man called Kopek whose first name was Daniel, which you've got to admit is pretty close to Danièle.'

In order to eliminate Kopek from the equation Neagle had asked United Airlines for any information they might have on him.

'I've already got Immigration going through their landing cards.' Neagle cleared his throat. 'Naturally they won't find a landing card for Kopek should he hail from a country within the European Union, but I'm pretty sure he doesn't.'

'Did you get Farid's credit card number from Airways Cranford Parking?'

Neagle said he believed the Egyptian had paid in cash, which probably meant he hadn't thought to ask.

'We need to know whom Farid banks with, the sort code of the branch and the number of his account. With that information we can probably—'

'Less of the royal "we",' Neagle said, interrupting him.

'You can't wash your hands of this because there is a slim chance Farid's death was crime related. The police took charge of his personal effects at the scene of the crime and cleaned out 62 Monk Road. They won't give me the information I need but Verco is your Special Branch link man and he can get it. All you have to do is ask him nicely.'

'I'm sorry, Will, but it seems to me your real concern is to protect Toby Quayle's reputation.'

'This isn't how the Combined Anti-Terrorist Organization is supposed to work,' Landon said icily. 'I don't mean to threaten you, Richard, but what do you suppose will happen when my DG becomes aware of your attitude?'

Not even Neagle's worst enemy could ever accuse him of lacking imagination. Consequently it took him less than a minute to conclude that perhaps he had been a little hasty.

*　　　*　　　*

It was the third meeting Ashton had attended that day. There had been the usual conference, commonly known as morning prayers, at 0830, followed two and a quarter hours later by Roy Kelso's moment of glory when heads of departments had learned how much money they were likely to receive in the financial year 1999/2000. The present conference had been called at short notice moments after Kelso had received forewarning from the police that they were going to name Toby Quayle as one of the murder victims when briefing the press at 5 p.m. As Hazelwood was quick to point out, they had little over four hours in which to construct a legend for the deceased.

'We have to manufacture a cover story that will stand up to critical examination,' Hazelwood told them. 'It's no use our claiming that Quayle was a middle-ranking civil servant and leaving it at that. We need to bury him in a boring job in an equally boring department of state.' He paused and looked around the table. 'Any suggestions?'

Nobody said a word. Rowan Garfield, the stop-gap Deputy DG, left the table, went over to the bookshelf and returned with an up-to-date copy of *Whitaker's Almanack*. 'The Home Office looks promising,' he announced presently, 'especially the Establishment Department. We could make him a Senior Executive Officer. After all, who's going to notice one extra when there are already thirty-one of them?'

'Are they named?' Ashton asked.

'Yes.'

'Then you had better demote Quayle to a grade where the incumbents are anonymous because you can bet some investigative journalist worth his salt will look for Toby in *Whitaker's*.'

Garfield consulted the *Almanack* again. 'OK. We make Toby a Higher Executive Officer, the grade doesn't even appear in the list.'

'And there is bound to be a small army of HEOs judging by the number of Senior Executive Officers,' Kelso observed chipping in. 'The Establishment Department is a big organization and like our own "Firm" you really only know the people who work alongside you. The others are just

61

faces you can't put a name to.'

'You make a valid point, Roy, one we should all bear in mind.' Hazelwood glanced in Ashton's direction. 'But I sense you are not happy with the proposal?'

Ashton wasn't, neither was Ralph Meacher for much the same reasons. Quayle had patronized Giordano's more than once and was known to the waiters. The staff had also told the police that Wednesday was not the first time he had entertained Anwar Farid to lunch. The restaurant was not some local deli frequented by civil servants who popped out of the office to buy a sandwich for lunch. Giordano's had already become known to reporters and they would begin to wonder how a Higher Executive Officer could afford to eat there, let alone wine and dine others.

'There's another factor we need to take into account,' Ashton continued. 'The time will come when Detective Chief Superintendent Roberts will find himself under increasing pressure to convince the public that the investigation hasn't come to a grinding halt. When that happens he will be forced to name Anwar Farid.'

And once the name was out how long would it be before some tout in B District gave his friendly reporter the whole story about the Egyptian for a small consideration? It would be the foretaste of a story that would run and run.

'We have to place Quayle in a job where, of necessity, he is obliged to sup with some pretty unpleasant people from time to time.'

'What are you going to do, Peter? Palm him off on to some other agency?' Garfield asked superciliously and drew a snigger from Kelso.

'No, we make him a member of the International Institute of Strategic Studies in Tavistock Street.'

The suggestion had Rowan Garfield thumbing through *Whitaker's* for the third time until he found what he wanted in the section dealing with societies and institutes. 'It's too small an organization, Peter, and surely he would look out of place? I mean the secretary is a retired lieutenant colonel and there are bound to be others from the armed forces.'

'I think you'll find the institute can call on a few retired members of the Diplomatic, Rowan. And let's not forget Toby's name appears in the FCO staff list.'

'I'm beginning to like it,' Hazelwood said.

'I think my department can put some flesh on the bones,' Meacher said. 'Over the years Toby has written various appreciations of the political situation in the Middle East. It would be comparatively easy to top and tail each paper and make it appear the document was written specifically for the Institute of Strategic Studies.'

There was no danger of the deception being betrayed. Unless ordered to brief the press, officers of the armed forces avoided all reporters like the plague.

'I'd like to distance ourselves from the operation,' Hazelwood said ruminatively.

'That's not a problem,' Ashton told him. 'I'll get Max Brabazon to brief the secretary of Strategic Studies.'

Brabazon was the retired Commander RN in charge of the SIS element of Military Operations (Special Projects). When justifying the reincarnation of the East European and Balkans Department, the then Deputy DG had added the

SIS cell in the MoD's Directorate of Military Operations for presentational purposes.

'Now I definitely like it.' Hazelwood bumped his chair back half a pace and stood up. 'So what are you waiting for, Peter?' he asked. 'Get Max over here and brief him.'

Garfield held his tongue until Hazelwood had left the conference room, then said, 'What happened to the concept of burying Toby in a boring job in an equally boring department of state?'

'Victor obviously changed his mind,' Ashton told him. 'It's not against the law to have second thoughts.'

*   *   *

Although only a stone's throw from the Bayswater Road the continuous noise from the nose to tail traffic did not reach Mews Terrace, Lancaster Gate. It was as if the cul-de-sac were protected by an invisible, soundproof cocoon. There were sixteen cottages in the mews, six on either side of the cobbled road and four across the bottom end of the close. Landon thought they had probably been built towards the end of the Victorian era, though clearly they had been skilfully modernized since then, possibly more than once. At one time there had been two fairly large rooms at the front on the ground floor, one of which had since been demolished to provide space for a garage. There was nothing tacky about the conversion, the pillars and the stonework beneath the room over the garage blended with the rest of the cottage.

There was a uniformity about Mews Terrace, as if a local by-law required every resident to have the same brass knocker, doorknob and coach lamp. The regulation apparently applied to the window boxes at the first-floor level, all of which had been planted with dwarf daffodils. Peaceful was an adjective that sprang to mind: at 1.26 that afternoon Mews Terrace was deserted.

'Where is everybody?' Hicks murmured.

'Be thankful the press aren't camped on the doorstep and there's no sign of the police.'

'Why would the boys in blue show up?'

'Kelso gave them Toby Quayle's address yesterday afternoon.'

'Terrific.'

'I thought you would be pleased. Now let's get this over soon as we can.'

The front door was fitted with a Yale lock; taking a bunch of skeleton keys out of his trouser pocket, Hicks tried them one by one. As he was doing this, Landon turned about and moved in front of him while giving the impression that he was making notes on the clipboard in his left hand. If anybody in Mews Terrace was watching he hoped the clipboard would lend them an air of respectability and allay whatever suspicions they might have.

'Cracked it,' Hicks said with evident relief. 'A double-handed job—Yale lock and doorknob.'

Landon followed him inside, closed the door and then left his clipboard on the hall table. The hall was much larger than he had expected. Halfway down a spiral staircase led to the landing above. Landon however was only interested in the two rooms at the back.

'What are we looking for?' Hicks asked as they entered the dining room.

'Anything of value,' Landon told him. 'What do

65

you know about silver, porcelain and works of art?'

'I can tell the difference between EPNS and the genuine article.'

The salver, vegetable dishes, servers and gravy boat on the sideboard were all electroplated nickel silver. The only hallmarked items were a Georgian coffee pot, cream jug and sugar bowl that had been put away out of sight in one of the cabinets. There were five Georgian desert spoons, three fruit knives, four fish knives and forks and two coffee spoons in the cutlery drawer that Landon thought were probably worth close on a thousand.

The drawing room was in fact over the garage and incorporated what had once been a bedroom overlooking a small walled garden. It was large enough to accommodate two three-piece suites and a couple of fireside chairs. There was also a baby grand, which provided a convenient platform for a picture gallery, presumably of friends and relations, displayed in silver frames of varying sizes. Diagonally across the room from the piano there was a mahogany cabinet with all three glass shelves crammed with porcelain ornaments. Unlocking the cabinet, Landon removed the figure of a country girl carrying a basket of freshly picked apples against her right hip, her hair covered by a cerise-coloured scarf. He turned the figure upside down and looked at the mark inside the base.

'My Lorna's got a statue with a mark like that,' Hicks said, standing on tiptoe to peer over his shoulder. 'Been in the family for donkey's years, claims it belonged to her great-grandmother. Meissen they call it.'

'Worth a bit then?'

'I should think so.'

Landon returned the figure, checked two others at random and found they both had the same mark. 'It doesn't make sense,' he said, giving voice to his thoughts.

'What doesn't?' Hicks asked.

'Nothing. Forget what I said.'

'We ought to be on our way, boss.'

Landon grunted but made no move to leave. Ashton had told him that Toby had been buying number 3 Mews Terrace with an endowment mortgage. If this was correct, Toby must have had a very understanding bank manager because the property was way beyond his means unless he had come into money. In this part of London the asking price for a place like Toby's would be in the region of one point five to two million.

'Shit!' Hicks murmured. 'Now we're for it.'

'The police?' Landon asked calmly.

'Yeah, two of them thanks to a nosy neighbour. I stand corrected—reinforcements have arrived.'

'Where did I leave my clipboard?'

'What?'

'My clipboard,' Landon repeated.

'Oh, for fuck's sake, it's on the hall table.'

'Thanks.'

'Maybe it's not too late to go out the back way and over the garden wall.'

'We're not doing anything of the kind,' Landon told him firmly. 'We are going to leave by the front door as though we have every right to be here.'

'We'll never get away with it. I've got a bunch of skeleton keys on me, remember?'

'Just leave the talking to me.'

'I intend to,' Hicks said grimly.

Landon went downstairs, picked up his clipboard

and opened the front door.

'Good morning, officers,' he said cheerfully. 'What can I do for you?'

Their answer was simple enough: they wanted Landon and Hicks to accompany them to the police station on Ladbroke Road. The fact that there was no sign of a forced entry did not impress the officers. The bunch of skeleton keys in Hicks's possession was more than sufficient to convince them they had been up to no good. Handcuffed and bundled into the police cars they were taken to the divisional station in Notting Hill where they were fingerprinted and subsequently interviewed. Landon declined to have a duty solicitor present and demanded they contact Detective Chief Inspector John Verco of Special Branch. It was a long time before they took him seriously.

Six

Ashton cleared his desk and locked everything away in the combination safe, then left his office. He had been expecting to hear from Dilys Crowther from four o'clock onwards; what was surprising was the fact that Victor Hazelwood had waited until Detective Chief Superintendent Roberts was about to brief the media before he sent for him. When he entered the PA's office Dilys Crowther already had her hat and coat on and metaphorically speaking was straining at the leash.

'We're giving a dinner party this evening,' she hissed. 'Seven for seven thirty and I was told I could leave at four fifteen.'

'So what stopped you?'

'His damned phone; it's been ringing all afternoon. Sir Victor's got the Deputy DG of MI5 on the line right now.'

'Well, get off home,' Ashton told her. 'I can switch all the incoming calls to his extension as soon as he puts the phone down.'

'That's very kind of you, Mr Ashton. The yellow bulb on the cradle will start winking when Sir Victor hangs up.'

'I think I can handle it,' he said smiling.

'Yes, of course you can.' Dilys picked up the plastic wildlife shopping bag that urged beholders to save the humpback whale. 'I'll be on my way then,' she said and fled the office.

Five minutes passed, then another five with Hazelwood still engaged in conversation with Colin Wales, the deputy DG of 'Five'. Ashton sat down at the PA's desk, lifted the receiver on the BT phone and rang Harriet intending to let her know he was going to be late—again. He never got the chance, the number was still ringing out when the yellow bulb on the secure speech facility started winking. He replaced the BT phone, switched all future incoming calls direct to Hazelwood and then went on through to the DG's office, to be greeted with the news that Landon and Hicks had been arrested.

'One of the residents saw them enter Quayle's house and thought they were behaving suspiciously. The woman called the police and they were there in no time. Couldn't be worse.' Hazelwood scowled. 'Did you know Mews Terrace is in B District?'

Ashton shook his head. Things were going from bad to worse. Roberts already had a low opinion of the SIS thanks to Anwar Farid's double identity. The detective chief superintendent probably thought Will and Terry Hicks had entered Quayle's house with the intention of removing any evidence that would prove the SIS officer had been engaged in criminal activity with his source. And that, Ashton thought, was not so very far removed from the truth.

'Where are the two of them being held?' he asked.

'Notting Hill. Hopefully they will be released very shortly.' Hazelwood opened the ornate cigar box on the desk and helped himself to a Burma cheroot. 'Without any fuss,' he added.

The way Ashton interpreted the remark, 'without any fuss' could only mean that Hazelwood had asked the deputy commissioner in charge of Special Branch to ensure Hicks and Landon didn't come into contact with the media.

'How long have Will and Hicks been in custody?'

'Since two o'clock this afternoon.' Hazelwood struck a match and lit the cheroot. 'The uniform branch at Notting Hill didn't get in touch with DCI Verco until a quarter to five. I think that was deliberate on their part. The moment Will Landon mentioned Special Branch the superintendent in charge at Ladbroke Road knew he would have to let them go.'

'So he dragged his feet to teach us a lesson?'

'Well, let's say he was encouraged to do so by Roberts. I can understand that; in his shoes I would be pretty angry if my investigation was being hampered by the SIS.'

'Hampered?'

'It must seem that way to him, Peter.'

The ability to see the other man's point of view was not something Victor had previously been noted for. Hazelwood had been seen as a thruster, someone who made things happen by riding roughshod over anyone or anything standing in his way. This new version was not the man Ashton had known from the day he had been assigned to the Russian desk all those long years ago, and the character change made him feel uneasy.

'What about the press briefing?' Ashton asked. 'Was it still on for five o'clock?'

'To the best of my knowledge it was. And yes I'm aware that the briefing was ten minutes old when Colin Wales rang me. But Roberts will make damned sure Hicks and Landon don't run into any reporters on their way out of the police station. You know why?'

'No, but you're about to tell me.'

'Roberts is a hugely ambitious officer and he has been left in no doubt that his career would be terminally blighted if some newshound linked Quayle to Landon and Hicks.' Without looking what he was doing, Hazelwood flicked the cheroot and, missing the cut-down brass shellcase, spilled ash over the desk top. 'The same applies to the superintendent in charge of the Ladbroke Road police station,' he added, using his other hand to brush the debris in the direction of the wastepaper basket.

'Sounds OK,' Ashton said. 'Let's hope bad luck doesn't enter the equation.'

'You'll know if it has when you debrief Landon and Hicks. Interview them separately and take whatever action you deem necessary should it become evident that either one has been

71

compromised.'

'Right. Is that it?'

'Not quite. Whatever your findings, Landon is to maintain a low profile until things quieten down. His investigation of Quayle's financial affairs is to cease forthwith.' Hazelwood broke off to crush the half-smoked cheroot in the ashtray. 'That task is down to you from now on, Peter.'

'Lucky me,' Ashton said dryly.

'You'll find this aide-memoire handy,' Hazelwood said and passed a slip of paper across the desk.

The aide-memoire showed that Toby Quayle had banked with the Kensington High Street branch of Coutts and Company for the past twenty-four years. Interestingly it seemed the bank prepared Quayle's tax return for signature, a service that had been provided from the day he had opened his account. The information had been provided by the Admin Wing but not the name at the bottom. That had been added by Hazelwood in his own hand.

'Who is Piers Felstead?' Ashton asked, looking up.

'He's the deputy chairman and finance director of Coutts. You're lunching with him at the Ivy next Tuesday.'

'I hope he's paying,' Ashton said with feeling.

*   *   *

His name was Jamal Haroon, he was thirty-nine years old and a major in the Parachute Regiment. Currently he was a Grade II staff officer at Headquarters, Northern Command in Islamabad. A graduate of the staff college, Quetta, Jamal

Haroon was regarded as a high flier and had been selected for promotion to lieutenant colonel in April when he would take command of the 5th Battalion of the Parachute Regiment.

Commissioned in 1980 he had spent the next six years at regimental duty, when he had attended such courses as weapons training at the Small Arms Centre, platoon tactics at the School of Infantry and mine warfare at 175 Engineer Regiment stationed in Lahore. In 1986 he had been sent to Peshawar to assist in the training of the disparate groups of mujahedin based in the Afghan refugee camps in the area. In the next eighteen months he had twice crossed over into Afghanistan with guerilla bands to demolish bridges, power stations and transmission lines in the Butkhak region. While still a captain he had also conducted operations against the Indian army of occupation in Kashmir and had participated in the assassination of the Deputy Commissioner of Police, Jamanu Province. A Muslim extremist, Jamal Haroon was a member of the fundamentalist Jamaat-e-Islami, as was his superior officer Seyed Sikander Zia, brigadier, General Staff (Intelligence).

Brigadier Zia's official residence was on Government Road South a mile from Headquarters, Northern Command. Haroon had been invited to dinner on several occasions with his wife, Izara, but this was the first time he had been asked to call at the house before attending evening prayers. To be more accurate he had been ordered to present himself at five o'clock. It had also been made abundantly clear that Izara was to be left at home with their children.

Haroon paid off the taxi on the main road

opposite the house, then walked up the drive and rang the bell. The door was opened by Zia's soldier servant, a lance corporal in the Khyber Rifles, who led Haroon into the drawing room where the brigadier was waiting for him.

Dismissing his soldier servant, he waved Haroon to a chair and poured him a glass of homemade lemonade from a pitcher. As a devout Muslim Zia neither drank alcohol nor smoked, though he sometimes enjoyed a smidgen of hashish as did Jamal Haroon. This evening, however, hemp was not being offered.

'Tara Rahim Khan,' Zia said abruptly. 'Perhaps you have heard of him?'

'No, his name means nothing to me.'

'He is one of us, a warrior of Islam.'

'Then I would be proud to meet him.'

'You shall, early tomorrow morning at the mosque. Tara Rahim Khan is here in Islamabad to strike a blow for Jamaat-e-Islami against the purveyors of a decadent alien culture and pornographic literature.'

'Who are we talking about?'

'Why the British and Americans of course. Have you forgotten how in February 1972 the UK was quick to recognize the breakaway state of East Pakistan that called itself Bangladesh? The old imperialists couldn't wait to afford Bangladesh membership of the British Commonwealth.'

'I haven't forgotten, Brigadier,' Haroon said stiffly.

'Then I assume you still recall how the CIA betrayed you.'

That was something Haroon would never forget, never forgive. In the struggle against the Soviet-

74

backed Karmal regime the weapons had been supplied by the People's Republic of China and the USA. Although the instructors training the mujahedin had been drawn from the Pakistan army, the CIA had also been involved, gathering intelligence by monitoring Soviet ground and air communications. The Americans had been well aware of the threat posed by MiG 27 fighter ground-attack planes and the MiL MI-25 gunship codenamed 'Hind' by NATO. To combat this threat they had promised to provide the mujahedin with 'Stinger', a man-portable, shoulder fired, guided anti-aircraft missile system.

The missiles still hadn't arrived when Haroon had made his second incursion into Afghanistan. This setback had in no way deterred the mujahedin and at first the operation had gone extremely well. The guerrillas had laid siege to the government troops in Butkhak and the Soviet relief column comprising three T64 main battle tanks and five BTR 70 eight-wheel armoured personnel carriers had been successfully ambushed. Unable to deploy off the narrow track in time, the column had been greeted with a barrage of RPG 7 anti-tank rockets. Every vehicle had been hit at least twice. Most of the sixty-odd casualties had been inflicted by the anti-tank missiles but at least eleven infantrymen who had abandoned their burning APCs had been cut down in the subsequent firefight.

The mujahedin had won a great victory and if ever there had been a time for guerrillas to melt away it had been then. But one obstinate Russian gunner in the turret of a BTR 70 had killed and wounded eight men and the mujahedin had wanted vengeance. They had continued the firefight until the Russians had surrendered. Except for the senior lieutenant in command of the column, the guerrillas had then cut the throats of the survivors including the wounded. The senior lieutenant had been tied up and buried alive in the slit trench he had been compelled to dig. By the time the mujahedin had decided to withdraw from the battlefield a flight of MiG 27 and two gunships based at Kabul were already airborne. The first strike had caught them before they had covered two miles and he had been lucky to survive when so many others hadn't.

'Syphilitic pigs,' Haroon roared.

'And who are you referring to?' Zia asked softly.

'The Americans, Brigadier. Things would have been very different if they had kept their word and supplied us with Stinger missiles.'

'You would do well to reserve some of your anger for the British. It is our intention to destroy their influence in the world. This will be achieved by forcing them to close their embassies one by one in the Middle and Far East. The British have already withdrawn their diplomatic representatives from Baghdad and Tehran. Now we shall begin the same process here in Islamabad.'

In contrast to everything that had gone before, the instructions Jamal Haroon received were concise and unambiguous. He was to provide every item Tara Rahim Khan asked for. In furtherance of this task he could count on the support of various members of the military intelligence arm whose names were known to Zia.

'Every one of them has links with the Taliban, which means they can be trusted implicitly.'

'I never doubted it,' Haroon told him.

76

'Good. Now it is time you were leaving.'

Charm had never been one of Brigadier Seyed Sikander Zia's attributes.

* * *

Ashton looked at his wristwatch and grimaced. Seven thirty and no one else left on the top floor except Landon, who was cooling his heels in the conference room, waiting to be summoned to his office. If the interview with Hicks was anything to go by, he would be lucky to get away by nine o'clock. That was the time Ashton had led Harriet to expect him when he had phoned earlier this evening. No way was he going to amend that estimated time of arrival before he was in a better position to judge how long the interview with Landon would take. Picking up the BT phone, he rang the extension in the conference room and told Will to come on in.

Although pure bad luck had triggered the foul-up in Mews Terrace Landon believed he had been at fault. He had made that clear on his return to Vauxhall Cross after he had been released from Notting Hill. That Landon still felt he was culpable was evident when he walked into Ashton's office and started to apologize again.

'It's my fault we were caught,' he said. 'Hicks urged me to leave but I ignored him. I was too busy examining Toby's possessions.'

'Listen to me, Will. You're not to blame, you couldn't know there was a curtain twitcher in Mews Terrace.'

'We could have been out of there before the police arrived if I'd listened to Terry Hicks.'

'Forget it,' Ashton said tersely. 'Just tell me what happened after you arrived at the police station.'

Hicks had taken a good half-hour to answer the question and for the most part that had been one long diatribe against the police. Landon however took less than five minutes to relate how he had been treated. In a nutshell, other than giving his name and home address, Landon had refused to answer any of their questions until they had produced DI Verco.

'They weren't exactly eager to oblige,' Landon continued. 'I guess they were trying to make us sweat.'

'Hicks was in the same cell?'

'No, we compared notes after we were released. Terry was pretty sore because the police had confiscated his bunch of skeleton keys and he nearly came to blows with the property sergeant over it. I stepped in and managed to calm things down. That was the only incident; there were no press photographers around when we left the station by the back yard.'

'Good. Now tell me what you made of number 3 Mews Terrace.'

'It's a very desirable residence,' Landon told him, 'but I don't see how Toby could have afforded to buy the property with an endowment mortgage even on a salary of £54K plus inner London weighting allowance.'

'What if the property was leasehold, like, for example, the Albany off Piccadilly?'

'In that case I wouldn't be quite so pedantic.'

Landon didn't know what to make of Quayle's possessions. The furniture was good quality, especially the Regency-style dining-room table, chairs and sideboard, but there were no antique pieces that would command a substantial sum at an auction. As for the assorted items of Georgian cutlery, there was only enough for three complete place settings.

'There was a display cabinet of Meissen porcelain but, like the silver, I had a feeling they were simply family heirlooms. There were no valuable paintings that I could see.' Landon shrugged. 'Of course, I'm no expert.'

'That's good enough for me.'

'I don't believe you, Peter, you never leave a job half done. I should have broken into the desk and—'

'That was never on,' Ashton said, cutting him short. 'It might have been a different proposition if we had been told to go in before Kelso gave Toby's address to the police.'

'So what happens now?'

'We'll have to see what Piers Felstead can tell us,' Ashton said.

Before lunching with Felstead on Tuesday he needed to read Quayle's security file. Better than a family bible, it would have been opened when Quayle had been positively vetted before joining the SIS. It would contain every subsequent quinquennial review, every senior officer's report, every subject interview and change of circumstance reports where applicable.

'Who's Piers Felstead?' Landon asked.

Deep in thought Ashton didn't hear him. Within the security file he expected to find details of Quayle's education, financial affairs and the background checks on him and his parents carried out by MI5 and the former Criminal Records

79

Office before it became the National Identification Bureau. Normally, only the DG, his deputy and the officer in charge of the Positive Vetting and Technical Services Division were allowed to see the file. But this was an abnormal situation and Ashton reckoned he could overcome any objection Victor Hazelwood might raise when he asked for the file.

'Who is Piers Felstead?' Landon repeated.

'The deputy chairman and finance director of Coutts and Company. Their Kensington High Street branch looked after Toby Quayle. Any other questions?'

'Only one: what do you want me to do now?'

'Well, you'll continue to look after the Balkans and remain our rep on CATO. OK?'

'Yes.'

'See you on Monday then,' Ashton said.

He waited until Landon had left the office before he tempted fate and called Harriet to let her know what time to expect him.

*　　　*　　　*

As Head of the British Council in Pakistan Keith Jenner was responsible for promoting a wider knowledge of Britain and the English language, as well as developing closer cultural relations between the UK and the host nation. He was also charged with administering educational aid programmes. To facilitate this Jenner received a proportionate slice of the hundred and thirty five million the Council received from the Foreign and Commonwealth Office and the Overseas Development Administration. The sum he was allocated by London enabled him to maintain three regional offices in Lahore, Peshawar and Karachi as well as the main office in Islamabad.

The cash flow was not all one way. In common with British Council offices throughout the world, there were gains from sources other than the British taxpayer. These included earnings from English language teaching, paid educational services and acting for international organizations including UN agencies.

The Council office in Islamabad was a good two miles from the High Commission in the Diplomatic Enclave, Ramna 5. The siting was intentional. Since the aim was to promote a wider knowledge of Britain, it was essential to be within easy reach of the indigenous population. And while Jenner didn't exactly live over the shop, his bungalow on Government Road North was a mere hundred and fifty yards from the Council Office.

Islamabad was not the best posting he had ever had. That accolade went to West Berlin, where he had met, courted and, at the age of forty-one, married an American divorcée fourteen years younger than himself. His colleagues at the regional office had said it would never last. Laura was an extremely attractive blonde; he was shorter by almost two inches and no way would anyone describe him as handsome. Laura had charisma and became the centre of attention whenever she walked into a crowded room. The amazing thing was that women, as well as men, really liked her. People liked him, too, but he was no extrovert and there were those who, on first acquaintance, couldn't understand what Laura saw in him. But the fact was they had been together for fifteen years and had two children, a boy of twelve and a girl aged ten, both of whom were at boarding school in England. This was the one aspect of their lives that made Laura unhappy, but Good Friday was only two weeks off and the children would be flying out for the Easter holiday next Wednesday.

Jenner turned over on to his right side and instinctively reached out for Laura. Still half asleep it was some moments before it dawned on him that she was no longer lying beside him. Rolling over on to his other hip, he groped for the lamp on the bedside table and switched it on.

'Put it out,' Laura hissed at him.

'What?'

'Switch the goddamned light off.'

Jenner plunged the room in darkness. He knew Laura was over by the window but he couldn't see her. His vision gradually returned as he slipped out of bed and moved towards her.

'What are you looking at, darling?' Jenner asked in a low voice.

'There's a cab parked right outside our bungalow. The driver's got the hood up and appears to be doing something to the engine. I think it could be the same vehicle I saw yesterday afternoon.'

Jenner slipped an arm round Laura's waist, hugging her close as he peered through the slats of the Venetian blind. 'It's a 1964 Ford Cortina built under licence,' he said. 'They're always breaking down.'

'That's comforting to know,' Laura told him dryly. 'I thought he was spying on us.'

As they watched, the driver slammed the hood down, got into the car and started the engine. There was a grating noise when he shifted into gear and the tyres squealed in protest when he took off as though on the race track at Silverstone.

'Doesn't seem to be much wrong with the engine, does there, Keith?'

'Do you really think it was the same vehicle that you saw yesterday afternoon?'

'I can't be sure. Maybe it's my imagination, but for the first time I no longer feel comfortable about living out here. In fact, I wish we could move into the diplomatic compound today.' She laughed nervously. 'It could be I've got those three o'clock in the morning blues.'

Seven

Landon had become accustomed to seeing the occasional different face representing the Defence Intelligence Staff at the weekly meeting of the Combined Anti-Terrorist Organization. This Tuesday morning, however, was remarkable in that the Defence Intelligence Staff was represented by two officers instead of one. Keith Amesbury-Cotton, the RAF Group Captain from D17, had attended the odd meeting in the past but the civilian from Science and Technology was representing a Ministry of Defence department that previously hadn't contributed any information to CATO.

In his capacity as chairman of the committee Richard Neagle liked to vary the batting order and for a change he had invited Michael York from GCHQ Cheltenham to lead off. Government Communications Headquarters was an intercept service assisted by specialist units provided by the armed forces. One such military organization was 14 Signals Regiment, which in addition to eavesdropping on potential enemies was also responsible for conducting electronic warfare. Normally stationed in Germany, one troop of the regiment was currently deployed in Kosovo. Starting on Sunday 7th March, the troop had been systematically jamming Serbian battlefield communications with the result that commanders at all levels from company to regiment had found it well nigh impossible to command and control their sub-units. The Serbs had tried switching frequencies but the waveband on their radios was limited and the electronic warfare specialists had experienced little difficulty in picking them up again.

The tactical advantage gained by jamming the enemy radio net had to be weighed against the potential loss of information. As yet this maxim had not applied in Kosovo. With a fine disregard for basic security procedures the Serbs had resorted to using mobile phones that could not be crypto-protected.

'Consequently we can pinpoint their locations, discover their intentions and jam them off the air whenever we like,' York announced triumphantly.

'One question,' Landon said crisply. 'What has this electronic warfare troop been doing with the high-quality information they've gleaned from time to time?'

York raised both eyebrows as if astonished Landon should have asked such a banal question. 'I should have thought that was obvious,' he said loftily. 'The transcript goes to Cheltenham with a copy to Force Headquarters, Kosovo.'

'Transcript? You mean every transmission is recorded and then translated?'

'That's exactly what I do mean.'

'And the Serbs made no attempt to encode any of their transmissions?'

'No, that assumption is not entirely correct. Not every message was sent in clear, but the code they were and still are using is so low level that the electronic warfare troop is able to crack it at will.' York turned to Neagle. 'I don't see where all this is leading, Richard,' he said plaintively.

'Neither do I,' Neagle smiled. 'Perhaps you can enlighten us, Will?'

'We've got eight SAS patrols in the region working to their own sub-unit commander who is nowhere near Force Headquarters. I think the patrols would be able to respond to any given situation much more quickly if their commander was to receive a transcript direct.'

'How about it Michael?' Neagle asked.

'I've no objection, provided the officer concerned has been cleared to receive signal intercepts.'

Landon was pretty sure the SAS officer had been cleared by positive vetting for constant access to top secret material. But that wasn't good enough for GCHQ. You needed more than a top secret clearance before the intercept service would allow you to see their stuff and Landon doubted if the sub-unit commander would have been indoctrinated before he left for Kosovo. That was something the Defence Intelligence Staff would have to rectify ASAP. Meantime he wasn't prepared to admit that there could be a problem.

'That's interesting,' Landon said before York could quiz him.

All the same it was something of a relief when Neagle turned the spotlight on the Defence Intelligence Staff. The man from Science and Technology claimed to have incontrovertible evidence that Saddam Hussein was attempting to obtain weapons grade plutonium from Russian dissidents in the Black Sea fleet. The information had been provided by a single source at the highest level.

'What do you mean by the highest level?' Neagle enquired.

'This man sits at the top table, that's all I'm allowed to tell this committee.'

'Well, in that case I am happy to accept the information without any qualification.' Neagle looked round the table. 'Comments anybody?'

'I don't like single sources,' Landon said reluctantly, 'even if they do have a seat at the top table. How do we know this Iraqi isn't stringing us along? I mean if he is that close to Saddam Hussein he's got to be walking the high wire with nothing to act as a counterbalance should he start swaying. Maybe he sees British Intelligence as his safety net and is feeding us with sensational information that can't be independently verified in the expectation that we will spirit him out of Iraq should things go pear shaped.'

'How would we do that when we have no diplomatic presence in Baghdad and the UN inspectors have been withdrawn?'

'The same way your agent in place gets his information out,' Landon snapped.

'That can take between five and eight days. Should he come under suspicion the source would be arrested, tortured and executed before he had time to pack a bag and he knows it.'

'I'm still averse to placing too much reliance on a single source.'

'Would it make you any happier, Mr Landon, to know that Talal Asir is the middleman between Saddam Hussein and the dissident Russians?'

'Is this from the same source?'

'No, this comes from someone else who is graded D5. Not the best assessment on record I grant you. But in this instance she is performing above her usual level. I also believe my colleague in D17 can support this contention to some extent.'

Keith Amesbury-Cotton opened the folder in front of him and passed copies of an enlarged satellite photograph round the table. The date/time group in the top left-hand corner of the print indicated that it had been taken on the 5th March at 1523 hours Greenwich Mean Time. The subject of the enlarged image was a villa in an unidentified street. There were two cars parked in the drive, a BMW 7 and a Cadillac Seville, the number plate of which was just visible. The satellite camera had also captured a slightly built man in profile as he walked towards the BMW.

Every week a USAF plane landed at Brize Norton with a consignment of satellite photographs, courtesy of the National Security Agency. These were then sent to JARIC, the Joint Air Reconnaissance Interpretation Centre at RAF Brampton, for analysis. Landon wondered what the photo interpreter had made of this particular frame. He did not have to wait long to know the answer.

'The villa is on the Boulevard Hafez el-Assad in Damascus,' Amesbury-Cotton informed them. 'The

BMW belongs to Major General Walid al-Kasam, Deputy Prime Minister and Minister for the Armed Forces. The CIA has tentatively identified the civilian in the photo as Talal Asir but they would like to know what we think.' Amesbury-Cotton smiled. 'I'm afraid nobody at JARIC has ever seen a photograph of the man,' he said apologetically.

'That's Talal Asir all right,' Neagle said cheerfully. 'I've got enough photographs of him to paper the office. How about you, Will, do you ID him?'

Landon looked up from the air photo he had been studying. 'Yeah, that's our Saudi banker all right.' The photocopy of the bloodstained note the police had found on Quayle's body was engraved on his mind. Four question marks followed by a capital 'L' and a lower case 'a'. Sixteen question marks then preceded a capital 'C' and the numerals '111'. 'Does this villa have a street number?' he asked.

Amesbury-Cotton flipped through his scratched pad, then said, 'Sorry about the oversight, the number is one eleven.'

'Anything else?'

'If there is, the CIA didn't inform us.'

'It would be interesting to know who owns the property,' Neagle mused.

'Even money the villa belongs to Major General Walid al-Kasam.'

'You could be right, Will.'

'Maybe so but we would have a hard time proving it. On the other hand, discovering who actually lives there shouldn't be too difficult . . .'

'For whom?' Neagle asked archly.

The reason for Neagle's swift response was transparent. There was just one MI5 officer on the staff of the British Embassy in Damascus and he was responsible for all aspects of personal and physical security in addition to screening locally employed personnel. He most certainly wasn't in post to act as a general dogsbody for the SIS.

'I guess it has to be Head of Station, Damascus.' Landon shrugged. 'Course that's only my opinion. Let's hope I can sell it to Ralph Meacher.'

'Amen to that,' Neagle murmured. 'Do you have anything else for us, Will?'

Landon shook his head. It seemed DCI Verco didn't have anything for the committee either, which was a little surprising considering the coverage the multiple slaying in Giordano's had received in the national press. The police had released an artist's impression of Danièle based on the photograph of the dead transsexual taken in the mortuary. It had appeared on the front page of every newspaper on Saturday morning under a variety of captions ranging from 'The unidentified fourth victim' to 'The mystery woman—who is she?'

'That's it then,' Neagle announced. 'And thank you, gentlemen. Same time, same day next week.' He smiled again. 'Unless in the meantime there's a major incident somewhere in the world.'

Verco was the first to leave but there was little in it. Only Landon remained behind.

'What's on your mind, Will?' Neagle asked.

'Is Verco holding something back?'

'That's a disturbing question. Suppose you tell me why you think he is.'

'Last Thursday the police removed Farid's

computer and three-drawer filing cabinet. I would have thought by now they would have at least discovered the name of his bank and which branch was looking after him. And I can't believe the contents of his filing cabinet are so negative that the police still have no idea what credit cards Farid had been using at the time of his death.'

Neagle snapped his fingers. 'That reminds me. I was mistaken when I said Farid had paid his bill at Airways Cranford Parking in cash. Seems he settled his account with MasterCard.'

'So you know his credit card number?'

'Detective Chief Superintendent Roberts does. Verco gave it to him.'

'Will he give it to us?'

'Cooperation is a two way street. I recall DCS Roberts asking you if Anwar Farid had family and friends living in Birmingham . . .'

'And I told him that nothing to that effect had shown up when he was screened by our Positive Vetting and Technical Services division.'

'When did you do this?'

'Yesterday,' Landon told him. 'It was the first opportunity I'd had.' Landon pushed his chair back and stood up. 'Now it's time Roberts honoured a quid pro quo.'

'I'm not promising anything,' Neagle said, 'but I'll have a word with Verco.'

There was, Landon thought, no point in holding his breath. What was it Roberts said to him? 'I answer to the commissioner of police, not the chief spook.'

*   *   *

In a city awash with restaurants the Ivy was in a class of its own and had long been a favourite haunt with those in the theatre, films, television, publishing and journalism. Unless you were a regular it was difficult to obtain a table at short notice, a regular being defined as someone who dined at the Ivy three or more times a week. With less than a third of the tables available for first timers, bookings were taken for days or even weeks ahead. Following this disquisition by Piers Felstead Ashton could only assume the deputy chairman and finance director of Coutts and Company was a regular.

At Felstead's suggestion Ashton had started with plum tomato and basil galette followed by rosemary-skewer lamb's kidneys with a barolo risotto. The Bramley apple crumble with Devonshire clotted cream had been his choice. Throughout the lunch the banker had discreetly drawn his attention to various celebrities he had recognized, and it wasn't until they were lingering over brandy that he spoke of Toby Quayle.

'A bad business all round,' Felstead murmured. 'Poor old Toby dies of wounds incurred in the line of duty and now his financial propriety is being called into question.'

'It's called guilt by association,' Ashton said quietly. 'Twenty-seven months ago Customs and Excise caught Anwar Farid with three hundred and fifty thousand pounds of cocaine in his suitcase. He was travelling under the name of Mahmoud Hassan Soliman and the evidence against him was overwhelming. But the evidence was never presented in court because somebody up high leaned on the DPP. We only became aware of

Farid's criminal activities and double identity after he was fingerprinted in the morgue.'

'And by inference Toby was also ignorant of the facts?'

'That's what we need to prove, Mr Felstead, because right now the police are treating the multiple homicide as a drug-related crime.'

'And Sir Victor wishes to know if Quayle could have afforded his lifestyle?'

'Yes. In particular we would like to be assured he could afford to buy 3 Mews Terrace on an endowment policy. I don't know how much the property cost three years ago when he bought it . . .'

'Neither do I,' Felstead said interrupting him. 'Furthermore, I am not aware of any mortgage or endowment policy. However, the deeds to the property are lodged with us for safekeeping.'

Ashton hoped he had managed to conceal his astonishment. Prior to 1996 Quayle had been one of those fortunates who were only required to pay a peppercorn rent for one of the grace and favour apartments in Dolphin Square. This had been from 1989 onwards, when he had completed his last overseas tour in the Middle East, having previously served in Jordan, Syria and South Yemen. Ashton just wondered if in those seven years Toby had amassed sufficient capital to purchase 3 Mews Terrace outright.

'Did Toby inherit a lot of money from his parents?' Ashton asked.

'His father was a spendthrift and an inveterate gambler. Much of his money went on the horses. He also had a roving eye, which didn't help matters. I understand he had hocked nearly everything of value before he died. The fact is he left his widow in dire straits financially.'

'What about Toby? Was he equally feckless?'

'Let me put it this way. Coutts and Company has looked after five generations of Quayles, but if Toby had been like his father we would have asked him to take his account elsewhere.'

It transpired that Toby Quayle had shown considerable financial acumen from an early age. From the day he had joined the SIS after leaving Cambridge in 1977 with an upper second in history, Quayle had made it a golden rule to save fifty per cent of his monthly salary, which he had then invested wisely on the stock market, choosing blue chip companies. By the time he had completed his last overseas tour and returned to England for good, his portfolio of investments had been worth a cool half million.

'He took advantage of the high interest rates that were on offer in '92,' Felstead continued. 'On the first of every month Toby would transfer three hundred thousand into a fixed-term deposit account that yielded between ten and twelve per cent gross depending on the market. The beauty of the scheme lay in the fact that tax was paid in arrears.'

'How long did that last?'

'Just over a year. Interest rates began to fall after we left the Exchange Rate Mechanism and the Inland Revenue demanded the tax up front based on the previous year's assessment. Toby got out of the money market and went into information technology. Did rather well out of it too.'

'What would Quayle have been worth when he purchased 3 Mews Terrace in '96?'

'On his instructions we sold some of his investments to raise two hundred thousand but that still left him with seven hundred and eighty thousand. The two hundred thousand was paid to Toby's solicitors, who were handling the purchase of 3 Mews Terrace.'

Ashton frowned. Two hundred thousand for the house in Mews Terrace? He hadn't seen the property but judging by Will Landon's description of the place that couldn't be right. 'I can't believe the property would have been so cheap,' he said.

'I think I may have misled you, Mr Ashton. The two hundred thousand amounted to only a fraction of the asking price. The rest came from Toby's account at the National Westminster. He was one of those lucky people who had a big win in the lottery.'

It wasn't so long ago that Quayle's PV clearance had been the subject of a quinquennial review. Although he had informed the Positive Vetting and Technical Services Division of his change of address, no mention had been made of his account with the NatWest. And the big win on the lottery? Shit, that was beyond belief. The whole business stank to high heaven.

'You look as though a second brandy wouldn't come amiss,' Felstead told him.

'You're right, it wouldn't,' Ashton said with feeling.

*　　　*　　　*

Unable to sleep Major Jamal Haroon lay flat on his back gazing up at the slowly revolving fan suspended from the ceiling, willing himself not to look at the alarm clock on the bedside table for at least another half-hour. The last time he had sneaked a glance it had been showing four minutes to one, which meant there were another fifty-six minutes to go before the English pornographer and the American harlot were abducted. He neither knew nor cared what Tara Rahim Khan intended to do with them, his job had been to supply the means to enable Khan and the others to carry out the operation. Following his meeting with the Jamaat-e-Islami fighter at the mosque on Saturday morning he had provided Khan with three disruptive pattern combat suits, bulbous silencers for the 7.65mm Type 67 pistol manufactured by the Chinese People's Republic, and a Gaz 4x4 command jeep borrowed from the Northern Command Vehicle park by a sympathizer in the Ordnance Corps. Another sympathizer had rented a house on Field Marshal Mohammed Ayub Khan Street in the midst of a rundown neighbourhood on the northern outskirts of Islamabad.

The house would be occupied for only a few hours while the Englishman and his American whore were in transit. Khan was convinced that vehicles entering or leaving Islamabad between midnight and daybreak were more likely to be stopped and searched by the police than at any other time of the day or night. It was his intention to remain at the house until there was more traffic on the roads before he moved on. There was, however, a conflicting requirement: Khan and his followers needed to be well clear of the city before the authorities learned that the British Council representative and his wife had been kidnapped. Haroon's involvement did not end with Rahim

Khan's departure; his superior, Brigadier Seyed Sikander Zia, had made it clear that he was required to check out the house on Field Marshal Mohammed Ayub Khan Street to ensure no evidence incriminating the army had been left behind.

Haroon rolled over on to his right side and peered at the alarm clock. In his experience waiting was always the worst part of any operation, each minute seeming more like ten. But not in this instance. A lot more than half an hour had elapsed since he had previously looked at the clock. In fact, if everything had gone according to plan the Gaz 4x4 jeep should now be turning on to Government Road North. The 'if' factor didn't bother him. He had embarked on a course of action from which there was no turning back. He felt under the pillow and caressed the butt of the 9mm Heckler & Koch self-loading pistol. There were nine rounds in the box magazine; should anything go wrong the police would never take him alive. He would shoot his wife, Izara, first as she lay beside him, then use the next seven rounds on the police before turning the weapon on himself. Completely at ease with his decision Haroon reached out and switched off the bedside light.

*   *   *

As they turned into Government Road North Khan tapped the driver's right arm, then pointed to the speedometer and instructed him to keep it down to twenty-five. Coming abreast of the British Council office and library, Khan swept the building with the spotlight attached to the nearside door and picked out the nightwatchman. He was sitting on a wooden stool outside the entrance, his hands interlocked to form a pillow for his head as they rested on the butt of an upturned shotgun. Khan judged the nightwatchman to be at least sixty years old, and he gave every sign of being fast asleep, which was only to be expected of a man of his age. The bungalow where the British infidel lived with his American harlot was only a hundred and fifty yards further on.

When Khan had looked at the bungalow five days ago no special security measures had been in force. This morning he had been warned that two police constables were now guarding the place. He had also been informed that the authorities did not believe the couple were at risk. They had assigned two policemen to watch over them simply to please the British High Commissioner.

'Don't do anything to alarm the police,' Khan told the driver. 'Come to a halt gradually, no stamping on the brakes.'

The driver nodded, pulled up opposite the bungalow, switched off and shifted into neutral. Khan unbuttoned the flap on his pistol holster in order to get at the 7.65mm Type 67 semi-automatic quickly when he needed to, then got out of the jeep and crossed the road. He carried himself well, head up, shoulders back, his turnout immaculate as befitted a senior NCO in the Provost Corps. Approaching the low stone wall that surrounded the bungalow on all sides, Khan crooked a finger at the police constable standing guard outside the front door and beckoned him to come forward.

'Have you anything to report, Brother?' he asked when the man drew near.

97

'No, everything is very quiet, same as I told my sergeant when he came by half an hour ago.' The constable eyed him suspiciously. 'He didn't say anything about an army patrol being in the area.'

'He must have forgotten. More to the point, I was told there were two of you on duty. Where's your friend?'

'Before I answer that question I'd like to see your ID card.'

'Whatever pleases you, Brother.'

Under the guise of unbuttoning the right breast pocket with his left hand, Khan snatched the 7.65mm automatic from the pistol holster and shot the constable twice in the chest. The bulbous silencer ensured the sound of each gunshot was reduced by ninety-eight per cent.

The gunman sitting in the back of the jeep saw the police constable go down and immediately climbed out of the vehicle, making as little noise as possible. He moved swiftly and silently, crossing the road to join Rahim Khan, whose hand signals told him the second policeman was somewhere behind the bungalow. The cook and the houseman were the only two live-in servants and they were quartered in a shanty at the bottom of the back yard. The sweeper, the gardener and the washerwoman arrived at 0730 hours.

The telltale glow of a lighted cigarette pinpointed the second policeman. Advancing to within ten yards of him without being challenged, Khan and the gunman opened fire simultaneously, each firing twice with deadly effect. Hit three times in the chest and once in the right eye, the constable was lifted bodily into the air before landing flat on his back. The only noise came from a dog barking somewhere down the street.

Dealing with the live-in servants could have been a problem but the cook and the houseboy made it easy for them. The door to their shanty had been left unlocked and they were sharing the same bed. They were still fast asleep when Rahim Khan shot them in the head one at a time.

Eight

A vehicle of some kind disturbed Keith Jenner, raising the level of his consciousness to the point where he was almost half awake. In his befuddled state it seemed to him that the driver had taken the vehicle down the far side of the bungalow and parked it somewhere in the back yard, as Laura was wont to call the garden. It was some moments before it dawned on him that the police sergeant, who had come by the house shortly after midnight, had returned to make sure the two constables were still alert and patrolling the grounds.

A lot had happened in the last forty-eight hours. He had seen the High Commissioner first thing on Monday morning and had asked if he and Laura could move into the diplomatic compound as soon as possible. The High Commissioner had asked him point blank if he personally believed they were being targeted and, like any loyal husband, he had supported his wife, even though he privately thought Laura's fears were groundless.

Although there had been no room for them in the diplomatic compound at the present moment, the High Commissioner had promised his request would be given every consideration as soon as suitable accommodation became available. In the meantime the Minister of the Interior would be advised of the situation and requested to take whatever security measures were deemed necessary. The response had been electric: less than an hour after returning to the council office Laura had phoned to say that the bungalow was now being guarded by two armed policemen. The fact that Laura was more like her old self again and was sleeping peacefully for the second night running made him feel less guilty for crying wolf.

Jenner closed his eyes and drifted back to sleep, but not so deeply that he didn't hear a van pull up outside the bungalow. 'Got to be the same vehicle,' he told himself drowsily and promptly dozed off. In the next instant a loud, splintering crack made him rear up in bed, his heart pounding like a steam hammer but twice as fast. The door was thrown open and a beam of light danced about the room before coming to rest on his face; then somebody found the switch and put the ceiling light on.

There were three soldiers in the room, all of whom were six feet tall or thereabouts. One of the soldiers was holding a tyre lever, which he knew instinctively had been used to break into the bungalow. Jenner started to demand an explanation from the NCO in charge and was promptly hauled out of bed to receive a pistol whipping instead that left him bleeding from the nose and mouth, and a gash over the right eye. He was then thrown face down on to the floor by the NCO, who twisted his arms behind his back in a grip of iron while one of his cohorts lashed them at the wrists and elbows.

Laura was shouting, mouthing four-letter words Jenner had never heard her utter before. Her face was repeatedly slapped and when that didn't have the desired effect she was punched in the stomach. The worst part for him was the fact that there wasn't a damned thing he could do to help Laura. With his legs now tied above the knees and at the ankles he couldn't even kick out at the intruders. Pinned down under the weight of the man who was sitting on his back, Jenner had to lie there passively while somebody removed the drawers from Laura's dressing table and tipped the contents on to the floor. Some moments later Laura stopped groaning and became silent.

Swallowing blood and almost choking on it, Jenner demanded to know what they had done to his wife. The question went unanswered and was, in any event, irrelevant. The man pinning him down grabbed a fistful of hair and yanked his head back. At the same time the NCO rammed a silk undergarment into his mouth and tied it in place with a nylon stocking. He then used a scarf to blindfold him.

Jenner was rolled over on to his back, picked up and carried out of the bedroom. He fully expected them to turn right in the hall and make their way to the kitchen at the back and was surprised when they left the bungalow by the front door. Four paces to cross the veranda, down three steps to the drive, another five paces on gravel, then a swinging motion and suddenly he was flying through the air. Jenner landed heavily, his head striking the steel floor with such force he lost consciousness. When he came to, they were on the move. He had no idea what time it was, how long he had been unconscious, what speed the driver was doing, or in which direction they were heading. For God's sake, he didn't even know if Laura was with him in the van. With some difficulty Jenner rolled over and over to the right until he came up against the side of the vehicle, then reversed direction. He had completed six revolutions when he bumped into something soft and drew a faint grunt of protest. For reasons he couldn't explain to himself it then became important to count the passage of time before they reached their final destination. Seventeen minutes and forty-one seconds after he'd started counting, the driver pulled up, shifted into reverse and, following several failures, finally managed to back into what had to be a narrow opening.

The driver switched off the ignition. In the ensuing silence Jenner heard the man get out of the cab and waited, expecting that at any moment he and Laura would be hauled out of the truck and carried into the building, where presumably they would be held until the ransom was paid. But nothing happened and he began to wonder where the other men had got to, because at least three bogus soldiers had participated in the kidnapping. And what of the two policemen who had been conspicuous by their absence when the intruders had broken into the bungalow? Had they taken a bribe and meekly allowed themselves to be overpowered?

Then it hit him: this had to be Wednesday morning, and the children would be departing from London Heathrow on British Airways flight BA119 at 0855 hours. Islamabad was five hours ahead of Greenwich Mean Time and that meant the

Pakistani authorities had to know they'd been kidnapped by 1200 local time at the latest, otherwise it would be too late. Even so it was doubtful whether the Foreign and Commonwealth Office would have sufficient time to arrange for the children to be intercepted at the airport and contact his brother or sister-in-law to inform them of the situation. Jenner wondered if the same train of thought had occurred to Laura and wished there was some way he could comfort her. He tried to entwine his fingers with hers, but she was lying on her back, unwilling or unable to move. Physically and mentally exhausted by their ordeal Jenner gave up the unequal struggle and allowed himself to be drawn into the dark bottomless pit that had opened at his feet.

*   *   *

Jenner surfaced in a blind panic, unable to breathe properly because his nose was blocked with congealed blood. The gag didn't help either; the silk undergarment filled his mouth and every time he tried to fill his lungs with air it seemed to come that much closer to blocking the windpipe. Didn't these people realize nobody was going to pay good money for a corpse? If they would just take a look at their prisoners, he could make them understand that he and Laura were in danger of choking to death. What did it matter that he couldn't speak a word of their dialect? He would wheeze, gasp and hold his breath until he went puce in the face. They would get the message all right; he hadn't been a leading light of the Berlin amateur dramatic society for nothing.

103

Suddenly and without any prior warning the rear doors were opened simultaneously, causing him to flinch. Recovering quickly, Jenner drew on all his acting skills to portray a man starved of oxygen fighting for his life. Nobody took a blind bit of notice, but that wasn't his fault, the audience he was aiming at was far too busy hauling Laura out of the van. He could hear his wife mewling in protest and he wanted to assure Laura that wherever they were taking her they would soon return to collect him. He could not have been more wrong. There was a metallic clunk that sounded like a car door, then a vehicle started up and moved off.

Time soon had no meaning for Jenner. In his anxiety after being separated from Laura the minutes seemed to fly past and he was sure a good hour had gone by when they finally came for him. The impression was strengthened as he was taken from the van and dumped in the boot of the car. Although blindfolded he was sure the sun had risen because it felt warmer than when he had been carried out of the bungalow.

There was not a lot of room inside the boot. Lying in a semi-foetal position his back was up against the spare wheel while his feet were pressed against the offside wing. Jenner could, however, bend his legs and then slam his bare feet against the panelling, which he planned to do whenever the driver was forced to stop at crossroads. With any luck a policeman on point duty might hear the noise and order the driver to pull over. Unfortunately the same idea had occurred to the kidnappers, and before Jenner knew what was happening his ankles and wrists were lashed together. The boot was then closed, entombing him. A few moments later the driver cranked the engine into life, shifted into gear and drove off.

*   *   *

Jamal Haroon was standing under the shower when his mobile emitted the personalized waking call of reveille sounded on a bugle. It stopped prematurely only to start again after a thirty-second interval. The signal lasted no longer than it had done on the first occasion but it told Haroon that the Jamaat-e-Islami cell led by Tara Rahim Khan had left Islamabad with their prisoners. He turned off the shower, got out and towelled himself dry. Haroon then went into the dressing room and put on the uniform the bearer had laid out for him the night before.

The transistor radio on top of the chest of drawers was already tuned to the local station, the volume turned down so as not to disturb Izara. He switched the set on in time to catch the 0600 hours news bulletin. Although there was no mention of an incident on Government Road North, Haroon had never believed in leaving anything to chance. It was conceivable the police had withheld news of the abduction from the media. As a senior officer on the intelligence staff of Headquarters Northern Command nobody would think it suspicious that he should phone the branch duty officer for a situation report. In the event of a major incident, and the kidnapping of the British Council representative was surely in that category, standing security orders required the police to inform the military authorities immediately. It took him less than three minutes to learn the police had not been in touch with Headquarters Northern Command.

Haroon went next door and sat on the edge of the bed. Izara lay on her stomach, head over to one side, her raven black hair draped like a curtain over the left eye. Her breathing was heavy as though she was fast asleep but Izara's play acting did not deceive Haroon.

'Wake up,' he said curtly. 'I've no time for playing games.'

Izara mumbled something unintelligible and snuggled lower in the bed. The day he had married Izara his mother-in-law had warned him she was an obstinate and wilful girl who would need to be forcibly reminded of her duties as a wife. Angered by her behaviour, Haroon fetched his regimental swagger cane from the dressing room and pulled the sheet back. In the event he had no need to thrash his wife; of her own accord, Izara turned over and sat bolt upright.

'I'm leaving now and taking the car,' Haroon said and scooped up the ignition key on the bedside locker.

'Ah, yes.' Izara was vagueness itself, and needed to be prompted.

'So what are you going to say to the police should they ask why I took the car this morning?'

'I shall tell them I was worried about the brakes, that perhaps the garage had not repaired them properly.'

There was more than a grain of truth in the story. He had collected the car from the garage only four days ago after sending it in to have the master cylinder looked at.

'Suppose then they ask why I didn't test drive the car last night?'

106

'I shall tell them I forgot to tell you about the problem until this morning, which made you very angry.'

'Good, in fact very good.'

'I'm pleased. Are you going to tell me what this is all about?'

'It is better you don't know,' Haroon said and left the house.

* * *

No assistant director had more experience in the field than Hugo Calthorpe, Head of the Asian Department. With the exception of eighteen months on the Soviet Armed Forces desk as a Grade III Intelligence Officer back in 1971, Calthorpe had spent his entire service abroad until he was promoted in 1998. He had done two stints with the British Embassy in Washington, and had had a lively time in Rome with the anarchist Brigate Rosse, who had specialized in kidnapping and murdering members of the judiciary. In addition he had spent a record six years as Head of Station, Moscow, and had been so highly thought of by Hazelwood's predecessor that the then DG had intended to employ him as the chief instructor at the training school before making him Deputy DG when Victor Hazelwood eventually moved into the top spot.

Although flattered that he should be considered for the appointment it was not a job he'd wanted. He'd had some experience of Hazelwood's methods when Victor had been the Assistant Director in charge of the Eastern Bloc, but the knowledge that they would be working hand in glove was not the reason he had turned the appointment down. The fact was he and his wife, Mary, both hated London, and had no desire even to live within commuting distance of the capital. When eventually he retired from the SIS they planned to settle in the Algarve and had already bought a villa at Albufeira with this in mind. However, in requesting to be considered for an appointment in Asia, the only relevant point Calthorpe had been able to make was the fact that he had never been employed east of Suez before.

The DG had been sympathetic but Calthorpe had only been assigned to Delhi because the resident physician to the British High Commission had insisted the Head of Station should be sent home on medical grounds. In the end the wheel had turned full circle and he had been recalled to London to take over the Asian Department following the suicide of the then incumbent twelve months ago.

Usually Calthorpe didn't have much to say at morning prayers. Although the Taliban regime in Afghanistan was of particular interest to the SIS they were entirely dependent on the Pakistan Inter-Services Intelligence Agency for information, and were prohibited from initiating intelligence gathering operations by the FCO. For once, however, he had something to say that hadn't come directly from the Pakistan authorities.

So far Hazelwood had received nothing but negative statements from his heads of departments. Ashton had told him the police still hadn't identified Danièle while Meacher had had to report that his department had lost track of Talal Asir. Furthermore he'd also let it be known that he doubted if Head of Station, Damascus would be able to discover who was actually living in the villa at 111 Boulevard Hafez el-Assad. This candid observation hadn't gone down at all well with Hazelwood.

'What have you got for me, Hugo?' he asked. 'More bad news?'

'I'm afraid so,' Calthorpe told him bluntly. 'The British Council representative in Islamabad and his wife appear to have been kidnapped.'

'When did this happen?'

'Sometime last night. The Jenners were under police protection and their disappearance only came to light when the sergeant in charge arrived with the relief constables and was unable to find the two officers who'd been on the 2200 to 0600 hours shift.'

However the sergeant did notice there were bloodstains on the drive midway between the veranda at the front of the bungalow and the low stone wall surrounding the property. Additional bloodstains discovered in the back garden led him to search the servants' quarters.

'The Jenners had two live-in servants,' Calthorpe continued, 'a cook and a house boy, both of whom had been shot in the head. It looks as if the two police constables were killed first and their bodies subsequently carried into the servant quarters after the occupants had been dealt with. The kidnappers then broke into the bungalow, forcing the kitchen door around the lock with some sort of crowbar. The Jenners' bedroom was in a hell of a mess and there were signs of a struggle. That's all we have so far.'

'No ransom demand?' Hazelwood asked.

'There's been no word from the kidnappers yet. But Head of Station has been talking to the Pakistan authorities and they reckon the kidnappers won't get in touch until they've gone to ground miles away from Islamabad.'

'Tell me something, Hugo, did we have any forewarning that the Jenners were at risk?'

Calthorpe shook his head. 'Apparently Keith Jenner saw the High Commissioner on Monday morning and asked if they could move into the diplomatic compound. He said his wife, Laura, was convinced they were being targeted. By all accounts Jenner himself was inclined to make light of her fears. Nevertheless, since there was no suitable accommodation available in the diplomatic compound, the High Commissioner persuaded the Minister of the Interior to place them under armed guard. The police were very quick off the mark; by 1200 hours that same day two constables were on duty at the Jenners' bungalow. It's worth noting the Ministry of the Interior were equally quick to inform the High Commissioner when it became evident the Jenners had been kidnapped. The date/time group of the signal Head of Station despatched to us is 24 0300 hours Zulu March. In other words 0800 hours local time.'

'What's your point, Hugo?'

'I believe the Pakistani authorities will keep us informed of developments a lot quicker than is normally the case.'

'Good. What do we know about the Jenners? Will they hold up under pressure?'

'I've never met them,' Calthorpe said, 'but according to the FCO they have two children, a boy and a girl aged twelve and ten respectively. They're at boarding school in England and are flying out to Islamabad this morning for the Easter holidays . . .'

'Jesus,' Ashton said under his breath but not so quietly that Calthorpe couldn't hear him.

'It's OK, Peter,' he said, 'the British Council office in Spring Gardens has been alerted and they are going to intercept the children at Heathrow.' He turned to Hazelwood. 'But of course the Jenners won't know that, and the possibility that their children will arrive in Islamabad and find there is nobody there to meet them will prey on their minds.'

'Thank you, Hugo,' Hazelwood said waspishly, 'you've made my day.' He looked round the table. 'How do we see the kidnapping? Is it simply a violent crime or is it political in some way? Comments anybody?'

Calthorpe didn't say anything. Victor's eyes had only lingered briefly on him before they focused on Ashton. He supposed it was almost inevitable that Victor should seek the younger man's opinion first. Victor and Ashton went back a long way and in many respects they were two of a kind. All the same, never had Rowan Garfield, the stopgap Deputy DG, seemed quite so superfluous as he did at that moment.

'Well, Peter?' Hazelwood said, prompting him.

'If the Jenners are wealthy then it's probably a violent crime. If they have no money then it's likely to be political.' Ashton paused, then said, 'There are a couple of things we ought to keep in mind. The kidnappers obviously knew the police were guarding the Jenners, and that smacks of inside information. Secondly, four people were shot in three different locations but apparently none of the victims heard the gunshots. This leads me to think

111

the kidnappers were provided with highly effective silencers.'

'What's your assessment, Hugo?' Hazelwood said, turning to Calthorpe.

'I agree with what Peter has said, except in that part of the world even a hundred pounds would be considered a fortune. All the same, in this instance I believe the kidnapping is political.'

'All right, political it is. This means that Neagle at MI5 should be informed because sooner or later CATO will be involved.' Hazelwood stood up and moved towards the door. 'Landon should also be kept up to speed,' he added and swept out of the conference room.

'I know somebody who's dying for a Burma cheroot,' Garfield said dryly.

*   *   *

The cell where Jenner was imprisoned was located in the basement of an abandoned tailor's shop on Jinnah Street in Peshawar City just over a hundred miles from Islamabad. Jenner of course had no idea where he was being held; he had remained blindfolded throughout the entire journey and the scarf had only been removed when he was safely under lock and key. The cell was roughly twelve feet by ten and was furnished with a wooden stool, latrine bucket and a charpoy, or string bed, complete with a thick bolster that would be nothing like as comfortable as a pillow.

The pyjamas Jenner had been wearing had been taken away and replaced with a pair of cotton slacks, a check shirt and a pair of leather sandals. Both items of clothing were at least one size too small around the waist for his frame. The cords that had bound him hand and foot had been removed and in their place he now wore handcuffs, leg irons and a steel collar. A chain attached to the collar was anchored at the other end by a ring bolt screwed into the wall. There was just enough slack in the chain for him to reach the latrine bucket when the need arose. Their consideration did not extend to providing him with sustenance; all he'd had was a few sips of water. Nor would his captors tell him what they had done with Laura.

A key turned in the lock and the door opened outwards. A faint hope that his wife was about to join him died when a fat man carrying a video camera entered the cell. He was dressed like a Pathan in sandals, baggy trousers, loose-fitting knee-length tunic and an untidy turban with long loops coming down round his neck. Pointing to the stool he ordered him to sit down.

'You speak English,' Jenner said in amazement.

'That's because I am British. Now sit down on the stool.'

The fat man told him to look into the camera and give his full name, date and place of birth. The shoot lasted no more than three minutes.

Nine

The Ford Transit van had been in the wars. The offside front wing had been buckled following a side-on collision and it was questionable who had inflicted the most damage—the driver of the other vehicle or the amateur panel beater who had tried to restore the wing to its original shape with a two-pound hammer. At some time in the distant past the van driver had also managed to put a V-shaped dent in the rear fender after reversing into a concrete bollard. The paint job had originally been a dark blue but too many summers in Karachi had taken the gloss out of the cellulose. Stencilled on both sides and the rear doors of the van was the legend 'Ishaq Khan—Fresh Fruit and Vegetables'.

At 0730 hours local time the Ford Transit was collected by the van driver and his youthful looking co-driver from number 3 Godown on West Wharf. From there their route took them through the Quaid-i-Azam section of the city to join the Ali Jinnah Road. Some eight miles after leaving West Wharf they turned off the Ali Jinnah Road and headed north. Passing Gandhi Zoo, they crossed the Layari River, skirted the zoological gardens and entered the Goth Goli Mar district. Their destination was a spare parts yard directly across the square from the Jama Masjid mosque. Here the van driver collected a brand new six-volt battery that had been charged up during the night. The girlish features of his co-driver, who refused to remain behind in the cab, were the subject of much ribald comment. One of the fitters went so far as to suggest that there was nothing like a young boy with taut buttocks to satisfy a man's appetite. Burning with rage, the driver opened the nearside door and placed the battery on the floor, then walked round the vehicle, got in behind the wheel and started the engine. From the Jama Masjid mosque they headed east, crossed the Layari River for the second time and rejoined the Ali Jinnah Road again in open country.

The co-driver was a twenty-two-year-old chemistry graduate from the University of Karachi. A thin, narrow face, flat chest and sinewy body practically guaranteed that she would be mistaken for a boy, especially when dressed like one, as she was on this occasion. As they headed out in the direction of the international airport, she coolly prepared the homemade bomb for detonation. Reaching under the dashboard she produced a reel of domestic insulated cable and cut off two equal lengths with a jackknife. She then bared the cables at both ends and bound the middle sections together with adhesive tape, leaving the bare wires exposed. Before lifting the six-volt battery on to her lap, she fished out the Cortex instantaneous fuse that had been concealed under her seat and plugged the loose end into the electric detonator she had been carrying in her shirt pocket. The detonator itself could only be activated by an electrical charge which was the reason why they had purchased a six-volt battery. Connecting the bared wires of the domestic insulated cable to the detonator was child's play, the tricky part came in preparing the other bared wires for attachment to the positive and negative poles of the battery. Carefully placing the detonator and attachments on the floor, she bent forward at the waist and lifted the battery on to her lap.

'You want to watch what you are doing,' the van driver told her. 'Make one mistake and there'll be a premature before we get to Malir Cantonment.'

'I know what I'm doing.'

Only two bare wires remained. Folding one back until it was flush with the insulated cable, she wound the other around the negative pole. When the time came she had only to straighten the bare wire and bring it into contact with the positive pole to detonate the two thousand pounds of Semtex packed into the cargo area of the Transit.

'We're almost there,' the driver announced unnecessarily.

In the days of the Raj the cantonment was where the army, police, civil administration, members of the judiciary and the top management of the railways, post and telegraph lived. Things weren't all that different now, fifty-two years after Independence. The European quarter had always been divorced from the city where the indigenous population dwelt and Malir Cantonment was a good seven miles beyond the outskirts of Karachi. With its metalled roads, broad avenues lined with trees, neat residential housing and unobtrusive public buildings, the cantonment was like an oasis surrounded by a scrub desert.

'Which way now?' the driver asked in a harsh but strained voice.

'First turning left then second on the right,' the woman told him calmly.

The British Council office was housed in a two-storey building located between a small shopping precinct on one side and a community health centre on the other. The ground floor was given over to an extensive library and a reading room where copies of the latest airmail editions of *The Times*, *Telegraph*, *Guardian*, *Independent* and *Herald Tribune* were available. Upstairs was a small theatre-cum-cinema, a cloakroom for the staff and the offices of the Council representative and his secretary. Apart from a brass plaque on the door, the building was completely anonymous.

At 0845 hours local time the Ford Transit supposedly belonging to 'Ishaq Khan—Fresh Fruit and Vegetables' stopped outside the British Council office. A split second later the twenty-two-year-old chemistry graduate straightened the bare wire that had been folded back and touched it against the positive pole.

The two-thousand-pound bomb blew the Ford Transit to pieces and reduced the British Council to a pile of rubble, trapping those who happened to be in the building at the time. The blast shattered every window in the shopping precinct and the community health centre. It also dislodged the roof tiles on buildings up to half a mile away from the epicentre of the explosion. Super-heated fragments of metal from the van cut down eight pedestrians in the immediate area and set fire to three cars parked at the kerbside. A column of black, oily smoke rose almost a hundred feet in the air before it began to disperse. Following the explosion there was a brief eerie silence before the panic stricken and the injured started screaming.

The first vehicle from the emergency services arrived on the scene ten minutes later.

*   *   *

Landon was the only Grade II Intelligence Officer to have a crypto-protected computer that was linked to MI5, the Defence Intelligence Staff and GCHQ. Every other officer of his seniority was locked in the standalone system, which meant that while they were able to access MIDAS, the Multi-Intelligence Data Access System containing the databases of SIS departments, they were cut off from external sources. Landon was the exception simply because he was the Firm's representative on the Combined Anti-Terrorist Organization. However, on a day to day basis he was a frequent user of the standalone facility and rarely found it necessary to contact other agencies. For that matter they seldom logged on to his terminal.

This morning was one of those rare exceptions to the general rule. Two minutes ago Richard Neagle had called him on the secure speech facility to ask if he was up and running. Now, as he sat there watching the VDU, details of the transactions on Anwar Farid's MasterCard appeared on the screen. Below the last entry, Neagle had included the number of Farid's current account with the National Westminster and the address of the branch which looked after him. The information was contained on a single sheet of A4 and, having already set the printer, he ran off two copies. Landon then shrouded the VDU and returned to his desk. From Ashton he had inherited this office on the fourth floor and, with it, an unrivalled view of the railway tracks between Vauxhall and Waterloo. How anybody from the vantage point of the tallest building on the South Lambeth Road would be able to read what was on the screen at a minimum distance of three hundred yards was beyond him. Scepticism was not, however, a valid reason for ignoring standing orders.

Landon scanned the printout. The first thing to catch his eye was the last transaction on Farid's MasterCard, which was dated 16th March, in favour of the Majestic Hotel, London. Since the Egyptian had arrived on United Airlines Flight 956 from JFK at 0720 hours, the entry meant he had stayed that night in London and had paid his hotel bill the following day before leaving for Wood Green. The sum of money shown against the preceding entry indicated that he had stayed at least one night at the Hilton Hotel, Union Station, St Louis. The satellite photograph of Talal Asir, which Amesbury-Cotton had produced at the CATO meeting two days ago, had been taken on Friday 5th March. Farid had left England on the 26th February, according to the docket at Airways Cranford Parking; timewise he could therefore have seen the Banker in Damascus. Unfortunately he had led Toby Quayle to believe he had run into Talal Asir on Thursday 11th March, the very day he'd settled his bill at the Hilton Hotel, Union Station. Looking at the very first transaction on the MasterCard, it was evident that Anwar Farid had a taste for the good things in life. Four days after leaving England he had run up a bill with the Sheraton Hotel in Amman amounting to four hundred and eighty-three pounds sixty-two pence. Between the 2nd and 11th March there was a yawning gap; the problem confronting Landon was how to fill it in. Before he could list the agencies that might be able to assist him, the Mozart secure speech phone issued a strident summons. Lifting the receiver Landon merely gave the number of his extension.

'So what do you make of the printout?' Neagle asked.

'It raises more questions than it answers,' Landon told him.

'Well, maybe his bank statement from the NatWest for the last twelve months will answer

119

some of your queries. Photocopies are on their way to you by special courier courtesy of Detective Chief Superintendent Roberts.'

'That's decent of him. What about the associated cheque books? Have they been included?'

'I wouldn't know, the bank statements are coming to you via Special Branch.'

'If they haven't been included we'd better hope that the payees have been notated against every entry on the statements. Without those details all we've got is a series of cheque numbers against varying withdrawals.'

'I like the way you keep saying "we".'

'Well, I wouldn't want you to feel left out, Richard . . . Has anybody talked to the manager of the Majestic Hotel?'

'Roberts has,' Neagle said tersely. 'Farid took a double room, claimed the woman who accompanied him was his wife. From the manager's description of her, Roberts is satisfied the "wife" was Danièle.'

'Is he any closer to finding out who she really is?'

'Nobody has come forward to identify the body. And before you ask,' Neagle said, pre-empting the question, 'the Daniel Kopek who was on the same plane as Farid is genuine. We interviewed him at the Grosvenor House Hotel yesterday, where immigration told us he would be staying. Kopek is a management consultant for Geldorf Sax. He's frequently over here, running his eye over the British subsidiary.'

Neagle was off down the byways, straying from the point as was sometimes his habit. Right now he wanted Landon to know Kopek was a bit eccentric. Travelling first class at the company's expense would have been one of the perks enjoyed by an executive of his status, but for some reason known only to himself Kopek was normally found in the world traveller or economy class.

'But on this occasion,' Neagle continued, 'world traveller was fully booked and he was obliged to fly club class.'

'What about Anwar Farid?' Landon asked.

'Oh, didn't I tell you? He was flying club class, but in his case I suspect he did so regularly.'

Landon felt like kicking himself. He should have guessed Anwar Farid would never travel with the hoi polloi; you only had to see the entries on his MasterCard statement to know that.

'I have a feeling we will never find out who Danièle is,' Neagle added.

'I disagree,' Landon told him.

'You're either an incurable optimist, Will, or you're on to something.'

'United Airlines Flight 956 arrived Heathrow at 0720. Correct?'

'Yes.'

'OK. Noon would be the earliest a room would be available for occupation at the Majestic Hotel or any other hotel for that matter.'

'I'm not sure I'm with you, Will.'

'I think Danièle was on a different flight that arrived within an hour or so of United Airlines 956.'

'From where?'

'America.'

'You want to give me the departure airfield?' Neagle asked sarcastically.

'Chicago, Newark, Philadelphia, Dulles International, Washington, maybe San Francisco or even Los Angeles. Don't rule any of them out just because they come into Terminal 4 instead of Terminal 3. It wouldn't take Anwar Farid more than an hour to collect his car from Cranford Airways Parking and meet Danièle at either terminal.'

'What you're asking for could be a colossal waste of time, Will.'

'Can you think of a better way of discovering what Farid was up to when he was out of the country?'

Neagle sighed. 'No, I can't, that's the trouble,' he said and put the phone down.

Landon picked up the BT phone, rang the chief archivist in Central Registry, and warned him he was expecting a package from Special Branch by courier. Barely five minutes later, Nancy Wilkins, the clerical officer he shared with Chris Neighbour, walked into the office and presented him with a large manila envelope. Ripping it open, Landon extracted a wad of bank statements for the previous twelve months. As he feared the police had not identified the payees.

'Are you busy, Nancy?' Landon asked, looking up.

'There's nothing on my desk that can't wait.'

'Good. Pull up a chair and sit down.'

With Nancy's assistance Landon intended to go through the twelve statements listing those entries in excess of a hundred pounds. He would then present Special Branch with the relevant cheque numbers and invite them to supply the names of the payees from the counterfoils in the cheque books. If nothing else Landon reckoned the search would identify the travel agent Farid normally dealt with.

*　　　*　　　*

Perestroika and glasnost had done very little for Chris Neighbour, who ran the Russian desk for Ashton. In 1996 he had been declared persona non grata by the Russian Minister of the Interior and deported from Moscow. He had been accused of espionage, which was the usual excuse, but it had been a bit more complicated than that. It had started with a plea for political asylum from Katya Malinovskaya, who, apart from being known to Ashton, had been a rising star in the Criminal Investigation Division of the old KGB before she had gone freelance.

Malinovskaya's security agency had been hired by Major General Gorov, Chief of Police, Moscow District, to protect Vladislav Kochelev, a government auditor. Kochelev was to have been a key witness in the forthcoming trial of President Yeltsin's former adviser on foreign affairs, who had misappropriated twelve million US dollars from the Kremlin's domestic budget. Some person or persons unknown had put a hundred thousand dollar price tag on Kochelev's head and Gorov had feared that some of his own men might be tempted.

Against the odds Malinovskaya had kept the government auditor alive for twenty weeks when she had run into an ambush on her way back from Moscow and the trial venue. Kochelev and her two most trusted operatives had been killed in the hail of gunfire and she had been incredibly lucky to survive. Having spent five months in the auditor's company Katya Malinovskaya had had every

123

reason to assume that the men who'd had Kochelev murdered would not rest until she too had been liquidated. She had therefore phoned the British Embassy and, presuming on her acquaintance with Ashton, had asked for asylum.

Neighbour had wanted to bring her in but Head of Station, Moscow had refused to sanction the operation. So far as he had been concerned Katya Malinovskaya had to make it to the British Embassy under her own steam before the application for asylum could be considered. It had been Neighbour's wretched task to convey this decision to her. That had been the last time he'd spoken to Katya Malinovskaya. Some time later Walter Iremonger, the AP correspondent in Moscow, had rung the embassy to report that she had been killed by a sniper from across the street shortly after she had taken refuge in his flat. Iremonger had already contacted the police but he hadn't wanted to face Moscow's finest on his own. Two police officers were already on the scene by the time Neighbour had arrived at the flat. They had been joined by a lieutenant, two detectives, a medical examiner, three technicians from the forensic science laboratory and a covey of uniformed officers. The chief investigating officer had wanted to arrest Iremonger and take him into custody for questioning. Responding to this, Neighbour had used the ambassador's name to threaten Major General Gorov with a major diplomatic incident. Consequently Iremonger had been released into his care on the understanding that the AP man would be required as a material witness should the killer be apprehended. To ensure Iremonger did not leave Moscow without their permission, the police had retained his passport.

As a cover appointment for his real job, Neighbour had been shown as Third Secretary, Consular Affairs on the embassy staff list. It had therefore been comparatively easy to issue Iremonger with a new passport under a different name and put the AP man on a British Airways flight to London that same day. Before the end of the week Neighbour had been declared persona non grata.

Although everybody had agreed that the Mafiozniki would have got to Iremonger and murdered him regardless of whether he was in custody or out on the street, Neighbour still reckoned his career had come to a grinding halt. He was a Grade II Intelligence Officer and was likely to remain one unless he turned in some good results. And the way things were going that wasn't likely to happen. He couldn't think what Ashton would make of this latest fiasco and wished now he hadn't asked to see him.

'Good, bad or indifferent?' Ashton asked him cheerfully when he entered his office.

'What?'

'Your news, Chris.'

'I've got a problem with the information Will was given by the Defence Intelligence Staff at the latest CATO meeting.'

'Is this to do with Saddam Hussein's quest for weapons grade plutonium?' Ashton enquired and waved him to a chair.

'Yes, I'm afraid it is. Soon as I received the information I asked George Elphinstone, Head of Station, Moscow, to find out what, if anything,

Russian Intelligence has on Talal Asir. I know we can't expect to hear from George before the weekend but I'm pretty sure he will draw a blank.'

Ashton smiled. 'George may not be an incandescent ball of fire but he's not hopeless.'

'I didn't mean to imply he is. But you know the Russians, Peter, they'll want more than just a quid pro quo and that's something I can't give them.'

'Of course you can't, it's not in your gift.'

The information concerning Talal Asir's role in implementing Saddam Hussein's nuclear ambition had come from the Defence Intelligence Staff. It was no use seeking permission to disseminate the intelligence report to the Russians. The rep from Science and Technology had claimed the information had been provided by an Iraqi who sat at the top table with Hussein. No way would the DIS allow their source to be compromised and put at risk.

'What you could do,' Ashton said thoughtfully, 'is to phone Science and Technology and ask them if their information on Talal Asir predates the satellite photograph D17 produced at the same CATO meeting.'

'Right.'

'What do you know about malcontents in the Black Sea fleet, Chris?'

'Morale is at rock bottom. Some personnel have not been paid in months, discipline is poor and the food is even worse. I don't think Hussein would have much trouble finding somebody who would be willing to sell him what he wants.'

'If morale is that bad we should capitalize on the fact.' Ashton leaned back in the chair and clasped both hands behind his neck. 'Pass the word around that we are offering half a million for Talal Asir, dead or alive.'

'Have we got that kind of money?'

'There's a hundred thousand in the imprest and the next financial year is just around the corner.'

'I thought the FCO didn't approve of assassinations,' Neighbour said doubtfully.

'They're not entirely inflexible. If you can show no blame will be attached to the UK, they won't throw a spanner in the works.'

'What about the politicians?' Neighbour asked.

'They would like to see Talal Asir stand trial for war crimes. It would drag on for years and cost the taxpayer a bomb but it would make them feel good.' Ashton suddenly straightened up. 'Let's not get sidetracked, Chris,' he said tersely. 'What I'd like from you is a non-attributable scenario for the liquidation of the Saudi banker. Come and talk to me again soon as you've got something down on paper.'

*   *   *

The date/time group of the emergency signal from Head of Station, Islamabad was 251417Z March. Classified confidential, it read: *British Council Office Karachi attacked and devastated by a suicide bomber at 0845 hours local time this morning. No details of casualties as yet.*

Hugo Calthorpe took it as read that there would be at least one follow-up, possibly more. While he had precious little information to give Hazelwood, it would be some hours before the Head of Station was in a position to add to his initial report. It was also a fact that Victor would undoubtedly spit blood if in the meantime he received the news second-hand from the FCO. Taking the signal with him, Calthorpe walked it down the corridor, passed through the PA's office and entered the adjoining room.

'You'll want to see this, Victor,' he said and passed the clear-text communication to Hazelwood. 'Of course, it's just the tip of the iceberg and it may be some time before we know the full extent—'

'Do you see a connection, Hugo?' Hazelwood asked, interrupting him.

'With the kidnapping of the Jenners?' Calthorpe paused briefly to consider the question, then said, 'Yes, I'm convinced both incidents are politically motivated. Unless I am completely wrong I believe we can expect these terrorists to go after the British Council office in Lahore and the newer one in Peshawar.'

'So what are you going to do about this latent threat?'

The short answer was nothing. The British Council offices were an adjunct of the FCO and it was up to the High Commissioner to warn Lahore and Peshawar to be vigilant. But Calthorpe knew this was not the answer Hazelwood was looking for. Victor wanted positive action and positive action he would get even though their man in Islamabad would think the people in London were teaching their grandmother to suck eggs.

'I'll signal our Head of Station and tell him to personally warn the council reps in Lahore and Peshawar to be on their guard.'

'Good.' Hazelwood flipped open the cigar box on the desk and took out a Burma cheroot. 'What about the expats working in Pakistan? Are they at risk?'

'Not at present. I've a hunch the terrorists are out to destroy our political influence in the entire region.'

'And the British Council offices are much softer targets than the High Commission?'

Calthorpe edged towards the PA's office. 'No one would dispute that, Victor.'

'These terrorists—can you put a name to them?'

'Jamaat-e-Islami,' Calthorpe told him on the way out.

*   *   *

A second emergency signal dated 251422Z March from Head of Station, Islamabad, was received by Hugo Calthorpe at 1527 hours British Summer Time. It was not the follow-up message he had been expecting. Instead, Head of Station reported he had just been informed that the British Council office in Lahore had been attacked by a suicide bomber.

Ten

At first Keith Jenner did not recognize the woman who was thrust into the cell where he was being held. There were no windows and the only source of light came from the adjoining room through the small metal grille set in the door. In the prevailing gloom there was some excuse for his failure to realize who she was. When she spoke to him, her voice didn't sound like Laura's; it was too shrill and unpleasant. It wasn't until she was standing right in front of him that he no longer doubted who she was.

His wife looked awful. Her face was puffy and blotched, the eyes inflamed and red rimmed while her hair was unkempt and resembled a ravaged bird's nest. The ivory coloured satin nightdress she had been wearing the night they were kidnapped was almost grey with dirt and she smelled of sweat and urine.

'What have they done to you?' Jenner asked in a hollow voice.

Laura regarded him through narrowed eyes. 'As if you cared,' she said.

He did care but no matter how he tried to express his love for her Jenner knew that Laura would never believe him in her present state of mind. 'What have they done to you?' he repeated softly.

'I've been sodomized.' Her voice became even more strained and she began to have palpitations, leaving her breathless so that she was forced to pause after every three to four words. 'I was bent . . . over a table . . . and they took it . . . in turns to bugger me.'

'They?' It was an instinctive response. The last thing Jenner had intended was to strike a note of incredulity that suggested he didn't believe Laura. But that was how she took it.

'You bastard,' she choked. 'You know their names . . . Rahim Khan . . . and the fat man . . . the one who claims . . . he is British.'

'I've met him.'

'His name is Khalef . . . as you know . . . damn well.'

He wanted to take Laura in his arms and comfort her but she stayed out of his reach near the door. He was sure it was deliberate. Somebody, possibly Rahim Khan or Khalef, had told her about the limits on his freedom of movement imposed by the collar and chain around his neck. Whoever it was had then ordered Laura to keep well back from him. Jenner could understand her anger but couldn't see why it should be directed at him. Before he thought to ask, Laura wanted to know why he had refused to cooperate with Khalef. Was it such a sin to lie about his involvement with the CIA if it meant her freedom?

'My involvement with the CIA,' he repeated blankly.

'Yes. They want you to admit you have been spying for the Company.'

'And if I do will they let you go?'

'Haven't I already said so?' Although Laura had recovered some of her composure her voice was still quavery and it wouldn't take much to push her over the edge.

Jenner said he would do it but he wanted Laura to know he had never refused to cooperate with their kidnappers. This, he learned, was only partly true. He had, in fact, got as far as giving his name, date and place of birth only to change his mind and refuse to read out the statement that had been prepared for him. There was, Jenner recognized, no point in arguing with Laura. The lie that he had refused to cooperate had been carefully nurtured. She also believed they had not been missed and that their children were now on their way to Islamabad and nobody would be there at the airport to meet them. Time had even less meaning for Laura than it had for him.

'All right, what are you waiting for?' Jenner said wearily. 'Go tell them I'm ready.'

Khalef did not keep him waiting. Literally moments after the door had been opened so that Laura could leave, the British Muslim, accompanied by two Pathans whom he hadn't seen before, entered the cell. One of the Pathans was carrying a folding canvas stool, which he erected and positioned as Khalef directed. The Islamic fundamentalist then sat down and trained the camcorder on Jenner. The other Pathan stood behind Khalef holding up a cue card.

'You will read what is on the card,' Khalef told him.

'Now?'

'Yes, now.'

'My name is Keith Jenner. I am head of the British Council in Pakistan.' Jenner paused and moved his lips a couple of times before continuing. 'I was born on the second of February 1943 at Peterborough in Cambridgeshire and was educated at Downside before going up to Queen's College, Oxford.'

Jenner thought he knew the source of Khalef's information. Where he had gone to school did not appear on the staff list produced by the British High Commission, only Laura could have supplied that kind of minutiae.

'I was appointed to my present position in September 1995. At the instigation of my wife, who is an American, I began working for the Central Intelligence Agency nineteen months later.'

Jenner paused a second time and worked his mouth like a goldfish in a glass bowl.

'Stop,' Khalef shouted. 'Why are you doing that?'

'Doing what?'

'Opening and closing your mouth?'

'I'm thirsty,' Jenner told him.

Khalef lowered the camcorder and nursed it on his lap, then called out to one of the Pathans. Presently a wall-eyed man entered the cell with a gourd containing water. Jenner managed a couple of sips before the gourd was withdrawn from his mouth. He did not feel deprived; although cool the water tasted brackish.

'Now we continue,' Khalef said and aimed the camcorder at him.

'My case officer at the American Embassy is Mr Warwick Moreno, First Secretary, Commercial,' Jenner intoned.

There were a lot of other names, officials whom Jenner had supposedly gone out of his way to cultivate. They included men like Malik Rahman, who was in charge of Pakistan's nuclear research programme.

*   *   *

Even before they assembled for morning prayers every head of department knew that Hugo Calthorpe would be invited to lead off. This tip had been spread by word of mouth by the duty clerks on the night watch. They had of course been in the right place at the right time to know that over ninety per cent of the communications received during the silent hours of the night 25th–26th March had been addressed to the Asian Department. In one sense, however, the duty clerks were not entirely correct. Before asking Hugo Calthorpe to update those present, Hazelwood felt compelled to give a resumé of the events at Karachi and Lahore just in case someone round the table had missed every single radio and TV newscast in the previous twenty-four hours.

Calthorpe glanced once more at the notes he had prepared, then said, 'I regret to say the loss of life was high in both incidents. There were, however, heavier casualties in Lahore simply because there were more people about on the street in the vicinity of the Council office than had been the case in Karachi. As at 0200 hours our time there were sixty-one confirmed deaths and a hundred and four injured.'

There was in addition an unknown number of victims buried under the rubble. Amongst those definitely unaccounted for was the Council representative in Lahore and his part-time secretary, who was the wife of the regional sales director for British American Tobacco. That the British Council rep in Karachi had come through unscathed was entirely due to luck. When the bomb was detonated he had been half a mile away, conferring with the Deputy High Commissioner. To date the death toll had risen to twenty-eight while sixty-two men, women and children had been injured. Sixteen people were thought to be entombed under the rubble.

'The bomb was transported in an old Ford delivery van.' Calthorpe glanced at his notes again. 'Earlier reports spoke of a suicide bomber; it now appears there were two people in the vehicle, one of whom had been identified as a young woman.'

'Anything else we should know?' Hazelwood asked.

'Neither bomb belonged to the home-made

variety. No garden fertilizer or sticks of dynamite stolen from a quarry. These terrorists were provided with Semtex to construct their device.'

'Could they have obtained the explosive from the Pakistan army?'

Calthorpe shrugged. 'The Karachi bomb was all of two thousand pounds. It's probable the one detonated in Lahore was just as powerful. Somewhere some explosives ordnance depot has a shortfall amounting to four thousand pounds of Semtex. I imagine hiding such a loss would entail a lot of paperwork and involve quite a number of officers.'

'I agree. Have there been any developments regarding the Jenners?'

'Absolutely none, Victor,' Calthorpe said. 'There's still no word from the kidnappers.'

'Out of interest,' Ashton asked casually, 'how far is Peshawar from Islamabad?'

'About a hundred miles,' Calthorpe told him. 'Why do you ask?'

'I'd like to know why the terrorists didn't bomb the Peshawar office.'

'I'm surprised at you, Peter,' Hazelwood growled. 'I've heard a good few damn fool questions in my time but your latest is in a class of its own. There are a dozen reasons why—'

'Yeah, I know,' Ashton said cutting him short. 'Maybe at the last moment the suicide bomber decided he didn't want to die after all. Perhaps the vehicle was so clapped out it wouldn't start or else when he parked outside the building and pressed the tit bugger all happened and he simply drove off planning to come back another day. On the other hand there could be another explanation.'

'Well, don't keep us in suspense, Peter. We're all dying to hear what it could be,' Garfield said and snorted with suppressed laughter.

Ashton ignored this and turned to Hugo Calthorpe instead. 'I assume things are pretty quiet now in Karachi and Lahore?'

'You've got to be joking. It's as if an ants' nest has been disturbed; the police are crawling all over the place in both cities.'

'Exactly. If you were holding the Jenners somewhere in Peshawar the last thing you'd want to have is the police turning the whole damned city upside down.'

'Are you serious?' Calthorpe asked.

'Of course he isn't,' Hazelwood snapped.

'It was just a thought,' Ashton said mildly. 'There's no need to get overheated about it.'

There was a lengthy silence before Hazelwood asked Ralph Meacher to outline what incidents had occurred in the Middle East during the previous twenty-four hours.

Around Whitehall it was jokingly said that successful administration was largely the wise manipulation of coincidence. Three days ago Meacher had been asked to find out who actually resided at 111 Boulevard Hafez el-Assad. The task had been passed to Head of Station, Damascus and nobody had expected to hear from him for at least a week. However, it so happened Head of Station already knew the answer, and since a Queen's Messenger was also passing through Damascus on his way back to London, it was a simple matter to hand the diplomatic courier a handwritten letter addressed 'Personal' for the Assistant Director in charge of the Mid East Department.

The letter was in the nature of a semi-official note from one old acquaintance to another. There was no originator's reference and it was unclassified. It simply stated the villa belonged to Miss Lana Damir Rifa, a close friend of Major General Walid al-Kasam, Deputy Prime Minister and Minister for the Armed Forces.

*   *   *

A cheque stub dated 18th February 1999 had led Landon to Mercury Travel at 7 Station Road, Hornsey. With the help of Nancy Wilkins he had gone through Farid's bank statements selecting the largest withdrawals. These cheque numbers had been given to DCI Verco, who had then obtained the relevant details from the police officer running the crime index for Detective Chief Superintendent Roberts. Of the seven cheque numbers that had caught Landon's eye the one in favour of Mercury Travel was the largest at one thousand four hundred and eighteen pounds. Only the owner or manager of the travel agency could tell exactly what this sum had purchased. Verco had insisted on accompanying him to Hornsey, which had suited Landon. There was a lot to be said for having a real policeman in tow should the people at Mercury prove difficult. It meant you didn't have to masquerade as a law enforcement officer, using one of the fake warrant cards the Positive Vetting and Technical Services Division kept under lock and key.

They met by arrangement at Scotland Yard and went on to Hornsey in an unmarked police car. There were forty-seven Station Roads listed in the

A to Z London Street Atlas and the one in Hornsey had a lot in common with others Landon had seen. Of the eight business premises in the precinct, three had been boarded up. Mercury Travel was at the top end nearest the station tucked between a newsagent's and a model shop selling radio-controlled aircraft. Most of the window space was taken up with adverts for last-minute bargain breaks over the forthcoming Easter holiday. At 10.30 on a weekday morning Mercury Travel was scarcely a hive of activity. The faded blonde behind the counter brightened visibly when they walked into the agency. A Dymo name tag pinned high up on the left shoulder identified her as Veronica.

Despite having left her early twenties a long way behind Veronica still dressed the part in black leather high-heeled boots with a mini-skirt that didn't leave much to the imagination. A patent leather belt and a deep mauve long-sleeved blouse completed the ensemble and created the impression Veronica had been out on the town last night and was still wearing the same clothes.

'We'd like to see the manager,' Landon said smiling.

'I am the manager,' Veronica informed him in a tone of voice that implied she expected some sort of apology.

'We're police officers; my name's Landon, this is DCI Verco.'

The woman looked them up and down disbelievingly. 'And I'm Lord Mayor of London.'

Verco took out his warrant card and placed it on the counter upside down so that she could read the inscription. 'This should remove any doubts you may have about us,' he said.

Veronica glanced at the warrant card, then looked up and nodded. 'Thanks. Sorry if I offended you but you can't be too careful these days. Now, how can I help you?'

Landon told her they were interested in one of Mercury's clients, a Mr Anwar Farid of Wood Green, from whom the firm had received a large cheque on or about the 18th February.

'The Mr Farid who was murdered ten days ago?' Veronica said in a husky voice.

'The same,' Verco told her. 'Now show us a copy of the invoice you billed him with.'

'I'll have to get his file,' she said and jerked a thumb over her right shoulder. 'It's in the office back there.'

'Then get it. But leave the door open so that we can see what you're doing.'

'I've got nothing to hide.'

'So prove it,' Verco said.

Veronica threw the door open and flounced into the office. The filing cabinets were not in view but they could hear her opening and closing a steel drawer. A few moments later she returned with a thick folder and placed it on the counter.

'Mr Farid's travel arrangements are on the top five folios.'

'You've obviously made similar arrangements for him in the past,' Landon observed.

'Yes, ever since 1994.'

'Farid lived in Wood Green.'

'I'm aware of that,' Veronica said frostily.

'Are there no travel agencies in that part of London?'

'I don't know, Mr Landon, I never bothered to

find out. Anwar Farid was a free agent and chose to do his business with us. Why should we turn him away?'

'No reason at all.' Landon opened the folder, removed the top five folios and placed them side by side on the counter.

Farid had flown British Airways to Amman on the 26th February and had subsequently spent four nights at the Sheraton Hotel. On the 2nd March he had flown to Cairo by Royal Jordanian. Thereafter Farid had open-ended plane tickets with Alitalia for Cairo to Rome and Rome to Boston; with United Airways from New York, La Guardia to St Louis and St Louis to New York, La Guardia. After Cairo there were only two occasions when his movements could be plotted with any degree of accuracy. On the 11th March he had settled his bill at the Hilton Hotel Union Station, St Louis, and on Monday 15th he had arrived back in London.

'I'm afraid we have to take this entire folder away with us,' Landon told the woman.

'You're going to do what?'

'We need to study it in detail, Veronica.'

'Like hell you will.'

'What's your objection? The client is dead and every transaction has been completed.'

'Nevertheless the folder belongs to the firm and I won't let you have it.'

'Unless we can produce a search warrant?' Verco suggested. Resting both elbows on the counter, he leaned forward. It didn't take a lot to anger the detective chief inspector and when riled he could be very, very intimidating. 'Now I'll tell you what's going to happen,' he grated. 'My colleague is going to remain here keeping an eye on you while I obtain a search warrant. And on my return I am going to take you in for questioning. In my experience people who are uncooperative usually have something to hide.'

'I'm going nowhere with you, my solicitor will see to that.'

'Listen to me,' Verco said ominously. 'We have reason to believe Anwar Farid was laundering money for Islamic Jihad and that puts you in the frame. Under the Anti-Terrorist legislation we can hold you up to three days without the bother of wheeling you in front of a magistrate.'

It was questionable who was bluffing whom. There was hardly a shred of truth in the story Verco had pitched to Veronica, and it was odds-on that she didn't have a tame solicitor on tap. Verco, however, was a more convincing actor.

Veronica pushed the folder closer to Landon. 'All right,' she snarled, 'if it means that much you can have the bloody documents. All you coppers seem to do is harass law-abiding citizens. Why don't you go out and catch a real criminal for a fucking change?'

*   *   *

The medium-sized Jiffy bag had been recycled at least once. It was addressed to the Chief Security Officer, British High Commission, Diplomatic Enclave Ranna 5, PO Box 1122, Islamabad, and was marked Special Delivery in English. Although the stamps had been franked, the postmark was virtually illegible. It was impossible to tell at what time or from where the package had been dispatched. Only two letters were readable; hazarding a guess, one of the locally employed clerks thought it might have been mailed at Mardon, a sizeable town midway between Peshawar and Rawalpindi. The chief archivist wasn't concerned to know where it had come from. The package looked suspicious, which was reason enough to send for the Chief Security Officer. In effect the archivist was killing two birds with one stone, although he personally wasn't entirely happy with the proverb.

The Chief Security Officer was seconded from MI5. While not trained in bomb disposal, he had served in Northern Ireland in the late 1980s, where he had acquired the basic skills second-hand. After inspecting the Jiffy bag visually, he put it through the X-ray machine and noted it contained what appeared to be a video cassette. He put the bag through again, this time upside down to satisfy himself that the video cassette had not been fitted with a pressure plate that would trigger an incendiary device when the packet was opened. Although the cassette had not been tampered with, he nevertheless took the Jiffy bag out into the garden before inserting a knife under the flap and slitting the envelope open. At the back of his mind was the knowledge that if the package was a sophisticated booby trap, no one else would have to pay for his mistake. Very gingerly he slid his hand into the envelope and gently withdrew the cassette. On a sticky label fixed to one side of the tape somebody had written *Introducing Mr Keith Jenner* in a spidery hand.

The Chief Security Officer lived in a government-provided quarter directly behind the High

Commission. All that separated the two gardens was a low metal link fence roughly two foot six high. Stepping over it, he crossed the lawn and let himself into the house. He went in to the smaller of the two drawing rooms, switched on the television and VCR, then drew the curtains, shutting out the late-afternoon sun. Inserting the cassette, he set it running with the remote control.

The camera panned round the cell, lingering in turn on a latrine bucket and a wooden stool that was low to the ground and far from comfortable. Then Jenner appeared on the screen wearing a pair of cotton slacks, a check shirt and a pair of leather sandals. He was shackled hand and foot in leg irons and handcuffs; there was also a chain attached to the steel collar round his neck that was anchored at the other end to a ring bolt set in the wall. His face was badly bruised, the nose in particular looked as if it had been broken, and there was an ugly gash above the right eye. In a shaky voice he said, 'My name is Keith Jenner. I was born on the second of February 1943 at Peterborough.'

The whole take lasted under three minutes. In his gut the Chief Security Officer knew the kidnappers would never demand a ransom for Jenner. There would of course be more tapes, each one more harrowing than its predecessor. However, what he needed to do now was to make extra copies of this tape for MI5 and the SIS.

*   *   *

Landon left the tube station at Gloucester Road and made his way to Stanhope Gardens. He had stayed on at the office trying to make sense of

143

Farid's travel arrangements until gone 7 p.m. At the end of the day he wasn't sure what he and Nancy Wilkins had achieved. There were gaps in the Egyptian's itinerary which could only be filled by guesswork. To quote but one instance, Farid had entered the US at Logan International Airport, Boston, on some unknown date and had flown from New York to St Louis also on some unknown date. There was no indication of how he had got from Boston to New York, which was where the guessing game had started. He could have made the journey by Amtrak, Greyhound Bus, Travelways or rented a car. Farid could even have used another airline to make the connecting journey, paying for his plane ticket with cash, though Landon thought this was unlikely. One thing Landon had learned about America was that hotels, airlines and Amtrak preferred plastic to cash.

The one intriguing thing was that since becoming one of Mercury's clients in 1994 Farid had visited St Louis in 1995, 1997 and 1998 prior to that final occasion a fortnight or so ago. Landon reckoned the SIS should endeavour to find out just who he had been seeing in St Louis. He had made this point in the report he'd prepared for Ashton, which at this moment was being typed by Nancy Wilkins.

Among the support staff there was no one quite like Nancy. She had left Essex University with a first in media studies but had scarcely been overwhelmed with job offers. In fact, only Horizon, a small commercial radio station in Buckinghamshire, had been willing to take her on. She had spent a year on the front desk answering the phone and generally making herself useful.

144

Nancy had learned shorthand and had improved her touch-typing, all in the hope of furthering her career. She had also learned that as far as the station manager was concerned she was always going to be the airhead on reception.

Convinced she could do better for herself, Nancy had responded to an advert in the appointments section of the *Daily Telegraph* and had applied for a clerical post in the civil service. At twenty-three she had been the youngest applicant and it said a lot for the selection board that her appearance hadn't put them off. On her first day at the office she had turned up in trainers, jeans and a denim jacket over a dark-blue cotton shirt. The betting among her fellow clerks had been that she wouldn't last three months.

They couldn't have been more wrong; four years on she was still with the SIS. In that time she had advanced from clerical assistant through clerical officer to acting executive officer, only to be bumped down a grade nine months ago for a technical infringement of the Data Protection Act. The DG had wanted to sack Nancy; Ashton had saved her. With any luck she would be restored to her former grade in three months' time, when her case was due for review.

Landon turned into Stanhope Gardens, walked on to number 25, and, using his swipe card, let himself into the apartment house. His flat was on the second floor. As he stood there on the landing going through his pockets for the key a voice behind him that he hadn't heard in nine months said, 'Hi, Will, how you doing?'

Landon turned slowly about and there was Ensley Holsinger just as he remembered her, glossy

145

dark brown hair, five feet eight in low heels. Same old Ensley, he thought, poised, very sure of herself, and too damned attractive by half.

'What are you doing in London?' he asked, turning his back on the American girl to open the door.

'You obviously haven't read my letter.'

'You're right, I'm afraid I haven't.' He couldn't bring himself to tell Ensley that her letter had ended up in the wastepaper basket unopened and torn in four. 'You'd better come in and tell me what it is I've missed.'

Landon stepped aside and waved Ensley to go ahead. Then, pausing only to pick up the post lying on the mat in the hall, he followed her into the living room.

'Make yourself comfortable,' he told her. 'It won't take me a minute to sort through this lot.'

'Now I know what happened to my letter,' Ensley said ruefully as she watched him consign everything except a postcard to the wastepaper basket.

'How did you get into the house?'

'Jonathan let me in.'

'Jonathan?'

'The nice old man whose apartment is opposite yours. We're old friends.'

A lopsided smile appeared on Landon's mouth. Well, of course they were old friends. Ensley had made Jonathan's acquaintance last June when she had suddenly decided to move in with him whether he liked it or not. She had persuaded Jonathan that she was the fiancée Landon was expecting to arrive from America on a later flight. He wondered how she had accounted for his absence this time but shied away from asking.

'How long are you going to be in London?'

'Indefinitely,' Ensley told him with evident relish.

'Doing what?'

'Headhunting, finding round pegs to fill round holes.'

'Sounds interesting,' he murmured.

'Don't look so worried, Landon, it's not your head I'm after.'

There was, Landon sensed, a hidden agenda behind her simple announcement.

Eleven

Landon woke up, stretched both arms above his head and yawned, then reluctantly turned over on his left side and, still half asleep, reached out to shut off the alarm. To his surprise he found the button had already been depressed and assumed he must have done it. It was a minute before the implication sank in; raising himself up on one elbow, Landon peered at the luminous face and saw it had gone eight o'clock. The effect was electric. Kicking the bedclothes aside, he went into the bathroom, stripped off and stood under the shower while simultaneously giving himself a dry shave with a cutthroat razor. He dressed just as quickly. When he left the flat barely ten minutes later, after skipping breakfast, the place looked as if it had been hit by a bomb.

There was little point in running to the Underground station. When you were going to be late into the office no matter what, two or three minutes either way was immaterial. It would of course be the second morning running, but no blame could be attached to Ensley Holsinger this time. Not that she had been responsible for him oversleeping yesterday. If he had wanted to retain some semblance of order in his life he should have shown Ensley the door on Friday evening. That had been his intention when he had found her waiting for him when he'd returned home late. Unfortunately his resolve had evaporated, something that had happened to a lot of people when they were exposed to Ensley's charisma. So instead of keeping the American girl at arm's length, he had spent the whole weekend in her company and had then come back for more on Monday evening. And at night when they were apart he had spent hours wondering what her motive might be in taking up with him again.

Landon turned into the Underground station and went down on to the eastbound platform to find the rush hour crowd lined up six deep with more arriving every minute. Although no explanation had been given for the hold-up by the staff, popular opinion was evenly divided between a train failure and a body on the line. The hard-bitten and knowledgeable hoped it wasn't a body because a corpse couldn't be moved until it was officially pronounced dead by a doctor. They were still none the wiser when normal service was resumed twenty minutes later.

Already an hour late by the time he arrived at Vauxhall Cross, his problems weren't over yet. Regardless of the fact that his face was known to the MoD police officer on duty in the entrance hall, he was still required to produce his ID card. And that, as he rapidly discovered, was in the jacket pocket of the suit he'd worn on Monday.

'I'm afraid you'll have to apply for a visitor's pass,' the constable informed him apologetically. 'It's laid down in the standing orders, sir.'

'Don't I know it.'

Landon went over to the reception desk, filled in a buff-coloured form, and waited for the redoubtable Enid Sly to stamp the date and time of issue on it. He was also given a fat slab of plastic bearing the word 'Visitor' embossed in block capitals that was attached to a chain worn around the neck.

'Sir Victor's been after you, wants to be informed the moment you arrive,' Enid Sly announced with satisfaction, as she picked up the phone and dialled a four-digit extension.

'So who's going to escort me?' Landon asked.

'I am, soon as I've spoken to Sir Victor's PA.'

The reception Landon received after Enid Sly had escorted him to the conference room on the top floor proved equally frosty.

'Good of you to join us, Landon,' Hazelwood said, greeting him with all the warmth of an Arctic winter.

'I'm sorry, Director.' Landon glanced in turn at Calthorpe, Ashton and Garfield. 'My apologies, gentlemen.'

'Never mind that,' Hazelwood growled, then added, 'If you're ready, Hugo?'

Calthorpe inserted a cassette into the VCR then returned to his chair at the table and aimed the remote control at the TV. The set had been installed on Monday so that they could watch a tape recording Calthorpe had just received from the Head of Station, Islamabad.

149

Yesterday, a haggard-looking Keith Jenner had appeared on screen to give his name, date and place of birth after the cameraman had panned the cell where he was being held. The entire clip had lasted under three minutes but even though the latest communication followed the same opening format, Landon sensed it would last a good deal longer.

As he sat there listening to Jenner confess that he had spied for the CIA it occurred to Landon that this was what the show trials of the Stalinist era must have been like. The number of Pakistani officials and scientists Jenner admitted to cultivating was beyond belief. The information he had allegedly obtained as a result covered the whole field of the Islamic Republic's nuclear, chemical and biological research programmes. The really sickening part for Landon was the fact that the confession ended with Jenner stating he deserved to be severely punished for the crimes he had committed.

'What are we to make of that?' Hazelwood demanded.

'Well, it's obvious, isn't it?' Garfield looked round the table. 'Is there anyone here who doesn't believe that Jenner was acting under duress? God knows how many times they must have worked him over.'

'No more than once, Rowan,' Ashton told him. 'Granted Jenner looks worse than he did on the first tape, but that's the bruising coming out.'

'Even if you're right, he was still acting under duress.'

'I've no quarrel with that, Rowan. Jenner is pleading for his life. What we've been looking at is the final moments of a show trial and he knows they mean to execute him.'

'If that isn't a quantum leap of the imagination, I don't know what is,' Garfield said.

'Think about it, the Jenners were kidnapped a week ago and there's been no talk of a ransom. For what it's worth I believe there will be one, possibly two more tapes. The first one will probably contain a plea in mitigation submitted by the accused before sentencing and in the other, if there is one, we will witness Jenner's execution.'

'Now that is pure speculation and we deal in facts,' Hazelwood snapped and then turned to Calthorpe. 'What about the scientists Jenner named? Do we know of them, particularly the physicist J. M. Siddiqi?'

'They're all known to us, Victor, some better than others.'

Among the more shadowy figures was J. M. Siddiqi. Although enjoying a considerable reputation in his own field, the Asian Department understood that he was currently engaged in the peaceful application of nuclear power. There had been rumours of his involvement in the development of nuclear weapons, especially after Pakistan had carried out six underground nuclear tests on the 28th and 30th May 1998.

'At the very least, Jenner was instrumental in giving the rumour some substance.' Calthorpe paused to clear his throat before continuing. 'Much of his confession contains highly classified material. From listening to that tape I'm convinced a number of senior officers in the Pakistan Inter-Service Intelligence Agency supplied the kidnappers with the relevant information and Jenner repeated it word for word.'

151

'Have you got anything to support that contention?' Hazelwood asked.

'Not really. However, Jenner was convinced the information he was supposed to have obtained from his many contacts was authentic. He was scared witless, you could see it in his eyes and the way he kept licking his lips.'

'I don't remember seeing his tongue,' Landon heard himself say.

'What!'

'His tongue, Director. I would expect to see the tip of it when he moistened his lips.'

'What's your point?'

'I think he was trying to tell us something,' Landon said quietly.

'When was this?'

'Right at the beginning, Director, when Jenner identified himself and again a few sentences later. His mouth kept opening and closing like a fish.'

'Then let's see it,' Hazelwood said.

Calthorpe rewound the tape and ran it again and again, sometimes freeze-framing the picture.

'He's just gasping for breath,' Garfield said dismissively.

'No, I think Will is on to something,' Ashton told him.

'So do I,' Hazelwood growled. 'Somebody get me a lip-reader.'

*   *   *

'Things can only get better' was, in Chris Neighbour's opinion, one of those banal sayings people tended to bandy about when nothing was going right. But only after you had hit rock bottom and there was nowhere else to go could it be said there was a grain of truth in that half-baked notion. So far as Neighbour was concerned he was still on the way down. Four days ago Ashton had suggested he should ring the Science and Technology Branch of the Defence Intelligence Staff and find out how recent their information was with regard to Talal Asir. As Neighbour had feared it predated the satellite photo of the Saudi banker in Damascus. What had disturbed Neighbour even more was the attitude of Science and Technology. When pressed by him they had refused to say whether or not they suspected their Iraqi source had sat on the information until he had deemed it safe to contact his case officer. Whatever business Talal Asir may have had with the Russian Federation, chances were it had been concluded some months past.

A week ago he had signalled George Elphinstone, Head of Station, Moscow, asking him to find out what, if anything, the Russian Intelligence Service had on Talal Asir. Yesterday George Elphinstone had replied to the effect that the Russians had never heard of the Saudi banker but could the SIS please supply an up-to-date photo of him? It was the request for a photograph that really stuck in Neighbour's craw. The RIS were just being cute, making out they were eager to help in any way they could.

Unfortunately Elphinstone hadn't left it at that. Before replying to his signal, he had obviously conferred with the ambassador and had then written a singularly unhelpful demi-official letter addressed to the DG with a copy to him plus the world and his wife at the FCO. The letter had arrived in the diplomatic bag just over an hour ago

153

and it had been panic stations ever since. He had phoned Dilys Crowther and urged her to withhold the DG's copy until he had had a chance to brief Peter Ashton.

To learn that both men as well as the Deputy DG were in the conference room attending a special briefing by Hugo Calthorpe was no comfort. There was going to be an almighty explosion and he was unlikely to emerge from it unscathed. The longer Neighbour was obliged to wait for the inevitable, the more screwed-up he felt. He was beginning to think he was unlikely to see Ashton before the lunch hour when Dilys rang to inform him the meeting had just broken up. He was also told that five minutes was the maximum head start she could give him.

Clutching the demi-official letter, Neighbour left his office, locked the door behind him and literally raced towards the bank of lifts midway along the corridor. There was no immediate response from any of the four lifts when he pressed the call button. One was on the way down from the top floor, a second was in the basement level, a third appeared to be held at the second floor and he had just missed the fourth, which was on the way up. Every second he stood there waiting for a car to arrive was precious time wasted. In his growing impatience he unconsciously transferred his weight from one foot to the other and back again like a man desperate to relieve himself. Unwilling to wait any longer Neighbour decided to use the staircase; by the time he reached Ashton's office the five-minute head start was down to less than three and he was out of breath.

'You'll want to see this letter from George

Elphinstone,' Neighbour said slowly. 'It's addressed to the DG . . .'

'So I see.'

'He will probably send for you any minute.'

'I daresay he will.' Ashton looked up. 'We've been warned off, no dirty tricks on Russian soil. Did you tell Elphinstone we are about to offer half a million for Talal Asir dead or alive?'

'Is that what you think?' Neighbour said hotly.

'Last Thursday I asked you to say how we might eliminate the Saudi banker without any blame being attributed to us. Then four hours later you produced an outline paper advocating we pay the Mafiozniki to kill him. Yesterday morning you came to see me and asked to withdraw the paper because you'd had a better idea . . .'

The BT phone interrupted Ashton but instead of lifting the receiver he let the instrument ring and ring until eventually it fell silent. Glancing at his wristwatch, Neighbour surmised the caller could only have been Dilys Crowther.

'Somebody who doesn't know you like I do might conclude you withdrew the paper because you'd had forewarning of this letter.' Ashton smiled. 'Remember what I said about George Elphinstone? He may not be an incandescent ball of fire but he's not hopeless. George put two and two together the moment he received your signal. He assumed the DG was behind the request for information and knowing Victor as the sort of man who likes to make things happen, alerted the ambassador.'

'I think I'm partly to blame for that,' Neighbour said. 'There is the little matter of my run-in with George over Katya Malinovskaya when I was stationed in Moscow. His antennae would have started twitching when he saw who had originated the signal.'

As far as Ashton was concerned just who had triggered the adverse response was immaterial. The fact was Elphinstone enjoyed the wholehearted support of the ambassador and the FCO was unlikely to ignore the advice of their man in Moscow.

'A question,' Ashton said. 'If we can't hire a Mafiozniki hitman or a member of the Russian armed forces, who do we get to do the job?'

'The Israelis,' Neighbour said unhesitatingly. 'I would be surprised if Talal Asir wasn't already on Mossad's Most Wanted list. According to Ralph Meacher the Israelis must know he is one of the paymasters funding Islamic Jihad.'

There was another, even stronger, reason for soliciting the Israelis. Most of the sighting reports received by the Mid East Department placed Talal Asir within an arc extending from Lebanon through Syria, Iraq, Jordan and to Egypt.

'Tell me something, Chris,' Ashton said quietly. 'Why didn't you plump for the Israelis in the first place?'

'Because the Foreign Office would have a fit if they learned we were colluding with the Israelis to take out a Saudi even if he is a terrorist.'

'Were you planning to visit Israel in order to enlist the support of Mossad?'

'No way. Mossad will have a man among the diplomats at the London embassy. I was hoping Ralph Meacher would be able to give me his name. However, if he couldn't identify the Mossad agent I planned to approach MI5.'

'You mean Richard Neagle?'

'Yes, but it wouldn't necessarily be me.'

'You're right, it's one for Will Landon. He knows Richard, you don't.'

The BT phone started ringing again. Although Neighbour recognized it was simply his imagination working overtime, it seemed to him that on this occasion its strident summons was louder and more demanding. Answering the phone this time, Ashton listened briefly, then said, 'Is this about the whingeing letter George Elphinstone saw fit to send to Victor?'

There was not the slightest doubt in Neighbour's mind that it was. It was also no surprise to him that Ashton was angry. What was surprising was the fact that his anger was directed at the Head of Station, Moscow and not at him. As far as Ashton was concerned, Elphinstone had no business to send one of his junior officers a copy of the letter he'd written to the DG. If anyone should have had a copy it was him, as George would discover to his cost.

'I'm not sounding off at you, Dilys,' Ashton said, winding up. 'But I'm not prepared to see the DG until I'm in possession of all the facts. So please inform Sir Victor I'll be with him in the next two minutes.'

There was no guessing what Dilys Crowther made of that; having said his piece Ashton put the phone down, terminating what had been a largely one-sided conversation. In the next two and a half minutes Neighbour learned what was required of him. He was to find a suitable rendezvous within a thirty-mile radius of London. The RV should not be so far off the beaten track that strangers in the area would be noticed and commented on. There was one final stipulation. It was essential to make sure the Mossad agent in London was not being followed. When selecting the rendezvous Neighbour was therefore to bear in mind that a three-car surveillance team would need to be deployed in hides five miles out from the RV.

*　　*　　*

The training centre run by MI5 was located in Bruton Place off New Bond Street. It was situated directly above a picture gallery and shared a common entrance. Since the Security Service did not advertise its presence the uninitiated frequently blundered into the picture gallery where attendants cheerfully redirected the lost and strays to the spooks department on the floor above. The description was inaccurate, the centre existed purely to train those civil servants from government ministries who had been designated as branch security officers in addition to their normal work. Since the number of one-day courses in a year rarely exceeded six there was no permanent staff as such. Instructors were therefore drafted in on an as and when required basis. The man who had been nominated as chief instructor for the one-day courses held on Tuesday 30th March was Richard Neagle. Consequently the CATO meeting scheduled for the day had to be postponed for twenty-four hours.

The course had just adjourned for a ten-minute coffee break when the chief clerk of Neagle's section had rung him on his mobile number. Of necessity their conversation had had to be conducted in veiled speech because the mobile was not crypto-protected. The message he had received from the chief clerk had been simple enough: Will Landon had phoned the office and had asked if he would phone him back ASAP. The trouble was the training centre was not provided with a Mozart secure speech facility and he could scarcely double back to Gower Street, leaving the course high and dry. The lunch break between 1300 and 1400 hours was the only free time Neagle had and it wouldn't be enough. A certain amount of juggling had been called for and he'd told the chief clerk to contact DCI Verco and inform him that his lecture scheduled for 1500 had had to be moved forward by an hour. Neagle had also asked the chief clerk to let Landon know that 1.15 was the earliest he was likely to hear from him.

At 12.50 Neagle called time on the morning session, giving himself a head start of ten valuable minutes. Leaving the training centre he made his way to New Bond Street and started looking for a cab; he didn't meet one that wasn't already taken. It was the same story when he reached Oxford Street and started walking towards the Circus. His luck had changed as he neared the tube station when a cab drew up alongside him and two women alighted.

Old habits die hard. On joining the Security Service Neagle had been told never to disclose the precise location of MI5. In the days when MI5 headquarters had been in Curzon Street, visitors from the various outstations routinely alighted at the Mirabelle restaurant. Observing this once cardinal rule Neagle asked the cab to drop him off at the British Museum, even though a photograph of the headquarters building had appeared in the newspapers. However, the basic security procedure would become relevant again in a month's time when 'Five' moved to Thames House near Vauxhall Bridge.

By the time Neagle reached his office he had exactly twenty-five minutes in hand before the course reassembled after the lunch break. The note on his desk from the chief clerk was hardly reassuring: Verco hadn't answered his phone all morning and he'd had to leave a message for the Special Branch officer. To make things worse, Landon's extension remained engaged for a good five minutes before he finally managed to raise him.

'You wanted me to ring you ASAP,' Neagle said tersely. 'I hope it's worth all the hassle I've been put through.'

'It is,' Landon told him. 'We received another tape of Keith Jenner this morning. According to the covering note you also have been sent a copy.'

'And?'

'In between confessing that he had spied for the CIA, he sent us a message. It consisted of two words: Khalef. British.'

'You think he meant Ali Mohammed Khalef, the Iraqi who gave us the slip in Bahrain last June?'

'We certainly do.'

'I don't believe it.'

'Then get a lip-reader and check it out for yourself.'

'I didn't mean it like that, Will.'

'I know you didn't. Call me again after you've seen the tape,' Landon said and hung up.

*　　　*　　　*

160

Jenner wasn't sure the woman who entered the cell ahead of the three Pathans really was Laura. She was about the right height and build but her face was hidden by a yashmak, and she wasn't close enough for him to see the colour of her eyes. The ivory coloured satin nightdress had been replaced by a pair of floral-pattern cotton trousers that were gathered at the ankles. He couldn't tell what else the woman might be wearing because she was enveloped in a black shroud-like garment that covered the head and reached to the knees.

In a sick way the Pathans reminded Jenner of the Three Wise Men, except they weren't bringing gold, frankincense and myrrh to the stable. One carried a ladder-back chair, the second a VCR, while the third had what appeared to be a clothesline.

'Where is Khalef?' Jenner asked and got no response.

The handcuffs, leg irons and steel collar were removed and the stool was replaced by the ladder-back chair. Nobody had to tell him to sit down; after God knows how many days without anything to eat he felt light headed. Numb with apprehension, he watched the third Pathan cut the clothesline into varying lengths. No great insight was required to guess what they intended to do with the ropes. What did surprise Jenner was the willingness of the woman to participate in his humiliation. As she approached him, he raised his head and gazed into her eyes. Grey blue. The lingering doubt born of wishful thinking vanished and he knew he was looking at Laura before she even spoke to him.

'I have to do this,' she murmured. 'For the children.'

'For the children?' Jenner repeated, genuinely puzzled.

'One of us has to be there for them.'

Comprehension dawned. 'These men have promised to release you?'

'Provided I assist them,' Laura told him.

'Then do what you have to.'

While one of the Pathans positioned his legs either side of the seat and lashed them to the chair legs, Laura tied his left arm to the frame at the wrist, elbow and immediately below the shoulder. In a matter of a few minutes he was totally helpless, unable to move so much as an inch. Almost comatose with shock he sat there listening to the recorded voice of Khalef sentencing him to death. At the end of the diatribe Jenner was ordered to enter a plea of mitigation that had been prepared for him.

To his intense shame he began to sob and could not read the words on the cue card that was held aloft by one of the Pathans. Eventually Laura read it for him, pausing frequently so that he could repeat the words she had just uttered. Jenner knew they would show him no mercy. How could they afford to let him go when the Pathans' leader had made no attempt to remain anonymous? Like a rabbit mesmerized by the headlights of an oncoming vehicle, he watched Tara Rahim Khan advance towards him knife in hand, then closed his eyes at the last moment. A hand undid the fly buttons on the cotton slacks, then reached inside and took out his testicles and penis. Jenner started screaming before the knife emasculated him. So

162

did Laura.

Twelve

For all the good they were doing, Landon thought that instead of postponing the CATO meeting for a mere twenty-four hours Neagle should have cancelled it altogether on the grounds that nobody had any worthwhile information to impart.

Defence Intelligence was uncertain whether the knee-capping of petty criminals and summary executions of so-called traitors that had occurred in Belfast and elsewhere constituted a breach of the Good Friday Agreement of 1998 or not. The Force Research Unit manned jointly by the Royal Ulster Constabulary and the army was however greatly alarmed by the number of convicted terrorists who were still being released from prison even though the Provisional IRA were failing to decommission their weapons on anything like the scale implied in the agreement. Many of these former prisoners were believed to have subsequently joined the various splinter factions like the Irish National Liberation Army, Continuity IRA or the Real IRA, who had rejected the Good Friday Agreement and were pledged to continue the armed struggle. What had come across very clearly was the fact that although Defence Intelligence could warn and advise, it was no longer in a position to influence events. The politicians were in the driving seat; where Northern Ireland was concerned they would decide what constituted a fatal breach of the Good

Friday Agreement.

The eavesdroppers of GCHQ had had little to contribute other than negative information, which in this instance had not been entirely without value. From their base in Cyprus, 9 Signal Regiment monitored military and civil communication networks in southern Russia and the Ukraine as well as maintaining a similar blanket cover over Azerbaijan, Georgia, Kazakhstan and Uzbekistan. Traditionally GCHQ had always targeted the Black Sea fleet and the Strategic Nuclear Force deployed in Kazakhstan. Following the report from the MoD's Science and Technology Department that Saddam Hussein was trying to acquire weapons-grade plutonium, GCHQ had reviewed every transmission captured in the past twelve months. Without wishing to denigrate the Iraqi source the fact was that they had found nothing to support the contention that Talal Asir had been in touch with disaffected officers and ratings in the Black Sea fleet.

Relying on the notes Chris Neighbour had given him, Landon had said much the same. Morale in the Black Sea fleet was at a particularly low ebb. Disaffected elements amongst the officers and ratings were known to be selling blankets, bridge coats and items of winter clothing to civilians and were doing a roaring trade with the Mafiozniki, supplying them with everything from the 9mm Makarov self-loading pistol to the AK 47 assault rifle and the RPG7 portable rocket launcher. But nuclear munitions was a different story. In order to carry out their programme for decommissioning the elderly nuclear-powered submarines of the Delta, Yankee and Golf classes, the Russians were receiving financial aid from the United States. No way was President Yeltsin going to stand idly by and see it withdrawn. Every precaution was being taken to safeguard nuclear warheads and fissionable material. Consequently US observers were satisfied that so far none had gone missing.

Neagle had had nothing new to report on either the Jenner kidnapping or the multiple homicide at Giordano's. Instead he had presented a list of asylum seekers who had gone to ground in the UK after their applications had been rejected and before a deportation order could be served on them. Of the eight names on the list, three were now linked to Islamic Jihad. The only good news was that the moderates had regained control of the mosque in Finsbury Park where Ali Mohammed Khalef had been an imam.

A meeting that normally lasted a full hour had finished in half the time. Landon had been about to join the exodus from the conference room when Neagle had caught his eye and signalled him to stay behind. It was only after the others had left that he learned why Richard had wanted to have a word with him in private.

'It's about the Jenners,' Neagle told him. 'The Pakistan police have made some progress in tracing their movements. You won't have seen the signal from the High Commission, Will, because it arrived shortly after you had left Vauxhall Cross.'

'Why didn't you put it on the agenda?'

'And have the other two Intelligence agencies thinking the left hand doesn't know what the right is doing?' Neagle smiled. 'I don't think so.'

'Are you going to tell me what's in the signal from Islamabad?'

165

'Of course I am. The Jenners were taken to a house on Field Marshal Mohammed Ayub Khan Street in the northern outskirts of Islamabad. They were held there for two or three hours before husband and wife were separated and moved out of the city.'

'How did the police find this out?' Landon asked.

The answer was simple enough, a Gaz 4x4 command jeep belonging to the army had been abandoned on August the 14th Avenue, which happened to be in the same neighbourhood as Field Marshal Ayub Khan Street. The vehicle had been collected by an NCO in the Transportation Corps around 1200 hours on Wednesday the 24th.

'This information only came to light after the authorities publicized the disappearance of the Jenners.' Neagle paused, then added, 'A reward of five thousand Pakistani rupees helped to jog a few memories. Money talks and the equivalent of a few hundred pounds sterling represents a considerable fortune in that part of the world.'

Consequently local police stations had been inundated with an army of informers all eager to claim the reward. Much of the information the police had received was pure dross but they had learned about the abandoned jeep from a beggar who slept on the street. Another vagrant had put them on to the house where the Jenners had been held briefly.

'There was an old five-hundredweight delivery van in the narrow alley next to the house,' Neagle continued. 'The police found bloodstains on the steel floor which DNA tests matched to those in the Jenners' bedroom. The vagrant also said he'd seen two American cars call at the house, one just

166

before first light, the other roughly an hour or so later when the sun was above the horizon. On the latter occasion two men had emerged from the alley carrying what appeared to be a large rolled-up carpet between them, which they had loaded into the trunk. The vagrant hadn't been in a position to see exactly what the two men were doing but it seemed the carpet was too big for the trunk and one end had to be folded back. They then slammed the lid down and drove off.'

'What about the Gaz jeep?' Landon asked. 'Was it used in the kidnapping?'

'The police think so. They reckon the men who shot the two officers guarding the Jenners were dressed as soldiers.'

'The jeep apart, what else do they have to put the army in the dock?'

'Jamal Haroon, a thirty-nine-year-old major in the Parachute Regiment. Currently he's on the staff of Northern Command where he holds a Grade II appointment in the Intelligence branch. However, right now Jamal Haroon is under arrest. Apparently he rang the Intelligence branch and asked the duty officer if the police had reported a major incident of any kind during the night as they are required to do under standing internal security instructions. His phone call was made shortly before the police discovered the Jenners had been kidnapped.'

'It could have been a coincidence.'

'There is that possibility, Will, but the thing is, it was the first time anybody could remember Haroon making such an enquiry.'

'Is that all they have against him?'

Neagle shook his head. 'An army officer was seen

167

to enter the house where the Jenners had been held. This was about an hour after the two men had driven off in an American car.'

'Presumably this information was provided by the ever so helpful vagrant?' Landon said acidly.

'He also identified Haroon in a line-up.'

'And got well paid for it.'

'You're probably right, Will. But what the hell, the police have got the right man and I'm not averse to applying a little psychological pressure. Physical, too, if it will loosen his tongue and lead them to Khalef.'

Landon thought it significant that Neagle had omitted the Jenners. He personally had known Keith Jenner was a doomed man when he'd heard him confess to spying for the CIA; now it seemed Neagle shared his opinion. It was, however, unrealistic of Richard to suppose Ali Mohammed Khalef would still be with the kidnappers in the unlikely event Jamal Haroon actually knew where they had taken the Jenners. Every terrorist organization the world over was based on the cell system. As a staff officer at Headquarters, Northern Command the paratrooper had been ideally placed to provide the necessary logistical support. In this capacity Haroon would only need to know one member of the operational cell. He certainly wouldn't be told where the kidnappers were going when they left Islamabad.

'I took your advice, Will,' Neagle said.

'What advice?'

'I got a lip-reader to view the tape and you were right, Jenner was telling us Khalef was involved. I should have taken your word for it.'

'No you shouldn't, I'd have done the same in your

position.'

'Well, you were wrong about Danièle. She didn't fly into Heathrow from Chicago, Newark, Philadelphia, Dulles International or anywhere else in the USA.'

'So what happens now?'

'An enhanced photograph of Danièle will appear in all the newspapers tomorrow.'

Landon snapped his fingers. 'What about that live-in girlfriend of Farid's who dumped him three days before he left for Amman?'

'You mean Jeanne Wagnall?'

'Yes, that's the woman.'

'Oh, didn't I tell you? The police interviewed Ms Wagnall in Birmingham. You want to know why the lady dumped Anwar Farid? The fact is, much as she liked to smoke a joint now and then, she drew the line at Class A drugs. Soon as she discovered Anwar was up to his old tricks again she was off.'

'I don't believe it.'

'Face it, Will, the police were right the first time around. What happened at Giordano's was drug related.'

'And Toby Quayle?'

'There'll be no comebacks on that score. I've persuaded Roberts to agree that Toby was simply in the wrong place at the wrong time.'

It was typical of Neagle that he should have waited for the right moment to drop his bombshell.

*　　　*　　　*

Resistance to interrogation had been one of the many courses Jamal Haroon had attended as a junior officer. He had learned how to inflict and

169

how to combat sleep deprivation, loss of sensory perception, physical and mental torture. Towards the end of the course the students had been subjected to a mock interrogation that had included a limited amount of violence. What the course instructors had done to Jamal Haroon in those far-off days was nothing compared to the treatment he was receiving at the hands of the Inter-Service Special Interrogation team.

Ever since the police had come for him on Sunday the 28th, Haroon had lost all concept of time. Confined in a cell that was constantly illuminated by a powerful light in the ceiling, he had not been allowed to sleep for more than a few minutes at a stretch. Whenever his eyelids began to droop, a guard would enter the cell and slap his face until he was wide awake once more.

When being questioned he was forced to embrace a wall. This was a subtle form of torture whereby Haroon was made to stand with legs wide apart some four feet away from the wall. He then had to lean forward within touching distance and was obliged to support his weight on fingertips. Denying every accusation levelled at him was no defence against maltreatment. To overcome what they regarded as his wilful obstinacy the interrogators would place a bucket over his head and hammer it with metal rods until he couldn't even hear himself screaming. They had also forced castor oil down his throat, a purgative that emptied his bowels and left him feeling weak and helpless every time it was administered.

But that hadn't been the only method they had used to make him foul his underpants. There was the time when they had given him water treatment.

While he lay flat on the floor, wrists lashed together behind his back, one of the team had covered his face with a towel and had then dripped water on to an absorbent cloth until it was saturated and he couldn't breathe. He remembered tossing his head from side to side in a vain attempt to dislodge the towel and fill his lungs with air. His bowels had moved as the darkness closed in and Haroon had been convinced he was about to die. They had of course brought him back from the dead, stubbing their cigarettes out on the fleshy part of both arms. Pain, their leader said, was a good resuscitator.

The door to his cell was suddenly thrown open and the four tormentors Haroon had come to know so well trooped inside. Two of them grabbed his arms and yanked him to his feet. Familiar with the drill by now, Haroon clasped his hands behind his back and waited for the handcuffs to bite into his wrists. As soon as they turned left outside the cell, he knew they were taking him to the ablutions. Nothing pleasant had ever happened to him in the washplace; it was in the shed that he had been forced to swallow enough castor oil to purge a horse and had nearly been drowned. Haroon told himself that whatever they had in mind to do to him he had already faced the worst. He could not have been more wrong.

Once inside the ablutions one of the interrogators pulled his underpants down around his ankles and ordered him to step out of them and bend over. A jet of cold water from a hosepipe struck his buttocks and the backs of his thighs before it was directed at the rectum. They laughed and made ribald comments about his physique, especially the size of his genitals, and how they had shrunk to half the normal size. Not knowing who they were he bestowed nicknames on his tormentors. The biggest and most dangerous was the Buffalo, the meanest the Hyena, the most bovine was the Ox while the man with the swollen belly and bulging eyes was, naturally, the Toad.

'Hang him up to dry,' the Buffalo said, and turned off the water.

It was, of course, the Hyena who threw one end of the rope over the nearest transverse beam in the roof and then tied it to the handcuffs. Giggling to himself, the Hyena hauled on the rope until Haroon was suspended and unable to even stand on tiptoe to relieve the agonizing pain in his shoulders. There were no accusations, no questions, instead they simply walked out of the ablutions and left him hanging there.

Thirty minutes passed, maybe forty-five. Haroon had really no idea; in his agony every minute seemed like five. When they finally returned to the washplace, he noticed that the Toad was carrying a reel of copper wire and a small hand-cranked generator, the kind combat engineers used in the field.

'You are a very stupid man, Mr Jamal Haroon,' the Buffalo said ominously.

'I am Major Jamal Haroon to you.'

'No, that isn't correct. You have been discharged from the army—services no longer required. Your superior officer Brigadier Seyed Sikander Zia was the driving force behind the decision to cashier you. He was satisfied that you supplied the terrorists with a Gaz jeep. What shook him was the statement we took from the transportation NCO

172

who collected the vehicle.'

'No,' Haroon said loudly. 'It's all lies.' His anger owed everything to a conviction that Brigadier Zia would never betray him.

'You also supplied the army uniforms—'

'No, I tell you again, it's all lies.'

'And the special weapons,' the Buffalo continued remorselessly.

'Listen to me, you are wrong.'

'What we want from you, Jamal Haroon, is the name of the terrorist you dealt with.'

'I don't know any terrorists.'

The Buffalo sighed as if he were genuinely sorry that Haroon was intent on making life difficult for himself. 'I said you were a stupid man.'

Acting on a signal from the Buffalo, the Toad paid out a length of copper wire from the reel and wound it around Haroon's penis and testicles while the Ox and the Hyena held his legs apart. From his jacket the Toad produced a roll of adhesive tape, which he wrapped over the copper wire to ensure it stayed in place and didn't slide off the penis. He then pushed the slack into what looked to be an electrical detonator, crimping the thin metal tube between his teeth so that it held the wire fast. Smiling lasciviously he passed the detonator between Haroon's legs and inserted it into his anus. After that all the Toad had to do was to connect the other end of the copper wire to the generator and crank it up.

'What happens next is up to you,' the Buffalo told Haroon.

'How can I give you a name when I don't know any terrorists?'

The Toad pressed the firing button and sent a

shockwave of agony through Haroon that made him dance in the air screaming.

'Was that a plea for mercy?' the Buffalo enquired.

Despite his experience to the contrary, Haroon decided that silence was his only means of defence. The way he saw it, to name anybody was tantamount to an admission of guilt.

A second shockwave more severe than the first was accompanied by an inhuman scream. The Toad cranked the generator and made him dance a third time just as Haroon realized that he had reached the limit of his endurance.

'My contact was Tara Rahim Khan,' he said in a low voice. 'I met him at the mosque I attend.'

'How did you recognize him?'

'I didn't. It was the other way round. He approached me.'

It was the most dangerous answer Haroon could have given. Apart from incriminating himself, it trigged a barrage of questions that were impossible to evade. What do you know about Tara Rahim Khan? Where does he come from? Who are his companions? And who ordered you to provide the necessary logistical support the Jamaat-e-Islami terrorists needed?

Haroon told them everything they wanted to know except for the last question. According to his own account Tara Rahim Khan came from the North-West Frontier Province and had been staying in Peshawar until recently. The only companion he had mentioned was Ali Mohammed Khalef, an Iraqi man who had given him money.

'You evaded one question,' the Buffalo told him. 'Who ordered you to meet Tara Rahim Khan?'

174

Jamal Haroon remained silent long enough to receive yet another shock that left him gibbering, his sense of loyalty totally destroyed. 'Brigadier Seyed Sikander Zia,' he gasped.

'The brigadier warned us you would say that,' the Buffalo told him amicably and signalled the Toad to increase the voltage.

*   *   *

A week ago Hazelwood had in principle been in favour of using the Israelis to run Talal Asir to ground, though it was fair to say he had jibbed at the idea of Mossad taking out the Saudi banker. Now that Chris Neighbour had come up with two possible locations for a face to face meeting with the Head of Mossad in London, it seemed to Ashton that Victor was having second thoughts.

'Apart from Neighbour and ourselves, who else knows about this proposal?' Hazelwood asked.

'Only Ralph Meacher.'

'Nobody outside this building?'

'We'll have to tell Five if we decide to go ahead. Hopefully this can be limited to your opposite number, Colin Wales, the Deputy DG and of course Richard Neagle.' Ashton frowned. 'They may want to inform Special Branch.'

'And they in turn will want to pass it on to the Diplomatic Protection Squad. And pretty soon the whole damned world will know what we are up to.' Hazelwood helped himself to a Burma cheroot from the cigar box. 'I don't like it one bit.'

Victor's attitude was understandable. The FCO would go ape if it came out that the SIS were getting into bed with the Israelis.

175

'Then let's abandon the idea,' Ashton said.

'I mean if we did approach the Israelis, could we trust them, Peter?'

'It's swings and roundabouts,' Ashton told him. 'They will probably ask themselves the same question about us when they learn we want to meet their Head of Station.'

'We would be taking an awful risk.'

Ashton made no comment. This was not the man he had known in the days when Victor had been running the East European Department. Hesitant, indecisive and worried, he wasn't even a shadow of the man who had been recalled to the Firm following the death of his successor. Maybe age had something to do with it. Victor was sixty-one, and while he had been given a two-year contract this could easily be revoked if the projected operation went pear shaped.

'What would you do in my situation, Peter?'

Somehow the question didn't surprise him. 'We could sound them out informally. Ralph's been doing it for years.' Ashton smiled. 'You never know, they might turn us down.'

Hazelwood struck a match and lit the cheroot. Then, suddenly making up his mind, he buzzed Dilys Crowther and told her to please give Ralph Meacher his compliments and ask if he would kindly spare him a few minutes. Meacher could not have responded any quicker had he been sitting by the phone expecting such a call.

'Peter tells me you have been in touch with the Israelis for years,' Hazelwood said the moment Meacher entered his office.

'Yes. It really started a year after Jill Sheridan was given the Mid East Department.'

176

'Nobody told me,' Hazelwood complained sourly.

'No reason why they should have done so in the beginning. It started as a friendship.'

'Who is the friend?'

'Samuel Levy; we're both members of the Moor Park Golf Club. That's how we met. Sam is a businessman, he buys and sells all manner of goods. It took me over twelve months to discover that unofficially he was a quasi Counsellor for Commercial Affairs on behalf of the embassy. That was when we started trading information and learned to trust one another . . .'

Strictly on the QT Jill Sheridan had allowed him to see top secret material GCHQ had gathered. Anything the Israelis had given the SIS in return was always attributed to another source. That had been part of the deal and it had suited Jill.

'It made her look good,' Meacher continued.

'Have you met the current Head of Mossad in London?' Hazelwood asked.

'Yes. I was introduced to him by Sam at an official reception at the embassy last May. This was to celebrate the fiftieth anniversary of Israel.'

'How often do you see Samuel Levy?'

'Often enough to put a strain on my marriage,' Meacher told him.

Hazelwood leaned forward and crushed the cheroot in the cut-down brass shell case that served as an ashtray. 'How soon could you get in touch with Levy?' he asked.

'Easter is almost upon us. I could have a round of golf with him sometime over the weekend.'

A slow smile appeared on Hazelwood's mouth. Turning to Ashton, he said, 'All right, Peter. Let's test the water.'

*   *   *

In the days of the Raj, Peshawar had been the last family station of any consequence on the North-West Frontier. Further up the frontier had been small family stations such as Palantra, where the European community had numbered under a dozen including the wife of the Political Agent. Beyond there lay the unadministered tribal areas, entry into which required a permit. Anybody who then strayed off the Government Road did so in the knowledge they were putting their life at risk.

But Peshawar itself had been and still was a largely peaceful city. The cantonment where the magistrates, senior civil servants, military, the Assistant Commissioner of police, post and telegraph officials lived was separated from the city by a large verdant park. Originally called Victoria Park, its name was changed to Mohammed Ali Jinnah in honour of the man who had created Pakistan. In commemoration of this event, the copper verdigris covered statue of the Empress of India had been replaced by one of Jinnah. Otherwise little had changed in the fifty-two years since Independence. Even the number of jackals that roamed the park at night had remained fairly constant.

It was the jackals that uncovered the shallow grave on the grassy knoll where Laura Jenner had been buried. They had gorged themselves on the limbs and departed shortly after daybreak, leaving the field clear for the vultures, which had begun to pick the bones clean.

The head gardener, who was in charge of four

underlings employed to look after the park, had gone to the local police station to report that his men had just found the body of a white woman. He had then guided the sergeant to the spot where the body lay, protected from the vultures by his assistants. With a length of picture cord still in place round the neck, no medical qualifications were required to establish that the cause of death was strangulation. The same applied to the approximate time of death. Since the flesh was only just beginning to putrefy, the sergeant considered the woman had been murdered a mere twelve hours ago.

Thirteen

As he always did, Landon collected his copy of *The Times* from the newsagent outside the entrance to the Underground station at Gloucester Road. On the way down to the eastbound platform he scanned the headlines and noted that Danièle had not made the front page. Before he had time to look inside the paper a District Line train pulled into the station and he was swept into the nearest car. No broadsheet was easy to read when space was restricted; it was impossible when people were jammed together like so many sardines in a tin. When the crush eased a little at South Kensington, Landon moved across the car to the far sliding doors and stood facing the glass partition. In the end seat a woman was reading the *Daily Mail*. As he watched she turned a page and he found himself looking at Danièle below a headline that asked

'Who Is this Woman?'

Verco had been unable to make up his mind what gender to use when describing Danièle; nobody else that Landon knew had any such problem. Except for the minuscule penis between the legs everything about the transsexual was feminine, and it made sense to refer to Danièle as 'her' or 'she'. Using the photograph taken in the morgue, somebody in the technical support unit had touched up the face and had made Danièle look more feminine than she had in life. The technician had also made her seem animated in a way that might stir somebody's memory where the description that had previously appeared in the newspapers had not. However, discovering who Danièle really was and where she had come from was no longer of paramount interest to the SIS. In the light of what Jeanne Wagnall had said about Farid reverting to his former bad habits, the Firm was far more concerned to evaluate the information he had given the Mid East Department over the years.

Ralph Meacher had tagged the Egyptian as a C3 source, meaning he had a reasonable track record and was regarded as a worthwhile asset. Late yesterday afternoon on Hazelwood's instructions Ralph Meacher had begun to question this assessment. The quality of the information was not the issue for the DG; what interested him was the timescale. Specifically he wanted to know if the SIS could have acted on any of the stuff they had received from Anwar Farid had they so wished.

As one who was not involved in the reassessment, Landon reckoned that discovering the attraction St Louis appeared to have held for Anwar Farid was the only useful thing he could do. The file Verco had obtained from Mercury Travel in Hornsey showed that the Egyptian had visited the city on four occasions between 1995 and 1999, the one gap year being 1996. There could be any number of reasons why Farid had broken the pattern. He might have been displeased with the arrangements Mercury Travel had made for him in 1995 and decided to do it himself the following year, only to discover the agency could get him a better deal after all. Alternatively, some unknown benefactor may have footed the bill for his expenses in the gap year or Farid could have used a travel agency nearer his home in Wood Green. Pursuing any line of enquiry that far back was going to be pretty difficult. The bank statements Special Branch had sent him merely covered the last twelve months and it was even money MasterCard could not produce photocopies of the statements issued in 1996.

Deep in thought Landon was carried on to St James's Park and had to double back one stop to catch a Victoria Line train. When he finally arrived at Vauxhall Cross the high-priced help was assembling for morning prayers and there was no time to see Ashton.

*   *   *

The immigration officer prided himself on having a good memory for faces, a faculty that was pretty essential in his job. There was, he thought, something familiar about the young woman whose photograph appeared on page 3 of the *Daily Express*, but at the moment he couldn't place her.

Below the picture he read that the woman had been known as Danièle and had been one of four victims shot to death at Giordano's Italian restaurant in Knightsbridge on Wednesday 17th March.

It was then that he recalled where and when he had seen the young woman. Terminal 1 on Monday the 15th, the day before he had left for Arosa on a ten-day family package holiday with Swiss Ski. He had been out of the country when Danièle had been murdered and he never bothered to read an English newspaper or listen to the BBC Overseas Service when he and the family were abroad. So why did he remember Danièle, aside from the fact that she was undoubtedly attractive? Because she had been petite, no more than five feet two? No, there had been more to it than that.

He snapped his fingers; it had been her complexion that had caught his eye. Olive skin, definitely not European. Could be Lebanese? So what was she doing coming through immigration with passport holders from the European Union? That had been his thought process at the time and he had nearly sent her back to join the passengers in the foreign nationals line who had just arrived from Istanbul. Fortunately he was, by nature, a cautious man and he'd decided to say nothing until he had seen her passport.

Suddenly everything fell into place and he remembered that Danièle had presented a French passport for his inspection. He also recalled that she had arrived on the early morning Aer Lingus flight from Dublin. It was with real regret that he was forced to admit he couldn't put a name to Danièle. Nevertheless, he assumed his information was not entirely without value. Retrieving his personal radio from under the desk, he called up the senior immigration officer on duty and asked to be relieved so that he could pass on certain information to the police.

*   *   *

There was a different face representing the Mid East Department at morning prayers that day. Ralph Meacher had phoned in sick and his place had been taken by Malcolm Ives, the Grade I Intelligence Officer in charge of the Gulf States and Arabian desk. He was also the man Meacher had designated to head the team of analysts, Special Intelligence whose job it was to reassess the information provided by Anwar Farid since he had been recruited by the SIS. His demeanour suggested he didn't know whether he was coming or going. Unsure what questions on what subjects he might have to field, he had arrived with briefing notes from the Egypt, Jordan, Lebanon, Israel, Iraq and Iran desks tucked in a folder which he was trying to put in some sort of order. The way Hazelwood kept drumming the fingers and thumb of his right hand on the table, Ives took as a sign of the DG's mounting impatience with him and he became even more flustered.

'Relax, Malcolm,' Ashton murmured, 'Victor is not getting at you. We're all waiting for Hugo Calthorpe and he's not likely to be the bearer of good news.'

In Ashton's experience, a classified signal carrying an emergency precedence was invariably a portent of a disturbing incident somewhere in the

183

world. In this instance most people round the table knew instinctively that the signal addressed to the Head of the Asian Department was from the Head of Station, Islamabad.

'We'll start with you, Hugo,' Hazelwood said as Calthorpe entered the conference room.

It came as no surprise to Ashton to hear that the body of a European woman had been found in Ali Mohammed Jinnah Park, Peshawar.

'When was this?' Hazelwood asked.

'Approximately half past six this morning local time. The woman had been strangled with a length of rope and buried in a shallow grave. It's almost certainly Mrs Jenner but that won't be confirmed until her dental records have been compared with those of the body.' Calthorpe harrumphed as though there was something distasteful in his mouth that he wanted to get rid of before continuing. 'I'm afraid the body wasn't buried deep enough and the jackals got to it.'

'Any word on Keith Jenner?' Hazelwood asked brusquely.

'No. I think we have to accept that he, too, has been murdered. No doubt our unfortunate Head of Station will receive a video of the proceedings in due course. Meantime the Pakistani authorities are organizing a massive search operation covering the whole of Peshawar and its environs.'

The inflection in Calthorpe's voice told Ashton that he didn't expect the police to catch the perpetrators. They were long gone, up through the Khyber Pass, over the hills and far away.

'It's a bad business,' Hazelwood said quietly.

'Yes it is. I'm assuming that the FCO will inform the State Department about Laura Jenner? For the record,' Calthorpe added.

Hazelwood nodded, then went round the table asking each head of department in turn for a resumé of incoming communications that had been received during silent hours. He left the Mid East until last, possibly out of consideration for Ralph Meacher's stand-in. By then Malcolm Ives was ready to answer anything except the one question he was asked.

'About Anwar Farid,' Hazelwood said casually. 'Do we know if he's ever been to Israel?'

Malcolm plainly didn't but he was not prepared to admit it. Instead he took a calculated risk and politely informed Sir Victor that there was no record of any such visit on the database of MIDAS.

'That was quick thinking,' Ashton told him as they left the conference room together.

'You don't think Sir Victor will have somebody to check it out?'

'You'll still be safe if he did. Jill Sheridan never allowed any source of hers to be recorded on MIDAS.'

Ashton left him, walked round the corner to his office and opened the combination safe. For the second time that morning he took out the filing trays and arranged them in order on his desk. That done, he plucked yesterday's float file from the in-tray and skimmed through it. Nothing classified higher than confidential ever found its way on to the float and the vast majority of the enclosures were of an administrative nature. Not surprisingly this meant Roy Kelso was usually the biggest contributor. Ashton made a note that a fire drill had been scheduled for next Tuesday, the day after the Easter break, then initialled the front cover and dropped the file in the out-tray. Landon called to ask him if he could spare him five minutes just as he was about to start drafting the monthly intelligence summary for March.

'So long as it is only five minutes,' Ashton told him.

Both of them knew that was an unattainable prerequisite. Ashton waited patiently while Landon spent longer than that making a case for discovering why Farid had been drawn so often to St Louis when he was in America.

'Leave it to the police, Will. It's probably drug related.'

'I don't think they are interested in the St Louis connection.'

'I can't see why we should be either. Besides, this is the end of the financial year and what money we have saved is already earmarked. Our number-one target in the next twelve months is Talal Asir followed by Ali Mohammed Khalef, and I'm not about to squander a single penny on any diversion.'

'What I'm proposing won't cost a penny,' Landon told him. 'I'll persuade Richard Neagle to involve the FBI.'

'And what if he refuses to play ball?'

'Then we will have to try the back-door approach using the CIA.'

'And have them picking over our dirty laundry? That's one thing I'm not going to have. Understood?'

'Yes.' Landon smiled lopsidedly. 'It was worth a try, wasn't it?' he added.

*   *   *

With the benefit of hindsight Meacher told himself that he should have known Moor Park Golf Club would be heaving over the Easter weekend. On the way home from Vauxhall Cross yesterday evening he'd phoned the captain to ask him when might be a good time to squeeze in a round of golf over the holiday. The advice he'd received had been somewhat discouraging: his chances of playing during the Easter break were minimal. His best hope was to arrive early on Maundy Thursday and trust to luck. By early the captain had meant no later than eight o'clock.

The idea of being ready to tee off at that hour in the morning hadn't appealed to Samuel Levy at all. In the end after much cajoling Sam had agreed to meet him at a quarter past the hour. How much better off they would have been had they been ready to start at eight was impossible to say. However, the fact was there had been an enforced delay of twenty minutes at the first hole while they waited for three foursome players to play off. Not until they had reached the hole furthest away from the clubhouse did Meacher indicate why he had wanted to see Sam.

'Talal Asir,' he said abruptly. 'Ever heard of him?'

'I can't say I have.'

'No matter, he's certainly known to your friends at the embassy. Same goes for Ali Mohammed Khalef.'

'Ah. Now I've heard of him.'

'I would have been surprised if you hadn't, the Iraqi cleric from Finsbury Park was forever appearing in the newspapers this time last year.'

Meacher checked the lie of his ball on the

187

fairway, reckoned the distance to the green was approximately a hundred and fifty yards and chose a number four iron. He tried a couple of practice swings, then addressed the ball and made the mistake of raising his head too soon on the follow-through and sliced the ball into the rough.

'Bad luck,' Levy called and brought a smile to Meacher's lips. Sam could afford to be generous, he played regularly off an 8 handicap, whereas Meacher was doing well if he justified his official handicap of 14. As he watched, Levy took a seven iron and effortlessly put the ball within six feet of the pin. The rest was a mere formality.

As they walked to the next hole, Meacher returned to the subject of Talal Asir.

'He's a bagman for Hezbollah, Hamas, Islamic Jihad and maybe other terrorist organizations we're not aware of yet. We do know he has bankrolled terrorist operations in Africa, the Far East, Chechnya. In addition he has provided financial support for the families of suicide bombers who have blown themselves up attacking vulnerable targets in Israel. In the last nine months MI5 has closed down his bank accounts in Haiti, Grand Bahamas, Barbados and Switzerland.'

'But he's still operating,' Levy pointed out.

'Unfortunately.'

'So what are you going to do about him, Ralph?'

'We intend to take executive action, to borrow an expression from the CIA.'

Meacher waited until Levy had driven off before delivering his bombshell. 'To this end we feel it would be to our mutual advantage if we joined forces with Mossad.'

'Are you people serious?'

188

'Never more so.' Meacher teed up his ball and this time did everything right. 'We are ready to finance the joint operation.'

'You are wasting your time and mine. It will never happen.'

'You won't know until you have spoken to your friend.'

'You're right. What do I tell him, Ralph?'

'We're suggesting Mossad's Head of Station should meet Peter Ashton—'

'Who's he?' Levy asked sharply, interrupting him.

'I guess you could say Ashton is the only one of our senior officers who has the ear of the Director General. He's a trouble shooter or a bit of a loose cannon, depending on your point of view.'

'Ashton is not exactly popular with the Foreign and Commonwealth Office then?'

'You could say that.'

'I don't find that particularly reassuring,' Levy said.

'I'll be present the whole time.'

'Can you guarantee this?'

'Who else is going to introduce the protagonists to one another?'

'Good. Is there anything else I need to know?'

There were a couple of points Meacher wished to make, both of them of an administrative nature. His colleagues thought the venue for the meeting should be within a thirty-mile radius of the centre of London. They had in mind somewhere not too far off the beaten track like Le Relais at Chalfont St Giles or the Jasmine restaurant at Beaconsfield. However, neither venue was cast in stone and Ashton was open to suggestions.

'OK, Ralph, I'll pass the word on.' Levy bent

down and picked up his ball.

'I'm conceding this hole,' he said.

'What!'

'I want to finish this game as soon as we can. I've got a business to run.'

*   *   *

Ensley Holsinger paid off the cab outside the American Embassy in Grosvenor Square and walked into the building.

'My name is Ensley Holsinger,' she told the woman on the enquiry desk, and produced her passport for inspection. 'Mr Virgil Zimmerman is expecting me.'

She had never met, never even heard of, Mr Zimmerman before he had phoned her at the office where she worked earlier that morning. Mr Zimmerman had said he would be very grateful if she would agree to see him during her lunch hour about a matter of some importance. Although he had been polite and had sounded apologetic Ensley had been left with the overwhelming impression that she had no option but to comply with his request. She was not kept in suspense for long. A few minutes after her passport had been returned, a Marine Corps sergeant arrived to escort Ensley upstairs to Zimmerman's office.

Virgil Zimmerman was not the handsomest man she had met. Nature had given him a long, thin face dominated by a hooked nose and lips that were too thick. He had black curly hair flecked with grey that made Ensley think he was in his late forties. When he stood up to greet her she thought Zimmerman must have lost a lot of

190

weight recently, judging by the loose-fitting jacket he was wearing.

'It's a pleasure to meet you, Miss Holsinger,' he said, shaking her hand. 'Do please sit down.'

'Thank you.'

'May I call you Ensley?'

'Of course.'

'Then I'll come straight to the point. Are you a patriot, Ensley?'

Ensley stared at Zimmerman dumbfounded. Although she had no idea what to expect, it had never entered her head that her loyalty might be questioned.

'I love my country,' she told him in a quiet but firm voice. 'I'm proud to be an American.'

'And if asked there is nothing you wouldn't do for your country?'

'What is it you want from me, Mr Zimmerman?' she asked.

'You're real friendly with a Mr Will Landon. Right?'

'I've made his acquaintance,' she said cautiously.

'Oh, I'd put it a lot stronger than that. Matter of fact, I'd say you were on intimate terms with the Englishman.'

'The hell I am.'

Zimmerman leaned forward and plucked a typewritten report from the pending tray.

'I don't mean to embarrass you, Ensley, but the fact remains you spent the whole of last weekend at his flat in Stanhope Gardens. You also called on him again last night and left this morning at 0700 hours.' Zimmerman returned the document to the pending tray and smiled, his eyes crinkling like he meant it. 'I don't imagine either of you slept on the couch.'

'You've been spying on me,' Ensley said indignantly.

'You're wrong, we've been watching Mr Landon. He's an officer in the British Secret Intelligence Service.'

'You're crazy,' Ensley said and was conscious he knew she was lying.

'He is known to us and the FBI. A couple of years ago Landon attended a symposium on international terrorism sponsored by us—'

'Us being the CIA?'

'Yeah. Along with the other British delegates he stayed at L'Enfant Plaza Hotel while in Washington. He was present when some Islamic fundamentalists bombed the Blue Marlin on State Highway 650. An English girl died of her wounds, that's how the FBI became acquainted with him.'

'I hadn't met Will two years ago.'

'But you've known he's in the SIS since last June, so don't get smart with me, Ms Holsinger.'

The sudden use of her surname and Zimmerman's harsh tone of voice startled her.

'That wasn't my intention,' she murmured. 'I'll do whatever I can for my country. I mean that.'

'Sure you do. And what I'm asking couldn't be simpler. There is an inner circle in the Intelligence world. It was spawned during World War Two and was originally confined to the exchange of what we call Sig. Int. material. Intercepts, in other words.'

Its members were the United States, Great Britain, Australia, New Zealand and Canada. What had begun with Sig. Int. grew over the years to include material gathered by other means.

'Right now, international terrorism is our

number-one priority,' Zimmerman continued, 'and we've reason to believe the Brits are withholding information from us. Nobody we could cultivate is better placed to find out what's going on than Will Landon. For chrissakes he's a member of CATO, the Combined Anti-Terrorist Organization.'

'You want me to pump him for information?' Ensley snorted in derision. 'Obviously you don't know Will Landon. To describe him as taciturn is an understatement. You raise something that Landon doesn't want to discuss and suddenly he's deaf and dumb.'

'I'm not asking you to interrogate him,' Zimmerman said lightly. 'I had pillow talk in mind.'

'You think Landon confides in me when we are in bed?'

'Are you or are you not prepared to help your country?'

There was a cutting edge to Zimmerman's voice now that made Ensley flinch. Somehow she made herself look the CIA officer in the eye and give him the unequivocal answer he wanted. For what seemed an eternity he gazed at her thoughtfully, then suddenly he produced a calling card from his billfold and wrote something on the back before passing it to Ensley.

'You can reach me anytime on one of those two numbers,' Zimmerman told her. 'Destroy the card as soon as you have committed them to memory. OK?'

'Yes.'

'Just remember you have been told things you've no business to know. If the Brits learned we were trying to subvert one of their own there would be hell to pay and you could find yourself in deep shit.'

193

Ensley put the card away in her shoulder bag and got ready to leave, then had to sit down again when Zimmerman asked her to wait while he summoned the marine corps sergeant to escort her out of the embassy's secure area. She was not held up for long; barely two minutes later she left the building, much to her relief.

Ensley crossed the road outside, entered the park in the centre of Grosvenor Square and sat down on the nearest bench. A spate of questions threatened to overwhelm her, all of them connected with Virgil Zimmerman. How did he know her name, where she lived, where to find her during normal office hours? Was it possible immigration had seen from her landing card that she had a long-stay work permit and had advised the United States Embassy accordingly? Will would probably know the answer but if she asked him his nose would start twitching and he would be off like a goddamned bloodhound running down the scent. Badly in need of a cigarette she opened her shoulder bag, took out a packet of Marlboro and lit one. The sun had disappeared and it had turned chilly while she was in the embassy but that wasn't the only reason why she couldn't stop shivering.

Fourteen

Meacher left the house in Beechwood Avenue at the usual time, ten minutes to seven, and walked to Ruislip station. In his jacket pocket was a letter from Sedgewick James, estate agents that, unbeknown to his wife Julie, had arrived on

194

Saturday morning. It informed him that the pre-war, four-bedroom, detached house he had purchased for eighty-five thousand in 1978 was now worth one and a quarter million. Even allowing for the two and a half per cent commission the estate agents would charge for selling the property and the fact that he might have to reduce the asking price by a hundred thousand, he would still be left with well over a million quid. That kind of money would enable them to move out of London and enjoy a better quality of life in the country. It was ridiculous to think it only took Ashton fifteen minutes longer to reach Vauxhall Cross from his cottage in Bosham on the coast than it did from Ruislip. Apart from an improved quality of life, there was another consideration: any move that made it impossible for Julie to remain in partnership with Sooby, Haines and McManus, chartered accountants, might just save their marriage.

For some months now he had suspected his wife was having an affair with Dermot McManus. His suspicion had been aroused by Julie's changing pattern of behaviour. She had never shown much interest in politics before but approximately fourteen months ago she had joined the Liberal Democrats and in a remarkably short space of time had become a committee member of the local branch. As such she was entitled to attend the annual party conference, and had done so, taking herself off to Scarborough for five days last autumn. Barely three weeks later Julie had attended a weekend convention for chartered accountants at the conference centre in Birmingham. In all the years they had been together he could not remember her attending a convention before. He had rung the hotel where Julie was staying several times over that weekend, and although she had always answered the phone he'd had a feeling someone else was in the room with her.

There were other pointers to Julie's unfaithfulness. Shortly before the Lib Dem party conference she had suddenly become fashion conscious and, in addition to having her hair done twice a week, she had begun to have regular facials. His wife was forty-two, her lover nine years younger, but no stranger seeing them together would guess there was a significant age gap,

There had been a number of occasions when he could easily have obtained proof of her infidelity but he'd always refrained from doing so. The truth was, Meacher didn't want to know. He loved Julie and, provided nobody rubbed his nose in it, he was willing to turn a blind eye to her sexual peccadilloes. That didn't mean he wasn't determined to break up her relationship with Dermot McManus; selling up and moving house was the easiest solution to the problem; one, moreover, that would avoid a damaging confrontation. It was, however, fraught with risk and he had yet to work out what he would do if Julie refused point blank to leave Ruislip.

Meacher had just reached the crossroads at the bottom of the high street when his mobile rang. Taking it out of his raincoat pocket, the eleven-digit number in the display strip told him that Sam Levy was trying to get in touch.

'Yes, Sam,' he said, accepting the call, 'what can I do for you?'

'It's the other way round,' Levy told him. 'The meeting you asked for is on for this evening.'

'Tonight?'

'Yes. Is there a problem?'

'Absolutely not,' Meacher assured him, even though he could foresee all kinds of difficulties. 'Where are we meeting?'

'The Jasmine restaurant in Beaconsfield. Seven thirty p.m. David will meet you there.'

'Right.'

'And bring your mobile,' Levy said, and disconnected before Meacher had a chance to come back at him.

Meacher crossed the road by the traffic lights, entered the station approach, waved his season ticket at the collector in the entrance hall and passed through on to the platform. His preoccupation with Julie's probable misconduct vanished, he had more important things to think about now. He thought it odd that David Ben-Yosef, the Mossad Head of Station, should have accepted one of the rendezvous suggested by the SIS. Such behaviour was unlike the normal working practice of Mossad; the Israeli Intelligence Service liked to be in control of even the most minor details. He wished he hadn't so readily accepted the date and time for the meeting they had chosen.

Two lines operating very different rolling stock served Ruislip, the Metropolitan and the Piccadilly. The journey from Ruislip to Vauxhall involved two changes, one at Baker Street, the other at Oxford Circus. Meacher had travelled the route so often now that he changed stations, platform and trains, boarded and alighted without having to think what he was doing. There were times when he walked into Vauxhall Cross with no clear recollection of the journey. Whenever this happened he would jokingly tell himself that such aberrations were only to be expected with the onset of senile dementia. The fact was he certainly hadn't been thinking straight this morning. He should never have committed Ashton and the others to a timetable that obviously suited Mossad without consulting them first. While he and most of his colleagues had spent the Easter break gadding about, the Israelis had been doing their homework.

By the time Meacher arrived at Vauxhall Cross he had exactly ten minutes in hand before morning prayers began. From the redoubtable Enid Sly on the reception desk, he learned that on this occasion Ashton had actually beaten him into the office. He found Ashton in the old map room that had been converted into an office for him when the Eastern Bloc of Cold War days had been resurrected as the East European and Balkans Department. He was conversing with his chief clerk, and while normally Meacher would have waited until they had finished what he had to say was a matter of some urgency.

'I'm sorry to butt in,' he said, 'but could I have a word with you in private, Peter? It's important you should hear about this particular development before morning prayers.'

Ashton turned to his chief clerk. 'Would you excuse us, Ron?' he asked.

Meacher waited until they were alone, then said, 'It's on, the Israelis are willing to discuss our proposal.'

'When?'

'Seven thirty this evening. I'm afraid I was caught on the back foot and went along with it.'

'Don't give it another thought, Ralph. I would have done the same in your place. Did they quibble about the venue?'

Meacher shook his head. 'They're happy with the Jasmine restaurant in Beaconsfield.'

'They've had four days to look the place over,' Ashton mused.

'What's your point?'

'I don't have to tell you how security conscious Mossad is. No matter what your golfing friend said to him, this Ben-Yosef may find it hard to believe the FCO is not aware of our intention.'

'And in his eyes the FCO is pro-Arab.' Meacher frowned. 'I guess he fears somebody in King Charles Street may leak details of the rendezvous to a third party. Wouldn't surprise me if Mossad's Head of Station didn't show up.'

'What exactly did Levy say to you, Ralph?'

'No more than what I've already told you. Except he did tell me to bring my mobile.'

'They mean to change the RV at the last minute.'

'That's very unsporting of them,' Meacher said, smiling.

'Well, we're going to do a little cheating, too,' Ashton told him. 'Chris Neighbour can draw three crypto-protected phones from Signals. I don't mind David Ben-Yosef and his friends monitoring your mobile but that's as far as it goes.'

*   *   *

Whenever he cared to think about it Landon had to admit there had been too many occasions lately when he had allowed himself to be manipulated. Twelve days ago he would never have used a

CATO meeting as a pretext for not going in to Vauxhall Cross first. Twelve days ago he should never have allowed Ensley Holsinger back into his life. He had been at her beck and call throughout the whole of Easter. For all she had seen of her rented flat in Bayswater that came with the job, Jerome, Sherman, Management Consultants were entitled to a rebate. So, all right, Ensley had charisma and it gave him a kick to see the envious glances cast in his direction when they were dining in restaurants like the Savoy Grill and other places he couldn't really afford. But that was tempered by the knowledge that over the last week he had put the American girl before his job and he despised himself for being like putty in her hands.

He should have got up at the usual time this morning and left Ensley to her own devices. As it was he would be going into a meeting ignorant of everything that had happened since Thursday morning. In particular he wouldn't know the final number of casualties from the bombing of the British Council offices in Karachi and Lahore that Calthorpe had expected to receive by the weekend. The only thing he could do was phone the officer in charge of the Pakistan desk from Neagle's office.

It proved impossible to obtain the information he needed on the QT. When he signed in at MI5 the duty clerk gave Landon a brief note from Neagle to the effect that he wanted to see him before the meeting began.

'I had hoped to catch you before you left Vauxhall Cross,' Neagle told him, 'but no such luck.'

'That's not surprising, I didn't go into the office this morning.'

'Yes, Chris Neighbour said he thought you would come straight here. Incidentally, he would like to have a word with you before the CATO meeting.'

'OK, may I use your phone?'

'Of course you may but could we deal with my point first?'

Neagle took his agreement for granted and plunged straight in. The enhanced photograph of Danièle that had appeared in the press on Thursday had produced a result. An immigration officer had recognized her and, while unable to remember her surname, he recalled she had arrived on the first Aer Lingus flight from Dublin on Monday 15th March and was travelling on a French passport. With the help of the Aer Lingus staff, Neagle had discovered that two days before her departure for London the lady had arrived in Dublin on an Aer Lingus flight from New York.

'That's terrific news,' Landon said.

'It gets better, Will. Aer Lingus still had her personal details on record. Her surname was Chirac, first name Danièle.'

'What are you going to do with the information? Pass it on to the French authorities?'

'I'm not really interested in the ins and outs of what is rightly seen as a drug-related crime. No doubt Scotland Yard will do so. For what my opinion is worth, I believe Danièle was Anwar Farid's mule. She smuggled the Class A drugs into the UK secreted inside her body. That's why they travelled separately.'

'And St Louis is where he usually collected his consignment of speed, mandies, H, M, or whatever he dealt in.'

'St Louis?' Neagle repeated quizzically.

201

'Farid was what they call a frequent visitor, he went to the city at least four times between 1995 and 1998 that we know of. It's likely there were other occasions.'

'Interesting.'

'It would do no harm to ask the FBI if they had ever come across him.'

'I think the Drug Enforcement Agency would be a more appropriate body.'

Landon forced a smile to hide his disappointment. Ashton had made it clear that the SIS wanted to distance the Service from Anwar Farid. Consequently he was not to approach the FBI to see what they had on the Egyptian. He either persuaded Neagle to involve the Bureau or forgot the whole business. A few moments ago it looked as if he had succeeded in talking Neagle into it until the DEA had entered his mind.

'What—no comments?' Neagle asked.

'I've got nothing against the DEA but they will only look at the information in relation to their own specific field. They are not, so far as I'm aware, hugely involved in counter-terrorist ops.'

'How many times do you have to be told, Will? The multiple homicide at Giordano's was drug related.'

'Fine, have it your way. But I tell you this, Anwar Farid was one of our stringers and he gave us some pretty good stuff from time to time. I just don't think you can afford to ignore the possibility that Farid was killed by a terrorist. Where is the harm in checking him out with the FBI?'

'Where's the harm in the SIS doing it?'

It was the equivalent of a fast in-swinger that he should have seen coming but hadn't. Caught off

202

guard, the ball scythed into his stomach and metaphorically speaking left him winded. What the hell could he say in rebuttal? Then suddenly the answer came to him.

'No harm at all but any request from the SIS would not be acted on with alacrity. Whether it was originated by Ashton or not they'd be convinced he was behind it and would look for some hidden agenda. Need I go on?'

There was no necessity to do so; Neagle was aware of Peter's record but Landon didn't believe in leaving anything to chance. Navajo Flats, Arizona, Lake Arrowhead, California, Nine Mile Drive outside Richmond, Virginia, Denver, Colorado, and, perhaps most telling of all with the FBI, St Louis, Missouri, where Ashton had tangled with the backwoods militia. Mayhem and sudden death had followed him wherever he went.

'Whitehall is not the only place where you will hear people describe Ashton as a loose cannon, there's a clique within the FBI which holds the same opinion. I doubt we will get anything like the same degree of cooperation as you would, Richard.'

Neagle glanced at his wristwatch. 'Time I got this meeting under way,' he said and moved towards the door.

'What are you going to do about Anwar Farid?'

'What you want me to do of course. I'll send his photograph to the Bureau and ask if he is known to them.'

'And Danièle Chirac?'

'The same,' Neagle called from the corridor. 'Now make that phone call to Chris Neighbour and join us soon as you can.'

Landon picked up the transceiver on the Mozart and put a call through to the Russian desk. He learned two things from Chris Neighbour. First and foremost he could forget whatever plans he may have had for the evening. At six o'clock they would be departing from Vauxhall Cross to meet a new-found friend with whom they had a lot in common. And secondly, in response to Landon's request, Chris Neighbour regretted he didn't have the latest casualty figures from Karachi and Lahore at his fingertips. Landon just hoped Richard Neagle wouldn't ask him for an update.

*   *   *

Morning prayers had been the most sickening and mind-numbing experience Ashton had ever endured. Hugo Calthorpe had given notice that the latest video received from Islamabad was not for the squeamish and suggested it should wait until the other departments had delivered their reports. Rowan Garfield and the acting head of the West European Department had nothing to contribute. Since the impending meeting with David Ben-Yosef was not for disclosure, Ashton and Meacher had also had little to say.

Normally, Roger Benton, the Head of the Pacific Basin and Rest of the World Department, had little to contribute. Today, however, had been the exception. Between 1992 and 1994 North Korea had embarked on a clandestine nuclear weapons programme despite being a signatory to the Non-Proliferation Treaty. The programme had been halted in November 1994; now reports from a number of sources indicated that the Democratic

People's Republic had resumed work on the weapons of mass destruction. Furthermore, work on a delivery system had reached an advanced stage and the North Koreans were expected to test fire a surface-to-surface long-range ballistic missile within the next four months.

The last to speak before Hugo Calthorpe had been Roy Kelso, who had wanted to remind everybody that there would be a fire drill sometime during the day, and had also announced that Toby Quayle's sister in New Zealand had finally been in touch to ask for the name and address of her brother's solicitor.

Calthorpe had begun by giving the latest casualty figures for the attacks on the British Council offices in Karachi and Lahore. The total number of deaths had risen from sixty-one to a hundred and nine while the number of injured had in fact decreased from a hundred and four to ninety-three. Dilys Crowther had then been invited to withdraw.

Even with the volume turned right down after Khalef had sentenced Keith Jenner to death, the video had still shocked, horrified and sickened everybody present. No great imagination had been required to hear the continuous inhuman screams from Jenner as he saw the knife descend, or smell the odour as he so obviously fouled himself. Ashton couldn't answer for the others but Hazelwood had certainly read what had been in his mind when he'd ordered Calthorpe to stop the video. A minute or so later, seven very shaken men had filed out of the conference room. With the exception of Hazelwood they had made their way to the coffee vending machine by the bank of lifts.

Ashton glanced at his wristwatch and rapidly

finished his coffee, then crushed the polystyrene cup and tossed it into the waste bin. 'Ten minutes', Hazelwood had said to him as he left the conference room, and the time was now up. Getting no reply when he buzzed Ralph Meacher, Ashton left the office and found the Head of the Mid East Department waiting for him in the corridor. When they walked in on him, Hazelwood had adopted a typical Churchillian posture, gazing across the river at the Houses of Parliament, hands clasped behind him, a Burma cheroot in one corner of his mouth.

'A bad business,' he said without turning about.

'It was,' Ashton said. 'What happened to Keith Jenner and his wife makes one more determined than ever to get Mohammed Khalef.'

Hazelwood turned round to face both men. 'I was referring to North Korea,' he rasped.

Ashton wondered if the harsh tone and callous attitude was simply a pose, that Victor didn't want them to think he had been emotionally affected by the video. Still determined to appear on top of things he reminded Meacher of their brief conversation before morning prayers when he had learned Mossad's Head of Station had agreed to meet his two assistant directors.

'Question is, do we want to keep the appointment?' Hazelwood asked rhetorically. 'Think about it, you might be walking into a PR trap.'

'What?'

'A public relations trap, Peter. It would be quite a coup if you and Ralph were photographed in conversation with David Ben-Yosef. You might find yourselves vulnerable to blackmail.'

'By whom?'

'The Israelis.'

'That's nonsense.'

'Is it? Listen, if pictures appeared in the newspapers your careers would be finished. They could hold that over you in the hope of obtaining at least one agent in place.'

'What are you really saying, Victor?' Ashton asked quietly. 'That we should back away from the Israelis?'

'I'm not having second thoughts, I'm just warning you to be careful.' Hazelwood brightened visibly. 'Now tell me how you intend to play it.'

'Chris Neighbour has drawn three crypto-protected Haydns,' Ashton told him. 'And Ralph and I will go straight to the Jasmine in Beaconsfield, where we'll wait for David Ben-Yosef. Will and Chris will be in the other two vehicles. It will be their job to make sure Mossad's Head of Station is not being followed. Chris will lie up off the A40 half a mile from the outskirts of Beaconsfield, leaving Will to cover the exit from junction two on the M40.'

'Are you going to shadow Ben-Yosef from his residential address?'

Ashton shook his head. 'He will run a series of checks to make sure no other vehicles are tracking him before he switches to a different car. I don't want either Chris or Will caught up in what could become a three-ring circus. I'm assuming Ben-Yosef is under the watchful eye of the Diplomatic Protection Squad or some other like body. One thing is certain, he won't show up in a vehicle displaying CD plates.'

'You won't know what sort of car Ben-Yosef will

be driving, never mind the registration number of the wretched vehicle. What do you expect Landon and Neighbour to do?'

'Their job is to make sure nobody from Special Branch or MI5 joins the party.'

'And how are they to do that if they don't know—'

'We've a solution,' Ashton said, cutting him short. 'His name is Terry Hicks and he has a portable scanner that can sweep every police frequency.'

Hazelwood grunted and leaned forward, elbows on the desk, shoulders hunched. There was no other reaction from him and his eyes looked blank, as if he'd suddenly switched off, like a victim of petit mal.

'You don't have much to say for yourself, Ralph,' he said presently.

'That's because Peter and I are in complete agreement.'

'How nice.' Hazelwood brooded some more, then said, 'This is a high-risk operation. Be careful, very careful. Above all don't commit us to anything we can't get out of. Understood?'

'I hear you,' Ashton said.

'Ralph?'

'We won't do anything rash, Director.'

'Good. I'm glad we're of one accord,' Hazelwood said, dismissing them.

'I don't like it,' Meacher said before he and Ashton parted company in the corridor. 'Seems to me the Director is suffering from a bad case of cold feet.'

'Well, he knows there will be hell to pay should the FCO learn what we're up to.'

'And we could end up being the sacrificial goats if things do go wrong.'

208

'Not if I have anything to do with it,' Ashton said grimly.

* * *

Mountford House was in Clarendon Terrace, a mere stone's throw from the Bayswater Road. It stood on the former site of numbers 1–3. These had been demolished during the mini Blitz of January 1944 by a one thousand kilogram bomb, which according to popular mythology had been aimed at the nearby anti-aircraft battery in Hyde Park. Mountford House had been completed in 1961 and, in accordance with an obscure section of the Town and Country Planning Act, the external appearance of the building had had to conform with the existing properties in the terrace. The house comprised thirty-six fully furnished apartments sharing a common entrance where number 2 Clarendon Terrace had once stood. Security was provided by a doorman who operated from a desk in the foyer where he could see the bank of lifts and the entrance.

The doorman was sorting the second delivery and had his back to the entrance while slotting the post into the appropriate mail boxes. He was not aware he had company until somebody behind him coughed discreetly. The newcomer was, he judged, about six feet tall, in his mid thirties and looked athletic.

'I'm Detective Chief Inspector Verco,' he said and produced a warrant card. 'I believe one of your residents is a Miss Ensley Holsinger from America?'

'That's correct.' The doorman took in the dark

209

grey suit and blue pinstripe shirt Verco was wearing and thought the police were obviously well paid these days.

'And this is the requisite authority from the Home Office to place her flat under electronic surveillance. That means bugging it to you and me, Henry.'

'It's Frank, sir,' the doorman said without thinking. 'What's she done?'

'That's not for you to know, Frank.'

'I'm not sure about this, sir. I mean I could find myself in all sorts of trouble.'

'Listen, if you're unhappy about this, phone Scotland Yard and ask for the Deputy Assistant Commissioner in charge of Special Branch. He will vouch for me.' Verco snapped his fingers. 'Better still you can watch me bug the place. Then you'll know I haven't stolen anything.'

'That won't be necessary, sir.'

'Suit yourself, Frank. Can I have the key to Miss Holsinger's apartment. I don't want to break the door down.'

'No, we can't have that,' Frank said and removed the key from the rack next to the mail boxes and handed it to the DCI. 'The number's 410,' he said.

The man who called himself Verco took one of the lifts up to the fourth floor and let himself into the apartment. He needed just five minutes to replace one of the plugs in the sitting room with an identical one incorporating a small version of the Ultimate Infinity Receiver. For good measure he bugged the television with a miniature battery powered transmitter that was good for three months. He then returned the key to the doorman and warned him not to say anything to Miss

Holsinger otherwise he might find Special Branch breathing down his neck.

Leaving Mountford House, he collected his car from the parking space he had been lucky to find in Connaught Place and drove round to Landon's flat in Stanhope Gardens.

Fifteen

Although Landon couldn't answer for the others he had a nasty feeling that, unless they were exceptionally lucky, the projected meeting with Mossad's Head of Station was going to come unstuck. Everything had been done in a hurry and they'd had to accept too many restrictions. In a ruthless application of the need to know principle Hazelwood had ruled that MI5 was not to be briefed, which meant that, without their cooperation, it would be ten times more difficult to track David Ben-Yosef. As a matter of routine Special Branch or the Diplomatic Protection Group were responsible for ensuring no harm came to Mossad's Head of Station.

To keep abreast of their movements they were therefore forced to rely on Hicks picking up the appropriate police frequency with his mobile scanner. Except the scanner wasn't exactly mobile because Hazelwood had ruled that in order to ensure total security only Ashton, Meacher, Chris Neighbour and himself could know the aim of the operation. Consequently Hicks had been left behind to set up the scanner in the attic of his semi-detached on Sunleigh Avenue in Alperton. Of necessity their communications were something of a lash-up. Since the Haydn transceiver had a maximum operating range of five miles Hicks had to use his mobile to pass information to Ashton.

Since leaving Vauxhall Cross Ashton had relayed just one message from Hicks. At 6.30 p.m. he had picked up an unidentified police unit in the middle of a transmission informing control that Foxbat and companion had arrived at the house in Kenton Lane where the cocktail party was being held. So far as Landon was concerned, whether the unknown police unit was Special Branch or the Diplomatic Protection Group was immaterial. Foxbat was obviously David Ben-Yosef and the message implied the police had known in advance where Mossad's Head of Station was going that evening. Chances were the Israeli gave the police a copy of his social engagements week by week, which made life easier for both parties. If this cosy arrangement had been going on for any length of time, the police might well be caught off guard. Landon certainly had no quarrel with Ashton's assumption that wherever the drinks party was being held in Kenton Lane, Ben-Yosef would enter the house by the front door and immediately leave it by the back with the keys to a car that had been pre-positioned for his use in a parallel street.

Of more concern to Landon at the moment was his deployment in Luxton Avenue on the outskirts of Beaconsfield. Although it was close enough to the roundabout where the slip road from junction 2 joined the A40, the side street had little else to commend it. The avenue might have seemed ideal for their purpose to Chris Neighbour, but he had seen it in the middle of the day when many of the

212

residents had been out at work. It was a very different story in the evening; by the time Landon arrived on the scene every inch of parking space at the kerbside had been filled.

He cruised up and down the avenue several times hoping that by some miracle a parking space would materialize, but no such luck. With time to spare before David Ben-Yosef put in an appearance, Landon decided he had better have a look at the Jasmine restaurant before one of the avenue's residents reported him to the police for kerb crawling. With the aid of the sketch map Chris Neighbour had provided it took less than ten minutes to find the restaurant.

The anonymous Lada 2110 with false number plates that the MT section had signed out to Ashton was parked outside the rendezvous, but there was no sign of the two men. That they were watching him from somewhere became evident when the background mush on his Haydn transceiver was suddenly stilled and Ashton came on their air to ask what he was playing at. Picking up the Haydn lying on the adjoining seat, Landon held the mike close to his mouth and pressed the transmit button. 'I wanted to find the quickest way to the RV,' he said.

'Well, now you have, don't hang around here,' Ashton told him.

'I don't intend to.'

'Good. Our friend could arrive at any time.'

Shifting into gear, Landon drove on to the nearest side road, reversed into it and then made a ninety degree turn to head back to the roundabout. The parking problem in Luxton Avenue hadn't improved during his brief absence. At the T-junction at the top of the avenue he made a three point turn with some difficulty, and crawled back down the road towards the roundabout at a walking pace. Only one semi in four had a garage attached. Out of neighbourly consideration it was noticeable that in every case nobody had parked on the road directly in front of a driveway. As a non-resident Landon had no inhibitions about blocking the exit from the garage. He told himself it would be for a few minutes at the most and who would complain about that?

Landon found out soon enough. As he sat there listening to Radio 2, one of the residents tapped on the nearside window to attract his attention. The plaintiff looked to be in his late thirties and was already bristling with indignation. 'You're blocking my exit,' he said in a yappy sounding voice.

Landon switched off the radio, unclipped the seat belt and leaned across the adjoining seat to lower the window. 'I'm sorry,' he said politely, 'do you want to come out?'

'That's not the point. I don't want you parking outside my house.'

'Well, you have my sympathy but I have to tell you, sir, you don't own the pavement or the road.' Landon produced his ID card and allowed the man to see his photo but not his name. 'I'm afraid I can't move on,' he continued. 'An operation is in progress and I have to—'

'I've been watching you cruise up and down the avenue and I know what your game is, you pervert.'

'Do me a favour, sir,' Landon said. 'Please go back inside your house and allow me to do my job.'

'Who do you think you are? I'm not taking orders from you.'

Landon counted slowly up to ten, something he always did when provoked beyond reason. Usually it helped him to contain his anger but not on this occasion. 'You're obviously looking for trouble,' he said in a quiet but menacing voice. For good measure he opened the door and started to get out of the car.

'Don't think I'm frightened of you,' the man said before retreating indoors.

Landon settled back into the Fiat Bravo, closed the offside door and fastened the seat belt again. There was just eight minutes to go before the 7.30 deadline. With Hicks apparently as silent as a Trappist monk, he could only assume the police officers who had tracked David Ben-Yosef to the drinks party were still sitting outside the house in Kenton Lane. On the other hand it could be that Mossad's Head of Station was still at the drinks party and had no intention of keeping his appointment with Ashton. The minutes passed slowly, then suddenly Ashton broke the silence to inform Chris Neighbour and him there had been a change of venue.

'We're moving to the King's Head at Amersham on the Hill,' Ashton said. 'That's map page 22, 9797. Join us soonest.'

Landon acknowledged the call, reached for the AA Big Road Atlas on the shelf below the dashboard and turned to page 22. The route was easy enough. All he had to do was leave Beaconsfield by the A355 and head north to Amersham approximately five miles from his present location. He put the map away, started the engine and moved off. As he waited for the break in the traffic at the roundabout, a police car turned into Luxton Avenue. Two miles up the road to Amersham, the police car appeared in the rear-view mirror, headlights flashing him to pull over and stop. As if to reinforce the signal the police driver blipped his siren a couple of times.

There were two police officers in the car. The long and short of it, Landon thought, eyeing them in the rear-view mirror as they approached the Fiat Bravo. The taller of the two looked to be in his late forties and it was he who did all the talking when Landon lowered the window on his side.

'Are you the owner of this car, sir?' he enquired politely.

'Yes I am. Why do you ask?'

'Because the registration number doesn't exist, sir. We've checked with the Driver and Vehicle Licensing Agency.'

'There must be some mistake,' Landon said.

'May I see your driving licence, sir?'

'I'm afraid I don't have it on me.'

'I see. What's your name and address?'

The fact that the officer had stopped addressing him as sir was a sign his attitude was hardening. No matter how he responded Landon knew he would be arrested. If he gave his real name and produced his ID card, there was no telling the extent of the subsequent fall out. There was, however, one cover name used by the SIS that the watchkeepers at Vauxhall Cross would recognize.

'My name is Messenger,' Landon told them, 'Peter Messenger. And before you ask, I can't prove it.'

'What about the ID card you showed Mr Porteous.'

'Who's he?'

216

'One of the residents in Luxton Avenue who told us you were behaving suspiciously. You told him you were a police officer.'

'That's a bloody lie,' Landon said with conviction.

'Mr Messenger, you are driving a motor vehicle with false number plates while displaying a tax disc belonging to a different car. You are also suspected of impersonating a police officer. I am therefore placing you under arrest. Do you understand?'

'Yes.'

'Good. Now please leave the key in the ignition and get out of the car. My colleague will drive the Fiat Bravo to the station.'

'And where's that?'

'In Amersham.'

His wrists handcuffed behind him, Landon was placed in the back of the Thames Valley Police car. At that moment in time, Amersham was the last place on earth he wanted to go.

*   *   *

The position Neighbour had chosen for himself on the A40 half a mile from Beaconsfield was ideal for keeping the trunk road under observation. Unfortunately it had proved to be a lousy site for the Haydn transceiver. The problem was he could hear Ashton but Ashton couldn't hear him. The solution was to find an alternative location where his transmissions wouldn't be screened either by a physical barrier or freak, localized atmospherics. By trial and error he had eventually found a suitable location two miles down the road in Belstock Park.

Nothing   was   ever   perfect;   although

communications had been loud and clear, his car could be seen from the road. With time running out, he had left his car in dead ground and had gone forward with the Haydn on foot to keep watch on the road. However, his problems hadn't ended there; the park was a favourite haunt for lovers and he had to make sure no one saw him, otherwise he would be labelled a peeping Tom followed by the inevitable altercation. The alternative RV announced by Ashton caught him on the back foot. His car was roughly a hundred yards from his position and even walking at a leisurely pace it should have taken him under two minutes to reach the Ford Escort. With a couple of latecomers having sex out in the open somewhere between him and the car he was forced to move with utmost stealth to avoid them, which meant it took far longer. Once inside the Ford Escort, Neighbour looked up the route to Amersham on the Hill in the AA Big Road Atlas and set off to the roundabout where the slip road from the motorway joined the A40.

He reckoned Landon had had at least an eight-minute head start and hadn't expected to see him before he reached the King's Head. Two miles north of Beaconsfield on the A355 he spotted a police car drawn up behind a Fiat Bravo parked on the verge. Slowing down to forty, Neighbour tripped the indicator to show he was giving the obstruction a wide berth and went on past without a sideways glance. When he looked into the rear-view mirror he saw Landon being led towards the police car, his wrists handcuffed behind him. A quixotic sense of loyalty to a colleague urged him to intervene, common sense and training dictated

218

he ignore the incident.

*   *   *

The King's Head in Amersham on the Hill was a good half-mile from the nearest house. How much of the coaching inn dated back to the early eighteenth century only a knowledgeable architect could say with any certainty, but some of the external brickwork definitely belonged to a later age. At first sight the interior was reminiscent of the Elizabethan era but even Ashton could see the oak beams were a comparatively recent innovation. On that Tuesday evening there were just seven people present in the snug, the smaller of the two bars.

'Our new-found friends are those sitting round a table over there in the corner,' Meacher said in a low voice, barely moving his lips. 'The good-looking guy with curly black hair is David Ben-Yosef, the man with him is Sam Levy. I don't know who the woman is.'

As they approached the table, Levy stood up. 'Good to see you, Ralph, and you, Mr Ashton,' he said warmly. 'You know David, of course, and this is Malka.'

Ashton wondered who Malka was and what she was doing there. He guessed Toby Quayle must have been equally disconcerted when Anwar Farid had turned up with Danièle in tow.

'What will you have to drink, Mr Ashton?' Levy asked.

'I'd like a tomato juice with Tabasco, Worcester sauce and ice, please.'

'Ralph?'

'I'll have a pint of Speckled Hen,' Meacher told him.

'David?'

'The same as before, Scotch on the rocks.'

'And Malka?'

'Nothing. I'm driving. Remember?'

Meacher said he would get them in and accompanied Levy to the bar, leaving Ashton to make small talk with the Israelis. Social chit-chat had never been his forte and the fact that he had no idea of the relationship between Ben-Yosef and Malka didn't help. He assumed she had something to do with Mossad or at least held an appropriate security clearance that allowed her to attend the meeting. In attempting to find something they could talk about he learned that she had no interest in sport, rarely went to the theatre but liked to go to pop concerts. Turning to Ben-Yosef he discovered the Israeli followed Manchester United and had been a member of their fan club for the past two seasons. The serious business began the moment Levy and Meacher returned with the drinks.

'I assume you and Ralph came alone, Mr Ashton?' Ben-Yosef said quietly.

Ashton resisted the temptation to confirm his supposition. The Israelis were no admirers of the SIS, which they regarded as little better than the Foreign and Commonwealth Office. The proposed alliance could only function on the basis of mutual trust and that was something he had to work at, starting now.

'No, we didn't come alone,' Ashton told him. 'Two of my officers were covering the A40 trunk road into Beaconsfield and junction two of the motorway.'

'And what orders were they given?'

'To make sure Special Branch and MI5 didn't gatecrash the party.'

'I admire your candour.'

'I don't,' Malka said bluntly.

'We know the police followed you to the house in Kenton Lane where the drinks party was being held.'

'You shadowed the police car?' Ben-Yosef asked incredulously.

Ashton shook his head. 'We used a scanner to find the frequency they were using and then eavesdropped on them. For what it's worth your codename is Foxbat, but I daresay you already knew that.' He smiled at Ben-Yosef's companion. 'They don't appear to have a separate codename for you, Malka.'

'That's no surprise, I'm Sam's sister.'

Ashton couldn't believe Sam Levy had any kind of security clearance that would satisfy the Positive Vetting and Technical Services Division at Vauxhall Cross. He was also absolutely convinced that Malka hadn't even been required to fill out a form giving her name, date and place of birth together with similar details for her parents, alive or dead, and her spouse, if any. This was the first basic step for the lowest security clearance. No way was he prepared to discuss a joint SIS–Mossad operation in front of the Levys.

'I think it's time we moved on, don't you?' Ashton said cheerfully. 'Obviously we can't all travel in the one car so why don't you come with us, David, leaving Sam and Malka to follow us in their car.'

Levy asked Ben-Yosef if he was happy with the

221

arrangement and looked affronted when the Israeli Intelligence officer raised no objection.

'Shall we go?' Ashton said and finished his tomato juice.

They left the snug talking animatedly amongst themselves as though they had just met up for a quick one before going on elsewhere. They split up in the car park, Meacher literally taking a back seat so that Ben-Yosef could sit up front next to Ashton.

'You want to tell me where we are going, Mr Ashton?'

'I'm going to pick up the A40 at Gerrards Cross and head into London. We'll probably drop you off in Northolt and go our separate ways. You'd better pass that on to the Levys.'

'What?'

'Sam appears to be wearing a deaf aid and I would be surprised if you weren't wired for sound.'

'You've got a vivid imagination, that's all I can say.'

Ashton glanced sideways at the Israeli. 'I imagine you would be pretty unhappy if the drinks party broke up before you rejoined it. So the sooner we get down to business the better it will be for you and us.'

'Fine. What's your quarrel with Talal Asir?'

'Ten months ago he financed the assassination of our Director General as well as the attempted assassination of his predecessor and the Minister of State for Foreign and Commonwealth Affairs. He is also behind the Islamic Jihad terrorists who packed two hundred pounds of Semtex plus half a ton of tubular steel pipes cut into jagged sections into a Ford Transit that they intended to detonate at the All England Lawn Tennis Club during the

Wimbledon championships.'

'What exactly are your plans for this man?'

'We intend to take him out,' Ashton said without the slightest hesitation.

'If what Sam has told me is correct, you would like us to flush him out of cover?'

'Yes. We are anxious to know where Talal Asir is in time to find him still at home when we call. That kind of information can only come from Humint sources and they cost money. That's why the SIS is prepared to fund half the cost.'

'How much are we talking about?' Ben-Yosef asked.

'We thought a down payment of two hundred and fifty thousand would be a fair offer. Plus of course another quarter of a million after the operation had been successfully completed.'

'You've underestimated the cost, Mr Ashton. My chief wants half a million up front with a further one and a half mil on completion. Take it or leave it.'

'We'll take it,' Ashton told him and provoked an audible gasp from Meacher.

'Ralph doesn't sound very happy about that,' Ben-Yosef observed.

'Ralph is merely suffering from heartburn. He shouldn't have had that pint of Speckled Hen. Beer disagrees with him.'

'In all fairness, I should tell you that, having located Talal Asir, we won't sit back and wait for your SAS people to arrive on the scene. We will in fact kill him at the first opportunity.'

'We won't complain if you do,' Ashton said. 'Matter of fact it would suit us.'

'We would probably use a helicopter gunship armed with air-to-ground laser-guided missiles.

They are extremely accurate and very effective. However, I can practically guarantee there will be collateral damage.'

To the uninitiated guided munitions were synonymous with pinpoint attacks, but there was no such thing as a surgical operation. The casualties were rarely confined to the bad guys; there were always the innocent bystanders, men, women and children who had happened to be in the wrong place at the wrong time. They were the collateral damage David Ben-Yosef had referred to. In drawing his attention to this issue, Ashton sensed the Israeli was trying to gauge the reaction of British Intelligence.

'Provided you get Talal Asir you won't hear any complaints from us about the slaughter of innocents. Of course, I can't answer for the FCO but I imagine you will shrug off any note of censure from our Foreign Secretary or the United Nations. It would be like water off a duck's back to you.'

'There was some talk of eliminating Ali Mohammed Khalef,' Ben-Yosef said, changing the subject.

'Didn't Sam tell you? He's part of the deal.'

'Two for the price of one. Is that what you are saying?'

'Yes.'

'You must think I was born yesterday,' Ben-Yosef said angrily.

'I'm not trying to pull a fast one, Levy was told the package would include Ali Mohammed Khalef. Isn't that so, Ralph?'

'It certainly is,' Meacher said.

'Why am I not surprised, Ralph? Mr Ashton is a colleague so you are bound to support him.'

224

'If you want more money I'll see what I can do,' Ashton said heatedly, 'but I'd be surprised if Khalef wasn't already on your most-wanted list. He's a one-man recruiting service for Hamas in the UK and has sent God knows how many British-born Muslims to training camps in Pakistan and the Lebanon. Until recently he was also an active fundraiser for the displaced Palestinians living in Ramallah. Only thing is, most of the money went to the families of those suicide bombers who had killed the most Israelis.'

Ashton waited for some kind of response from Ben-Yosef, but the Israeli didn't say anything, he just sat there gazing straight ahead as though in a trance. Chalfont St Peter and Gerrards Cross were behind them now and in a few minutes they would pass under the M25 orbital motorway and join the M40 at junction 1.

Ashton calculated he had something under fifteen minutes in which to bring the meeting to a successful conclusion. By then the motorway would have become the A40 and they would be approaching the turn-off near the Polish war memorial.

Either Landon or Neighbour blipped the transmit button on their Haydn a couple of times, then repeated the signal after failing to get an immediate answer. Reacting instinctively, Meacher turned the volume right down on his transceiver, then half turned his back on Ben-Yosef to answer the call in a low voice that was virtually inaudible above the noise of the engine. Ashton was about to switch on the car radio, then suddenly changed his mind.

'Something you didn't want me to hear, Mr

Ashton?' Ben-Yosef said mockingly.

'No, I was going to put the radio on because you didn't have much to say for yourself. Then I realized Ralph might not be able to hear what was being said to him.'

'That was quick thinking.'

Ashton ignored the jibe. 'Who was that, Ralph?' he asked.

'Chris, I told him he was no longer required and to go on home.'

'You did right.'

Northolt aerodrome was coming up on the left now. With darkness closing in fast, Ashton switched on the main beams and automatically adjusted the rear-view mirror to the anti-dazzle mode. The Levys, he noted, were still behind him. Easing his foot on the accelerator, he gradually reduced speed from seventy down to forty miles an hour and signalled his intention of turning left some distance before reaching the slip road. Ben-Yosef continued to play it close to his chest after he had turned into West End Lane and swept past the Polish war memorial.

'There's a pub a mile ahead,' Ashton said. 'I'll drive into the car park and we'll part company there, OK?'

'Suits me.'

'Go past the Central Line station on the right, then under the railway bridge and it's immediately on your left.' Ashton recalled the directions Chris Neighbour had given him and tripped the indicator in good time. There were only two other vehicles in the car park adjoining the pub, but it was a Tuesday night and things were bound to be quiet after the Easter break.

'Well, here we are,' Ashton said unnecessarily, and unclipped his seat belt. 'Are you coming in for a drink?'

'I don't think so,' Ben-Yosef told him. 'I don't want to be the last guest to leave the drinks party.'

'Yeah. I can see it could be embarrassing.'

Ben-Yosef reached inside the top pocket of his jacket and produced a business card. 'You'll be needing this, Mr Ashton.'

'Federal Construction Works, Thun, Switzerland.' Ashton looked up. 'Who are they?'

'One of our overseas investments. Turn the card over and you will see who they bank with and our numbered account. We're in business soon as the bank notifies us they have received the down payment of half a million.'

Ben-Yosef got out of the Lada, walked over to the Merc that had just entered the car park, opened the nearside rear door and literally slithered into the back. Somehow he managed to close the door behind him and bury himself on the floor as Malka turned the car around and drove off.

'A little flamboyant,' Meacher observed.

Ashton grunted. 'I still feel like a drink, how about you?'

'I reckon we both need one. Will Landon's got himself arrested. Neighbour saw the police had handcuffed him as he drove past. He didn't get involved.'

'Good for him.'

'So what are we going to do about Landon?'

'Nothing,' said Ashton. 'Will's a big boy now, he can look after himself.'

Sixteen

Landon was six feet three and had weighed two hundred and seven pounds at his last medical review board. There wasn't a spare ounce of flesh on his body; he was, in fact, built like a heavyweight minus the scar tissue around the eyes normally associated with a prizefighter. Finding seven men of similar physique to stand in line with him on an identification parade hadn't been the easiest of tasks. However, by a quarter to nine the police had succeeded in rounding up seven volunteers who might loosely be described as lookalikes.

The line-up was held indoors in a specially adapted room divided into two by a large sheet of one-way glass from floor to ceiling. Powerful overhead lights threw Landon and the volunteers into sharp relief. Witnesses like Mr Porteous of Luxton Avenue, Beaconsfield were the other side of the glass partition where they couldn't be eyeballed or feel intimidated by the mere physical presence of the suspect under arrest.

The parade itself was over in a flash; moments after Landon had taken his chosen place in the line-up he was picked out by a witness. He subsequently changed place with the end but one man on the right and was again identified without the slightest hesitation. Nevertheless, the duty inspector had not been a happy man. He became even more uneasy on hearing the prisoner was prepared to make a statement and answer questions but only to the superintendent in charge of the Amersham sub-division. In his time the duty inspector had been threatened by more than his fair share of bombastic characters who had claimed to be on first name terms with the chief constable or any other establishment figure who came to mind. But this man who called himself Peter Messenger was different; he wasn't overbearing or arrogant like some the duty inspector had met. He made no threats and never once raised his voice. But there was an air of authority about him that was intimidating. It was, however, the Haydn transceiver that was the clinching argument for the duty inspector. Until the property sergeant produced it he had never seen anything in the communications field to touch it. Somehow this sophisticated piece of equipment explained the false number plates and persuaded him to send for Superintendent Oakham.

The superintendent in charge of the Amersham sub-division had been attending the initiation of a new member of his Masonic Lodge and was not best pleased to be called away shortly before 10 p.m. And he didn't really like it when Mr Peter bloody Messenger imposed yet another condition by insisting no one else should be present during the interview.

'I would also like you to remove the cassette from the recorder,' Landon told him.

'You can forget that,' Oakham snapped.

'What's your security clearance, Superintendent? Are you NV or PV cleared? In other words, were you interviewed at any time? This would be after the referees you had nominated and your superiors had had their say.'

'Not that I recall,' Oakham said.

'Then you were probably cleared by normal vetting. That would give you occasional access to top security material.'

'And what if I hadn't been cleared, where does that leave you?'

'Well, Superintendent, I have to say you would be the first senior police officer I've met who was not allowed to see even a confidential memo. Now shall we stop all this nonsense and get down to business?'

'I don't like your attitude, Mr Messenger.'

'That's OK, I don't care for yours either.' Landon went through his pockets, found a scrap of paper and, borrowing a pen from Oakham, wrote down a phone number, then passed it to the superintendent. 'Please ring this number. When the operator answers ask for the senior watchkeeper. If she feigns ignorance, tell her you want extension 4126.'

'And then what?'

'You give me the phone and I ask the man to confirm that Peter Messenger is a colleague.'

'Do you see a phone in this interview room?'

'Oh come on,' Landon said wearily, 'don't tell me you haven't got a mobile.'

'All right, Mr Messenger, I'll humour you just this once.'

Oakham produced a mobile and tapped out the number Landon had given him. Rebuffed by the exchange operator at Vauxhall Cross he asked for extension 4126 and was immediately connected. 'It's all yours,' he said and passed the mobile to Landon.

'This is Messenger,' Landon said. 'I'm going to put Superintendent Oakham back on the phone and I'd like you to confirm my identity.'

There were no hiccups, which was no more than Landon had expected. Standing orders for the senior watchkeeper laid down the action to be taken in the event of an incoming call being received from a Mr Messenger. The procedure was a model of clarity, and provided they stuck to the guidelines only somebody who was totally incompetent could foul things up.

'Who is this senior watchkeeper?' Oakham demanded. 'What government department does he work for?'

'Have you got a Special Branch officer in the Thames Valley force?'

'What is this? I came here tonight because you told the duty inspector you could only talk to me.'

'And I will,' Landon said. 'But if you want to know which government department the watchkeeper and I belong to, ask your Special Branch officer to check out the phone number I gave you.'

Oakham stared at him long and hard, then suddenly got to his feet and stormed out of the interview room. A police constable took his place and kept Landon company. The property sergeant had taken Landon's wristwatch and, since the police constable was unwilling to tell him what time it was, Landon could only guess that at least twenty minutes had elapsed when Oakham finally returned.

'How long have you been working for the Ministry of Defence?' Oakham asked after the constable had left the room.

'Eleven years this coming September,' Landon told him.

'And Messenger is not your real name, is it?'

'No, it's a covert one all of us use whenever it's necessary to protect our real identity.'

'And you are not going to disclose yours. Right?'

'I would be in hot water if my name and what I did became public knowledge. And in this instance public knowledge means any police officer apart from yourself. You tell the duty inspector or even the chief constable himself and the Home Office will be down on you like a ton of bricks when they hear what has happened tonight. It's not my intention to threaten you, I'm merely indicating what will happen in the worst case.'

It was all a huge bluff. In accordance with his standing orders the senior watchkeeper would inform the DG that one of his officers had been arrested but Hazelwood was unlikely to take up the cudgels on his behalf. His attitude in the matter of co-opting Mossad to hunt down Talal Asir and Ali Mohammed Khalef was ambivalent. One minute he was all in favour of the idea, only to develop cold feet the next. If the government ever learned what the SIS was up to his head would be well below the parapet.

'Our Special Branch officer told me you weren't the usual kind of civil servant,' Oakham said quietly. 'He reckons you are either MI5 or SIS.'

'You don't want to believe all you hear,' Landon told him.

'I don't. What were you doing in Luxton Avenue, Mr Messenger?'

'Keeping the roundabout under observation.'

'Why?'

'That's not for you to know,' Landon said.

'I'm cleared for occasional access to top secret,

you said so yourself.'

'It wouldn't matter if you had been positively vetted, Superintendent. Your name would have been on the codeword list for access, tonight's operation was that sensitive.'

'Didn't stop you threatening Mr Porteous with violence, did it?'

'Mr Porteous is a nasty, territorially minded little prick. The joke is the territory in question doesn't belong to him.'

'He claims you were kerb crawling up and down the avenue.'

'I was looking for somewhere to park.'

'This isn't how Mr Porteous recollects your behaviour.'

'I bet it isn't. He called me a pervert, meaning I was a paedophile.'

'And that made you angry,' Oakham said insidiously.

'What do you think?'

'I think you meant to teach him a lesson, Mr Messenger.'

'Rubbish.'

'You got out of the car with that intention in mind.'

In a measured voice Landon related how he had asked Porteous to go back indoors and allow him to do his job. Yes, he had opened the car door and had started to get out of the Fiat Bravo but at no stage had he contemplated hitting Porteous.

'He reminded me of one of those yappy little dogs who are all bark and no bite. He said he wasn't scared of me as he retreated inside the house and that's the crux of the whole business. You've got a small man who feels humiliated and wants his revenge. Making a complaint to the police is the only way he knows how to get it. But the odds are that when push comes to shove you won't get him to testify in court.'

'There's more than one witness,' Oakham told him.

'No, there was only one man on the street. The second witness may have seen me driving up and down the road but that's it. The question is what happens now?'

It took Oakham all of five seconds to reach a decision. 'You're free to go,' he announced.

'Thanks.'

'If you really want to thank me you won't come near Beaconsfield again.'

Landon signed for the Haydn transceiver, his wristwatch, mobile, fountain pen, ignition key and leather wallet containing sixty-five pounds.

'No credit card, no membership card of any description, no charge card,' the property sergeant intoned. 'In fact, no cards at all.'

'I believe in travelling light,' Landon told him poker faced.

'Your Fiat Bravo's in the yard.'

'Good.'

'I'm surprised it passed the M.O.T.,' the property sergeant said, determined to have the last word.

Landon collected the car and headed south east on the A413. Just short of Chalfont St Peter he pulled off the road and contacted the senior watchkeeper on his mobile. In guarded language he informed him everything was now OK, then continued on his way to Vauxhall Cross. Taxis were few and far between south of the Thames at the witching hour of midnight and it was getting on for one o'clock by the time he reached his flat in Stanhope Gardens.

There were four messages on his answer phone, all of them from Ensley Holsinger. She rang a fifth time moments after he had cancelled them out.

'You're back,' she said. 'We had a dinner date. Remember?'

'And I left a message with your secretary saying something had come up and I wouldn't be able to keep it.'

'Where have you been?'

'Working.'

'You work funny hours, Landon.'

'Like I told you once before, it's a funny old job,' Landon said and slowly put the phone down.

*   *   *

It was the first time Roy Kelso had had anything to report at morning prayers since the allotment of funds to heads of departments for the financial year 1999/2000. As on that occasion he had produced a diagram that was back projected by a Vugraph on to a portable screen. His subject on this occasion was the move by MI5 from their headquarters on Gower Street to Thames House on Millbank. With the aid of a pointer staff he indicated the order in which the various sections would be relocated.

'The redeployment starts tomorrow,' Kelso announced. 'It will be completed by the weekend. Since all the phone numbers will remain the same wherever the instrument is positioned we will not be affected at any stage. In fact, anybody who phones Richard Neagle tomorrow won't know if he's in Gower Street or Thames House. When he does physically move house, the phone in the old office will be closed down.'

'Does this duplication of equipment apply to the Mozart secure speech facility?' Ashton enquired.

'It certainly does,' Kelso told him. He looked round the table, oozing with confidence. 'Are there any other questions?'

'Will they still be using Box 500 as their postal address?' Garfield asked.

'Yes.' Kelso cleared his throat. 'I've produced an aide-memoire for distribution by heads of departments. If you would like to help yourselves to however many copies are needed on the way out.'

'Thank you, Roy,' Hazelwood said. 'And you too, gentlemen,' he added, then pushed his chair back and stood up.

Ashton collected ten copies of the Admin King's masterpiece and returned to his office. That the BT phone started ringing before he had time to open the safe was no surprise in view of everything that had happened last night.

'Has Sir Victor sent for Ralph Meacher?' he asked Dilys Crowther.

'No, he wants to see you first.'

'Then tell him I'm on my way.'

Ashton put the phone down. Clearly Hazelwood was more interested in learning what Landon had told the police than the outcome of the meeting they'd had with David Ben-Yosef. It was yet another sign that the DG was becoming less and less enthusiastic about getting into bed with Mossad.

For once the atmosphere in Hazelwood's office

didn't reek of Burma cheroots and there was only one cigar in the cut-down brass shell case where normally there would have been three or four by mid-morning. Instead, when Ashton entered the room, Hazelwood was holding a puffer to his mouth.

'How long have you had asthma, Victor?'

'Since last August.' Hazelwood took a deep breath. 'It was the high pollen count.'

'There's no pollen around at the moment.'

'You think I don't know that,' Hazelwood said irritably. 'The attacks flared up again shortly after Toby Quayle was murdered. I put it down to stress, the doctor said heavy smoking was the root cause of my asthma. That's why I limit myself to four cheroots a day.'

'Since when?'

'I started on Good Friday.' Hazelwood stabbed a finger at him. 'I would be grateful if you would keep it to yourself, Peter. Only two other people know about my condition, one is my wife, Alice, the other is Dilys Crowther. I've got a medical board in late June and a lot of Whitehall mandarins would like to see me fail the review. It would give them an excuse to get rid of me.'

'Nobody is going to hear about your asthma from me, Victor.'

'Thank you. I've always known I could rely on you, Peter, which is more than can be said for Landon. I take it you have questioned him?'

'I had a long session with Will before morning prayers. He had a slight altercation with a poisonous householder who reported him to the police for kerb crawling. The police subsequently arrested Will for displaying false plates on the Fiat.'

In Ashton's opinion nobody could have handled a difficult situation better than Landon had. He had held out, refusing to make a statement to anyone other than the superintendent in charge of the Amersham sub-division.

'Will knew we were meeting Ben-Yosef at the King's Head in Amersham on the Hill so he set out to give us time to conclude our business and leave the area.'

'Who was the superintendent?'

'His name is Oakham. Will gave him the phone number of our exchange and told him to check it out with the Thames Valley Special Branch. They told Oakham it was a Ministry of Defence number and he was persuaded to let Will go. From first to last Oakham never discovered Landon's real name.'

'What about his personal effects? Didn't he have to surrender them when he was arrested?'

'The only thing Will had on him was a wallet containing sixty-five pounds.'

'Thank God for small mercies.'

Hazelwood couldn't have made his relief more apparent had he sighed out loud. It prompted Ashton to find out just how far he was committed to enlisting the support of Mossad in the hunt for Talal Asir and Ali Mohammed Khalef.

'We had a very successful meeting with David Ben-Yosef,' Ashton said casually.

'Oh yes.'

'Don't you want to hear about it?'

'Of course I do,' Hazelwood said with a conspicuous lack of enthusiasm.

'OK. The facts are Mossad will target both men as soon as their bank in Switzerland notifies them they have received our down payment of half a million. They will require a further one and a half million after the operation has been successfully completed.'

It was difficult to tell what perturbed Hazelwood the most, the sum of money involved or the fact that the Israelis hadn't rejected the SIS proposal out of hand. He became even more alarmed on learning the Israelis wouldn't wait for the Special Air Service to arrive if they located Ali Mohammed Khalef anywhere within striking distance of their special forces.

'Where is the two million coming from?' Hazelwood asked curtly.

'We've only got to find half a million initially and that shouldn't be a problem. My own department had a surplus of three hundred thousand at the end of the last financial year and we've just been told how much we've been allocated for 1999/2000.'

'Your total budget for the whole year amounts to one point seven million. Deduct the second payment to the Israelis and you are left with a pittance to run your department for the rest of the year.'

'Ralph Meacher had a modest surplus at the end of last year and has indicated he would be willing to contribute a percentage of his current budget. If the worst came to the worst I was hoping the contingency fund would bail us out.'

'You can forget the contingency fund,' Hazelwood said, 'and I would need a lot of convincing before I was persuaded the Mid East Department was financially able to support the operation.'

'I don't see that,' Ashton told him. 'The hunt for

Khalef and Talal Asir is primarily the responsibility of Ralph Meacher and his department.'

'I'll decide whose responsibility it is,' Hazelwood growled.

The financial debate had nothing to do with whether or not the operation was affordable. It was simply a smokescreen. Hazelwood had changed his mind yet again and was looking for any excuse to abrogate the alliance Ashton had made with Mossad at his behest.

'It won't do, Victor,' Ashton said icily.

'What are you talking about?'

'You've suddenly decided you don't want to have anything to do with Mossad.'

'Did you hear me say that?'

'You didn't have to, nothing could have been plainer.'

'Really?'

'Just remember I gave my word to David Ben-Yosef.'

'And the last thing I said to you yesterday was don't commit us to anything we can't get out of. So what you may have said to Ben-Yosef is not my problem.'

'It is now, Victor, because I'm not going to be the one who tells him the deal is off.'

Ashton got to his feet and walked out of the room. As he went through the PA's office he heard Hazelwood gasping for breath.

*   *   *

Although described as management consultants Jerome Sharman was in reality an employment agency for those people belonging to the AB

240

socio-economic group who had either been made redundant or were looking for a more prestigious and better paid appointment. The registered office was in Dover Street but applicants who wanted to be placed on the firm's book were interviewed at Astra House in the Strand. When she had arrived at the office that morning Ensley Holsinger had been scheduled to interview three potential clients commencing at 10 a.m. However, a fourth name had been added shortly before she left for Astra House.

According to Ensley's secretary, who had compiled the list, the fourth man was Hiram J. Dirlwinger, a twenty-eight-year-old graduate from the Massachusetts Institute of Technology. The man who was waiting for Ensley in the interview room when she returned from a hasty lunch was more than twenty-eight and was better known to her as Virgil Zimmerman from the American Embassy.

'What are you doing here?' Ensley demanded.

'You are expecting to interview Mr Hiram J. Dirlwinger at two o'clock.' Zimmerman smiled and touched his chest. 'I am he, at least for this afternoon.'

'What do you want?'

'I'd like you to repeat the two phone numbers written on the back of the calling card I gave you.'

'Why should I?' Ensley asked defiantly.

'Because I'm asking you politely.'

Ensley stared at him in disbelief, then shrugged her shoulders. 'Well, OK, if it means that much to you, the office number is 020 7499 9007, your residential one is 020 7373 8866.'

The fact that she had complied with his

instructions and committed the numbers to memory made her feel like a puppet.

'So why haven't you phoned me?' Zimmerman asked.

'This is crazy. Why would I phone you?'

'I was hoping you would have something for me. You spent the whole of Easter with Landon.'

'You had us followed.'

'Damn right I did. You guys returned from Dartmouth on Monday afternoon.'

Ensley shivered at the memory of three utterly miserable days on the Devon coast. Cold grey sea matching an equally grey sky with a chilling breeze coming from the south west, though to her it had seemed more like a howling gale. However, that had been the least of her problems. All the hotels along the coast had been fully booked, as Landon had prophesied, and they'd had to settle for an olde worlde pub miles from the sea whose landlord had never heard of central heating.

'You know what intrigues me?' Zimmerman murmured. 'The fact that someone like Landon can take off for three days and nights and nobody turns a hair.'

'Peter knew where to find him.'

'Peter?'

'Landon's boss, he touches base with him every day, sometimes more than once.'

'Peter's in the office and Will is playing fast and loose.' Zimmerman shook his head as though genuinely perplexed. 'I guess I'll never understand the Brits.'

'He rang Peter at home,' Ensley told him.

She did not believe she had betrayed a confidence. After all, Landon had made every

242

phone call in her presence and what he had said to Peter Ashton concerning their movements each day was no big secret. At the back of her mind was the hope that in passing on such trivia Zimmerman would eventually conclude she was of no use to him.

'Where did he take you last night, Ensley?'

'Nowhere, we didn't have a date.'

'Yeah?' His voice sounded full of doubt.

'What's the matter, don't you believe me?' she asked, confronting his scepticism head on.

'Did you phone Landon yesterday evening?'

'No, absolutely not.'

'Why so vehement, Ensley?'

'We'd quarrelled. I said what I thought of the pub where we had stayed, its landlord and the food he'd set in front of us and Landon told me to stop bitching. Nobody talks to me like that and gets away with it.' Feisty, convincingly angry at the way she had been treated. If she said so herself, Ensley reckoned it was a five-star performance. 'Now, Mr Zimmerman, are you serious about coming aboard with us?'

'You know I'm not.' Zimmerman got up and walked to the door. 'Stay in touch, Ensley,' he said, and waved her goodbye.

*   *   *

First Karachi, then Lahore, and now the British Council offices in Ekaterinburg, Moscow and St Petersburg had been simultaneously bombed. The incidents had been reported by the BBC on Radio 2 at ten minutes to one, almost half an hour before George Elphinstone, Head of Station, Moscow had

243

originated an emergency signal to Vauxhall Cross. His initial report had been no more detailed than the newscast. However, where international terrorism was involved, Elphinstone had a direct line to Sergei Stepashin, chief of the FSB, the Federal Security Service and successor to the KGB's Second Chief Directorate. Hence, subsequent reports from Head of Station, Moscow had been far more authoritative and detailed than those of the BBC.

Despite the spate of signals from Moscow, Hazelwood demanded more and more information, in handwritten memos that were hard to decipher. Not quite the 'action this day' exhortations but close enough. *Are we under attack!!!* with three exclamation marks. *Are you sure the terrorists don't belong to Islamic Jihad?* The first three words had been underlined in green ink even though the FSB had stated categorically that the suicide bombers had been Chechens. And finally, *When can I expect to see your analysis of the situation?*, a message that invited a caustic reply. Ashton was in fact trying to get something down on paper when Meacher asked him if he could spare a minute.

Ashton looked up and saw a broad smile on Meacher's face. 'What's happened to make you happy, Ralph?' he asked.

'Victor has just sanctioned the down payment to Mossad, three hundred thousand from your department, one twenty from mine, eighty grand from the contingency fund.'

'Well, I'll be damned. I can't believe Victor changed his mind.'

'You can take the credit for that,' Meacher

told him.

'Me?'

'He asked you if you were under attack and you returned his memo with the word "YES" printed on it in capital letters. I guess when you go to war you need all the allies you can get.'

Seventeen

A change of scenery was said to be as good as a rest. Landon supposed there was some truth in that old adage, although in his case the change of scenery merely involved a train journey to Petersfield where a staff car from the SIS training school would be waiting to convey him to Amberley Lodge. Delivering a lecture on the organization and role of CATO to the induction course also represented a change, because this would be the first time he had been required to do it, but no way could the experience be described as a rest. He hadn't known about the commitment until he'd returned to the flat late on Saturday night to find Ashton had left a message for him on the answer machine.

'Something's come up,' Ashton had said, 'and I'm afraid you will have to give the lecture in my place. You should do it anyway, you know far more about CATO than I do.'

'Something's come up' sounded vaguely ominous and there had been any number of questions he had wanted to ask Ashton, but not while Ensley was with him. On the assumption Ensley would return to her apartment in Mountford House on

Sunday evening he had planned to phone Peter later that night. Ensley, however, had been less than obliging and had stayed over, so that when he did call Ashton he'd had to use veiled speech.

In the space of seventeen days Ensley had swiftly moved back into his life as if she had never walked out on him in June last year. Some of her clothes were now hanging up in his wardrobe and, in the absence of a dressing table, she had arranged just about everything Estée Lauder provided on the glass shelf above the hand basin in the bathroom. He wondered how much longer it would be before she moved in lock, stock and barrel.

Landon went into the kitchen, measured two level dessert spoonfuls of Colombian coffee into the cafetière and put the kettle on, then popped two slices of bread into the toaster. Accustomed to eating breakfast on the run, he recalled Ensley liked muesli and was looking in the cupboard for the remains of a packet he had bought last May when she walked into the kitchen.

'Just a cup of coffee and an orange juice for me, please,' Ensley said.

'On the run, standing up or sitting down?'

'What?'

'I wanted to know if I should lay the kitchen table.'

'Let's not stand on ceremony, Landon. From what I've seen of your domestic arrangements it would probably take you all morning to find a tablecloth.'

Landon binned the toast, looked out two large wineglasses in the cupboard under the worktop and filled them from the carton of orange juice in the fridge. Finding himself short of milk he managed to convince Ensley he preferred black coffee.

They left the flat three minutes later, Ensley preceding him. As he emptied the letter box and turned about to place the mail on the hall table, he heard her say, 'Well, hi there, Jonathan, how're you doing?'

'All the better for seeing you, my dear,' the old gentleman gallantly told her, and raised the milk bottle he was holding as if to toast Ensley. Then, catching sight of Landon, he said, 'I trust your friend from Special Branch solved the problem you were having with the telephone?'

'My friend in Special Branch,' Landon repeated, the alarm bells beginning to ring in his head. 'When was this, Jonathan?'

'Last Tuesday. Must have been about eleven o'clock. I had been shopping at the local supermarket and bumped into him as he was leaving your flat. He wasn't in uniform and I was a bit alarmed in case he was a burglar. I mean you're not safe anywhere these days, but I needn't have worried. He was very nice, commended me for my vigilance and showed me his warrant card.'

'Are you sure it was a warrant card, Jonathan?'

'Well, it certainly looked like one, Mr Landon. He was a detective chief inspector if that's any help.'

'Did he tell you his name?'

'I think he said it was Verity.' Jonathan frowned. 'No, that's not right.' His face suddenly brightened. 'Verco. That's it, Detective Chief Inspector Verco.'

Landon was aware of Ensley frowning at him in mounting impatience. She wasn't tapping her foot yet but he sensed it wouldn't be long before she did, not that he would take any notice. 'Can you describe him, Jonathan?' he asked.

'Of course I can. He was almost as tall as you are, Mr Landon, perhaps three or four years older and I remember he had blond hair. It was cut very short, so close to the scalp that it was standing up like the bristles on a scrubbing brush.'

'Thank you, Jonathan, you've been very helpful.'

'Nothing's wrong is there?'

'Absolutely not,' Landon assured him cheerfully and went on downstairs.

'What was that all about?' Ensley asked when they were outside on the street.

'I know DCI Verco,' Landon told her. 'He's a small man no more than five feet seven. Furthermore he has grey hair and is in his mid to late fifties. I doubt very much if the Metropolitan Police have two DCIs called Verco in their Special Branch.'

'What are you saying, Will? That the man Jonathan saw was an impostor?'

'I'd bet a month's pay on it. And he didn't have to force an entry because he had a bunch of skeleton keys guaranteed to open any lock.'

'I don't like the sound of that.'

Landon walked on towards the Underground station on Gloucester Road, deep in thought and oblivious to what Ensley had just said. If Jonathan hadn't bumped into the impostor he would never have known some stranger had been inside his flat. The place hadn't been ransacked because theft was not what the intruder had in mind. His only interest had been to bug the place.

The flat would have to be spring cleaned, and that was a job for Terry Hicks. Normal office hours were observed by the whizzkid of the Technical

Services Division and it was now too late to catch him at home. For basic security reasons Landon decided to do nothing before he arrived at Amberley Lodge. Towards the end of last year the training school had been linked to the Mozart network and it was only sensible to use this secure speech facility.

'Have you been listening to me?' Ensley demanded.

'Of course I have.'

'Then what have I just said?'

'Well, there you have me,' Landon said smiling. 'I don't recall your exact words but to put it in a nutshell you wanted to know what I was going to do about the intruder.'

'That's not a bad guess,' Ensley conceded reluctantly, then asked him again what he was going to do.

'I'm going to have my flat spring cleaned,' Landon told her. 'That's what we call it in the trade.'

'Maybe I should have my apartment spring cleaned as well?'

'Why so?'

I would have thought that was obvious,' Ensley said. 'If Jonathan regards us as an item, so will Verco, and it would be foolish to suppose he wouldn't have taken steps to discover where I live.'

Although there wasn't anything Landon could put his finger on, he knew Ensley well enough to sense she was holding something back. This, however, was not an appropriate time to challenge her when they were about to part company.

'Will I see you tonight, Landon?' she asked.

Ensley stood there facing him in a tidewave of

249

people that separated on meeting them and passed by on either side as if they were a breakwater.

'I'll call you on your mobile after I've been spring cleaned.' Landon wrapped his arms around Ensley and drew her close. 'And when I call take your mobile into the bathroom and set the taps running before you answer.'

*   *   *

Ashton left the conference room and returned to his office knowing that Hazelwood wanted to see him in ten minutes' time. Ever since the possibility of co-opting Mossad in the hunt for Talal Asir and Ali Mohammed Khalef had been mooted, morning prayers had been followed by a second, more intimate meeting. Usually it was attended by Ralph Meacher, but not this morning, for the simple reason that what Victor had to say concerned Will Landon.

The brouhaha had started on Friday evening and had reached a crescendo twenty-four hours later. The man who had sparked it off was Oakham, the superintendent in charge of the Amersham sub-district. He had submitted a report to the assistant chief constable in charge of operations complaining about the activities of a Mr Messenger and others in the Beaconsfield area during the evening of Tuesday 6th April. Oakham had believed he'd been dealing with an officer of the Security Service, a mistaken impression MI5 had been swift to correct when the Home Office had asked Colin Wales, the Deputy DG, for an explanation. Knowing Messenger was a cover name used by the SIS, Wales had simply pointed the Home Office in the right direction. As soon as the complaint was received by the Foreign and Commonwealth Office, the Permanent Under Secretary of State had immediately asked the Chairman of the Joint Intelligence Committee to investigate.

To explain what the SIS had been doing in Beaconsfield Hazelwood needed a believable story that would hold up under scrutiny. There was a further complication for him: in admitting that the SIS had been conducting a clandestine operation within the UK, he would undoubtedly receive a severe reprimand in writing. There was one possible solution to his dilemma: he could imply to the chairman of the JIC that Landon had been acting on his own and had not been on duty when he was apprehended by the police on the 6th April. Without actually saying so Hazelwood could imply Landon had indeed been kerb crawling and had used the Messenger procedure to get himself out of trouble. From little things Victor had said to him over Friday and Saturday Ashton believed this was the way his mind was working.

Ashton suddenly noticed there was a buff-coloured note from Nancy Wilkins attached to the blotting paper on his desk with a paper clip. Brief and to the point it said, *Mr Neagle would like you to phone him ASAP on the Mozart network.* Glancing at his wristwatch it was clear he had enough time in hand to find out what was so urgent.

'It's me, Ashton,' he said when Neagle answered. 'What's the problem?'

'There is no problem, Peter. Six days ago Will Landon persuaded me to ask the FBI if their field office in St Louis had anything on Anwar Farid. It seems they had indirectly. Farid came to their

251

notice because he supplied Bauer & Deutsch with carpets and artefacts from the Middle East. The firm had other furniture stores in New Orleans, Las Vegas, Kansas City, Kansas, Memphis and Louisville. Goods from the Middle East and Asia destined for Bauer & Deutsch are shipped into New Orleans and then transported up river by barge to Memphis and St Louis.'

The FBI had entered the picture when a rig belonging to Bauer & Deutsch en route from St Louis to Kansas City had been hijacked. The vehicle had subsequently been found abandoned near Calwood off Interstate 70. The trailer had been broken into but according to Bauer & Deutsch nothing had been stolen. However, the bodies of the trucker and an unidentified hitchhiker had been found in the trailer. Both men had been shot in the head.

'Particles of white powder were found in the clothes of the hitchhiker,' Neagle continued. 'This was subsequently found to be pure cocaine.'

'When did this happen?' Ashton asked.

'Two years ago. The FBI alerted the Drug Enforcement Agency. They've been watching the firm ever since, convinced it is a distribution centre for cocaine.'

Neagle wanted him to know that although the DEA had failed to intercept a significant quantity of cocaine on its way up river so far, Bauer & Deutsch were living the good life on borrowed time. They had grown too big too fast and the IRS was going to put the partners away for tax evasion and money laundering.

'Did they have Anwar Farid in the frame at any time before he was murdered?'

252

'Well, that's not an easy question to answer, Peter. Let's say the Bureau was aware of his existence.'

Time in hand was fast running out for Ashton and he couldn't afford to let Neagle ramble on. 'Yes or no, Richard?' he said interrupting him.

'The answer's no, they didn't have Farid in the frame.'

'What about Danièle Chirac?'

'Before they received my cable the Bureau had never heard of her. Same goes for the DEA.'

Ashton thanked him and hung up. As he left his office the BT phone rang and he guessed Victor had told his PA to find out what had happened to him. It was not, however, the question Hazelwood raised when they were face to face.

'Where is Landon?' he demanded.

'Down at Amberley Lodge delivering the lecture I should have given,' Ashton told him and promptly sat down in one of the two leather armchairs provided for visitors. 'Your curiosity regarding his present whereabouts wouldn't have anything to do with the Chairman of the Joint Intelligence Committee, would it?'

'We wouldn't be in this mess but for Landon.'

It was obvious to Ashton that Victor still regarded Will Landon as a convenient scapegoat. He needed to be reminded that the blame lay elsewhere.

'And you and I, Victor, wouldn't be having this conversation if we hadn't courted the Israelis.'

'You're no help,' Hazelwood growled. 'What we need is a convincing story that will satisfy the Chairman of the JIC.'

'Well, the best legends contain more than a grain

253

of truth.'

Hazelwood snorted. 'If I take your advice I might just as well clear my desk now.'

'What if we told the Chairman the Saudis had made us an offer we couldn't refuse?'

'I think you had better run that past me again,' Hazelwood said.

The story Ashton had in mind was based on a single truth. The Saudi ruling family hated and feared Talal Asir. The possibility that he might organize a popular uprising was a perpetual nightmare for them. Given the opportunity the Saudi authorities would willingly chop off his head tomorrow, if they believed they could get away with it.

'They could get away with it,' Ashton said, 'provided they made it possible for our special forces to kill Talal Asir. Now if this was for real and the Saudis did come to us with such a proposition, where do you suppose we would meet them?'

'Somewhere out of town.' Hazelwood frowned. 'But what if the Chairman demands to know the name of the Saudi negotiator?'

'You tell him we've no objection but what will he do when the Saudi diplomat denies all knowledge of such a deal? I mean he is bound to do that in real life.'

'And if that doesn't satisfy the Chairman, what then?'

'We indoctrinate him for codeword material. In joining such a select group he incurs certain restrictions, one of them being that all foreign travel is banned for the next five years.'

'He has a house in Spain,' Hazelwood said thoughtfully.

'Yes, that could make life difficult for him. You might also remind him how the FCO reacted the last time relations between our two countries were impaired. As I recall the Saudis took grave exception to a documentary on TV called *Death of a Princess*, and a defence contract worth millions nearly went down the pan.'

'You're really quite a devious fellow, Ashton.'

'Well, I had a great tutor in you, Director,' Ashton told him, smiling.

*   *   *

Hicks was a man who enjoyed his creature comforts. Not for him the peculiar tasting coffee and tea dispensed by the vending machines on every floor. He kept a jar of Maxwell House and a packet of chocolate digestive biscuits in the bottom drawer of his desk. Except when he was away from Vauxhall Cross for the whole day he made a point of bringing half a pint of fresh milk into the office in a vacuum flask. When Nancy Wilkins walked into his office Hicks was enjoying an extended mid-morning coffee break.

'Mr Landon would like to have a word with you, Terry,' she said.

'He knows where to find me,' Hicks said truculently.

'Upstairs on the Mozart in his office on the fourth floor,' Nancy told him briskly.

'No peace for the wicked,' Hicks observed and helped himself to another chocolate digestive.

'Now!' Nancy snapped.

'You're a hard taskmaster, Ms Wilkins,' he mumbled, his mouth half full with a chocolate biscuit.

'That's part of my charm.'

Not from where I'm looking, Hicks thought. Below the narrow waist Nancy was really something—slim hips, mouth watering legs and buttocks you itched to pat. His wife, Lorna, would have plenty to say had she been there to see him ogling Ms Wilkins. But what the hell, where was the harm in admiring a beautiful object so long as you didn't touch it?

Alighting from the lift at the fourth floor he caught up with Nancy and thereafter walked beside her in case she twigged he had been deliberately hanging back.

'I take it you know the MoD number of the training school?' she said, and ushered him into Landon's office.

'Does it have the same area code as Petersfield?'

'It's not on the BT network.' Nancy walked round the desk, lifted the transceiver, tapped out the number on the Mozart, then checked to make sure Landon was on the phone before handing the receiver over.

'It's me, Terry,' Hicks said.

'I've got a job for you,' Landon told him. 'I think my flat is infested with bugs. In fact, I'm sure it is.'

'So where do I meet you?'

The simple direct question elicited a simple direct answer. After delivering his lecture Landon planned to catch the 1302 from Haslemere, arriving London Waterloo at 1355. Hicks was to wait for him at W. H. Smith in the centre of the concourse opposite platform 9.

'I'll be there with my kit,' Hicks told him.

'Good.' There was a brief pause, then Landon

256

said, 'I think you had better warn Lorna you may be home later than usual this evening. It could be you'll have more than one job on your hands.'

*   *   *

Some would call it moral cowardice, others would say it was only sensible of him to withhold bad news until he was able to do something about it. Ashton wasn't in the business of courting popularity and didn't care what people said behind his back. He hadn't told Hazelwood what he'd learned from Neagle earlier in the day for the simple reason that the report didn't shed any fresh light on Anwar Farid. It was only some hours later that he began to see how the potentially incriminating evidence could be used to their advantage. The trick was to catch Hazelwood when he was in a receptive mood. The opportunity to do so presented itself in the form of a draft letter to the Chairman of the JIC, which Victor had sent to him for comment.

'Well, what do you think of it, Peter?' Hazelwood asked as he entered the DG's office. 'Is there anything that needs to be rephrased?'

'No, I wouldn't change a word. The letter is succinct, firm but polite, and is written in such a way that anyone would think twice before questioning its authenticity.'

'Good. Perhaps you would be kind enough to give the draft to Dilys on your way out?'

'Right. However, there is another matter you should be aware of before I go.'

'Bad news?'

'You may think so but I believe we can use it to our advantage.'

257

Hazelwood opened the cigar box and helped himself to a Burma cheroot, then had second thoughts and put it back. There was just one stub in the brass ashtray and only the thinnest wisp of tobacco smoke eddying near the extractor fan.

'Tell me the worst,' Hazelwood said.

'It concerns Anwar Farid and a chain of furniture stores owned by Bauer & Deutsch of St Louis.' As briefly as he knew how, Ashton went on to relate what the FBI knew about Bauer & Deutsch. And, more importantly, how little the Bureau knew about Anwar Farid. To the local FBI office in St Louis the Egyptian was one of the legitimate businessmen who supplied Bauer & Deutsch with soft furnishings.

'That happy state of affairs will be unravelled by the IRS,' Ashton said in conclusion.

'And Farid will be front-page news again just when I thought he had ceased to be of interest.' Hazelwood picked up the paperknife on his desk and beat a slow cadence on the blotting pad. 'Worse still the spotlight will fall on Toby Quayle once more. And this time the media won't accept that he was a member of the International Institute of Strategic Studies who happened to be in the wrong place at the wrong time. Everything's going to come out.' Hazelwood looked up, a sour expression on his face. 'Would you mind telling me how this can possibly help us?'

'Remember when we learned Anwar Farid was known to the police as Mahmoud Hassan Soliman? He was never prosecuted for smuggling Class A drugs into the UK because someone on high leaned on the Director of Public Prosecutions. I said then MI5 had probably brought pressure to bear on the grounds there was a good chance that Farid was working for them as well as us?'

'Well?'

'Well, now I've changed my mind. I believe Jill Sheridan was behind it when she was in charge of the Mid East Department.'

'I don't believe this,' Hazelwood said angrily.

'Hear me out, Victor. I looked up Farid on MIDAS and there was very little on him. In other words I believe Jill expunged any reference to Mahmoud Hassan Soliman on the Multi-Intelligence Data Access System. It would be like her: she was hugely ambitious and ruthless in her determination to be the first woman to run the SIS. No way was Soliman going to blot her copybook.'

'I don't know, Peter. I mean she was just an assistant director at the time and as such she didn't have too much influence around Whitehall.'

'But Robin Urquhart did, still does for that matter.'

There was no need for Ashton to elaborate. Robin Urquhart was the senior of four deputy under secretaries at the Foreign and Commonwealth Office. He had a brilliant mind and was considered honourable on two counts. After sixteen years of married life, his wife, Rosalind, had left him and moved in with the junior but well-heeled partner in the biggest firm of commercial lawyers in the City.

From childhood, Rosalind had ridden to hounds. One frosty morning in November 1989 she had put her horse at a six-foot-high hedgerow by a ditch and the animal had balked. Rosalind had been thrown and, landing awkwardly, had broken two vertebrae, leaving her paralysed from the waist down. The lover had disappeared while she was still in Stoke Mandeville Hospital. Urquhart had taken her back, which in the eyes of friends and acquaintances practically made him a saint. Urquhart had taken care of Rosalind, seen to her every need and for his pains had been constantly reminded that it was her money that paid for the live-in nurse.

He had met Jill Sheridan shortly after she had been promoted to head the Mid East Department and had been very much taken with her. He had regarded her as the brightest of all the assistant directors in the SIS and had been convinced she would eventually become the Director General. He had worked behind the scenes to foster Jill's career and had become so infatuated with her that in the end, after years of bitterness, he had divorced Rosalind. It was almost inevitable that Jill would lose interest in him once he was free to marry her.

'Are you suggesting we should use Robin Urquhart in some way?' Hazelwood asked.

'Supposing he was to admit that he had used his influence to persuade the DPP not to prosecute Soliman? We'd have a powerful ally within the FCO, someone who could nip trouble in the bud if the Israel deal went pear shaped.'

'I like it,' Hazelwood said. 'I like it very much. Who would set the ball rolling?'

'I think you would have to do that,' Ashton told him.

Eighteen

Ensley looked at the notes she had made during the interview and saw no reason to revise her original opinion of the client. First impressions were often wrong but not in this instance. The client, who was arrogant, opinionated, bumptious and rude, appeared to think he was doing Jerome Sharman a favour by signing up with them. His CV had been misleading. Supposedly an Oxford man he had in fact attended Oxford Brookes University as a mature student, where he had read chemistry before switching to political studies after the first year. Subsequently he had qualified as a certified accountant.

He was thirty-seven, divorced, his wife having custody of their two children, a girl aged twelve and a boy of ten. He had moved out of the family home in Reigate eleven months before his ex had sued for divorce. He was now living in Basingstoke with his partner, a veterinary surgeon. Currently he was employed in the finance department of Hampshire county council and was responsible for fiscal control. By implication he had suggested he was only one grade lower than the chief executive of the county council. Although new to the game, Ensley thought his salary was not commensurate with the job description he had given her and she suspected he had exaggerated his importance in the scheme of things. In her opinion he also had an exaggerated idea of his worth. He saw himself as the financial director of a major company and had let it be known he wasn't interested in a job where his salary was less than £60K per annum plus a company car appropriate for his position. 'I see no point in being on your books for more than six months,' he'd said in conclusion. 'If Jerome Sharman cannot place me by then I've obviously chosen the wrong management consultants.' Amen to that, Ensley thought and then flinched as the musical chimes on her mobile broke the silence. Unzipping her shoulder bag she fished out the phone and accepted the call.

'Whereabouts are you?' Landon asked.

'I'm at Astra House in the Strand.'

'Anyone with you?'

'No, I've just finished interviewing a client.'

'OK. My flat has been spring cleaned and it was bugged. Question is, would you like us to give your place the once over?'

'I surely would.'

'Right. What time will you be home?'

Ensley calculated that with the rush hour approaching it would take her approximately twenty to twenty-five minutes to reach the office in Dover Street from the Strand. She would need to allow another ten to open a file on the latest client and clear her desk. In theory the quickest way to Mountford House in Clarendon Terrace was probably by Underground but that involved changing from the Victoria Line to the Central at Oxford Circus as well as a half-mile walk at either end. On balance she decided a cab was more convenient and added a further half hour.

'One hour from now,' she told Landon.

'Then this is what we'll do.'

On arrival at the apartment house she was to inform the doorman that she was expecting her financial advisors, Messrs Landon and Hicks, to call on her at 6.15. The doorman would undoubtedly volunteer to let her know when they arrived and it was up to her to actively discourage him from doing this.

'We don't want the eavesdropper to know you've got visitors,' Landon continued. 'Assuming you have been bugged we want him to believe the listening device had simply malfunctioned.'

'I can't hang around the lobby waiting for you guys to show up. Frank will get suspicious.'

'Who's Frank?'

'The doorman, he will probably still be on duty when you arrive.'

'No problem,' Landon said confidently. 'I'll call your mobile as soon as we arrive and you can then meet us in the lobby.'

'I could have figured that out for myself, Landon.'

'And when your phone does ring, take it into the bathroom and run the taps before you answer.'

'Yes, sir,' Ensley said and pulled a face.

'Last but not least, don't answer your landline phone should it ring.'

'You're really something, Landon,' she said, but he had already hung up.

*   *   *

Hicks examined the Ultimate Infinity Receiver he had removed from the power point by the writing desk-cum-bookcase and wrinkled his nose in disgust. It had taken him less than five minutes to find the bug, but he'd spent the next two hours going over Landon's flat with a fine-tooth comb

263

because he couldn't believe anybody who knew his job would have used such an antiquated piece of equipment. 'It's downright unprofessional,' he said aloud, 'the guy must be a bloody amateur.'

'Any idea who it might be?' Landon asked.

Hicks pursed his lips. 'It ain't MI5 that's for sure. Their gear is light years more sophisticated than this piece of junk. Mind if I ask you a personal question, boss?'

'Feel free.'

'You're not having it off with some married bint, are you?'

'I don't have suicidal tendencies. My face appears in the tabloids and that's me finished. The Service hates any kind of publicity.'

'What about the Yankee girl, could the intruder be working for her?'

It was not the sort of question Landon could answer off the cuff. The fact was he didn't entirely trust Ensley. Only this morning he'd felt she was holding something back when she had tentatively suggested that perhaps her apartment ought to be spring cleaned as well. The truth was he honestly didn't know, and admitted it to Hicks.

Landon picked up the phone, called Ashton on the BT line and related everything that had happened from the moment Ensley had left the flat to the discovery of the Ultimate Infinity Receiver.

'The intruder told my neighbour, Jonathan, he was DCI Verco, Special Branch. According to Jonathan the man was over six feet and had spiky blond hair. In short, he was nothing like the Verco I've met. I suppose there could be two DCIs—'

'I know what you are going to say,' Ashton said, cutting him short. 'So leave it with me, I'll get in

264

touch with Richard Neagle.'

'One small request, Peter. Tell Richard to stay away from Jonathan; he's an old man in his eighties and it will only worry him needlessly if Plod turns up on his doorstep. Besides, the police won't get a better description of the intruder than the one he has already given me.'

'Consider it done. What's your next move, Will?'

'Hicks and I intend to give Ms Holsinger's apartment the once over. If we find her place has also been infested I think we should encourage Verco to sink his fangs into the doorman.'

'And where does the delectable Ms Holsinger reside when she is not with you?'

'Mountford House in Clarendon Terrace off the Bayswater Road,' Landon said and hung up when he heard Ashton put the phone down. 'Time we were going, Terry.'

'Bit premature isn't it? It's not half five yet.'

'You don't see too many cabs plying for hire in this neck of the woods. We'll use my car, it's nearer than the Tube station.'

The car, a twelve-year-old Aston Martin V8 vintage model that Landon had lovingly restored to mint condition, was kept in a lock-up garage on Gloucester Road. With its souped-up engine the Aston Martin was capable of speeds in excess of a hundred and fifty. In the rush hour he was lucky to rack up ten. There was also a double yellow line outside Mountford House, which didn't help, but further down the terrace he spotted a Jaguar pulling away from the kerb and nipped into the vacant slot before anybody else could claim it. While still in the car he rang Ensley on his mobile. Her number rang out for just over thirty seconds

265

before she answered. The rushing noise in the background told him she had every tap in the bathroom going full blast.

'We've arrived,' Landon told her. 'We're parked approximately one hundred yards beyond Mountford House and will be with you in two minutes.'

'I'll meet you in the lobby then.'

'Good. Don't forget to turn off Niagara Falls.'

Before leaving Vauxhall Cross for Waterloo Station Hicks had packed the gear he needed into an attaché case. Consequently he could pass for a financial advisor working for an insurance company. But it was Ensley who stole the show, greeting Landon as though they'd never met before and shaking hands with Hicks when he introduced him.

'Ever thought of going on the stage?' Landon said after they'd entered the lift and were on their way up to the fourth floor.

'Only briefly, when I was a student.'

'Pity, the theatre lost a born actress.'

'What do you mean by that?' Ensley asked sharply.

'Take it as a compliment.'

'The hell it was.'

'Listen to me,' Landon said irritably. 'The moment we enter your apartment nobody says a word. You and I go straight to the bathroom and leave Terry to get on with the job. OK?'

'Yeah, yeah.'

'Good. You lead the way.'

Ensley alighted from the lift, turned right and walked along the corridor to the first apartment at the far end. A good deal more opulent than 25

266

Stanhope Gardens, it comprised an entrance hall, lounge, dining room, kitchen, a master bedroom with bathroom en suite, and a second smaller bedroom with a separate WC and shower. The television was on low, turned to ITV. Using sign language Hicks indicated he wanted Ensley to switch the set off before she left him to sweep the lounge. Moving past Hicks, she pressed the on/off button, then went into the master bedroom. Landon followed her inside and closed the door behind him. As he did so, Ensley turned on the taps in the bathroom.

'This is ridiculous,' she said quietly. 'Why do we have to stay cooped up in this room? Does Mr Hicks seriously believe we can't be trusted to keep our mouths shut?'

'It's standard procedure,' Landon told her. 'Nobody is allowed to see Terry at work. That rule applies equally to embassy staffs in the secure area. The ambassador himself has to leave his office when Terry arrives to sweep it clean.'

'Why the exclusion?'

'I guess it prevents careless talk. The theory is, if you were present when Hicks was doing his stuff you couldn't help taking an interest. Later there might come a time when in all innocence you recount how your office was spring cleaned, and that could get back, second or third hand, to a hostile intelligence service. The information could explain why their audio surveillance equipment was failing and enable them to improve it.' Landon smiled. 'Of course, Hicks undoubtedly gets the job done a lot faster without an audience.'

'How long did it take to spring clean your place?'

'A little over two hours.'

'Ye gods,' Ensley said and rolled her eyes. 'Two hours stuck in the bathroom. Life is never dull when you're around, Landon.'

I could say the same of you, Landon thought. She was easily the most exciting and desirable woman he'd met. Charismatic, fiery, exhilarating, amusing, poised, exuberant: a dozen adjectives came to mind, but trustworthy was not amongst them.

'Why are you looking at me like that?' Ensley demanded.

'I was just wondering how you got a job with Jerome Sharman.'

'That's easy, their head office is in Chicago.' A mocking smile appeared. 'And, no, for once Daddy didn't call in a marker. Jerome Sharman ran a full-page advert in the *Chicago Tribune*. As a result I applied to have my name included on their executive register and submitted a CV. I was subsequently interviewed and they offered me a job in their London office.'

'Just like that,' Landon said and snapped his fingers.

'I guess I must have impressed them.'

Apparently it was not unknown for Jerome Sharman to recruit staff from the names on the executive register, but for an applicant to be offered a plum job on the spot struck Landon as quite exceptional. The appointment called for a number of social skills, the ability to empathize with applicants, to put them at their ease and draw them out. Just how good Ensley was at this he discovered for himself.

'You're a bit of a recluse, Will,' she suddenly announced. 'Your private life is a closed book. Yet you know everything about me, where I was born, my lush of a mother living in California with her toyboy, my father, the hot shot lawyer, with a team of bimbos in tow, and my meteoric rise and fall as a literary agent. Whereas you . . .'

'I'm not very interesting,' Landon told her but she wouldn't allow him to get away with that feeble excuse.

'Well, all right, I was born in Weston-super-Mare, which is where my parents still live.' He had two sisters, one older than himself; the other, Charlotte, known within the family as Charlie, was the younger. She was reading chemistry up at Oxford and would sit her finals in June. Susan, the elder, was married to an accountant, lived in Chester and had three boys, aged seven, eight and ten. What else was there? Well, he enjoyed flying and had once qualified as a pilot at his own expense, but the licence had lapsed because he had been unable to put in the requisite number of hours to retain it. He had a brown belt at judo but the urge to progress further in the sport had deserted him.

'And that's it,' Landon said. 'I told you I wasn't very interesting.'

'No personal relationships then?'

'I was engaged to a newly qualified barrister in '92 but she suddenly got cold feet six months before the wedding and called it off. Shortly afterwards I was posted to the British Embassy in Lima, which spared me a lot of embarrassment.'

'No romantic attachments?'

'There have been other girlfriends, none of them serious.'

'You make it sound like a challenge,' Ensley told him with a ghost of a smile.

She was perched on the laundry basket, her back against the wall, legs outstretched and crossed at the ankle. She was wearing dark grey slacks tailored to fit her like a glove and a Prussian blue silk shirt. He had never seen her look more enticing than she did at that moment. He grasped both hands and drew Ensley to her feet, then folded his arms around her in a bear hug. Riven by a frenzy that was alien to him Landon crushed her, moulding their bodies into one. A hand pressed against his shoulder and she freed her mouth just far enough to suck air into her lungs.

'Jesus, Landon, I'm dying, I can't breathe.'

Dying or not Ensley came back for more of the same, thigh to thigh, mouth open on his, tongue darting, pelvis writhing, heralding the onset of an orgasm. A woodpecker suddenly tapping on the communicating door separated them in a split second before Hicks poked his head into the bathroom to inform Landon that he had spring cleaned the rest of the apartment.

'I don't expect to find anything in the bathroom,' Hicks said, 'but I'll wave my magic wand over it to be on the safe side. Shouldn't take more than five minutes.'

If anything, five minutes was a gross exaggeration. As Hicks had anticipated the bathroom had not been tampered with; he had, however, located an Ultimate Infinity Receiver in the lounge.

'The guy also bugged the TV as a back-up. It would of course have been rendered totally ineffective whenever the set was switched on.'

'Do you think this was the handiwork of the same man who did my flat?' Landon asked.

'He was certainly using the same electronic equipment. You'll know for sure if the doorman's description of the intruder is similar to Jonathan's.'

Landon glanced at his wristwatch. 'What time does Frank go off duty?' he asked.

'Six o'clock,' Ensley said. 'He was still here when you arrived this evening because the relief doorman was late.'

'Then I guess that's it for now.' Turning to Hicks, Landon said, 'Thanks for all your help, Terry. I'll run you home.'

'Are you sure, boss?'

'It's no trouble,' Landon assured him. Then, on the spur of the moment, he asked Ensley if she would like to come along for the ride. He did not have to ask her twice.

*   *   *

Twenty-seven days ago four people had been shot to death in Giordano's Italian restaurant and the murder team of 'B' District were no closer to making an arrest than they had been on day one. In Verco's opinion nothing he did that morning would bring the police any nearer to getting a result. For the life of him he couldn't see the connection between the multiple homicides and the bugging of two apartments by an intruder masquerading as himself. Of course, it gave him a personal motive to run the man down, but the only common denominator linking the two crimes was the fact that Quayle had been a serving officer in the SIS and Landon still was. Nevertheless, the two crimes were unrelated. Neagle had said as much that morning but he'd still asked him to investigate

Landon's allegation. Sometimes he thought MI5 was being run by those people across the river at Vauxhall Cross.

The doorman was on the phone when Verco entered Mountford House and walked over to the desk. As he drew nearer, the doorman turned about and continued a private conversation with someone called Rod. Verco waited patiently for him to finish for a good two minutes before he reached for the phone and depressed the cradle, thereby terminating the call.

'We've met before,' Verco growled as the doorman swung round to face him, his eyes narrowing in anger. 'Detective Chief Inspector Verco,' he added.

'I don't remember you.'

'It was a week ago today. I was at least six feet tall then, well built and had blond hair cut very short so that it stood up like the bristles on a scrubbing brush.'

'What is this?'

'You gave me the key to Miss Holsinger's apartment. Number 410 as I recall.'

The doorman's eyes were wide open now and the anger he'd shown earlier had dissipated. Instead he looked apprehensive. 'What is this?' he repeated.

'It's Frank, isn't it?'

The doorman nodded, unable to find his voice.

'The man you dealt with last week was an impostor. If you don't believe me, this is my warrant card.'

'He had one just like that,' Frank said. 'And a form he said was from the Home Office authorizing him to bug Miss Holsinger's apartment. He used a more technical expression—I think it

272

was electronic surveillance. Anyway, I asked him what she had done and he said it wasn't for me to know.'

From the jargon the impostor had spouted at the doorman, Verco reckoned the man was a professional eavesdropper. It could be he had a military background.

'Any idea what time he arrived, Frank?'

'I was sorting the second delivery when he walked in.'

'Around noon then?'

'No, it was earlier than that, Mr Verco. The second delivery arrives mid-morning in this part of town, wouldn't have been later than eleven fifteen.'

Timewise it didn't add up. Neagle had told him that Landon's eighty-two-year-old neighbour had seen the impostor leaving Landon's flat at approximately 11 a.m. Nobody could be in two different places at the same time. Either there had been two impostors or one of the witnesses who'd met him face to face had got the time wrong.

'This impostor,' Verco said. 'Do you agree with my description of him?'

'Yes, I do.'

'Well, is there anything you'd like to add?'

The doorman pinched the bridge of his nose between his finger and thumb. 'Well, yes, he had a cleft chin.'

'Thank you Frank, you've been very helpful.'

'What about the bugs in Miss Holsinger's apartment?'

'Oh, they were removed yesterday evening.'

'Well, I'll be damned,' Frank said in a hollow voice. 'She told me they were her financial advisors.'

273

'Yeah, it's amazing the lies people tell.' Verco cleared his throat. 'Is there somewhere private where I can phone my guvnor?'

'The janitor's office,' Frank said and pointed to the door behind him. 'He phoned in sick this morning.'

Verco borrowed the telephone as well as the office to call Neagle at Thames House. As succinctly as possible he told him what he'd learned from the doorman.

'The times don't fit,' Verco said in conclusion. 'Either Jonathan or the doorman at Mountford House is mistaken. I know Landon doesn't want to bother the old man but he is more likely to have lost account of time and just whose residence was bugged first could be significant.'

'You mean to question Jonathan?' Neagle asked.

'Yes, very gently,' Verco told him and hung up.

*   *   *

The latest offering from Head of Station, Islamabad had been received far too late for the content to be divulged at morning prayers. After reading the signal a second time Calthorpe couldn't see that it contained anything so urgent that he should walk it along the corridor to Hazelwood. The facts were simple enough; thirteen days after the body of Laura Jenner had been found in Mohammed Ali Jinnah Park on the outskirts of Peshawar the police had discovered the dismembered remains of her husband. Keith Jenner had been interred in a shallow grave dug in the basement of an abandoned tailor's shop on Jinnah Street in Peshawar City. What amazed

274

Calthorpe was the length of time it had taken the police to find the body, considering how often that neighbourhood had been searched. According to the Head of Station, who had seen the basement for himself, it was immediately apparent that Keith Jenner had been executed at the burial site. In attempting to expunge the bloodstains on the floor and walls the murderers had only succeeded in drawing attention to their crime.

It was already known that Laura Jenner had been present when her husband had been executed on camera. Her voice had been captured on the final videotape mailed to the British High Commission in Islamabad. Snatches of what she had said to Keith Jenner in the last few minutes of his life had been enhanced by Terry Hicks and subsequently identified by a number of diplomats at the High Commission who had known her. Now evidence had been found suggesting that she, too, had been murdered at the tailor's shop. Buried in the shallow grave were remnants of an ivory coloured satin nightdress.

There had been one other development. Seyed Sikander Zia, Brigadier, General Staff (Intelligence) at Headquarters, Northern Command had been taken into custody. The brigadier was only one of a number of senior officers who had been arrested in what *Azad*, the daily Urdu newspaper published in Lahore and Karachi, had described as a crackdown on the fundamentalist Jamaat-e-Islami movement. Calthorpe believed the brigadier had been implicated by his subordinate Major Jamal Haroon, who had been arrested a fortnight ago. There was a limit to how much pain a man could stand before he betrayed a comrade and it was

275

known that Jamal Haroon had undergone rigorous interrogation from the day he had been arrested. Counter-terrorist operations were not for the squeamish, and if what had been done to Haroon eventually led to the arrest of Ali Mohammed Khalef, Calthorpe imagined not too many people at Vauxhall Cross would care how it was effected.

*　　　*　　　*

Landon had never been a clock-watcher before today. Ever since an ebullient Richard Neagle had phoned him shortly before one o'clock he had been willing the time away. 'Guess what,' Neagle had said. 'British Summer Time wrong-footed your neighbour Jonathan. He altered all the clocks in his flat with the exception of the one in the hall. That was still running an hour slow when Verco called on him this morning.' There had been no need for Neagle to spell it out for him, he was quite capable of drawing the right conclusion for himself. When Jonathan had bumped into the impostor on his return from the local supermarket, he'd taken the time from the clock in the hallway. Consequently, this meant it was 12 noon and not 11 a.m. when he'd seen the bogus DCI Verco.

Normal office hours for the support staff were nine to five thirty, Monday to Friday, but few of the clerks, typists and translators observed them, much to the anguish of the Civil Service Union. Nevertheless, Landon rang Ensley on her mobile half an hour before the official exodus began and arranged to meet her at Mountford House. Never had time dragged quite so much as it did during that thirty minutes; conversely the tube journey

276

across town to change on to the Central Line at Oxford Circus passed all too quickly. By the time he alighted at Marble Arch and started walking towards Clarendon Terrace Landon wished he hadn't called Ensley and had simply allowed things to slide.

Frank was no longer on duty when he entered the lobby. Approaching the desk he asked the relief doorman to phone Miss Holsinger in 410 and inform her that Mr Landon had arrived. A premonition that things were about to go pear shaped took hold before Ensley arrived to collect him.

'Where are we going tonight, Will?' she asked.

'Nowhere. There are things we need to discuss.'

'Sounds ominous,' Ensley said flippantly and pressed the button for the fourth floor.

Nothing more was said. From the moment he had left Vauxhall Cross Landon had thought of nothing else but how he proposed to tackle the American girl. He was still undecided when she opened the door to her apartment and he followed her into the lounge.

'So what's this all about, Will?'

'DCI Verco had a word with Frank this morning and his description of the intruder matched the one given by Jonathan.'

'No surprise there then. You were expecting as much last night when Terry Hicks found the impostor had used the same sort of gadget to bug this place.' Ensley crouched in front of a drinks cabinet. 'What'll you have?' she asked.

'Nothing for me, thanks.'

'Suit yourself. I'm for a Jack Daniels.'

'The curious thing is the impostor was in two

277

different places at eleven a.m.,' Landon said, feeling his way.

'There's an obvious explanation for that, Will. Either Frank or Jonathan was mistaken.'

Ensley still had her back to him but if her voice was anything to go by it seemed to Landon she was completely unfazed. 'Jonathan was mistaken, he forgot to advance the clock in his hall by one hour for British Summer Time.'

'I need some ice,' Ensley said and disappeared into the kitchen.

'Why do you suppose your place was bugged before mine?'

'I haven't the faintest idea, Will.' Ensley held the ice tray under the hot water tap until she was able to break off half a dozen cubes. 'Perhaps for him Clarendon Terrace was on the way to Stanhope Gardens?'

'Can I trust you?' Landon asked quietly.

'WHAT!' She spat the word out, angry and incredulous at the same time, but he was sure it was just a class act.

'Why don't you look at me? What are you hiding?'

Ensley swung round to face him, her eyes glinting. 'I think you had better come clean, Mr Landon, and tell me what goes on in that mind of yours.'

'Why would anyone want to bug your apartment? That's something I can't figure, unless it was a back-up.' He watched Ensley closely and saw in her eyes that he was on the right track. 'A fallback in case you failed to deliver. Who's on your back, Ensley?'

The answer was a long time in coming but it was

worth the wait. 'Virgil Zimmerman,' she said faintly. The rest came staccato fashion, in short bursts punctuated by frequent breaks, as if she needed to give some thought to what she was going to say next. 'He's a CIA officer at the American Embassy. He sent for me on the Thursday before Easter—wanted to know if I was a patriot and then invited me to spy on you. He said international terrorism was America's number one priority and the CIA had reason to believe you people were withholding information. He came to see me last Wednesday when I was interviewing applicants at Astra House. He'd made an appointment under an assumed name. He wanted to know why he hadn't heard from me when I'd spent the whole of Easter with you. I had to repeat the two goddamned phone numbers he'd given me.'

'One was obviously the office,' Landon mused. 'The other being his home number?'

'I guess,' Ensley said miserably.

'OK. Give me his home number.'

'What!'

'I already know the office one,' Landon said calmly.

'Are you serious?'

'Never more so.'

'Too bad, you'll get nothing from me.'

'There's a close relationship between the two intelligence agencies,' Landon told her, 'and Zimmerman doesn't feature in the list of CIA personnel in London supplied by the station chief. This means Zimmerman is operating under cover in the UK.'

'You're not listening to me, Landon.'

'Virgil Zimmerman is engaged in criminal

279

activity; he hired somebody to break into my flat.'

'Where's your proof?'

'Special Branch will find the impostor and he'll talk. You can bet on it.'

'Good. In the meantime I'll not betray my country.'

'You don't know how pompous you sound,' Landon told her.

'I'd like you to go,' Ensley said with quiet dignity.

'Sure. There's nothing here for me.' Landon paused on his way out of the kitchen and looked back. 'For the record,' he said, 'Zimmerman is not worthy of your loyalty.'

Nineteen

Every government ministry in Whitehall had its own security organization. The department which looked after the Foreign and Commonwealth Office was situated in a quiet backwater off Storey's Gate, a bare ten-minute walk from Downing Street. Located in what resembled a four-storey Edwardian house fronted by an impressive wrought-iron gate and railings, the property deserved a grander name than number 4 Central Buildings. It was, however, an appropriate venue for the Chairman of the Joint Intelligence Committee to conduct an inquiry into the activities of the SIS in the Beaconsfield area during the evening of Tuesday 6th April.

Ashton had been a frequent visitor to number 4 Central Buildings back in the days when he had been on the Russian desk. At the height of the

Cold War he had played a leading role in the debriefing of officers in the Diplomatic Service, defence attachés and support staff on their return from Moscow. As for Ralph Meacher, he had practically taken up residence in the Edwardian building, but, to the best of Ashton's knowledge, today was the first occasion Hazelwood had set foot in the place.

They had been subpoenaed to attend the inquiry at different times: Victor at nine fifteen, himself one hour later, followed by Ralph Meacher at a quarter past eleven. Allowing a mere sixty minutes in which to cross-examine the DG was, in Ashton's opinion, unduly optimistic. He was therefore not surprised to find that Hazelwood was still giving evidence when he arrived. An usher met Ashton at the reception counter and escorted him to the ancient lift that whirred and clanked its way to the fourth floor, where the inquiry was sitting. A second usher steered Ashton into a small office that had been set aside as a waiting room. The desk, swivel chair and three-drawer filing cabinet had been moved out into the corridor to make room for two armchairs and a round pedestal table. This was covered with back numbers of *Field*, *Country Life*, *Punch*, the *Spectator*, the *Economist* and the *New Statesman*, the most recent of which was two months old. While waiting to appear before the Chairman, Ashton decided reading the Christmas number of *Country Life* was better than doing nothing. At twenty-five minutes to one, almost two and a half hours later than the appointed time, the Chairman of the Joint Intelligence Committee finally sent for him. Although Ashton had neither seen nor heard

Hazelwood leave, there was no sign of the DG.

There had been no convening order setting out the terms of reference and composition of the Board of Inquiry. All Ashton had seen was a copy of the letter the Permanent Under Secretary of State and Head of Her Majesty's Diplomatic Service had sent to the Chairman of the Joint Intelligence Committee. It was, therefore, something of a shock to find that the Foreign and Commonwealth Office was represented by Robin Urquhart, the Senior Deputy Under Secretary. The board was assisted by a shorthand writer and a court orderly. There was nothing informal about the proceedings: once Ashton had identified himself to the chairman, the court orderly thrust a bible into his left hand, told him to raise his right and then swore him in.

'My name is Gavin Pearce,' the chairman informed him. 'I understand you already know Mr Urquhart?'

Ashton smiled at the Foreign Office man. 'Good morning, Robin,' he said cheerfully and got a brief nod in return.

Ashton supposed he shouldn't be too surprised by the underlying antagonism Urquhart had shown him. After all, he was the man who, in May 1997, had gone to Jill Sheridan's house in Highgate and invited her to sign a letter of resignation, allegedly on the grounds of her ill health. Jill Sheridan had, in fact, sailed too close to the wind once too often and the letter had been a face-saving ploy to spare her the embarrassment of being dismissed with all the attendant publicity that that was bound to attract. But in Urquhart's eyes Ashton was responsible for destroying her career in the SIS and ultimately doing irreparable harm to the relationship he'd enjoyed with her. The truth was, Jill had dropped Urquhart because there was nothing he could do for her after she had left the Firm.

'Do you understand the purpose of this inquiry?' Pearce asked. 'Or would you like me to repeat the directive I've received from the Permanent Under Secretary?'

Ashton hadn't heard a word but he wasn't about to admit it. 'Thank you, but that won't be necessary,' he said.

'Good. We have been told that you were in charge of the illegal operation conducted in the Beaconsfield area on Tuesday the sixth of April. Is that correct, Mr Ashton?'

'I was in charge of the operation; there was nothing illegal about it,' Ashton told him with controlled anger.

'Did the Thames Valley Police receive any forewarning of the operation?'

'No, there was no time to liaise with them.'

'Sir Victor has stated that you were engaged in a counter-terrorist operation. This being the case, should you not have informed MI5?' Pearce allowed himself a brief smile that conveyed all the warmth of an Arctic winter. 'After all, the Security Service did establish CATO for that very purpose.'

'You're mistaken. The Combined Anti-Terrorist Organization was conceived by Jill Sheridan, as Mr Urquhart will confirm. MI5 implemented the proposal following a bout of the political in-fighting that Whitehall indulges in from time to time.'

'MI5 was not informed. Correct?'

'Absolutely, and for the same reason Thames Valley wasn't.'

'And this alleged lack of time is presumably the reason why the FCO was not briefed,' Urquhart said coldly.

'I'm afraid it is.'

'Perhaps you would care to explain how the lack of time arose?' Pearce suggested.

'Certainly. A friendly source contacted Ralph Meacher at 0700 hours on Tuesday morning stating he knew the present whereabouts of Talal Asir and Ali Mohammed Khalef, numbers one and two on our most wanted list. Time was at a premium for two reasons. Talal Asir and Ali Mohammed Khalef have so far evaded arrest because they never spend four nights running under the same roof. Secondly, the source was in this country for less than twenty-four hours and had specified the meeting had to take place outside London. In fact, the RV was chosen by the source. So we had to move fast to obtain the information and act on it.'

The story contained several grains of truth: Levy had phoned Meacher a few minutes after seven o'clock on the Tuesday morning, the RV had ultimately been chosen by David Ben-Yosef and for security considerations the SIS had decided the RV had to be outside the London area. The rest was a complete fabrication put together by Hazelwood, Meacher and himself. Provided they all adhered to the same story nothing would come of the fact that he had committed perjury.

'And the identity of this elusive source?' Pearce enquired sarcastically.

'A Saudi businessman not connected with the embassy. He is, however, related to the ruling

284

family.'

'And you are not prepared to reveal his name?'

'Damned right I'm not.'

Ashton didn't bother to elaborate. Hazelwood would have reminded Urquhart what had happened after *Death of a Princess* had been screened. Had he repeated that argument, Pearce would have known that before testifying he and Victor had conspired together. Collusion had been the name of the game.

'We have been given to understand that your source was David Ben-Yosef, Head of Station in London,' Pearce said, almost purring like a cat. 'What do you say to that?'

'It's a load of bollocks,' Ashton said and laughed. 'Who gave you that cock and bull story?'

'Ben-Yosef was invited to a drinks party given by Mr and Mrs Bernard Greene at their house in Kenton Lane. He arrived at six thirty and was among the last to leave at nine fifteen, which is not like him. In between time Ben-Yosef sneaked out of the house to meet you at a prearranged RV.'

'And where was that?' Ashton enquired icily.

'Why ask when you know very well where it was.'

'Humour me.'

'Beaconsfield,' Pearce said and avoided his gaze.

'Whereabouts in Beaconsfield?'

'I've had enough of this nonsense.'

'So have I, Mr Pearce. I'm aware Ben-Yosef is looked after by either the Diplomatic Protection Group or Special Branch. Unless they were completely incompetent his minders would have shadowed him to Kenton Lane. And if he had sneaked away from the party, they would have followed him. Right?'

'It's gone one o'clock. I suggest we adjourn for lunch and reconvene at two fifteen.'

'I agree,' Urquhart said mildly.

'We can wrap this farce up in five minutes,' Ashton told them. 'The fact is the police didn't follow Ben-Yosef anywhere after they had escorted him to Kenton Lane. He isn't a great one for socializing at parties but that night he stayed on to the bitter end. Since this was so unusual the police assumed he must have slipped away for a couple of hours. And on the strength of a complaint from Superintendent Oakham, whose nose is out of joint, the Home Office put two and two together and managed to make five.'

'What role was assigned to Messrs Landon and Neighbour on the sixth of April?'

The question rocked Ashton. Only Victor Hazelwood, Ralph Meacher and himself had been subpoenaed to attend the inquiry. Will Landon had declined to give Oakham his real name and Chris Neighbour's involvement was not known to the police or the Permanent Under Secretary of State and Head of HM's Diplomatic Service. That being the case there were grounds for thinking Hazelwood had talked out of turn.

'Their role?' Ashton said, recovering quickly. 'Well that's easy. The Saudi demanded total secrecy. Landon and Neighbour were there to ensure the press didn't join the party.'

'How were you going to do that?' Urquhart's scepticism was apparent in every inflection of his voice.

'They were waiting for the Saudi outside Beaconsfield. As he drove past their position, Neighbour tucked in behind him and was followed

286

by Landon. As they entered the built-up area, Landon and Neighbour slowed right down to a crawl, the aim being to create a logjam. This was to enable our Saudi friend to lose the media circus and drive on to the RV.' Ashton shrugged his shoulders. 'Personally, I didn't see how the press would learn about the meeting when our Saudi was only spending twenty-four hours in the UK. But he laid down certain conditions and we had to humour him.'

'Was your meeting worthwhile?' Urquhart enquired silkily.

'The answer is yes in the long term.' Ashton looked from one man to the other. 'Do you need me any more?' he asked.

'Only to sign your statement,' Pearce told him.

Ashton said he presumed the statement would be sent to Vauxhall Cross for his signature, a cool assumption Pearce didn't contradict, possibly because he was somewhat flabbergasted. However, things didn't go all Ashton's way. The presence of the court orderly who escorted him to the lift meant he couldn't go looking for Meacher. He just hoped Ralph would not be caught cold when asked what role had been assigned to Landon and Neighbour.

*   *   *

Offhand, Landon could not recall a previous occasion when he had been summoned to the DG's office. Although Dilys Crowther hadn't said why Hazelwood wanted to see him he was sure it wasn't for a career assessment. Or was it? Right now, thanks to him, Ashton and Meacher were being

287

interrogated by the Chairman of the Joint Intelligence Committee. Ashton had repeatedly said he wasn't to blame, that encountering a cretin like Mr Porteous of Luxton Avenue had been sheer bad luck. While that might be true, he could have handled Superintendent Oakham better. He should have recognized the superintendent was rank-conscious and quick to take offence if he wasn't treated with respect. So, OK, Oakham had rubbed him up the wrong way but he should have been big enough to shrug that off. What would it have cost him to have massaged his ego and taken the man into his confidence? Had he done so, chances were Oakham wouldn't have written a letter of complaint to the assistant chief constable in charge of operations.

Alighting from the lift at the top floor Landon walked slowly down the corridor to the PA's office. Thames Valley Police weren't the only people he had tangled with. Four weeks ago tomorrow, he and Hicks had been arrested for breaking into 3 Mews Terrace. That particular fracas was certainly down to him and the DG had had to really get his coat off in order to save their hides. No matter which way you looked at it he had committed two sackable offences in a month. Correction, three sackable offences. He had taken up with Ensley Holsinger again in the full knowledge she wasn't to be trusted. And what had been the end result? His flat had been bugged. Who was going to believe he hadn't committed a breach of security by letting something slip in an unguarded moment? He was for the chop, no two ways about it. The only thing which made him think he was perhaps being a trifle pessimistic was the smile Dilys Crowther bestowed on him. It was a friendly smile rather than a sympathetic one.

'Do go in, Mr Landon,' Dilys said, rewarding him with another. 'Sir Victor is expecting you.'

Landon opened the communicating door and, bracing himself, walked into the lion's den, still expecting to have his head bitten off. He could not have been more mistaken.

'Sit down, Will,' Hazelwood said warmly. 'How well do you know Robin Urquhart?'

'I've never met him, Director. Of course I know something of his background.'

'Such as?'

'He left Cambridge with a double first in Modern Languages and Politics, Philosophy and Economics. He met his wife in Berlin. By all accounts she was an unpleasant woman.'

'Don't mince words,' Hazelwood told him. 'The woman was a first-class bitch and Robin is well shot of her.'

'So I understand, Director.'

'Well, go on, what else do you know about him?'

'He was very keen on Jill Sheridan.'

'Keen isn't the word,' Hazelwood growled. 'He was besotted with Jill, did everything in his power to further her career.'

Landon sensed Hazelwood had a lot more to say on that subject but the Mozart phone interrupted him and he broke off to answer it. Cupping a hand over the mouthpiece he told Landon to stay where he was.

It was said of the DG that he had a soft spot for the forces. The evidence was there for anyone to see from the cut-down brass shell case on his desk to the signed prints on the walls. The three services were represented by Terence Cuneo's *The Bridge at Arnhem*, a battered-looking corvette on a storm-tossed Atlantic entitled *Convoy Escort* and *Enemy Coast Ahead*, which depicted a vic of three Wellington bombers on a moonlit night approaching a smudge of land on the horizon. There was also a personal connection for Hazelwood. His father, a wartime officer in the Queens, had been killed in action at Salerno in 1943 when he was only six years old.

Landon was also aware that Hazelwood himself had been called up for National Service in 1955 and had joined the Parachute Regiment after completing basic infantry training at the depot of the Royal West Kents. Less than twelve months after being conscripted into the army he had been commissioned into his father's old regiment, after being awarded the sword of honour at the passing-out parade from the officer cadet training unit at Eaton Hall. By pulling a few strings he had managed to join the 2nd Battalion of the Paras and had seen active service in Cyprus. He would have taken part in the Suez operation had he not broken his right leg and ankle in a practice jump.

That injury had in fact pointed Hazelwood in the direction of his future career. Medically downgraded as a result of his injuries, he had been sent on a six-month course at the School of Military Intelligence. He had expected to hate every minute but had come away completely enthralled and knowing exactly what he wanted to do in life. After demobilization he had studied Russian at London University and in due course had applied to join the Foreign Office.

Hazelwood put the phone down, plucked a beige-coloured folder from the top of the files in the pending tray and pushed it across the desk at Landon.

'This will give you a much more detailed picture of Robin Urquhart's private life and how it impinged on his career.'

Landon had no idea why he had been given the folder and merely nodded dumbly.

'The folder also contains a photocopy of the enclosures on BM/05/ME/Cairo,' Hazelwood continued. 'The branch memorandum concerns two complaints of sexual assault by Anwar Farid. The victim was Louise Appleton, the cultural attaché at the British Embassy in Cairo from September 1994 to July 1995.'

'I don't understand,' Landon began.

'It's really very simple, Will. Jill Sheridan received the original document from Robin Urquhart around the time Anwar Farid was caught smuggling Class A drugs into the UK. He was charged with possession with intent to supply and was remanded in police custody. It never came to court because Urquhart leaned on the Director of Public Prosecutions.'

'Why did he do that?' Landon heard himself ask.

'Jill Sheridan had only just been appointed to head the Mid East Department and he didn't want to see her go down for something that wasn't her responsibility. He was also very enamoured of her.'

'Why do I need to know all this, Director?'

'Well, you are going to interview him, Will.'

Landon sat there transfixed by what Hazelwood was telling him. Robin Urquhart had been very badly treated by Jill Sheridan and there were reasons for thinking that, possibly out of spite, he

291

was prepared to admit he had brought undue influence to bear on the DPP on her behalf. If he did, it would solve all kinds of problems, of which limiting the scope of the investigation into the incident at Beaconsfield by the chairman of the Joint Intelligence Committee was but one example.

'Robin has a cottage on the outskirts of Longstock,' Hazelwood continued. 'It's a small hamlet about two miles from Stockbridge and the cottage is called Wyvern. Now that spring has officially arrived Urquhart spends every weekend there, acting the part of the country gentleman— long walks in the fresh air, fishing for trout in the River Test. That sort of thing. If he doesn't change his mind, you'll go down to meet him at the cottage at eight p.m. this coming Friday.'

'And if he should change his mind at the last minute?'

'You will be informed in good time, Will.' Hazelwood smiled. 'Any other questions?'

'Not at the moment.'

'Good. One last point: I want that document you're holding to be returned to me personally by close of play this evening.'

There was one final stipulation that Landon found particularly disturbing. On no account was he to mention his assignment to anyone.

*   *   *

Since the pay branch formed part of the Admin Wing, Hugo Calthorpe decided that, as a matter of common courtesy, he should tell Roy Kelso why he needed to seek advice from the officer in charge.

'You want to buy gold.' Kelso fingered his upper

292

lip as if to draw attention to the moustache he was endeavouring to grow, even though it was practically invisible to most of his peer group. 'Well, I'm afraid Ken is away on holiday in South Africa. However, I'm sure I can help you. What are we talking about, gold coins or ingots?'

'Coins. They will be easier to distribute.'

'Quite so. As you probably know gold ceased to circulate during the First World War and consequently controls on buying, selling and holding gold coins have been imposed at various times. However, under the Exchange Control Order of 1979 gold coins may be imported and exported without restriction, with one exception. Any coins which are more than fifty years old or in total are valued at in excess of eight thousand pounds cannot be exported without specific authorization from the Department of Trade and Industry. You'll have to pay VAT, though I hear this will be revoked next year.'

'I can't wait that long, Roy,' Calthorpe said.

'How much do you want?'

'Forty thousand.'

'Gold coins come in denominations of one hundred pounds, fifty, twenty-five, ten, five, two, sovereign and a half sovereign.' Kelso smirked. 'That's fifty pence in today's money.'

'I'll take forty thousand in sovereigns. The clients would view the larger denominations with the utmost suspicion.'

Kelso gawped at him, mouth open to form a near perfect circle. 'Dear God, the coins will weigh several hundred pounds. How do you propose to send them?'

'By air freight.' Calthorpe edged towards the

door. 'I've no idea how long it will take you to acquire forty thousand gold sovereigns but I'm going to need them by the weekend.'

'That might not be too easy. It will have to be done in secrecy and those special arrangements take time.'

'Then perhaps you had better start now, Roy,' Calthorpe said and backed out into the corridor before Kelso had a chance to tell him just what this would entail.

Calthorpe retraced his steps and was about to enter his own office when he saw Ashton appear from the direction of the lifts. Before and after lunch he had phoned him no less than four times and every call had gone unanswered. Now it looked as if Ashton was making for the DG's office and there was no telling when he would reappear.

'Peter.' Calthorpe raised his voice and called him again as he hurried after him. 'Can you spare me a couple of minutes? I need your advice.'

Ashton stopped and turned about, clutching a polystyrene cup in his left hand. 'Of course I can. What's the problem?'

'Is there somewhere private where we can talk?'

Ashton raised an eyebrow. 'What's wrong with my office?'

'Nothing. I thought you were about to see Victor.'

'Not this afternoon.'

Terse almost to the point of being hostile, that was Ashton. Calthorpe wondered what had happened to upset him.

'So what's on your mind?' Ashton said, waving him to a chair.

'Well, to put it in a nutshell, are you offering a reward for information leading to the arrest of Ali

294

Mohammed Khalef?'

'Me!' Ashton exploded. 'Who gave you that idea?'

'Nobody. I just thought you would know, because Landon is a member of the Combined Anti-Terrorist Organization. Obviously I have caught you at a bad time, Peter—'

'I'm sorry, please don't go, Hugo. I realize it's no excuse but things didn't go well at the inquiry. Matter of fact I've spent the last two hours stomping around Green Park trying to decide whether or not it's time I made a career change.'

'And what's the decision?'

'The jury is still out. On another matter, we have, in fact, offered half a million for Talal Asir and Ali Mohammed Khalef dead or alive.'

'Is any of the money going to Pakistan?'

Ashton leaned back in the chair, and clasped both hands behind his neck. 'Suppose you tell me why you are interested.'

'Late this morning I received a letter from our Head of Station, Islamabad. The Pakistani government is fed up with the Taliban infiltrating the tribal areas. They are going to send the army in to clear them out and restore the authority of the political agents in the federally administered tribal areas. It's been suggested to the Head of Station that we might like to divvy up forty thousand in gold sovereigns. The political agents would spread the gold around the tribal leaders with the promise of more to come if they produce Khalef.'

'You go right ahead, Hugo. Not one penny of our half million is going to Pakistan.'

'Thank you, Peter. That's all I wanted to know.'

'Is it OK for Landon to mention this at the next

meeting of CATO?' Ashton smiled. 'You never know, MI5 might ante up some of the dosh.'

It all sounded a little too mercenary for Calthorpe's liking but that didn't mean he would turn up his nose should the Security Service make him an offer of financial support.

Twenty

The more Landon thought about the tête-à-tête he was due to have with Robin Urquhart the more disturbing he found the prospect. What Hazelwood wanted him to do was akin to blackmail; the very fact the Director had ordered him not to discuss the assignment with anyone suggested he knew full well they were skating on very thin ice. With midday approaching the possibility that Urquhart would either forego his usual weekend in the country or refuse to see him was becoming remoter by the hour. Landon promised himself that if there had been no word from Hazelwood by twelve noon he would brief Ashton. So, OK, he would be ignoring the instructions he had received. But Ashton was closer to Hazelwood than anyone else and if the DG went down he would take Peter with him. In the circumstances he had a right to know what was going on.

The decision made, Landon couldn't see the point of waiting a further eighteen minutes, until it was twelve noon. It was a bit like going to the dentist: once you realized there was a bad tooth that had to be extracted, nothing was gained by being dilatory about it. He lifted the receiver on the BT phone, tapped out Ashton's number to see if he was free and got no answer. He tried again five minutes later with the same result. As he put the phone down a second time, Nancy Wilkins entered the office and placed two thick files in the in-tray.

'Where did they come from?' Landon asked.

'The top one is from Chris Neighbour, the other has been minuted to you by the Pakistan desk. No action is required on either file, though you may wish to make a few notes for the next CATO meeting.'

'Is that what you recommend, Nancy?' Landon said, teasing her.

'I took the liberty of sidelining the more interesting paragraphs in pencil. It might save you a bit of time.'

'Well, thank you, Nancy.'

Landon removed the top file from the in-tray and read the latest enclosure, which happened to have been originated by George Elphinstone, Head of Station, Moscow. The intelligence summary contained the final list of casualties from the bombing of the British Council offices in Ekaterinburg, Moscow and St Petersburg. In total 624 men, women and children had been killed and a further 1672 had been injured. The dead and injured included some twenty-six locally employed personnel and five Britons, of whom two had been killed.

In an earlier report Sergei Stepashin, chief of the FSB, had been adamant that, although Muslims, the Chechen suicide bombers had nothing to do with Islamic Jihad. According to George Elphinstone, the Head of the Federal Security Service had modified his previous opinion. While still maintaining the attacks had been planned and executed by Chechens with the aim of killing Russians, Stepashin was now of the opinion heavier casualties would have been inflicted had the insurgents targeted the more crowd-drawing landmarks. As examples he had quoted the Hermitage and the Nevsky Prospekt shopping centre, both situated in St Petersburg. In Chris Neighbour's assessment Sergei Stepashin appeared to infer that while the Chechens had not changed their primary aim, they had gone out of their way to hit those centres where there was a British presence. Nobody imagined they had done that purely out of brotherly love.

The file marked up for Landon's attention by the Pakistan desk contained a brief note from Hugo Calthorpe. Referring to the previous folio, Calthorpe stated he was in the process of sending forty thousand pounds in gold sovereigns to the Head of Station, Islamabad, for distribution to the political agents administering the tribal areas. The money would be a reward for information leading to the capture of Ali Mohammed Khalef.

Landon initialled both files and transferred them to the out-tray, then tried Ashton's number again and was third time lucky.

'This is very embarrassing,' Landon said, 'but I need to see you in private.'

'How private is private?'

'Anywhere but the top floor.'

'I see. It's like that, is it?'

'I'm afraid it is,' Landon said, colouring still more.

'Then I'll be right down,' Ashton told him and hung up.

Less than three minutes later Peter walked into his office. It seemed twice as long to Landon.

'So what's this all about, Will?' he asked.

'I'm seeing Robin Urquhart this evening, eight o'clock at his cottage outside Longstock. The name of the game is blackmail.'

'What the hell are you talking about?'

Landon started again, right from the beginning when Hazelwood had sent for him. He told Ashton about the branch memorandum on Anwar Farid and how he had been given photocopies of the enclosures to study together with a background briefing on Robin Urquhart's career and personal life.

'I was instructed to return all the documents to the DG by close of play yesterday evening. When I did as he'd asked, I was given a photocopy of a letter Jill Sheridan had written to a Mr Alvin Dombas at the Zenith Corporation in New York.'

'That's a dummy corporation set up by the CIA,' Ashton said.

'So I've been told. Anyway, she was staying at the Shakespeare Hotel in downtown Manhattan.'

'Have you still got the letter?' Ashton asked.

'Sure.' Landon got up, walked over to the safe and returned with four sheets of headed notepaper. One was a photocopy of an envelope postmarked in Manhattan and addressed to Alvin Dombas, Zenith Corporation, 127 Battery Place, NY 10006. The other sheets comprised the letter Jill had sent to him shortly after she had arrived in New York.

'That's Jill's handwriting all right,' Ashton said.

'No chance it could be a forgery?'

'No, it's her style, the way she expresses herself, I'd know it anywhere. We were engaged once, lived in Surbiton. The original letter and envelope must be on Jill's security file and you can bet that that particular document has now joined the other seven which are held in perpetuity.'

Normally an officer's security file was destroyed when he or she had reached the age of sixty-six. Even if death had occurred prior to that the document was still retained until the deceased had reached the theoretical age of sixty-six. There were, however, exceptions to every rule and, including Jill's, there were now eight files that would be retained for all time because of their content. They were held in a twin combination safe positioned in the strongroom next to the office occupied by Roger Benton, Head of the Pacific Basin and Rest of the World Department. To Ashton's knowledge both combinations were routinely changed every six months by Hazelwood and Rowan Garfield, the Deputy DG. A slip of paper bearing the combination sequence was then sealed in an envelope with a red star label across the flap. A signature from the appropriate officer covering both the label and the flap was a further security measure.

Benton was the third man in the trinity; Hazelwood knew the first combination, Garfield the second, Benton wasn't aware of either sequence of numbers. The beauty of the arrangement lay in the fact that neither the DG nor his deputy could make use of the knowledge without obtaining the key to the strongroom from the head of the Pacific Basin and Rest of the World Department. This entailed signing for the key and recording why they needed to get into the strongroom.

'We slipped up,' Ashton said. 'We should have put a tail on Jill when we demanded her resignation. Cunning little minx admits she went straight to the CIA Head of Station in London, told him she was off to America shortly and had certain Humint material she wished to share with the CIA concerning Mid East terrorist groups.'

Jill's letter to Dombas had also made it clear that she was uniquely qualified to disclose the FCO's strategy regarding the Middle East thanks to her intimate friendship with Robin Urquhart.

'The DG is convinced that what Jill had written about her former lover will persuade Urquhart to toe the line.'

'Her betrayal will certainly make him bitter,' Ashton observed. 'I don't see it will induce Robin to admit he leaned on the DPP to drop the case against Anwar Farid, which was my idea. I wanted to get him on side in case the Israel deal went pear shaped.'

'The DG went along with your idea,' Landon told him. 'However, Sir Victor wasn't quite so ambitious; he merely wanted to limit the scope of the investigation into the incident at Beaconsfield.'

Hazelwood had already tried to forestall a formal investigation by writing a sanitized account of the incident to the Chairman of the JIC; unfortunately, the FCO had been unimpressed. It prompted Ashton to ask if he thought he could handle the interview with Robin Urquhart.

'Yes. I'm not happy about the assignment but I can cope with Urquhart even though he might be a Deputy Under Secretary.'

'Well, I don't like it,' Ashton told him. 'You could end up as a sacrificial lamb.'

'Thanks. I've been called a few names in my time but never a sacrificial lamb.'

'Maybe we can cancel the meeting,' Ashton mused.

'I was hoping Robin Urquhart would cry off at the last moment, but that seems very unlikely and you won't get the DG to call it off. He's very fired up.'

'I'm going to meet Robin at the cottage.'

'You?' Landon said incredulously. 'From what I've heard he won't open the door to you.'

'You're going in first, Will. I'll arrive five minutes later.' Ashton planned to leave the office earlier than usual, catch a fast train to Portsmouth Harbour and collect his Volvo from the car park at Havant station. 'We'll RV in Stockbridge,' he announced.

'Whereabouts?'

'Any pub in the centre of the town. Call me mobile to mobile and tell me which one. Failing that I'd recognize your car anywhere.'

*   *   *

It was a celebratory lunch given by Dermot McManus following his selection as the Lib Dem candidate for Hillingdon and Ruislip at the next general election. There was only one guest—Mrs Julie Meacher. He had, in fact, entertained his estranged wife, Barbara, the previous evening, and a very dull business it had been too, but the constituency party expected their candidate to be happily married. He had returned to Barbara and the matrimonial home last October when he had learned his name was on the shortlist, and she had been willing to take him back. A curious, rather sexless woman, that was Barbara. But she could

302

play the candidate's wife to perfection, appearing with him at all the fundraising events, being nice to everybody. Why, even the women liked her. Nobody seeing them together in public would ever dream that, despite living under the same roof, they did not share the same bed. There was one notable exception: Julie Meacher knew just what a sham their relationship was.

Apart from being great in bed, the nice thing about Julie was the interest she showed in his political ambitions, for there was not the slightest doubt in his mind that he would be returned as the member for Hillingdon and Ruislip. No, his sights were set on what he would do when he was in the House.

'I want to be a recognized Lib Dem spokesman, someone the media will seek out when they want the party's view on policy.'

'You could become an authority on Treasury matters,' Julie suggested.

'There are too many accountants and economists in the party already.' McManus signalled the waiter to bring the bill. 'I need to broaden my horizons. Foreign affairs, that's where the real action is.'

'You're a good accountant, Dermot. It would be a pity if you didn't make use of your qualifications.'

'Oh, I will.' McManus glanced at the bill the waiter had placed in front of him, then covered it with his gold MasterCard. 'But only as a sideline,' he added.

'You're in a hurry,' Julie remarked in the direction of the retreating waiter. 'Anxious to return to the office, are we?'

'It wasn't the office I was thinking of.'

'Surprise, surprise.'

303

'A friend of mine has lent me a house in Pinner.'

'That's very decent of him,' Julie murmured.

'Well, I've known him most of my life; we went to the same grammar school—Harrow County.' McManus signed the chit the waiter presented to him, retained the duplicate together with the itemized bill and returned the MasterCard to his billfold. 'Shall we go?' he said smiling.

'I thought you'd never ask.'

They walked round to the car park behind the restaurant side by side as though they were merely colleagues and not lovers. After he had released the central locking, McManus made no attempt to help Julie into the Mercedes. The touchy-feely bit and much, much more would happen after they arrived at the borrowed love nest in Elm Tree Grove.

'Ralph is worried about something,' Julie remarked casually.

'I see.' McManus moistened his lips. 'Does he suspect we are having an affair?'

'Oh, no, it's something that happened at the office yesterday. He won't talk about it other than to say they've made a big mistake.'

'The office being the FCO?' McManus said tentatively.

'In a manner of speaking.'

It was the first time Julie had ever come close to admitting her husband was connected with the diplomatic service. Hitherto, when moaning about the late hours he worked, she had always referred to the office or the firm.

'Is Ralph in a stressful job?' he asked casually.

'He has the Mid East Department.'

McManus digested the news in silence. If

304

Meacher was only loosely connected with the Foreign Office, could it be he was a senior officer in the Secret Intelligence Service?

'The Mid East is stressful for any man,' he said presently.

Elm Tree Grove was a comparatively new development consisting of twelve cheek-by-jowl three-bedroom houses lumped together in a cul-de-sac. There was a sign in the window of the first house warning would-be burglars there was a neighbourhood watch in operation. There was, however, nobody at home in the cul-de-sac during the day from Monday to Friday. The asking price for properties in Elm Tree Grove required a double income to service the mortgage.

McManus parked the Mercedes outside number 12 and waited for Julie to join him on the pavement before tripping the central locking.

'Would it help you if I found out what was troubling Ralph?' Julie suddenly asked.

McManus opened the front door and ushered her into the hall. 'What made you say that?'

'You want to make a name for yourself as a spokesman on foreign affairs, don't you?' she said and mounted the stairs.

'Yes, of course I do but . . .'

'But what?'

'Well, won't Ralph think it unusual?' McManus floundered. 'I mean do you really discuss his work with him?'

'You worry too much, Dermot, I can handle my husband. Now which bedroom are we using?'

'The small one over the porch,' he told her.

*   *   *

The description of the impostor whom DCI Verco was determined to find was extremely vague. Apart from blond hair that had been cut close to the scalp, he was approximately six feet tall and had a cleft chin. Verco believed he either worked for a security company or was employed by a private detective agency. The fact that the man had bugged Ms Holsinger's apartment in Mountford House shortly after 1100 hours and then had done the same to Landon's flat an hour later suggested he might possibly be self-employed.

The first thing Verco had done was to obtain a list of those firms and agencies that had come to the notice of the Met for one reason or another. With the help of a detective constable he had then gone through all the Yellow Pages for the London area and extracted those firms specializing in security service and equipment. They had also ploughed through a great pile of Thomson's Local directories only to find that many of the companies were already listed in Yellow Pages. Although private investigators were few and far between they still added to the daunting number of firms that had to be checked out.

To complete the task within a reasonable period of time it had been necessary to group firms in order of priority. The range of the Ultimate Infinity Receiver that had been used to eavesdrop on both addresses had a great bearing on this. Consequently, firms located in the outer suburbs had been accorded the lowest priority. Verco had resisted the temptation to eliminate them altogether on the grounds that a recording station might have been positioned within two thousand yards of both targets. Conversely the security firms given the highest priority had been those inside a circle with a radius of two thousand yards centred on each address. Between the highest and lowest priorities there was a wide band embracing many of the Inner London boroughs. After Verco had prioritized individual firms, he had grouped them by addresses and then divided the list in two, splitting the workload between himself and the detective constable.

It had taken a full working day to draw up the programme. On Thursday they had put in an eight-hour shift working through the first priorities. Today they had started on the Inner London boroughs. Verco had taken those located south of the river, and by mid-afternoon he was working his way through the London borough of Wandsworth.

Verco parked his car in front of Stress Free Security Services in Purcell Road near Wandsworth station. The firm shared a two-storey, comparatively modern, red-brick building with Acme Electrical Goods. The less weathered bricks indicated that the third-floor towers at either end of the building had been added at a much later date. Each firm had its own entrance. Passing through the swing doors on the right, Verco produced his warrant card for the benefit of the woman on the reception counter and informed her he would like to see the managing director.

'It's nothing serious,' Verco assured her, 'and all I need is five minutes of his time.'

The MD's office was on the third-floor extension, which was no surprise. What did surprise him was why the developer hadn't installed a lift while the building was being elevated. The nameplate on the desk identified the MD as Malcolm Todhunter.

Todhunter was a short, tubby man with thick dark hair brushed straight back. It was a warm day and the office was mostly glass so that in the absence of an air conditioning unit the interior was akin to a greenhouse. Consequently Todhunter was in shirtsleeves and sweating freely.

'It's very good of you to spare me the time,' Verco said, shaking hands with Todhunter. 'I won't keep you long.'

'What can I do for you, Chief Inspector?'

'We've been given a vague description of a man who may be able to help us. He is said to be around six feet tall, with short blond hair sticking up like a scrubbing brush and a cleft chin.'

Verco waited for the inevitable apology he had received from so many other managers who'd expressed their regret at being unable to help him.

'Sounds like Gordon Portland to me,' Todhunter said, breaking the trend.

'Is he in the security business?'

'No. Portland's a PI specializing in bogus insurance claims. Does the odd bit of snooping for the DHSS, rooting out all those bastards who claim unemployment benefit or income support while they are raking it in on the black economy.'

'That must involve surveillance?'

'Yes, I guess.'

Verco didn't need to press it. Todhunter's slight hesitation before answering his question told him he knew Portland's snooping included electronic surveillance.

'Where do I find Mr Portland?'

'Wandsworth High Street between the community law centre and the betting shop.'

'Thank you, Mr Todhunter, you've been very helpful,' Verco said as they shook hands. 'If there were more like you, our job would be a lot easier.'

Finding Portland's inquiry service was easy given the directions he had received. Finding somewhere to park his car was a lot more difficult and took far longer. But the hassle was worth it. The moment Verco met Portland he knew he had a good collar. Three phone calls would be enough to set the ball rolling: a courtesy one to Detective Chief Superintendent Roberts of B District to inform him what had happened, a second to Notting Hill police station to request arrangements be made for an identity parade and a third to the DC, instructing him to collect Frank, the doorman, and Jonathan, the very senior citizen, and convey them to Notting Hill.

'My name's Verco,' he told the PI. 'You've been a very naughty boy, Mr Portland.'

There is an old saying that less depends on the size of the dog in a fight than the size of the fight in the dog. For all that he was physically a big, hard-looking man, Mr Gordon Portland crumpled like a paper bag.

*   *   *

Landon backed the Aston Martin out of the parking area fronting the Grosvenor Hotel in Stockbridge and continued on the A30 trunk road to Salisbury. After crossing the River Test he turned right into a narrow lane that led to Longstock, where Urquhart had a cottage on the outskirts of the village. So far everything had gone like clockwork: Ashton had had no difficulty in locating the RV and had joined him in the hotel bar barely six minutes after Landon himself had arrived. With better than a quarter of an hour in hand they had been able to review one last time what he was going to say to the Deputy Under Secretary. But for all Ashton's confident assertion that they were holding all the trump cards, Landon was not looking forward to the next half hour.

The cottage was something from the lid of a chocolate box. Slate roof, wisteria reaching up to the bedroom windows, its blooms just beginning to turn purple, new growth on the rose bushes either side of the flagstone path that led from a wooden gate set in a low stone wall. On the far side of the cottage part of the hedge bordering the lane had been ripped out and the ground behind levelled to provide a parking area for up to three vehicles. By a dint of manoeuvring, Landon reversed his car into the bay and parked it alongside a Rover that he presumed belonged to Urquhart. Keen to get it over and done with, he locked the Aston Martin, walked up the front path and rang the bell. Urquhart kept him waiting a good two minutes before he came to the door.

'You must be Mr Landon,' he said in a condescending manner. 'Do come in. We are in the drawing room, first on your left.'

Landon didn't like the sound of the royal 'we', liked it even less when he entered the drawing room and came face to face with a tall, elegant lady whose beautifully coiffured hair was flecked with grey.

'This is Helen,' Urquhart said and left him to draw his own conclusion. 'And this, my dear, is Mr Landon, the gentleman I was telling you about.'

Just what Helen was doing there became clearer when Urquhart made no attempt to curb the social pleasantries and get down to business. At some time during the day he had evidently changed his mind and decided that no way was he going to meet Landon on a one-to-one basis. Helen's presence served a two-fold purpose: she was meant either to deter Landon from raising the subject of Anwar Farid altogether, or else she was to be a witness to his crude attempt at blackmail. Whatever her role Landon refused to be sidetracked.

'I think you should read this letter Jill Sheridan wrote to Alvin Dombas,' he said and produced the photocopy from his jacket pocket. 'Try not to take offence at her remarks concerning you, Mr Urquhart. Concentrate on what she has to say about Anwar Farid.'

'I've never heard of the man.'

'You would know him better as Mahmoud Hassan Soliman. Customs and Excise arrested him over twenty-seven months ago for smuggling Class A drugs into the UK. As a favour to Jill Sheridan you persuaded the Director of Public Prosecutions to drop the case.'

'That is a monstrous lie.'

'You know it isn't,' Landon said coolly. 'You gave Jill the branch memorandum you had opened on Mahmoud Hassan Soliman. It was a quixotic gesture to reassure her that Soliman would cease to exist once she destroyed the file. Unfortunately for you, Jill simply re-labelled the file under Anwar Farid.'

'Why would she do that?'

'I wouldn't know, Mr Urquhart.'

311

'This letter is a forgery. It's the handiwork of one of the grubby little back street calligraphists you people are known to use from time to time.'

Landon thought the angry rebuttal was more for Helen's benefit than his. In the midst of the diatribe he heard a vehicle drive slowly past the cottage. The door bell rang a couple of minutes later while Urquhart was still ranting.

'That will be Ashton,' Landon said interrupting him.

'Ashton!' Urquhart's face contorted with rage. 'What is that swine doing here?'

'I'll let him in, shall I?' Landon asked.

'Please do,' Helen told him.

Landon went out into the hall and opened the front door. In a low voice he told Ashton about Urquhart's companion, then showed him into the drawing room. Urquhart had calmed down a little but the atmosphere still reeked of hostility and Urquhart left it to Helen to introduce herself.

'What do you want?' Urquhart demanded.

'I'm going to brief you, Robin, and explain what exactly lay behind the incident at Beaconsfield.'

'Why me? Why not the Permanent Under Secretary?'

'Listen to me,' Ashton said in measured tones. 'What I'm about to disclose is top secret codeword material. Do I make myself clear?'

'You do to me, Mr Ashton,' Helen said quietly. 'I'll wait in the dining room while you talk to Robin.'

'Thank you, Helen.' Ashton caught Landon's eye and jerked his head. 'You too, Will.'

'What?'

'Go keep the lady company.'

It was the last thing Landon had envisaged doing that evening.

Twenty-One

Landon thought it was all very well for Ashton to tell him to keep Helen company, but what do you say to a lady you know nothing about other than her first name? Correction: Helen was wearing a gold wedding ring and a half hoop of diamonds on the same finger. Did that make her a widow or had she merely separated from her husband, or had he run off with another woman? They hadn't met under the happiest of circumstances, either, which was another stumbling block. He wondered what sort of olive branch he should offer the lady or whether it was necessary to offer one at all.

'I'm sorry,' he said, breaking the silence between them that had gone on for far too long.

'What for?' she asked, and seemed genuinely puzzled.

'We understood Robin would be alone, otherwise I wouldn't have come barging in here,' Landon said and paused, but she refused to be drawn.

'It's Helen.'

'And I'm Will.'

'I know, Robin introduced you. Who's Jill Sheridan?'

'A shooting star that burned out. Her father was an executive with the Qatar General Petroleum Corporation and she spent most of her childhood and adolescence in the Persian Gulf, with the result that Arabic had naturally become her second

313

tongue. Persian, or Farsi, was an additional language she acquired at the School of Oriental and African Studies. Jill was appointed to run the intelligence network in the United Arab Emirates from Bahrain in October '89. On paper she was made for the job, but unfortunately a woman is definitely a second-class citizen in that part of the world.'

To get the job done she had had to run the network through her Grade III assistant. Whenever there was a conference with Arab intelligence officers in the Emirates, Jill Sheridan had been obliged to pass herself off as a secretary. It had been an intolerable situation but she had stuck it out until the Iraqis had been defeated and Kuwait liberated before she had requested to be relieved in post.

'It could have meant the end of her career if Robin hadn't intervened,' Landon continued.

'He was already obsessed with her in those days?'

'No, they didn't meet until much later. He just believed Jill was by far and away the best of her intake and it would be criminal to lose her. He blamed the then Director General for placing her in an impossible position.'

Landon wanted her to know it had been a very different story after they had met. Jill Sheridan had really set her cap at Robin Urquhart and had extracted one favour after another from him, ruthlessly exploiting his affection.

'Thank you for answering my questions, Mr Landon.'

'My pleasure, Mrs Helendon.'

'Coppinger,' she said, instinctively correcting him.

'Right.'

314

'How much longer do you suppose your friend will be?'

A door opened and there was a sound of footsteps. 'I think he must have heard you,' Landon said and went out into the hall to meet Ashton.

'Are you ready, Will?' he asked.

Landon nodded, called out goodbye to Helen Coppinger and followed the older man out of the house. Urquhart didn't bother to see them off.

'Were you successful?' Landon asked.

'I believe Robin has got the message. We'll talk about it when we stop off at the Grosvenor on the way back.'

'Maybe we'd better find somewhere else, Peter. Somebody might remember us if we returned to the Grosvenor less than an hour after leaving the hotel. And you never can tell, that could prove an embarrassment at a later date.'

'You could have a point, Will. Suppose you lead the way and find us a suitable place?'

Landon got into the Aston Martin, started up and pulled out of the bay. What he didn't need to find was a quiet, half-empty village pub where a new face would be noticed. The proven way to remain anonymous was to pick a popular haunt in a town. The nearest was Winchester, some nine miles from Stockbridge. Although Landon was not familiar with the city and could not recall the last time he had visited Winchester, he anticipated little difficulty in finding a place. In the event it took him twenty minutes of criss-crossing the city before he finally came across the Wessex in Paternoster Row. He was also lucky enough to find a couple of parking spaces in the courtyard.

'Local knowledge, Will?'

315

'Damned right,' Landon told Ashton with a straight face. 'I thought I'd show you something of Winchester while I was at it.'

They went inside, ordered a couple of beers and grabbed a corner table where they could talk more or less freely without being overheard.

'Let's talk about this woman Helen for a minute or two, Will.'

'I think her surname's Coppinger.'

'You think,' Ashton repeated. 'Why the doubt?'

'Because she didn't really introduce herself. At one point during our conversation I paused just long enough hoping she would take the hint and give me her family name. But she merely smiled sweetly and reminded me it was Helen. The next time I tried it on, I gave her a bogus surname and she automatically corrected me.'

'That was a clever move, Will.'

'I would like to think so. However, Helen is a pretty smart woman and I'm not a hundred per cent sure I did catch her off guard. It could be she had anticipated I would try to catch her out and had been ready with a name.'

'OK, she's a smart woman. What were your other impressions?'

'Helen Coppinger is elegant, poised and I believe widowed rather than divorced.' Landon frowned. 'I reckon she and Urquhart are more than just good friends. I do know she is jealous of Jill Sheridan and what she had meant to him at one time.'

'Any guesses as to why she was at the cottage this evening?'

'Perhaps she was there to inhibit me?'

'Not as a witness then?'

'To what?'

'What you said to Urquhart might have sounded like blackmail to some people.'

'Thanks a bunch.'

'Ralph Meacher was called on to testify at the inquiry again today. He didn't perform too well.'

'That's terrific,' Landon said. 'Have you got any other good news?'

'You and Chris Neighbour will probably be subpoenaed to attend the inquiry on Tuesday April the twentieth. If you are, stick to the script. The source who contacted us is a Saudi businessman related to the ruling family. You were told he had dictated where, when and what time we were to meet him. The man conducting the inquiry is Gavin Pearce, Chairman of the Joint Intelligence Committee. You need to be wary of him. He tried to pull a fast one on me, claimed he'd heard our source was actually David Ben-Yosef, the Mossad Head of Station.'

Landon felt his stomach turn over. Maybe Ashton was right, maybe it had been just a shot in the dark inspired by the fact that the Israeli had given his Special Branch minders the slip and had gone missing for a couple of hours or so. But the allegation was too close to the truth for comfort.

'Don't look so worried,' Ashton told him. 'You will have an ally in Robin Urquhart; a reluctant one, admittedly, but he will rein Pearce in if he shows signs of going down the Israeli route again.'

The photocopy of the letter Jill Sheridan had written to Alvin Dombas had reminded Urquhart how vulnerable he was. There was enough documentary evidence in the files to indict him for perverting the course of justice. That Mahmoud Hassan Soliman had walked when they had had him bang to rights was something the police had not forgotten nor ever would.

'There's another reason why he will muzzle Pearce,' Ashton continued. 'He believes the Israelis approached us to propose a mutual aid package aimed at neutralizing Talal Asir and Ali Mohammed Khalef.'

'Where did he get that idea?'

'From me,' Ashton said calmly.

'Jesus.' Landon felt his stomach plunge to even greater depths.

'Hear me out, Will. I told Urquhart the arrangement was classified top secret with a codeword caveat, meaning only those named on the need-to-know were aware of the impending operation. I further told him the list comprised the government minister who'd authorized the project, Sir Victor Hazelwood, Ralph Meacher and myself. Robin understands he is now the fifth name on the list.'

As one of the names, it meant Urquhart could not voice whatever concerns he might have to any outsider. This included the Permanent Under Secretary of State and Head of Her Majesty's Diplomatic Service.

Although he could be prosecuted under the Official Secrets Act should he ignore this restriction it occurred to Landon that there was a possible loophole.

'Did Robin sign a certificate of any kind?' he asked.

'He didn't have to.' Ashton reached into his jacket pocket and brought out a miniature cassette recorder some three inches in length. 'Courtesy of Terry Hicks,' he added.

318

'You were wired for sound?'

'Yes. And I played the tape back to Robin.' Ashton pocketed the cassette and finished the rest of his beer. 'I don't know about you, Will,' he said, 'but I'm going home.'

*   *   *

In Verco's experience identity parades could be an iffy business at the best of times. Put a suspect in a line-up with seven men of similar height, build and age, and a witness who'd only caught a fleeting glimpse of the perpetrator could become confused and pick out the wrong man. But not this evening. Frank the doorman and Jonathan the very senior citizen had been spot on, no hesitation whatever from either man. They had ignored the other seven and had gone straight to Mr Gordon Portland. The proceedings had been conducted with a solicitor present to represent the accused and to make sure the witnesses were not primed to recognize Portland. The parade over, Portland had been transferred to Paddington Green, the most secure police station in London. After the custody sergeant had taken care of his personal possessions and the clothes Portland had been wearing when arrested, he had been issued with an orange-coloured coverall and escorted to the interview room.

'We've got you bang to rights,' Verco informed him gleefully. 'Breaking and entering, two years minimum with the right beak.'

'Not according to my solicitor. He reckons I'll get a suspended sentence and probation. Six months max—no previous form see.'

'You know something, Gordon? More suspected terrorists have been held at Paddington Green while they were being interrogated than at any other centre in mainland Britain.'

'Why are you telling me this? I'm not a terrorist.'

'Convince me.'

'I don't know where to start.'

'The beginning is as good a place as any,' Verco said.

'Well, OK, there is this guy Holsinger who's separated from his wife, Ensley. He's worth scads of dosh and if he has anything to do with it she won't see a penny. Claims his wife left the matrimonial home and is having an affair with a man called Landon. Mr Holsinger said they were very smart, lived under separate roofs but come together whenever they felt in need of sex. He reckons they arrange where and when to meet over the phone. That's why I was hired—'

Verco slapped the table between them with the palm of his right hand with enough force to sound like a pistol shot. 'You must think I'm still in nappies,' he said angrily. 'You've been walking around using my name and passing yourself off as a detective chief inspector in Special Branch with a warrant card to prove it.'

'I'm only telling you what I was hired to do.'

'And you believed all this crap about an unfaithful wife with the hots?'

Portland gave the matter some thought, then said, 'I took his story on trust. Maybe I was a little naïve.'

'You've a tattoo on each arm. One shows a tarty looking Aphrodite with the legend "Cyprus" underneath, the other depicts a winged messenger.'

320

'What is this?'

'You've served in the army with 9 Signal Regiment stationed in Cyprus, a GCHQ unit. Right?' Verco held up a cautionary finger. 'And think before you answer,' he added.

'I won't deny it.'

'Good. Now we're getting somewhere. Who hired you?'

'I've already told you, it was a man called Holsinger, first name Frederick.'

'Did he provide the fake warrant card?'

'Yeah. And before you ask, it was his idea I should become DCI Verco. He said the doorman at Mountford House would cooperate a lot more readily if he believed he was dealing with an officer from Special Branch.'

'And masquerading as a police officer didn't bother you?'

Portland took a sudden interest in the table and lowered his head. 'The money was good,' he muttered.

'All right, let's have a description of the benefactor.'

'I can't tell you what he looks like, I've never met him.'

'Don't give me that shit,' Verco snarled.

'No, listen, he was just a voice on the telephone. Honest, I thought he was a practical joker until the package arrived by Special Delivery. It contained a thousand pounds in fifties.'

'And that was when you began to take him seriously, was it?'

'I suppose so.'

'Well, you can take this seriously, Mr Gordon Portland. You are going to stay here until I get some straight answers.' Verco pushed his chair back and stood up. 'I'll see you on Monday bright and early.'

'I'm not having that; I want to see my lawyer.'

'Go whistle for him.'

'I've got my rights.'

'You've got no rights, you're a bloody terrorist,' Verco told him.

*   *   *

Like a thief in the night Meacher had entered the house stealthily and had immediately taken refuge in the study. To keep himself company he had purchased a bottle of Johnnie Walker Black Label whisky from the off licence in the high street on his way home. He had also bought a dozen polystyrene coffee cups and a packet of paracetamol from Sainsbury's. At seven thirty he had heard Julie ring the branch duty officer on the BT phone in the hall to ask if her husband was still there at the office. Moments after slamming the phone down she had picked the receiver up again and called the steward at the golf club. Finally she had tried the Levy household and had had a stilted conversation with either Sam or his wife. At no stage had Julie looked in on the study, but then why would she when there was no light showing under the door?

For someone who limited himself to the occasional weak whisky and soda after dinner he had imbibed pretty freely this evening. However, despite consuming half the bottle, the whisky had not had the desired effect. Furthermore, a double dose of paracetamol taken at seven o'clock and nine thirty had failed to relieve a splitting

322

headache. Everything that could go wrong had gone wrong; that was the underlying reason why he was so stressed out and unable to unwind.

Meacher switched on the table lamp, then opened the centre drawer in the desk and took out the letter he'd received almost a fortnight ago from Sedgewick James, the estate agents. There was no longer any point in telling Julie he proposed to sell the house for one and a quarter million in order to move out of suburbia and enjoy a better quality of life in the country. It had never been his intention to take early retirement; on the contrary, he had seen himself commuting to the office, but that was now a pipedream. In view of all that happened since Toby Quayle and Anwar Farid had been murdered, it could only be a question of a few weeks before he was compelled to submit his resignation. When that had happened he would need to find another job, and they were hard to come by in rural England. Meacher poured himself another whisky by way of consolation, returned the letter to the centre drawer and switched off the table lamp. His eyes were just beginning to adjust to the darkness when the door opened and the ceiling light with its two 100-watt bulbs blinded him. Julie shrieked and literally jumped in the air.

'Bloody hell,' she screamed. 'What in God's name are you doing sitting in the dark?'

'I was thinking,' Meacher told her and was conscious that his speech was slurred.

'You frightened the life out of me, Ralph.'

'I'm sorry.'

Julie moved to the window and drew both sets of curtains. 'You've been drinking, too,' she observed, her back towards him.

'Best way I know to drown one's sorrows.'

Julie turned slowly about. 'What sorrows?' she asked anxiously.

'You are wearing pyjamas.'

'I've just had a bath. Anyway, stick to the point, Ralph. What sorrows?'

'I haven't seen those before.'

'You're drunk.'

'And with good reason.'

'What's wrong? Is it something I've done?'

'No, it's to do with the office.'

'Can you tell me about it?'

Meacher gazed at his wife. He could not recall when she had last shown an interest in what he was doing. But that was scarcely her fault; except for the stuff that was already in the public domain there was little he could tell Julie without committing a breach of security.

'It's to do with Toby Quayle and Anwar Farid,' he said suddenly, taking the plunge.

'Were they the two men killed in that Italian restaurant?'

Certain aspects of the case were still classified but he no longer felt inhibited by security implications. He told Julie everything there was to know concerning the criminal activities of Anwar Farid and how, at the behest of Jill Sheridan, pressure was brought to bear on the Director of Public Prosecutions to drop the case against the Egyptian.

'Roughly a month ago we learned Anwar was up to his old tricks again. He probably never stopped, which shows how well he conned us.' Meacher laughed bitterly. 'You want to hear a good joke? Jill Sheridan had him down as a reliable source and I agreed with her assessment.'

'Are you telling me that you've changed your mind, Ralph?'

'I was told to check out all the information Anwar Farid has ever given us and you know what? The stuff was solid enough but we always got it just a day or so too late.'

'I don't see why you should blame yourself when Jill Sheridan was the one who wrote him up.'

It was a comforting thought but the fact remained he should have conducted his own assessment of Farid the day he became the acting head of the Mid East Department. Still, it was nice to hear Julie stick up for him and he was tempted to confide in her.

'Have you eaten, Ralph?'

'Not yet.'

'I put your dinner in the oven but it will be ruined by now. How would you like scrambled egg with smoked salmon?'

'Sounds mouth watering,' he said, his eyes on her satin pyjamas.

'You like them?' she asked.

'What do you think?'

'Well, I'm wondering if yellow suits me.'

'From where I'm standing it does. But then I've always found you attractive,' he said and followed her out of the study.'

'Have you?' Julie turned about. 'You obviously do at the moment,' she said and stroked his crotch, then unzipped his flies to reach inside his trousers to fondle an already erect penis. 'Which would you like first?' she teased. 'Scrambled eggs or this?'

'I'm surprised you need to ask,' he said.

Landon backed the Aston Martin into the lock-up on Gloucester Road, then switched off the lights and cut the ignition. After leaving the Wessex they had made their way to the M3, Ashton to head south to pick up the M27 and trunk road to Chichester, while he drove north east to link up with the orbital motorway. Sixty-four miles from city centre to city centre and how long had it taken him? The answer was one hour thirty-five because he had acquired two convictions for speeding and six penalty points on his licence since last November that were positive inducements to keep well under whatever speed restrictions were in force.

It had been one of those days that were best forgotten. He'd put in the hours and earned the salary but with little satisfaction. Talal Asir and Ali Mohammed Khalef were recognizable enemies but not Robin Urquhart. He was simply a man who, as a result of personal prejudice, had become an obstacle that could not be ignored.

Landon released the bonnet, got out of the car and removed the rotor, which was the most effective way he knew of immobilizing a vehicle. He then locked the Aston Martin, closed the garage up and turned about to find he had company.

There were three of them, male Caucasians whose ages ranged from late teens to early twenties. Two had metal studs in their noses while the third sported a curtain ring through the lobe of the right ear. They were well built and, though shorter than him, they looked mean, ugly and intimidating. They weren't drunk nor were they high on drugs and that made them twice as dangerous. He was hemmed in, his back to the garage, the three yobs positioned in front of him at nine, twelve and three o'clock, all of them within touching distance. He was alone, there were no pedestrians about on the street and there wasn't a police car in sight.

The man with the earring said, 'Give me yer fucking mobile and yer dosh and we'll let you walk away in one piece.'

Two cars went by but the drivers, and in one case the front seat passenger, avoided looking in his direction. If anything both vehicles speeded up as they drew level with the lock-up.

'Did you hear what I said, dickhead?'

The earring moved a pace nearer and, guessing what was coming, Landon reared back but still took a headbutt in the face that brought the blood flowing from his nose and split upper lip. While he was still dazed, his arms were pinioned by the mugger on his right.

'We need to teach this wanker a lesson,' the youngest of the trio said, 'and I'm just the man to do it.'

Landon allowed himself to be swung round to face left. Hunching both shoulders to protect his jaw, he kept his eyes on the teenager while the earring used the right side of his face as a punchbag.

The teenager shuffled forward, clenched fists held high, his shoulders rolling like a prizefighter. Timing it perfectly, Landon pivoted on his left leg, shot out the right and slammed his foot into the teenager's kneecap with enough force to break it and wipe the smirk from his face. As he went down screaming in agony, Landon stooped low enough to grab the testicles of the man behind him. Then, like a compressed spring reasserting itself, he shot up and smashed his adversary under the jaw with his head while maintaining a firm grip on his scrotum.

The ethics of judo were forgotten, and so too were the techniques Landon had mastered on his way to becoming a brown belt. He simply attacked the third man with the utmost ferocity. Intent on inflicting the maximum pain and damage, he ripped the curtain ring from the ear lobe, then battered him senseless with forearm blows to the head, jaw and neck.

None of the assailants attempted to detain Landon as he walked away in the direction of Stanhope Gardens. Stopping at a public phone box two hundred yards down the road, he made a 999 call and reported the incident to the police without disclosing his name, address or present location. By the time he let himself into his flat he had stopped bleeding from the nose and mouth.

There was the usual quantity of junk mail waiting for him in the letter box plus a notelet in a now familiar hand. The invitation to apply for a credit card offering zero per cent interest for the next nine months went straight into the waste bin, the note from Ensley he left on the combined drop-leaf desk and bookcase until he'd cleaned himself up.

The bloodstained shirt was consigned to the laundry basket and the lapels of his jacket obviously required something more than Dab It Off. The face in the mirror looked a little battered, the nose swollen, the right eye beginning to close as the bruise on the cheekbone came out, and the strip of elastoplast Landon applied to his upper lip did nothing to improve his appearance.

The note from Ensley was brief and to the point. It read: *You were right about Zimmerman, I was wrong. The number you asked for is 020 7373 8866.* Picking up the phone he rang Ensley at her flat in Mountford House.

'Hi,' he said, 'it's me.'

'Hello, you.'

'I got your note,' he continued, 'and I know what it must have cost you. It can't have been easy.'

'You were right, let's leave it at that.'

'Well, I'll make sure you are kept out of it.'

Landon wasn't too certain how he was going to manage that. First thing on Monday he would pass the phone number to Special Branch through Richard Neagle. There would be enough time to figure out what they were going to do about Mr Virgil Zimmerman once they had his private address.

'Are you OK?' Ensley suddenly asked.

'Yeah, I'm fine.'

'You don't sound it.'

'I'm just a little beat up, that's all.'

'Metaphorically or literally?'

'It's nothing.'

'I'll be right over.'

'What are you planning to do?'

'Emulate your Florence Nightingale,' Ensley said and put the phone down.

Twenty-Two

The black patch over the right eye was infinitely preferable to the sunglasses that had made him the butt of much ribald humour when he had worn them yesterday. The weather had been against him on Monday; polaroids don't go with a low overcast and frequent showers. Far from disguising the injuries the dark glasses had in fact drawn attention to the bruised cheekbone. One advantage of the black patch was that it ensured nobody could accuse him of trying to hide the injuries from other members of the Combined Anti-Terrorist Organization seated around the table. It also made his explanation attributing the injuries to a domestic accident seem more plausible.

The black patch had been Ensley's idea. In case his injuries were reported to the police she had also insisted on accompanying him when he had visited the local medical centre to have a couple of stitches in the upper lip. On the basis of getting your story in first, she had then given the nurse on duty her version of how Landon had come to injure himself.

Before going to the medical centre Landon had phoned Ashton to let him know what had happened. As he related the incident in detail Landon could not help thinking that the affray on Gloucester Road would probably be the final nail in his coffin. In the five weeks since the multiple slaying in Giordano's, he had been arrested for breaking into Quayle's house in Mews Terrace, had been stopped and taken in for questioning by Thames Valley Police and had had a run-in with

Superintendent Oakham that had ultimately led to an official inquiry. Finally he had put one man in hospital with a seriously damaged kneecap and may have killed a second. Ashton might tell him that none of it was his fault, the fact remained that in the last thirty-four days he had been more of a liability than an asset.

A part of him wanted to make a clean breast of it to the police, the baser element urged him not to be a bloody fool. If a man with an earring had snuffed it, the police were unlikely to be satisfied with simply charging him with manslaughter. So far as a number of senior officers in the Met were concerned he had been a real pain in the arse and the incident in Gloucester Road would be a golden opportunity to get even. Chances were all three yobs had criminal records or at the very least were known to be troublemakers, but in this instance they would be regarded as innocent victims who had been viciously assaulted. It wouldn't matter that they had had him penned in, that the odds had been three to one in their favour and they had started the affray. Maybe Ensley had a point, maybe he should sit tight and do nothing. The police could find him, they knew exactly where the fight had occurred. There was blood on the pavement outside the lock-up. Once they learned who rented it they would come knocking on his door on some pretext, and if he was still showing signs of wear and tear that would be it.

Landon glanced at the notes with which Keith Amesbury-Cotton, the RAF group captain from DI7, had provided each committee member, realized he was nearing the end of his presentation and hastily consulted his own notes in case Richard

Neagle called on him next. From Hugo Calthorpe there was a brief memo to the effect that the forty thousand pounds in gold sovereigns were now in the hands of the political agents operating in the tribal areas. Ever a cautious man, Hugo had stressed that nobody should look for quick results. In view of his role in the abduction and subsequent murders of the Jenners, Ali Mohammed Khalef was likely to give both the tribal areas and the North-West Frontier Province a wide berth for some time.

The notes provided by Chris Neighbour were a little more fulsome. The scuttlebutt in Moscow concerned Vladimir Putin, the former career officer in the KGB turned politician. Sources known to be reliable were predicting that within the next four or five months Putin would be appointed Prime Minister by President Yeltsin. The same sources were taking wagers that before the end of the year Yeltsin would resign, which meant that under the constitution Vladimir Putin would become the acting President until such time as elections could be held. The Foreign and Commonwealth Office was not exactly overwhelmed with joy at the prospect.

There were also indications that Islamic rebels based in Chechnya were preparing to invade the neighbouring republic of Daghestan. If this should happen, Russian forces would undoubtedly intervene. Although the last Russian troops had been withdrawn from Chechnya in January 1997, armoured and mechanized infantry formations had remained within striking distance of the republic. Since this report had been confirmed in the satellite photographs furnished by DI7, Landon thought it was only sensible to make this his main talking point when Keith Amesbury-Cotton finished his presentation.

Given his sense of theatre Landon wasn't surprised that Neagle should have kept the best until the last. The man who brought the curtain down after his own dissertation was Michael York, the representative from Government Communications Headquarters. For years GCHQ had been trying to find a way of monitoring the mobile telephone network used by Islamic Jihad and other Mid East terrorist groups. As of today Michael York was delighted to inform the committee they had cracked the problem.

'We had a gigantic stroke of luck,' York informed them. 'After Ali Mohammed Khalef had disappeared last June the police searched the house in Finsbury Park where he had been living. Among the many items taken away for further examination were a couple of microchips that had been found wrapped in cotton wool in an empty box of Swan Vesta. The microchips were unique; they were in fact a secure-speech component for mobile phones. A bulk order for sixty chips was placed with CFS Electronique, Boulogne-Billancourt by Talal Asir when he was living in an apartment on the Rue de Ponthieu in the 8th arrondissement.'

CFS Electronique were the acknowledged experts in the field of secure telephonic communications and GCHQ were familiar with their various products. Consequently when York's colleagues saw one of the microchips that had been found in Mohammed Khalef's flat they were able to identify the manufacturer. At the request of

Michael York, MI5 had then asked their French counterparts, the Direction de la Surveillance du Territoire, to ascertain whether Talal Asir had had any dealings with CFS Electronique. In due course the French authorities had sent the Security Service a photocopy of the appropriate invoice.

'How long have you known about this?' Landon asked, dividing his attention between the two men.

'Since the beginning of last December,' Neagle said.

'So why did you keep the news to yourselves for over four months?'

'Because we didn't have one lousy phone number we could monitor,' York informed him. 'We had to write a programme capable of identifying mobile phones that had been fitted with that particular CFS microchip.'

'And now you have?'

York nodded. 'Currently we are eavesdropping on three mobile phone numbers. Two of the subscribers are definitely active members of Hamas, one is operating in Gaza City, the other in Ramallah.'

As yet GCHQ hadn't managed to identify the two men by name but that was only a question of time. Both were leaders of a terrorist cell and spoke to each other quite frequently. From the general tenor of their conversation it was evident they were financially supported by Talal Asir.

'In fact they are expecting to see the bagman within the next seven to ten days,' York said in conclusion.

'When did you intercept this?'

'Yesterday afternoon, 1429 hours our time.'

'And do you believe the bagman is Talal Asir?'

334

'Yes, Will, we do.'

'We think the bagman could be Ali Mohammed Khalef,' Landon told him, 'but it doesn't matter who's right or wrong. Asir and Khalef are numbers one and two on our most wanted list.'

'And you would like to be apprised of the bagman's movements the moment GCHQ learns of them?' Neagle suggested.

'Yes, we would,' Landon said. 'We aim to put a few two-legged bloodhounds on to his scent.'

'I see.' Neagle looked round the table. 'Are there any other points you would like to raise, gentlemen?' he asked. 'No? That's it then. Same time, same place next Tuesday.'

Even before Neagle said it, Landon knew he would be asked to stay on. He also knew what was on Neagle's mind, and wasn't surprised when he was asked if his superiors were preparing a contingency plan to lift the bagman.

'Nobody has said anything to me about mounting an operation to kidnap him,' Landon said carefully. 'But should we learn that he was in Amman, Cairo or Beirut we would certainly expect the FCO to ask the host nation to detain him.'

'What if he were in Syria, Iran or Libya or any other country that is not well disposed towards us?'

'What else could we do except grin and bear it.'

'Assassination is an option, Will, especially if you could persuade some foreign agency to do the job on your behalf.'

The two cell leaders of Hamas were in hiding close to the Israeli border. Normally the bagman was a fleeting target, but he would be extremely vulnerable when he visited the Palestinians in Ramallah and Gaza City. It didn't take a genius to work out who was best placed to mount an operation at short notice.

'I imagine the FCO would have something to say about that,' Landon said coolly.

'Quite so.' Neagle left the table, went over to the window and looked out on to Millbank, then turned about. Perching one buttock on the windowsill, he braced the other leg to prevent himself slipping off. 'Verco found his impostor,' he continued. 'A man called Gordon Portland, who used to be an Operator, Special Intelligence, in the Royal Signals. He left the army at the nine-year point in the rank of corporal and set himself up as a private investigator.'

'Is Verco going to charge him?'

'He already has, Will. I'm only telling you this because your name will undoubtedly appear in the newspapers along with Miss Holsinger's.'

'What about Virgil Zimmerman, the man who hired Portland? Is he going to get away with it?'

'Possibly. Much as he is willing to do so Portland can't give evidence against Zimmerman because he has never met him. The American was just a voice on the telephone. Portland believed he was working for a Mr Frederick Holsinger on what was going to be a very bitter and messy divorce.'

'Couldn't he identify the voice if he heard it again?'

'I doubt it. Portland is convinced the American was using some gizmo to distort his voice. That brings us to the phone number you gave me yesterday. 020 7373 8866 is ex-directory.'

'Are you telling me you couldn't get the name and address of the subscriber?'

'No, Will, I just wanted you to know why Portland

couldn't get hold of it. The subscriber is listed as Mr V. Zimmerman and the address is 384 Drayton Gardens. The question is, what are we going to do with the information?'

To Landon the answer was obvious. The Home Secretary should be invited to summon the American ambassador to his office, lay the facts before him and make it absolutely clear that Zimmerman's conduct was unacceptable. If necessary the Home Secretary should be supported by the Secretary of State for Foreign and Commonwealth Affairs, but regardless of his intervention Zimmerman would be recalled. Verco could take his pound of flesh from Portland's hide but on no account should Ensley Holsinger be dragged through the mire.

'I wouldn't like the CIA to take it out on her, because she gave me that vital phone number.'

'The simple solution is always the most convenient. Right, Will?'

'It is in our line of business,' Landon said grimly.

'Well, I guess that's it.' Neagle straightened up. 'Let's hope you stay lucky.'

'What?'

'At the Board of Inquiry this afternoon.'

Landon began to wonder what, if anything, was secret about the Secret Intelligence Service.

*   *   *

Toby Quayle might be dead but he wouldn't go away. It seemed to Ashton that time and again he returned to haunt Ralph Meacher in one form or another. On this occasion his latest resurrection was in the shape of a letter Roy Kelso had received

337

from the sister in New Zealand. In view of its contents he had felt Meacher should read the letter before he showed it to Victor Hazelwood. A difference of opinion between the two men had prompted Ralph Meacher to suggest they seek the opinion of a third party. That the third party was Ashton hadn't greatly pleased Kelso.

'Alladyce, Bardolph and Benjamin,' Ashton intoned and looked up. 'I presume they're her solicitors?'

'They are now,' Kelso said heatedly, 'and I only found that out quite by chance. I thought she was only interested in the will Quayle had left with them when she asked me for the name and address of his solicitors.'

A lot more than the Last Will and Testament of Tobias (Toby) Quayle was involved. Ms Annabel Quayle was in dispute with Alladyce, Bardolph and Benjamin concerning the amount of inheritance tax she would be liable for as the sole beneficiary. She was also outraged that the deeds to 3 Mews Terrace were in her brother's name and not hers. The covering letter addressed Personal, for Mr Roy Kelso, c/o the Secretary, Box 850, London W1Y 8HD merely drew attention to the enclosed correspondence.

'What do you make of her claim, Ralph?' Ashton asked. 'Do you believe that except for the initial deposit of two hundred thousand the property was purchased with her money?'

'Well, the solicitors agree they received a further one point three million from Toby Quayle's account with the National Westminster in the Strand.'

'And she certainly didn't get her brother's

338

account number with the NatWest from Alladyce and Co.' Ashton frowned. 'The thing is, Piers Felstead of Coutts and Co. told me Quayle was one of those lucky people who had had a big win on the lottery.'

'That's the story he got from Toby,' Meacher reminded him. 'It depends on who you believe, the brother or the sister.'

In her letter to the solicitors Annabel Quayle had maintained the one point three million had been in the nature of a personal loan to her brother and therefore should not be included in the estate. The loan was to have been repaid by the 31st December 1999. Ashton reckoned that when he had acquired 3 Mews Terrace in 1996 this would have been an impossible stipulation. However, in the following three years the value of the property had more than doubled and Quayle would have had little difficulty in securing a loan to pay off the debt to his sister.

'He had probably been shrewd enough to foresee this,' Ashton said. 'The question we have to ask ourselves is do we believe Annabel's claim that the money had been left to her by her employer?'

'You surely don't believe her cock and bull story about thumbing her way around the world?' Kelso said incredulously.

Annabel had set off on her travels in May 1967 immediately after graduating from Leicester University at the age of twenty-two. Eight months later she had fetched up in New Zealand. By her own admission she had fallen in love with the country and had decided to stay. With her degree in English Annabel could have gone to a teacher training college and pursued a career in education, but she hadn't been ready to settle down until she had seen more of the country. It was during this backpacker stage of her life that Annabel had answered an advert for a full-time nanny to a forty-one-year-old widower. The bereaved parent, whose wife had died of cancer, happened to be one of the biggest sheep farmers in New Zealand. Tragically, his only child had succumbed to motor neurone disease at the age of nineteen. After her death, Annabel Quayle had stayed on as a housekeeper. Reading between the lines, it was apparent she had gradually made herself indispensable. There had been no next of kin and in due course she had inherited the property and all that went with it.

'It's decision time,' Ashton said. 'You obviously don't believe her story, Roy, and Ralph does. That's why you came to see me before waltzing the letter into Victor. Right?'

'Correct.'

'Are you still of the same opinion?'

'If anything I'm more convinced than ever,' Kelso told him.

'Well, I'm sorry, Roy, I agree with Ralph. I find her account the more creditable.'

'So why did he tell Piers Felstead he'd had a big win on the lottery?'

'I think it was a matter of pride; he didn't want to admit his sister had lent him the money.' Ashton smiled. 'Look, we all would like to believe that Toby was clean and this letter from Annabel Quayle is strong enough to remove any doubts we might have had about his integrity.'

'So if Hazelwood asked your advice you would recommend we do nothing about her letter,' Kelso

340

said.

'Damned right I would,' Ashton informed him. 'The dispute is between the lady and her solicitors and we shouldn't get involved, because the financial arrangement between sister and brother never was any of our business.'

'There is another practical consideration,' Meacher said quietly. 'So far as the media is concerned Toby Quayle was an innocent victim who happened to be in the wrong place at the wrong time. That letter strengthens our case and will see off any investigative journalist who reckons he has a nose for a good story.'

'It's two to one, Roy,' Ashton observed. 'You want to make it unanimous?'

Kelso pursed his lips and looked judicious. It was his stock expression whenever he found himself in a minority of one and was intended to convey he had serious reservations about the proposed course of action. But as always he nodded his assent after a suitable pause.

*   *   *

The inquiry had started on Thursday 15th April when Hazelwood, Meacher and Ashton had been subpoenaed to give evidence. Ralph Meacher had been recalled the next day for some reason that was a mystery even to him. That same evening Landon had been told that he and Chris Neighbour would be required to give evidence on Tuesday 20th, though why the inquiry was not sitting on Monday had never been explained to him. Roy Kelso had received a message on Monday afternoon to the effect that Chris Neighbour should report at 1100 while he wasn't required until 1400 hours. There had still been no sign of Chris when Landon left Vauxhall Cross to make his way to 4 Central Buildings.

Landon arrived five minutes before the appointed time and was shown into the waiting room. Fifteen minutes after the appointed time he was collected by the court orderly.

The Joint Intelligence Committee was pretty much a closed book to Landon and he had never come across Gavin Pearce before, which was not altogether surprising. All he knew about the JIC was that it was staffed by civil servants and acted like a filtration plant between various intelligence agencies and the Cabinet Office. In this capacity its members were responsible for summarizing the intelligence data in a more digestible form.

Pearce had passed the fifty mark but Landon would never have guessed it if he hadn't looked him up in the latest edition of *Who's Who*. He was immaculately dressed in a grey pinstripe that had a Savile Row cut about it. Sleek was the adjective that readily sprang to mind and best described him.

'I understand you are already acquainted with Mr Urquhart?' Pearce said.

Landon nodded. 'We met quite recently,' he added and received a frosty smile in return.

'What have you done to your face, Will?' Urquhart enquired.

'I had a quarrel with the fridge freezer. One of the cork tiles in the kitchen had come unstuck and I tripped over it.'

'Nasty,' Pearce said and proceeded to acquaint him with the directive the Board of Inquiry had received from the Permanent Under Secretary of

State at the Foreign and Commonwealth Office. He then came straight to the point.

'Tell me, Mr Landon, how many covert operations have you participated in?'

'Two, one in the UK, the other in Switzerland almost a year ago.'

'Were both operations in the nature of a clandestine meeting with a source?' Pearce asked.

'They were.'

'Did you know the identity of the source beforehand?'

'I did in the case of the senior Russian intelligence officer we met in Geneva.'

There was no point in denying it. Pearce had been Chairman of the JIC last June and knew all the grisly details of when that operation had gone pear shaped in a big way. The Russian had proposed to trade Ali Mohammed Khalef for two Chechen rebels who had gone to ground in London. Since the Iraqi cleric was said to be involved in the planning of a major terrorist spectacular directed against the UK, SIS had naturally been interested in the proposition. Unfortunately, despite the presence of four bodyguards, the Russian had been taken out by a Chechen woman who had walked right up to him as he was leaving the Café Simplon in the botanical gardens and blown herself to pieces.

'Strange that you should know the identity of the Russian but not the Saudi,' Pearce observed.

'It was one of the conditions the Saudi imposed. We were given to clearly understand there would be no meeting if we didn't respect his wishes.'

'And you weren't the least bit curious about his identity?'

'Oh, come on, Mr Pearce, I'm sure you are aware of the need-to-know principle.'

The fencing match continued for the best part of half an hour with Pearce constantly striving to trip him up. It was evident to Landon that the Chairman of the JIC was convinced the man they'd met on the 6th April was not a Saudi national. Mentally prepared for a long siege, he was taken aback when Pearce thanked him for being so co-operative and announced he was free to go.

Leaving 4 Central Buildings Landon walked to Parliament Square and picked up a cab at the corner of Whitehall. Ten minutes later he strolled into Vauxhall Cross, flashed his ID card at the armed security guard on duty in the entrance hall and took the first available lift to the top floor. Following the CATO meeting that morning, he had tried to see Ashton twice only to find he was locked in conference with the DG. On this occasion it was a case of third time lucky.

'How did it go, Will?' Ashton enquired before he had a chance to say anything.

'Not too bad. Gavin Pearce did his best to throw me by talking about the incident in Geneva last June. I was quite open about it and told him everything I knew. I figured he should have seen the after-action report and the subsequent internal inquiry.'

'You did the right thing,' Ashton told him.

'The funny thing is, Urquhart never said a word other than to ask me what I had done to my face. I just wonder what he had said before and after I was questioned.'

'Did you stick to the party line?'

'Absolutely.'

'Then you've nothing to worry about, Will.'

Landon thought differently and related what Michael York from GCHQ had told them at the CATO meeting, with particular regard to the Hamas cell leaders in Ramallah and Gaza City whose phone calls they were intercepting.

'That's a real breakthrough,' Ashton said.

'Yes it is.'

'And I presume GCHQ will let us know the moment they learn Ali Mohammed Khalef has arrived in Gaza City?'

'I specifically asked them to do just that.'

'So why are you less than enthusiastic?'

'Because Richard Neagle took me aside after the meeting and made it very obvious that MI5 believed we were relying on Mossad to grab him.'

'Believing is one thing, proving it is quite a different matter,' Ashton said coolly.

Twenty-Three

Seventeen days on and Landon's face was showing definite signs of improvement. The swelling that had virtually closed his right eye had gone, the bruise on the cheekbone had faded to a very pale yellow, his nose was back to its normal shape and the stitches had been removed from the bottom lip a week after the injury had been inflicted. Long ago the absence of any notices appealing for witnesses had told Landon the assailant he'd beaten unconscious was still alive. From the lack of police activity it had also become evident that all three men had declined to make a statement. It was as if the affray had never taken place. Nevertheless, he had moved the car from the lock-up on Gloucester Road to a slightly less accessible underground garage in South Kensington that was a good deal more secure. While the thugs he'd tangled with were unlikely to come at him a second time they wouldn't hesitate to break into the lock-up and trash the Aston Martin.

The Home Secretary had had an informal word with the American ambassador with the result that Virgil Zimmerman had departed towards the end of April. It had been clearly understood that in return there would be no reference to an American involvement when Portland appeared in court charged with breaking and entering. For this to happen it had been necessary to offer Portland an inducement he couldn't refuse. Provided he pleaded guilty, Portland was assured he would be sentenced to a term of imprisonment amounting to no more than two years suspended for eighteen months. In his revised statement to the police there was no reference to Ensley Holsinger, her apartment in Mountford House or the fact that Portland had masqueraded as a detective chief inspector in Special Branch. He'd admitted to entering Landon's flat in Stanhope Gardens for the purpose of installing a listening device, which he had done at the behest of a business rival who had since left the country. As the officer Portland had impersonated, DCI Verco had been loud in his condemnation of the offer until, that is, the deputy assistant commissioner in charge of Special Branch had had a quiet word with him.

Things had quietened down after that spate of activity. There had been no fresh developments regarding the present whereabouts of the two most wanted men on the SIS list, and Landon had come away from the last two CATO meetings at Thames House with nothing to report.

The Balkans was Landon's primary area of responsibility. Although not much was happening in Bosnia there were enough intelligence reports coming in from Kosovo to keep him occupied. In the last two weeks the role of the eight SAS deep penetration patrols had changed following the intensification of attacks on Albanian civilians by the Yugoslav national army. To combat this they were now acting as forward air controllers to NATO aircraft bombing JNA infantry, armoured and artillery units.

A Serbo-Croat or Albanian speaker was attached to each patrol to provide linguistic support. Two such specialists had independently submitted a paper to Military Operations (Special Projects) questioning their continued presence in Kosovo now that the SAS were effectively under NATO control and engaged in an all-out war. Their arguments had certainly impressed Max Brabazon, the retired naval commander in charge of the SIS element of Military Operation (Special Projects). And Landon could see why this should be so; both linguists were former servicemen, one of whom had won a Military Cross in the Falklands.

When the Mozart rang he was in the middle of penning a memo to Ashton supporting the recommendation the two linguists had made.

The caller was Michael York from GCHQ. Grabbing his scratchcard, Landon made a few brief notes, then asked a couple of questions. As soon as York had finished, he rang Ashton on the BT line, said it was vital he saw him ASAP and was told to come up.

'So what's up?' Ashton asked and consigned the file he had been reading to the pending tray.

'I've just been informed by GCHQ that Ali Mohammed Khalef has arrived in Gaza City.'

'Really? When did they learn this?'

'This afternoon—1305 hours our time.'

Ashton glanced at his wristwatch. 'Seventeen minutes past one,' he murmured. 'They didn't waste much time. When did York say the Hamas leaders in Gaza City and Ramallah were expecting to see Khalef?'

'Between the twenty-sixth and twenty-ninth of April,' Landon told him.

'And it's now the seventh of May. He's at least a week late, Will.'

'Yes. I asked York if Khalef had told the Hamas leaders he was going to be late and he said being a bagman for terrorists wasn't a nine to five job. As of now Khalef is in the Zeitoun district of Gaza City and it isn't known whether he intends going to Ramallah. However, GCHQ will contact me the moment they hear anything.'

'But you don't have a Mozart secure-speech facility at your flat, Will.'

'I plan to sleep in the office.'

'Get back to York, tell him that after seven thirty p.m. the duty officer at GCHQ is to call me at home.'

'OK.'

'Is Ralph Meacher aware of this development?'

'Not yet. There's something else you should know. York reckons GCHQ has identified the mobile Talal Asir is using. If they're right, he's currently in Istanbul.'

'So there's an element of doubt in their minds?' Ashton smiled. 'Don't answer that.' Lifting the transceiver on the BT phone he tapped out an internal four-digit number and invited Meacher to pop along to the office.

'How many of those special microchips did you say Asir purchased from CFS Electronique when he was living in Paris?'

'Sixty.'

'I wonder how many he kept back for himself?'

'The microchip had nothing to do with it,' Landon told him. 'GCHQ identified Asir by the number of calls he made to different numbers and the content of each one.'

'What's going on?' Meacher demanded as he walked into the room.

Ashton said, 'It's a red-letter day, Ralph. Will's friend at GCHQ has just told him that Mohammed Khalef is in Gaza City.'

'How long has he been there?' Meacher asked as he slipped into the chair Landon had just vacated.

'Since five past one today. At least that's when they intercepted his transmission. He could have arrived yesterday, the day before that or even a week ago. A visit to Ramallah may or may not be on the cards.'

'And he may or may not be about to move elsewhere.'

'Anything is possible, Ralph.'

'So what are we going to do?' Meacher asked. 'Wait for confirmation?'

That was the last thing Ashton had in mind. The way he saw it they had to go with what they had. That meant Ralph needed to contact Sam Levy immediately and give him the information. To set up a face to face meeting with Ben-Yosef first would eat into what little time they had. The important thing was for Mossad to know Mohammed Khalef was holed up in the Zeitoun district of Gaza City. The Israeli intelligence service could then have a strike force at five minutes' notice to move while the SIS tied up the finer points with Mossad's representative in London.

'Am I to tell Sam exactly how we came by this information?' Meacher asked.

'I'm afraid you must, otherwise Mossad won't attach much credibility to the information.'

'The ability to identify a mobile belonging to a terrorist has got to be top secret.'

'You're right it is,' Ashton said.

'Well then . . . ?'

'Nailing Khalef is more important than preserving the security status of a technique that won't remain a secret for long.'

'I'm still not happy about it, Peter.'

'All right, let's take the problem to Victor and get a decision from him. God knows he's changed his mind about involving Mossad often enough, maybe he'll change it again.'

Meacher got to his feet and moved towards the door. 'Forget it, I'm not going through that rigmarole again.'

'Where are you off to, Ralph?'

'I'm going to tell Malcolm Ives he is in charge of the Mid East Department for the rest of the day, which will hardly be a new experience for him. Then I'm going to have a cosy little chat with my friend Sam.'

'I'd better phone GCHQ,' Landon said and made to follow Meacher out of the room.

'Hang on a minute,' Ashton told him. 'I've got another job for you.'

The job entailed the collection of certain statistical data. Specifically, Ashton wanted to know what type of helicopter, if any, could make the round trip from RAF Akrotiri in Cyprus to an unprepared landing zone in Israel and back again without refuelling. He was not, repeat not, to seek advice from the RAF. Instead he was to use the library on the second floor and extract the technical information from the latest edition of *Jane's All the World's Aircraft*. He would probably find the geographical details in the forty-fifth edition of *The Middle East and North Africa* published by Europe Publications Limited.

'Am I allowed to know what this is all about?' Landon asked.

'We may have to provide a pick-up service, Will.'

'I think I'm with you.'

'Good.' Ashton lifted the transceiver on the Mozart. 'I'd like the answers before I see Max Brabazon,' he added.

*   *   *

Max Brabazon was a confirmed bachelor who had been wedded to the Royal Navy ever since he had been a cadet at Dartmouth. The evidence was there for all to see who were invited to his rented apartment in Dolphin Square. It was displayed in the photographs of the ships he had served in, like HMS *Gloucester*, the Type 42 destroyer, the frigate HMS *Broadsword* and his first command, the 'ton' class minehunter HMS *Maxim*. Pride of place, however, went to his last command, the modified Type 12 Rothsay class frigate HMS *Plymouth*.

In a long, distinguished naval career Brabazon had participated in the Suez invasion, the anti-terrorist quarantine of Cyprus at the height of the EOKA campaign and the confrontation with Indonesia over Borneo and Brunei from '63 to '66. Finally, at the age of forty-six, he had taken part in the Falklands war. But it wasn't only his experience of what it was like to be under fire that had prompted the SIS to offer Brabazon a job when he retired from the navy. Where other officers had specialized in gunnery, navigation or anti-submarine warfare, he had gravitated to signals, a year-long course that had included electronic warfare and electronic counter-measures. As a senior officer he had done a three-year stint at the MoD as a member of the Defence Intelligence Staff. Two years after being promoted to lieutenant commander he had been posted to the British Defence Staff in Washington DC as a naval attaché. It was the long signals course and the two shore appointments that had given him the edge over the other contender, a retired lieutenant colonel in the Intelligence Corps.

His job was to find round pegs for round holes from within the ranks of serving and retired members of the armed forces. Until 1997 he had taken his instructions from the Deputy DG. In March of that year there had been an organizational change that had seen the resurrection of the East European Department under the leadership of Peter Ashton. To justify this submission to the establishment committee the chain of command had been amended and Brabazon had found himself answering to a man twenty years the younger. It could have been a difficult working relationship but Ashton was no armchair warrior. He, too, had entered the SIS by the back door, having spent nine months in Belfast as an undercover agent with the army's Special Patrol Unit and had also fought in the Falklands with 22 SAS.

Life with Ashton was never dull. A phone call from him at 1340 hours was the reason why Brabazon had left his office in the main building of the MoD and set off for the Army and Navy Club in Pall Mall. Mindful that he shared an office with the lieutenant colonel commanding the military element of Special Projects, Ashton had been pretty cagey even though he had come through on the Mozart link. The younger man had merely said he was to leave without arousing the suspicion of his colleague and meet him at the club. Picking the right moment to slip away had taken longer than expected and consequently he was not surprised to find Ashton waiting for him in the entrance hall when he arrived.

'I've booked a conference room on the third floor,' Ashton told him. 'I don't know whether you would care to have a drink before we begin?'

'Perhaps another time,' Brabazon murmured.

The conference room was big enough to seat twenty at a large mahogany table. At Ashton's suggestion they chose to sit nearest the window overlooking St James's Square.

'This is a pick-up job, Max. Hopefully it won't come off but we have to be at instant readiness to collect Ali Mohammed Khalef.'

'From where?'

'Israel,' Ashton said tersely. 'We're looking at a round trip of five hundred and twenty-one miles without a refuelling stop. Landon's been doing some research; he reckons a Westland Sea King Mark 4 with maximum standard fuel at six thousand feet will do the job with a safety cushion of over three hundred miles. But check that with whatever company you are going to hire.'

'You may take that for granted.'

'We need three minders, ex-servicemen currently employed by a good crisis management firm. For preference, the men should have served in Special Forces.'

'Are they to be armed?' Brabazon asked.

'Yes, for personal protection only, 9mm P7 Heckler & Koch pistols. They will be delivered to the minders on their arrival in Cyprus. Chris Neighbour will be flying out tonight on BA664. The weapons will be travelling with him in the diplomatic bag.'

The enormity of what they were planning to do was not lost on Brabazon but there was more to come. Logotype and registration letters that could identify the owners of the helicopter were to be obliterated on arrival at RAF Akrotiri. Normal air traffic control procedures were to be observed except when entering and leaving Israeli air space.

'This whole business is fraught with risk,' Brabazon observed. 'All it will take is one tiny misunderstanding and we will be faced with a major disaster. There's something else you should bear in mind: this operation won't come cheap.'

'The money is not a problem,' Ashton told him. 'However, the risks involved do alarm me. That's why I'm hoping it won't come off.'

'Hoping is all very well but is it realistic, Peter?'

'Mossad's Head of Station in London told me that having located the target they would in fact kill him at the first opportunity. This they would do using a helicopter gunship armed with air-to-ground laser-guided missiles. Of course, he was talking about Talal Asir but, make no mistake, they will deal with Ali Mohammed Khalef in like fashion.' Ashton smiled. 'Do you have any other questions, Max?'

'Plenty. Who will our mercenaries look to for a go or no go decision?'

'Chris Neighbour, and he will get the word from me.'

'I'm glad to hear it. I wouldn't be happy if the decision was taken too far down the ladder.'

'Any other questions?'

'Just one,' Brabazon told him. 'What are your movements?'

'I'll leave the office at six fifteen and I won't have access to a Mozart for the next two hours. Thereafter you can catch me at home all over the weekend.'

'I think we can survive a two-hour breakdown of communications,' Brabazon said dryly. 'When do you hope to see our mercenaries in position?'

'We should aim for eighteen hundred hours Greenwich Mean Time tomorrow.'

'You obviously believe in miracles.'

'Well, if anyone can work a miracle, it's you, Max.'

'Just don't bank on it,' Brabazon growled.

They left the club together, turned right outside and walked up to Pall Mall, where Ashton flagged down a passing cab. 'You take this one, Max,' he said, 'you're more pressed for time.'

Brabazon didn't argue with him.

*   *   *

Sam Levy ran his business from the second floor of Peel House, an anonymous office block some two minutes' walk from Baker Street station. Today would be the second time Meacher had been there, the previous occasion being early on in their friendship long before he had discovered that Sam was a quasi Counsellor for Commercial Affairs on behalf of the Israeli Embassy. Thereafter they had met on neutral ground either at Moor Park Golf Club or at some restaurant in town that was off the beaten track. Entering Peel House, he signed in as Ralph Messenger, representing self to see Sam Levy, and was given a visitor's pass. Nobody asked him for proof of identity. For the sake of appearances he made himself known to the clerks and waited while one of them rang Levy to announce his visitor had arrived.

'Good to see you, Ralph,' Levy said, then waved him to a chair as he closed the door. 'Where's the fire?'

'What?'

'I got the impression from your phone call that something was about to implode.'

'Something is. Ali Mohammed Khalef has arrived in the Zeitoun district of Gaza City.'

'Is that a rumour or a fact?'

'The information is a hundred per cent reliable,' Meacher said. 'And you need to pass the word to David Ben-Yosef right now, because our Iraqi

356

cleric won't be there for long. I imagine Mossad will know who is the Hamas cell leader in that particular district and the safe houses that are at his disposal?'

Levy held up a hand to silence him before he went any further. 'Wait a minute, Ralph, how do you know this information is so kosher?'

It was the question Meacher had been dreading. The ability of GCHQ to identify the Talal Asir network by the type of microchip they were using to make their mobile phones secure was classified top secret. The fact that Ashton had said they might well have to breach this security classification simply meant both of them would be put through the mincer should MI5 hear about it. Nevertheless Meacher decided to chance it.

'The eavesdroppers have the ability to identify which mobile phones are in the hands of the terrorists,' he said and then explained how the breakthrough had come about.

'I don't know about David Ben-Yosef, Ralph, but you've convinced me.'

'Thanks for your vote of confidence,' Meacher said tersely. 'Now pick up the phone and convince him.'

*   *   *

Ashton paid off the taxi at Vauxhall station, entered the subway as the cab driver moved off and then retraced his steps when satisfied the vehicle was out of sight. It had gone three o'clock when he entered the SIS building and took the first available lift up to the top floor. Kelso was in the habit of slipping off early on a Friday afternoon and it was essential Neighbour's travel arrangements were firmed up before he disappeared. The greeting Ashton received was unusual even for him.

'Ah, there you are, I've been looking for you,' Kelso said with evident satisfaction. 'What's all this nonsense Landon has been giving me about one of your officers having to fly out to Cyprus tonight, or maybe tomorrow or even the day after tomorrow, first class if necessary. I ask you, what does he think I'm running here? A travel agency?'

'I hope you took notice of what he said, Roy.'

'What?'

'Will was showing good anticipation. I want Chris Neighbour on a flight to Cyprus this evening,' Ashton told him. 'It has to be British Airways because he will be taking a diplomatic bag with him. World traveller, club or first class; get him on a flight even if it costs you an arm and a leg.'

'And if every seat is taken?'

'All airlines overbook at times. Ask British Airways to find an amicable customer and offer him a generous financial inducement to give up his seat. And be sure to tell the airline we will foot the bill.' Ashton backed out into the corridor. 'Chris will need a hundred Cyprus pounds for incidental expenses. Also, please ring the armourer and tell him to have three 9mm P7 Heckler & Koch pistols with thirteen rounds for each weapon ready for collection by Chris Neighbour at six p.m.'

'He can't board an aircraft carrying three semi-automatic weapons,' Kelso protested.

'He isn't going to,' Ashton said. 'They'll be in the diplomatic bag.'

'Does Hazelwood know about this?'

Ashton walked away without saying anything. It was safer to ignore the question and leave Kelso in doubt. Given any kind of positive response, he would be on the phone to Hazelwood to verify what he had just been told and that would put the cat among the pigeons. What he needed was a little more breathing space to complete the preparatory phase of the operation; after that there would be time enough to brief Victor.

He called Neighbour into his office and told him he was going to Cyprus and would be at thirty minutes' notice to move with effect from five o'clock. Head of Station, Nicosia would be asked to provide accommodation and Neighbour was to use the Mozart link at the High Commission to keep in touch with Vauxhall Cross. He would receive the latest intelligence update through this link as well as the composition and time of arrival of the collection party. Ashton had almost finished the briefing when Kelso came through on the line with details of the arrangements he had made.

'Good news,' Ashton said and put the phone down. 'You're on British Airways flight BA664 departing Heathrow 2030 hours tonight. Pick up your flight ticket and a hundred pounds in local currency from Roy Kelso, then ring the transport section and order a car to pick you up from your flat and allow enough time to collect the diplomatic bag from here.'

'OK.'

'One final point. If the pick-up team is despatched to collect Ali Mohammed Khalef you don't go with them. Understood?'

'Yes, but it doesn't seem right.'

'I'm not interested in appearances, Chris. There's

359

a fifty-fifty chance the operation could go badly wrong, that's why we have to distance ourselves from it. Clear?'

'Yes.'

'Then you'd better get moving.' Ashton picked up the Mozart and punched out Landon's number. 'Well done, Will,' he said when the younger man answered.

'What have I done to deserve a pat on the back?' Landon asked.

'You anticipated somebody would have to go out to Cyprus and acted on the assumption, so now you know.'

'There's no answer to that.'

'Well, I need a couple of answers from you,' Ashton told him. 'Has GCHQ picked up any more transmissions from Ali Mohammed Khalef?'

'No, he's still in Gaza City so far as they're aware. York did say they had lost track of Talal Asir and think he may have left Istanbul.'

'Congratulations, you've just answered my second question,' Ashton said and hung up.

There was no longer any reason to put off informing Victor of exactly what he had set in motion. Had he been a smoking man, a cigarette would have been welcome at that particular moment. However, contrary to what he had anticipated, Hazelwood did not erupt, nor did he give the impression that he had gone cold on the operation.

*　　　*　　　*

The signal from Head of Station, Bern could hardly have been more mundane. It referred to a

360

large property on the Waldstrasse halfway between the ski resorts of Arosa and Maran and stated that after standing empty for sixteen months the Villa Bergman was now occupied by a couple in their late thirties and a male companion of North African appearance. The signal was classified restricted and accorded a routine precedence, which practically guaranteed it wouldn't be looked at before Monday 10th May.

The Villa Bergman had been purchased by Talal Asir in the days when he had been the vice president in charge of overseas investments at the National Bank of Saudi Arabia.

Twenty-Four

The first grey light of dawn roused Ashton at 0300 hours. For a panic-stricken moment he couldn't think what he was doing lying in bed next to Harriet when he should have been at Vauxhall Cross within touching distance of a Mozart secure line. Then he recalled that Ralph Meacher had relieved him on Sunday evening shortly before 7.30 and his pulse rate fell back to a normal seventy-two. On reflection he could not recall a more frenetic time than the last sixty hours from three o'clock on Friday afternoon.

Getting Chris Neighbour off to Cyprus with three Heckler & Koch 9mm semi-automatic pistols in a diplomatic bag had been the least of his problems. Head of Station, Nicosia, who had met him at Larnaca airport, hadn't been too happy when he'd learned what was in the diplomatic bag. However,

British Airways flight BA664 had been scheduled to arrive at 3.10 a.m., and precious few people were happy as Larry at that hour of the morning. The three-man team charged with collecting Ali Mohammed Khalef from the Israelis had been provided by Sentinel, a crisis management consultancy the majority of whose personnel were former members of the SAS and Royal Marine Commandos. Without exception all of them were self-employed; consequently, the administrative staff at the registered offices of Sentinel had had to ring up individuals on their books to find out who was available and wanted a job in the sun for a strictly limited time. The bait had been a tax-free salary of seven fifty a day with all expenses paid. By the early hours of Saturday morning Sentinel had two firm takers whom they had despatched to Athens by British Airways flight 632 and then onward to Larnaca by Olympic Airways. The third man had travelled the same route overnight and had arrived in Cyprus midday on Sunday.

Long before then Sentinel had encountered one major problem. Although able to provide the requisite aircrew, obtaining a Westland Sea King Mark 4 was beyond them. They had also informed Brabazon it would be impossible to pre-position a helicopter at Akrotiri by the deadline set by Ashton. They were therefore faced with two stark choices: either they cancelled the operation or Hazelwood briefed the Cabinet Office and obtained the necessary helicopter support from the RAF. Since from the outset Victor had wanted to keep the whole business within the immediate family, Ashton had assumed he would be instructed to stand everyone down. To his surprise

362

Hazelwood had told him to proceed on the assumption that the requisite helicopter support would be forthcoming. Just how this would come about when the Cabinet Office was still in the dark was beyond Ashton.

He peered at the alarm clock on the bedside table again, saw that it was now seventeen minutes past three and decided it was time he made a move. Trying not to disturb Harriet, he eased the bedclothes aside and put one foot on the floor.

'I'll get breakfast while you're dressing,' Harriet said quietly.

'How long have you been awake?' he asked.

'Probably half an hour longer than you.'

'Was I snoring?'

'No, just tossing and turning, the way you always do when there's a flap on and things aren't going too well.'

Harriet got out of bed, went to the window and opened the curtains. She was a tall woman, half an inch under six feet, a fact of life she had once tried to disguise by wearing low heels and hunching her shoulders. That was the way she had walked into the office the day they'd first met all those long years ago when she had been seconded to the SIS from MI5. By the end of that first day, the slouch and hunched shoulders had disappeared for ever.

'Coffee, fruit juice, eggs and bacon,' Harriet said on her way out of the bedroom.

'Only toast, please.'

'I wasn't asking what you would like.'

'You were just telling me what I would get?'

'Exactly. God knows when you will eat again and I don't want you fading away.'

Although he'd shaved the night before Ashton

ran a razor over the new growth of stubble, then freshened up under the shower. Returning to their bedroom, he slipped the washbag into the holdall Harriet had packed for him on Sunday evening, then quickly dressed and went downstairs into the kitchen.

'Two minutes more,' Harriet informed him. 'Meantime, help yourself to coffee.'

'Thanks.'

'You're not going away, are you, Peter? Because every time you're sent abroad I wonder if you will come home in one piece.'

It was an oblique reference to an incident five years ago up at Lake Arrowhead, California, when a man called Gillespie had put a bullet in his shoulder with a 6.35 Walther PPK semi-automatic.

'You've no worries on that score,' Ashton promised her. 'My days as a foot soldier are over.'

'You can't know how relieved I am to hear you say that.'

Although people who met Harriet for the first time were aware she had a good figure, it was the perfect symmetry of her face that claimed their attention and remained firmly imprinted in their minds afterwards. To most of the village she was the very attractive young woman whose husband was something big in the City and who lived in Roseland Cottage with their three children, Edward, Carolyn and four-month-old Bernadette.

No one knew just how tough life had been for Harriet. He had nearly lost her six years ago in Berlin when her skull had been fractured by a Turkish Gastarbeiter during a race riot in the Kreuzberg district. Her mother had committed suicide by suffocating herself with a plastic bag after learning she had terminal cancer, and barely three years ago her father had succumbed to Alzheimer's. If that wasn't enough, she had also miscarried between Edward and the birth of Carolyn.

'What's wrong, Peter?'

Ashton was suddenly aware of the bacon and eggs she had placed in front of him. 'With breakfast—absolutely nothing.'

'I was referring to the office. There's some kind of major problem, isn't there?'

'We've gone out on a limb and embarked on an operation that almost certainly will go horribly wrong. And it will be my fault because I talked Victor into it.'

'Nonsense,' Harriet said firmly. 'No one ever talked Hazelwood into doing something he didn't want to do. And don't let him convince you otherwise.'

Harriet had never understood the bond that existed between Hazelwood and himself. In her opinion loyalty extended in both directions, down as well as up. There was a time when he would have denied the assertion vehemently, but it seemed to him that in the last twelve months Victor's chief concern had been to look out for himself.

Eating quickly, Ashton finished the eggs and bacon, swallowed the cup of coffee, then wiped his lips on the napkin. 'Time I was going,' he said and stood up.

'Drive carefully and no heroics.'

Ashton smiled. 'How can you be heroic behind a desk?'

'Then just remember to stay there.'

365

Harriet wrapped her arms around his shoulders and hugged him close, her body ramming into his. She was wearing a cotton nightshirt that barely covered her thighs and the temptation to raise it proved irresistible as their tongues fenced. Presently she placed a hand against his chest and gently pushed him away.

'I think you had better go,' she said in a husky voice that was lodged somewhere in the back of her throat.

Ashton kissed her one more time, collected the holdall from the foot of the staircase and left the cottage. Backing the Volvo out of the driveway, he picked up the Portsmouth road on the outskirts of the village and headed west to link up with the A3 to London. There was very little traffic on the road and he had a clear run all the way to Vauxhall Cross.

*   *   *

The sun was well above the horizon when Ashton walked into the Art Deco building and showed his ID card to the armed security guard on duty in the entrance hall. At 5.36 in the morning he didn't have to wait for a lift and the car took him straight up to the top floor without any intermediate stops. Pausing only to obtain a cup of dubious-looking coffee from the vending machine near the bank of lifts, he turned right in the corridor and made his way to Ralph Meacher's office.

The office Ralph Meacher had inherited from Jill Sheridan when she had been promoted from Assistant Director in charge of the Mid East Department to Deputy DG overlooked the Thames and was three times larger than the cubbyhole allocated to Roy Kelso. This was a bone of contention with the Admin King, who conveniently forgot how he had fought tooth and nail for an office on the top floor. In the days when the SIS had occupied Century House, Roy Kelso's fiefdom had been farmed out to Benbow House in Southwark, and he had been determined never to be divorced from his peer group again.

'Good morning, Ralph,' Ashton said cheerfully. 'Any developments while I've been away?'

Meacher turned away from the window where he had been gazing out at the Houses of Parliament across the river. 'Chris Neighbour rang from Nicosia at ten to eight last night with details of the signals plan.'

'And?'

'It's a recipe for a disaster. We're relying on Radio Tel Aviv to tell us when to go, in Arabic and Hebrew.'

The Israelis had borrowed heavily from the BBC. Throughout World War Two and particularly in the run-up to D-Day, the Overseas Service had broadcast a series of coded messages to Resistance groups in occupied Europe. Each message was a simple quotation the meaning of which was known only to the originator and the recipient. Of the two quotations allocated to the collection team 'There is a distant sound of drums' signified that Mossad had launched the operation to snatch Ali Mohammed Khalef, while 'Even the ranks of Tuscany could scarce forbear to cheer' was the signal for the collection team to lift off.

'The moment the helicopter enters Israeli air space, the pilot will be given the bearing he should take for the landing zone. This will be marked on the ground with a luminous recognition panel. The wind direction will be indicated by a smoke pot. Chris Neighbour has of course been told what radio frequency the pilot is to use.'

'What language will the air traffic controller use?' Ashton asked.

'Hebrew,' Meacher said tersely.

'And what have we done about that, Ralph?'

'We're an educated lot in the Mid East Department. The Grade II intelligence officer who runs the Levant desk is fluent in Hebrew. I ran him to ground in Farncombe where he lives and got him on the last flight to Athens yesterday.' Meacher glanced at his wristwatch. 'His flight arrived on schedule at 0440 hours local time, which means he's been on the ground for approximately four and a quarter hours now.'

'What's the departure time of the first Olympic Airways flight to Cyprus?'

'It left at 0905 hours their time but we don't know if he was on it. Olympic is looked after by the British Airways desk at Heathrow and they couldn't tell us because the Olympic desk in Athens closed down for the night at 2100 hours Greenwich Mean Time. It wasn't possible to pre-book the onward flight.' Meacher stretched both arms above his head and yawned. 'I think that about covers everything.'

'One question. Who told Chris to monitor Radio Tel Aviv and gave him the two quotations?'

'You met her at the King's Head in Amersham. Her name is Malka and she claimed to be Sam Levy's sister.'

'I don't care who she is related to,' Ashton said angrily, 'she's a Mossad agent. Maybe she is even more important than David Ben-Yosef. Between them they probably cobbled together this crazy signals plan soon after they received the down payment of half a million.'

'Well, I did tell you it was a recipe for disaster. If it's OK with you, Peter, I'm going to have a wash and brush-up.'

'Go ahead, I'll hold the fort.'

'Oh, by the way, the operation is now to be known as "Harpoon". That was Hazelwood's contribution.'

Hazelwood had insisted the need-to-know list should be kept to the bare minimum, by which he meant no more than four to five officers. MI5, GCHQ Cheltenham and the Defence Intelligence Staff had all been kept in the dark. As far as Ashton was concerned, the world and his wife would know about Operation Harpoon before much longer.

*   *   *

Landon had gone into the office on Saturday to see if GCHQ had intercepted any further calls from Ali Mohammed Khalef that would indicate the Iraqi cleric was still in Gaza City. If ever a journey had been unnecessary his most certainly had been. The fact was Ashton would have contacted him if he'd heard anything from Michael York. Much to his surprise he had found Peter ensconced in Meacher's office, which was being used as a makeshift ops room. He'd hung around until gone one o'clock trying to make himself useful but there had been little for him to do other than act as a telephone orderly whenever Ashton was conferring

369

with the DG.

Sunday had been even more frustrating. Landon had stayed away from the office on a promise from Ashton that he would ring him at the flat or on his mobile should GCHQ have anything for him. Depending on the time of the day Ashton would suggest they met for a drink at his local or had a bite to eat somewhere or caught the latest box office attraction, but there had been no coded message for him. He had resisted the temptation to ring the office until eight o'clock, when curiosity had finally got the better of him. The moment Landon had found himself talking to an irate Ralph Meacher he knew he had made a big mistake and had promptly broken the connection.

Landon hadn't known quite what to expect when he came into work that Monday morning. He checked with the chief archivist in Central Registry, who was busy sorting the first delivery, but there was nothing for him that required action this day. Ashton had nothing for him either, other than the codeword for the abduction of Ali Mohammed Khalef.

'Is Harpoon going to come off?' Landon asked.

'Put it this way, Will. The collection team is in position, so is the Hebrew speaker from the Levant desk, and Chris Neighbour is waiting for the first quotation to be broadcast on Radio Tel Aviv. The only trouble is we still don't have a helicopter and, as of this minute, the DG is locked in combat with the secretary of the Cabinet Office, hoping to get his backing for RAF support. My guess is he—'

Ashton broke off to answer the BT phone. The conversation lasted barely longer than a minute and Landon found it impossible to guess what was being said either from his responses or by his expression when he put the phone down. In the silence that followed Landon couldn't resist prompting him for an explanation.

'Well?' he said.

'That was Victor, he's back. I was going to say my guess is he won't get the backing he wants, but he has. The Cabinet secretary is going to support his request.' Ashton stood up. 'Morning prayers is going to be very interesting,' he added cryptically.

Landon thought the same would apply to the next meeting of the CATO committee. As was his usual practice when preparing for the weekly meeting, he visited each department in turn and sounded out those desk officers whose area of responsibility included some of the world's hotspots. It was also his habit to deal with the quietest areas first in order to give himself more time with the real flashpoints. Nowhere was quieter than the South Central region, embracing Austria, the Czech Republic, Slovakia and Switzerland. It was such a dormant area that desk officers were rotated every six months. The present incumbent had only been in post since the beginning of April and was still feeling his way.

'Tell me something, Will,' he said, holding up a slip of paper, 'why should I be interested in the Villa Bergman on the Waldstrasse? It's midway between Arosa and Maran.'

'I know where it is,' Landon told him. 'Is that a signal from Head of Station, Bern you're holding aloft?'

'It is.'

'May I see it please?'

'Be my guest.'

Landon read the brief text and immediately had a gut feeling that the man of North African appearance was Talal Asir.

'There's been a cock-up in Central Registry; this signal should never have come to you. Leave it with me and I'll get it sorted,' he said and walked off with the signal before the desk officer could think of objecting.

Back in his own office Landon fired off a signal to Head of Station, Bern suggesting the Swiss police should be requested to keep the occupants of the villa under surveillance round the clock. He then checked the flight times to Zurich and connecting trains to Arosa with the friendly travel agent used by Roy Kelso.

The delayed morning prayers seemed to last for ever and it was gone ten o'clock before they finally broke up and he was able to get hold of Ashton and show him the signal.

'Very interesting, Will,' he said, 'but is the Villa Bergman one of the properties Talal Asir misappropriated for his own use?'

'According to our records it is. The place has been unoccupied for the last sixteen months and suddenly there are two men and a woman staying there. I know that doesn't make one of the men Talal Asir.'

'All right, Will, I'm going to talk it over with Victor.' Ashton smiled. 'I don't say anything will come of it but to be on the safe side you'd better collect your passport from the flat.'

*   *   *

Ruislip Lido would not have been Dermot

McManus's first choice as a venue for a lunchtime assignation with Julie Meacher. Unfortunately, the friend in Pinner who had lent him his house in Elm Tree Grove a little over three weeks ago had not been disposed to do so on this occasion. His wife Barbara was an assistant floor manager at Selfridges and Ralph Meacher was someone pretty big in the Mid East Department of the FCO, and it was therefore ironic that two very comfortable love nests should be going begging. But of course neither of them could afford to take any chances. Julie didn't want to lose a husband without the prospect of immediately acquiring another, and as the Lib Dem candidate for Hillingdon and Ruislip he was not in a hurry to get himself deselected. Discretion was the name of the game and this lunchtime he had picked up Julie in Ruislip Manor, where she had gone allegedly to see one of her clients. He had also thought it expedient to avoid parking the Mercedes near the lido itself.

'You seem very preoccupied,' McManus observed. 'You've hardly put two words together since I picked you up from the station.'

'Well, there is a reason. Ralph behaved very strangely the whole weekend from the moment he arrived home on Friday evening till he suddenly decided on Sunday that his presence was required in the office.'

'Had it anything to do with us?' McManus asked, trying not to sound alarmed.

'He would have me believe it didn't, said the way things were going he would be lucky if he still had a job by next Friday.'

'Did Ralph say why?'

Julie nodded. 'It was all very involved and Ralph

373

kept alluding to something he called a high-risk strategy and how it could all go horribly wrong. I was almost convinced but then this morning I went through his desk and found a letter from Sedgewick James, a firm of estate agents in Harrow. It was dated the first of April and in response to his request for a valuation. They reckoned our house would fetch one and a quarter million if it was put on the market.'

Julie's eyes narrowed in anger, her face transformed and ugly with spite. She reminded McManus of a domestic cat confronting the one next door, tail puffed up like a fox's brush, claws unsheathed and ready to lash out.

'Ralph never said a word to me; the swine was planning to sell the house behind my back. Look at the sneaky way he went about it. He didn't bother to consult any of the estate agents in Ruislip. Oh no, he goes to a firm in Harrow, four miles away.'

'Has Ralph ever accused you of having an affair?'

'No.'

'Well then, there could be another explanation for his behaviour.'

'Like what?' Julie snapped.

'Just three weeks ago you told me Ralph was worried stiff and was talking wildly about finding himself on the scrapheap. Maybe he was feeling under pressure even before that.'

'My husband has always been withdrawn,' Julie sneered.

'So when did you first notice the change in him?'

'It must have been around the middle of March, though why that should be of interest—'

'Bear with me,' McManus said, aware of her growing impatience. 'If Ralph did lose his job how would it affect his pension?'

Julie nibbled at her bottom lip and looked pensive. 'He would expect to retire in 2007, which means he would lose the normal rank increment for the next seven and a bit years. And since he was only promoted to assistant director a year ago he's still on the bottom rate of pay in the appointment.'

'In other words you would feel the pinch,' McManus suggested.

'Our lifestyle would certainly change,' Julie agreed, and half turned towards him.

'Exactly. Of course I am only guessing, Julie, but I think Ralph wanted to know how much the property was worth in case he was compelled to resign on a reduced pension.'

'He'll have to resign all right if only half of what he told me is true. Remember Mohammed Khalef, the Iraqi cleric who claimed he was on Saddam Hussein's death list but wasn't?'

'What about him?'

'We want Khalef so badly we're paying the Jews to catch him.'

It was sensational stuff and he knew there was a lot more to come.

Twenty-Five

Ashton stepped into the lift and pressed the button for the underground garage where he had parked the Volvo. Landon had already left for Zurich on British Airways flight 214 departing at 1200 hours, and unless he encountered a traffic jam on the way to Heathrow he would only be a couple of hours behind him. The passport in his jacket pocket came from the blanks held by the Technical Services division and had been processed by Terry Hicks and the clerks of the Admin Wing. In the space of seventy-five minutes his photograph had been taken and his surname, given names, nationality, date and place of birth had been recorded on an insert together with his passport number and a facsimile of his signature that had subsequently been laminated to page 31.

Alighting from the lift, Ashton aimed the remote control at the Volvo and released the central locking. As he walked towards the car the transport supervisor called him over to the office.

'The Director for you,' he said, and passed the phone to him.

'Neighbour has just called from the High Commission in Nicosia,' Hazelwood informed him. '"There is a distant sound of drums" was broadcast by Radio Tel Aviv ten minutes ago. I thought you would like to know, Peter.'

'Thanks.'

'If we can get Talal Asir as well as Mohammed Khalef in one day it will be a tremendous feather in our caps.'

'Yes it would. We must hope Talal Asir is staying at the Villa Bergman.'

They also had to hope the Swiss would keep him in jail while the necessary extradition papers were being prepared, but that was not what Hazelwood needed to hear right now.

'You never know, some of my luck may rub off on you,' Hazelwood said and hung up.

Ashton returned to the Volvo, dumped his holdall on to the adjoining seat, then got in behind the wheel, started up and drove out of the underground garage. Hazelwood was lucky all right. It was one thing to get the backing of the Cabinet secretary, but for the Cabinet to order the RAF to provide the necessary helicopter support was something not far short of a miracle. He wondered what story Victor had pitched the Cabinet Secretary. There was no point in speculating what it might have been, the fact was RAF Akrotiri had had a search and rescue Sea King at immediate readiness with effect from 1115 hours. By now, Chris Neighbour would be on his way to the airfield to give the aircrew and three ex-servicemen from the Sentinel Agency their final briefing.

Morning prayers had been a bad-tempered affair. Rowan Garfield, Roy Kelso, Roger Benton, Hugo Calthorpe and the acting head of the West European Department had wanted to know why they had had no forewarning of Operation Harpoon. Victor had had a difficult time convincing them they had been excluded on the need-to-know principle. As the proponent of the operation, Ashton had felt morally bound to stand shoulder to shoulder with Victor, but he could see

377

Ralph Meacher was uncomfortable with it. At one point in the heated discussion Dilys Crowther, who had lost count of the number of meetings she had attended, had intervened to ask how much of the exchange should be recorded in the minutes of the meeting. Before Victor had a chance to answer her question Rowan Garfield had told Dilys he wanted a verbatim report or as near as she could make it. Victor had been against the demand but had been forced to put it to the vote. As it happened only Ralph Meacher had sided with the Deputy DG.

Morning prayers had started late and lasted far too long. It had cut into what little time Ashton had had to act on Landon's hunch about the occupants of the Villa Bergman. While Landon was in Stanhope Gardens collecting his passport, he had battled hard to get Victor to agree that they should at least check out the villa. He had also persuaded him that the legal department of the FCO should be asked to prepare a warrant for extradition. He had then called Head of Station, Bern on the Mozart link and requested him to meet Landon at the railway station in Arosa. That done, he had landed Kelso with the problem of getting Landon on the first available flight to Zurich and providing him with sufficient Swiss francs to cover the return train fare to Arosa and incidental expenses. There was to be no respite for Kelso: one hour after despatching Landon, Ashton had informed him that Hazelwood had decided he should join Will in Arosa.

After crossing the river by Battersea Bridge, Ashton headed north to Sloane Square, then cut across to join the A4 trunk road in Brompton. It was slow going all the way, and, until the trunk

378

road became the M4 motorway, it looked as if he would miss the Swissair flight. Leaving the Volvo in the long-stay car park, he reported to the Swissair desk in Terminal 2 at 1324 hours, a mere twenty-six minutes before take-off.

*   *   *

Mossad was aware that Ali Mohammed Khalef had arrived in Gaza City twenty-four hours before their Head of Station in London relayed the same information from the SIS on Friday 7th May. Their source, as was so often the case, was a Palestinian who was a semi-active member of Hamas. It had then taken the Israeli intelligence service a further seventy-two hours to pinpoint the block of flats where Mohammed Khalef was staying. By that time Mossad was also satisfied that the Iraqi cleric had no intention of visiting Ramallah. On the recommendation of the intelligence service, executive action was approved by the Cabinet and passed to the air force with orders to effect soonest.

Two Apache attack helicopters under the command of Captain Yehuda Gur were assigned to the mission. Each was armed with a McDonnell Douglas M230 Chain Gun 30mm automatic cannon located between the mainwheel legs in an under-fuselage mounting with Lear Siegler electronic controls. For this mission the main armament consisted of four laser-guided air-to-surface Hellbore anti-tank missiles. The target itself was on the south-west outskirts of Gaza City less than a mile from the border with the Egyptian province of Sinai.

From their base at Ashdod, thirty miles south of Tel Aviv, Captain Gur and his wingman flew out to sea at wave top height until they were out of sight from the land, then headed south west on a bearing of 208 degrees for twenty-four miles before beginning their approach to the target. The pilots came in fast, their helicopters in echelon at twenty feet and close to their never-exceed speed limit of 227 miles an hour. Ten miles from the target they reduced speed to 60 mph.

The four-storey block of flats was on the sea front. Ten minutes flying time from the shore the target acquisition and designation sight in Gur's Apache indicated there were two vehicles parked outside the entrance. As Gur closed to within fifteen hundred yards both vehicles began to move off. Reacting to the situation, Gur's co-pilot/gunner seated forward of him fired two Hellbore missiles, in rapid succession. At the time of the launch each laser-guided munition weighed slightly in excess of one hundred pounds.

The first missile hit and totally destroyed a Mercedes 600, the second just missed the pick-up truck in front of the limousine and ripped into the building at first floor level, severely damaging the reinforced steel joists supporting the ceiling. The blast overturned the pick-up and tossed the four armed men in the back into the air like so many rag dolls. As Gur increased speed and banked to starboard his Apache came under fire from a 25mm Oerlikon anti-aircraft cannon deployed in the adjoining street. Completing a 180-degree turn, Gur engaged the Oerlikon, putting down suppressive fire with the chain gun while his wingman attacked the third floor of the building with four Hellbore missiles aimed at the flats directly above the entrance where Mohammed Khalef was known to be staying. Huge slabs of concrete blasted from the facing fell into the street below giving the impression that the building itself was melting. Progressively weakened, the third floor at the front collapsed on to the second, which in turn gave way. A huge, dense cloud of dust rose into the sky obscuring the block of flats. As the two attack helicopters turned away from the target and headed out to sea the first Green Crescent ambulance arrived on the scene followed by a fire truck. A news reporter and camera crew from an Arab TV station were not far behind.

Once clear of the target area Captain Yehuda Gur checked to make sure his wingman was OK then reported mission accomplished to the control tower at Ashdod and was asked if he didn't have another message. There occurred a somewhat testy exchange before it dawned on Gur what the air traffic controller was getting at.

'You mean that thing about the ranks of Tuscany?' he asked.

'That's exactly what I do mean,' the air traffic controller told him. 'Over and out.'

*   *   *

There had been no further word from Mossad since Radio Tel Aviv had broadcast the first quotation. The aircrew had been given the call sign and frequency they were to use on entering Israeli air space, when air traffic control would tell them the location of the landing zone. There was a limit to the number of times the collecting team could be told what was expected of them. Their job began when Mohammed Khalef was delivered into their custody by the Israelis. On the return leg to Cyprus their task was to ensure the Iraqi cleric was denied the opportunity to endanger the safety of all on board. There was nothing more Neighbour could do except wait patiently to hear from Lawrence Durnford, the Levant desk officer, whom he had left behind at the High Commission to monitor Radio Tel Aviv. At the invitation of the group captain commanding RAF Akrotiri, Neighbour had moved into his office, where there was a Mozart secure-speech facility.

From where he was sitting, at a small table facing the window, he could see the Westland Sea King parked on a hard standing outside the apron. All six men involved in Operation Harpoon were sitting cross-legged on the ground in the shade afforded by the helicopter. One of the pilots was facing the station commander's office waiting for the signal to go. Neighbour reckoned the longer they were forced to wait the more likely it was that the operation would be cancelled. He could not have been more wrong. The Mozart rang ten minutes after the group captain had left the office to attend a conference held by the administrator of the British sovereign areas. Answering the phone on the assumption the call was meant for him, Neighbour heard Lawrence Durnford say, 'Could I speak to Mr Neighbour please?'

'I'm here, Larry,' Neighbour told him. 'What have you heard?'

'The quotation or at least part of it. Naturally the broadcast was in Hebrew and therefore something might have been lost in translation. Instead of

"Even the ranks of Tuscany could scarce forbear to cheer" what the announcer actually said was "The ranks of Tuscany could scarcely cheer".' Durnford paused as if hesitant to say at first what he was thinking. 'It's not exactly the message you were expecting, is it? Do you suppose it was intended to convey a different message, Chris?'

Go or no go? Neighbour havered, unable to make a decision, then had a brainwave. 'Call our Head of Station in Tel Aviv and get him to verify the situation with Mossad. You'll have to brief him about the operation first. Meantime I'm going to despatch the Harpoon team. We can always recall them if the Israelis haven't got a live body for us. OK?'

'Yes. Leave it with me.'

'I intend to,' Neighbour said and hung up.

The Sea King was approximately two hundred yards from the office and there was no way he could make himself heard over that distance. Leaving the office, Neighbour ran full pelt towards the helicopter, which in itself conveyed the message he had to deliver. Before he had covered half the distance the co-pilot, winchman and the Sentinel team had boarded the helicopter. Out of breath and blowing hard, he briefed the pilot and warned him to listen out for a recall. He was still recovering his breath when the two Rolls Royce Gnome turboshaft engines fired into life. The downdraft from the whirling rotor blades forced him to keep his eyes closed against the dust, then the Sea King lifted off and he walked slowly back to the office.

*   *   *

383

Landon had left the Zurich express at Chur and changed to the funicular single-track railway that for nineteen miles snaked up the mountainside on an average gradient of one in six to Arosa. Limited to a maximum speed of twenty it had taken the six-car unit an hour to climb almost six thousand feet to the resort. From the moment he had cleared customs and immigration, the journey from the railway station at Zurich international airport to Arosa had taken three hours twenty minutes.

Head of Station, Bern, who was waiting for him outside the railway station, was no stranger to Landon. He had met him almost a year ago following a terrorist incident at the botanical gardens in Geneva when a young Chechen woman had blown herself up.

'It's good to see you again, Morris,' Landon said, greeting him.

'And you, Will. I've left the Volkswagen in the car park near the ice stadium,' he said, pointing across the lake.

Stolid was an apt description of Morris, who rarely showed any animation. Competent and staid were two more adjectives that sprang to Landon's mind whenever he was asked for a thumbnail sketch of Morris. Social chit-chat was definitely not his forte.

'Have you been waiting long?' Landon enquired for want of something to say.

'Not really. I only arrived an hour ahead of you and most of that time was taken up in hiring a self-drive vehicle.' A faint smile touched his mouth. 'Your Peter Ashton must think this country is not much bigger than Liechtenstein. Arosa is quite some distance from Bern, and if I hadn't broken the speed limit I would never have got to Zurich in time to catch the train leaving an hour ahead of yours. Incidentally, did you know Peter is on his way?'

'No, I didn't.'

'Well with any luck he should arrive on the ten to eight train tonight.'

Morris turned into the car park and looked around him. After aiming the remote control at two other Volkswagens, he eventually found the right one.

'Sorry about that,' he said, 'I forgot the damned colour.'

Landon followed Morris over to the VW Golf, dumped his overnight bag on the back seat and got in beside him.

'Where are you taking me?' he asked.

'The police station. I thought I would introduce you to the inspector in charge before we looked for a hotel.'

'Good idea. Do you know if the police are keeping the Villa Bergman under observation?'

'Your signal to me was despatched today at 0930 hours Greenwich Mean Time. I'm not sure how much you know about this country, Will, but there are forty-one cantons, each of which has its own government. First thing I had to do was talk to the member responsible for justice and the police in the National Council. She in turn put your request to her opposite number in the canton government and from there it gradually trickled down to the officer responsible for policing Arosa. When I saw the inspector minutes ago, he assured me the matter was in hand, whatever that may mean.'

'We must hope Talal Asir is still at the Villa Bergman,' Landon said.

'We've yet to see proof that he's ever been in residence,' Morris reminded him dourly.

*   *   *

The Sea King had been airborne for twenty-five minutes, and in that time Neighbour calculated he must have walked close on a mile and a quarter slowly pacing up and down the group captain's office. Given a cruising speed of 132 knots the helicopter would have covered seventy-six miles by now. Although there was still a long way to go, the Israelis would have been tracking them soon after lift-off and there was no telling how Tel Aviv would react if they believed the British understood the rest of the operation had been cancelled. They certainly wouldn't acknowledge their call sign when the pilot or co-pilot switched to the frequency they had been told to use on entering Israeli air space. What happened next depended on the mindset of the air defence commander for the region. If he believed the helicopter represented a terrorist threat he might launch a surface-to-air missile. Neighbour was just working his way through that nightmare scenario when the Mozart came to life.

'Neighbour here,' he said, lifting the transceiver.

'You can scrub Harpoon,' Durnford told him. 'The Israelis have done the job for us. They knocked hell out of the block of flats where Mohammed Khalef was staying. Head of Station, Tel Aviv told me pictures of the destruction have already appeared on Arab television. The flats on the second and third floors directly above the

386

entrance have gone, and you can look right into those on the top floor. A car in front of the building has been reduced to scrap metal and an overturned pick-up is burning nicely.'

'Is Khalef dead?' Neighbour demanded.

'The Arab TV station says he is, along with the local Hamas leader.'

'That's it then. Would you get through to Vauxhall Cross and tell Ralph Meacher what's happened while I recall the team and debrief them?'

'Of course.'

'Thanks a lot, Larry,' Neighbour said and hung up.

Neighbour left the office and made his way to the air operations centre and asked the senior watchkeeper to recall call sign Tango 22. He felt vaguely guilty that neither he nor Durnford had thought to ask if there were any civilian casualties.

*   *   *

The pilot acknowledged the transmission from RAF Akrotiri and turned on to a reciprocal course for home, then told the winchman to inform the foot soldiers the mission had been cancelled. Being at immediate readiness for hours on end and then finally getting the word to go only to be recalled forty-five minutes later was a very deflating experience. Curiously, it was a very exhausting one.

They were four minutes from Akrotiri when they were involved in a freak mid-air collision with a member of a freefall parachuting club who had jumped from a Cessna 208 six hundred feet above and behind the Sea King. The parachutist struck the tail rotor and was killed instantly; the structural damage to the tail assembly was such that the blades chopped into the tail pylon and destroyed the stabilizer. The whole airframe began to rotate, with the result that the helicopter fell like a brick from an altitude of four thousand feet and plunged into the sea, breaking up on impact.

There were no survivors but two bodies were recovered by the motor launch assigned to pick up the skydivers.

*   *   *

The sun was rapidly disappearing below the mountaintops when Ashton arrived on the 1850 from Chur. In what little daylight was left Landon took him on a quick tour of Arosa, which Ashton likened to a travel brochure after being shown the tennis hardcourts, golf course and hiking trails.

'Whereabouts is the Waldstrasse?' he growled.

'It's midway between Arosa and Maran off the Eichornliweg,' Landon told him. 'From where it branches off and then rejoins the Eichornliweg. The Waldstrasse is roughly a thousand yards long. There are only two properties on what is no more than a lane.'

'Have you seen the Villa Bergman?'

Landon shook his head. 'The inspector in charge warned me off, said I would never get near the place without being spotted. The house is built on a shelf bulldozed out of the hillside and is surrounded by tall fir trees. There are a lot of nature trails in the area but you need to be dressed the part.' Landon smiled deprecatingly. 'In my jacket and slacks I wouldn't look right. That's why

Morris supported the inspector.'

'The police are all dressed in lederhosen, are they?' Ashton said acerbically.

'Something like it.'

'Where's Morris?'

'At the police station; this is his car I'm driving.'

In the short time it took Landon to follow the bus route out to Maran and then back into Arosa, he found himself answering one question after another from Ashton, who wanted to know exactly what the police proposed to do about the occupants of the Villa Bergman. The fact was the inspector had a sergeant and five officers to police an area of two hundred square miles and could only afford to assign two officers to keep the house under observation. However, in response to his request for assistance the chief of police at Chur had agreed to send him four additional officers.

'And when do they arrive?' Ashton asked.

'One minute to midnight. Duty rosters have to be rearranged and that's the earliest they can be made available.'

Even after the reinforcements arrived the inspector was not prepared to effect a forcible entry in the early hours of the morning before first light for two reasons: no one could say with any certainty that Talal Asir was staying at the villa and, secondly, the officers from Chur wouldn't have seen the area in daylight.

'So what's he going to do, Will? Wait until it's broad daylight before knocking on the front door?'

'Well, he is all in favour of the softly, softly approach.'

'How many officers will he have watching the house tonight?'

'Three. One either end of Waldstrasse, while the third covers the rear of the building.'

'And the inspector—what will he be doing?'

'He will be roving in his vehicle. All his officers will have a personal radio.'

'Do they know who they are looking for? More importantly, will they be able to recognize Talal Asir should they encounter him?'

'I doubt it,' Landon said. 'To the best of my knowledge we haven't sent Morris any photographs of him.'

'There's an international arrest warrant for Talal Asir. The French initiated it after they let him slip through their fingers when he was living in Paris. There's a photograph of him on the warrant.'

If Talal Asir had managed to give the Direction de la Surveillance du Territoire the slip, Ashton didn't believe Arosa's finest would be able to keep him bottled up until the cavalry arrived when they had so few men on the ground.

'The police will have to be reinforced ASAP.'

'Who by?' Landon asked.

'You, Morris and me. Provided, of course, we can convince the inspector he needs help.'

Landon pulled into the kerb and switched off the ignition. 'Well, now's your chance, Peter. This is the police station.'

*　　　*　　　*

Ashton reckoned the inspector was in his early thirties; he was about five feet eleven and had the physique of a light middleweight. He looked extremely fit, but that was hardly surprising considering he probably spent every spare minute on the ski slopes for five months of the year when he wasn't on duty. He was probably good at his job and the fact remained his remit extended over two hundred square miles. In his shoes Ashton was sure he would be pretty angry if three foreigners descended on his patch and tried to tell him how to do his job. At least that would be the inference the inspector would draw from their presence. Mindful of this, Ashton trod carefully. For a man with a reputation for being a loose cannon, he showed considerable diplomatic skills. With the utmost tact and infinite patience he persuaded the inspector that the surveillance detail should be reinforced before the men from Chur arrived and volunteered himself, Landon and Morris to make up the numbers. That the police officers from Chur were due to arrive in just over an hour was probably the deciding factor.

'I can't allow you to be armed, Herr Ashton.'

'That's understood but we do need to be in radio contact.'

There were supposed to be four spare radios but it transpired there was only one set on the shelf because the other three were in for repair. To overcome this problem the inspector suggested that Morris should stay with him while Ashton and Landon took the radio from the officer they were relieving on the Waldstrasse.

'I don't like this,' Morris complained when the inspector was out of earshot. 'If anything goes wrong the Swiss will say it's our fault.'

'If the worst should happen, you can tell the DG you were acting on my orders,' Ashton told him.

A few minutes later they left the police station,

Morris travelling with the inspector while Ashton and Landon continued to use the car he had rented. The night life of Arosa was beginning to wind down as they headed in convoy towards the railway station opposite the Obersee. Shortly before reaching the Union Bank of Switzerland they cut through a back street and picked up the Eichornliweg. Approximately two hundred yards beyond the junction with the Waldstrasse, the inspector pulled into a cut and signalled Ashton to overtake him.

'I assume he wants us to relieve the officer at the other end of the Waldstrasse,' Landon said.

'That is his intention,' Ashton said.

Leaving their car on the Eichornliweg they went forward on foot. Although the officer had been warned to expect them, Ashton decided to approach his position boldly. Had they crept up on him stealthily he might have jumped to the wrong conclusion and treated them as hostile. Somewhat reluctantly the officer handed over his radio and moved off to join the third man, who was keeping the rear of the villa under observation. Once he was no longer in sight, Ashton turned the volume down on the radio to eliminate the background mush, then held the microphone close to his mouth and reported they were in position.

The moon was in the last quarter and their field of vision was strictly limited. What they needed was an image intensifier that captured the ambient light from the stars and magnified it a hundred fold. Such an aid would have extended their vision from a mere ten to fifteen yards to in excess of a hundred.

There were only two things they could do to combat the lack of a night vision aid. The first was to lie flat on the ground and hope that if the occupants did try to leave the villa and came towards them they would be silhouetted against the skyline. The other was to use their ears to catch the slightest sound of movement.

And sound did carry in the still night air. They heard the officers from Chur arrive and get out of their vehicle even though they were obviously trying to make as little noise as possible. Long before they reached their position, Landon could tell the inspector had sent two officers to relieve them.

A woman screamed just after they had been relieved and were on the way back down the slope to where they had left the car. She went on screaming at the top of her voice and there was no doubt in Ashton's mind where her agonized cries were coming from. Up till now the police had thought they were on a wild-goose chase; a woman's screams convinced them otherwise. For a moment Ashton, too, thought she was fighting for her life, then it dawned on him that this was precisely what they were meant to think.

'Stand fast, it's a trap,' Ashton roared, then repeated the warning in German.

Landon didn't hesitate; whirling about he ran after the two police officers while Ashton used the radio to warn the others. According to the signal Morris had sent them, the villa was occupied by two men and a woman. At some stage in the late afternoon they had become aware that the police were watching the villa and had decided to slip away during the night. They probably knew just

393

how many officers the inspector had at his disposal and were prepared to bide their time. The arrival of additional manpower had forced them to think again. They had decided to break out in the direction of Maran and had planned to sucker the officer guarding that exit into a lethal trap.

And the plan was working only too well. Landon was approximately twenty yards behind the two officers when somebody inside the villa opened up with a sub-machine gun fitted with a noise suppressor. At such close quarters the gunman couldn't miss.

It was the signal for a brief but bloody firefight. Two of the reinforcements were armed with high-powered semi-automatic rifles and they began to pump round after round into the villa. Landon had already thrown himself flat and was crawling towards a fold in the ground to his left that would afford better cover when the door opened and a man came out of the villa. To Landon's horror the gunman appeared to be running straight at him, but whether or not he'd seen him was never put to the test. When he was less than a dozen yards away he was hit several times in the back and went down like a log, spilling the sub-machine gun from his grasp. Landon crawled after the weapon on his belly and grabbed hold of it in the same instant that a second figure emerged from the house firing shot after shot at him with a pistol. There was never any question of taking him alive. Pointing the machine gun in his direction, Landon emptied the rest of the magazine in one long burst of fire. When the firing eventually stopped, the body of a woman was found in the doorway.

Landon was still shaking when Ashton joined

him. 'My God, Will,' he said, 'what a bloody mess.'

It was some time before Landon realized he wasn't just referring to the carnage around them.

Twenty-Six

In one day they had removed the two most dangerous men in the Middle East: Talal Asir, the banker who had financially supported every known terrorist organization, and Ali Mohammed Khalef, the bagman who had disbursed the monies on his behalf. Hazelwood had deemed it a magnificent achievement. So what if they had cut a few corners and had blackmailed Robin Urquhart into keeping Gavin Pearce, Chairman of the Joint Intelligence Committee, on a tight leash when he had conducted the inquiry into the Beaconsfield incident? In ridding the world of Asir and Khalef they had made it a better and safer place.

There had been a number of close shaves. Two additional bodies had been reclaimed from the sea: the RAF winchman and a second civilian, whose 9mm P7 Heckler & Koch pistol was still in his shoulder holster. The Greek Cypriot government had demanded to know what an armed civilian was doing on an RAF helicopter and the local newspapers had described the two men as spies. Matters could have got out of hand but fortunately the administrator of the British Sovereign Areas was on friendly terms with the Head of State. A statement issued subsequently by the Minister of Defence, Mr Andreas Kofou, had dismissed the allegation as pure fantasy, with the result that the press had soon lost interest.

There could have been serious repercussions following the deaths of the two police officers at Arosa. The Minister for Justice and Police in the Graubunden canton had wanted to detain Ashton, Landon and Morris for questioning in connection with the terrorist incident. Had the minister got her way it would have come to light that Ashton, Landon and, to a lesser extent, Head of Station, Bern had all been involved in another terrorist incident in the botanical gardens in Geneva the previous June. However, the chief of police in Chur had reminded her that Interpol had issued an international arrest warrant for Talal Asir. Consequently, one of the dead officers was credited with killing the Saudi banker, having somehow managed to wrestle a sub-machine gun from him. Pressure to let the Britons go had also been brought to bear on the minister by her opposite number in the Federal Council. Finally, Landon had identified the dead woman as Lana Damir Rifa, owner of a villa on the Boulevard Hafez el-Assad in Damascus. That she was a close friend of Major General Walid al-Kasam, Deputy Prime Minister and Minister for the Armed Forces was something the Swiss authorities had been determined to keep from the public. They could scarcely do that if Ashton, Landon and Morris were held for questioning.

The secret deal with Mossad had been seen by Meacher as their Achilles heel but, as Hazelwood had pointed out, the Cabinet had tacitly sanctioned the agreement with the Israeli intelligence service by authorizing the use of an RAF helicopter to collect Mohammed Khalef. The Firm was of course in bad odour with the police officers of B District investigating the multiple homicide at Giordano's, but they could live with that. A month after the event the danger of exposure seemed remote.

The whole business began to unravel at a garden fête and strawberry cream tea held by the Liberal Democrats on Saturday 5th June. As the fête was drawing to a close, the chairman of the local branch called on Dermot McManus, the Lib Dem candidate for Hillingdon and Ruislip, to give a short address.

'And I do mean short,' the chairman had added to a faint ripple of laughter.

McManus had begun conventionally enough, thanking everyone present for attending the function and stressing how important it was to raise funds to fight the next general election in two years' time. He then went on to castigate the government for failing to control the Secret Intelligence Service.

Sitting in the audience was Julie Meacher, who listened with mounting horror as McManus revealed everything she had told him in their intimate moments together. She thanked God Ralph had refused to attend the fête and vowed to make sure he didn't see the *Ruislip Herald* when the weekly newspaper appeared next Friday. Also in the audience was a freelance journalist and stringer for the *Sunday Observer* whose accountant happened to be Dermot McManus. Forewarned what to expect, he had prepared a short report for tomorrow's edition. The piece was in the nature of a warning shot across the bows of the intelligence community to see what kind of reaction it would provoke. It was also intended to capture the interest of the big national dailies and the BBC, which regarded the freelance journalist as one of their reporters.

The ploy succeeded beyond McManus's wildest dreams. On Sunday night he was telephoned by *The Times*, the *Telegraph* and the *Independent* wanting to know his source, which he had refused to disclose. On Monday morning he was contacted by the BBC and asked to appear on *Newsnight* at 10.30 p.m.

Morning prayers had lasted barely twenty minutes. Thereafter Hazelwood, Ashton and Meacher had been locked in conference on and off for the rest of the day. A spokesman for the Prime Minister's office stated that it was not government policy to comment on speculative journalism. However, behind the scenes the Cabinet Office, Home Office and FCO wanted a minute-by-minute assessment of the unfolding story from Hazelwood. Specifically they wanted to know if there was any danger the allegation of collusion with Mossad could be made to stick. Throughout the day Hazelwood had confidently maintained the media had no evidence. Not surprisingly the responsible minister had declined the BBC's invitation to be present when Dermot McManus was interviewed on *Newsnight*, a fact the anchorman had commented on.

As he watched the programme at home, Ashton thought McManus started nervously but gained in confidence as the interview progressed. Timing it perfectly he delivered the bombshell in the last four minutes.

'The RAF helicopter which crashed into the sea off Cyprus on Monday May tenth had been on the way to collect Ali Mohammed Khalef. On board were three civilian guards provided by a security company—'

'But can you prove this?' the anchorman asked.

'Oh, yes.' McManus faced the camera with a faint smile etched on his mouth. 'They were supplied by Sentinel.'

The Mozart in the study started ringing almost immediately. Even before he left the sitting room to answer it, Ashton knew it was Hazelwood.

'Meacher will have to go,' Hazelwood announced when he picked the phone up.

'What?'

'Meacher lives in Ruislip, so does that little creep McManus. Furthermore, Julie Meacher is a partner in the same firm of chartered accountants.'

'You can't be serious, Victor.'

'I had Julie Meacher checked out when she joined the Lib Dems. She's having an affair with McManus. Ralph talked too much about Harpoon and his tart of a wife passed it on to her lover.'

'Don't you think I should go as well?' Ashton asked. 'After all, no one did more than me to launch the operation.'

'Don't be a bloody fool,' Hazelwood growled and hung up.

1	21	41	61	81	101	121	141	161	181
2	22	42	62	82	102	122	142	162	182
3	23	43	63	83	103	123	143	163	183
4	24	44	64	84	104	124	144	164	184
5	25	45	65	85	105	125	145	165	185
6	26	46	66	86	(106)	126	146	166	186
7	27	47	67	87	107	127	147	167	187
8	(28)	48	68	88	108	128	148	168	188
9	29	49	69	89	109	129	149	169	189
10	30	50	70	90	110	130	150	170	190
11	31	51	71	91	111	131	151	171	191
12	32	52	72	92	112	132	152	172	192
13	33	53	73	93	113	133	153	173	193
14	34	54	74	94	114	134	154	174	194
15	35	55	75	95	115	135	155	175	195
(16)	36	56	76	96	116	136	156	176	196
17	37	57	77	97	117	137	157	177	197
18	38	58	78	98	118	138	158	178	198
19	39	59	79	99	119	139	159	179	199
20	40	60	80	100	120	140	160	180	200

201	211	221	(231)	241	251	261	271	281	291
202	212	222	232	242	252	262	272	282	292
203	213	223	233	243	253	263	273	283	293
204	214	224	234	244	254	264	274	284	294
205	215	225	235	245	255	265	275	285	295
206	216	226	236	246	256	266	276	286	296
207	217	227	237	247	257	267	277	287	297
208	218	228	238	248	258	268	278	288	298
209	219	229	239	249	259	269	279	289	299
210	220	230	240	250	260	270	280	290	300

301	(310)	319	328	337	346
302	311	320	329	338	347
303	312	321	330	339	348
304	313	322	331	340	349
305	314	323	332	341	350
306	315	324	333	342	
307	316	325	334	343	
308	317	326	335	344	
309	318	327	336	345	